THEY PLAYED THEIR ROLE

THE GLINTCHASERS SERIES

THEY PLAYED THEIR ROLE

CamCat Publishing, LLC
Fort Collins, Colorado 80524
camcatpublishing.com

Hardcover ISBN 9780744311457
Paperback ISBN 9780744311471
eBook ISBN 9780744311495

Library of Congress Control Number: 2024938698

Cover and book design by Maryann Appel
Map illustration by Maia Lai

5 3 1 2 4

To Wings,

Never let anyone stop you from flying.

To Sue,

O Captain! My Captain!

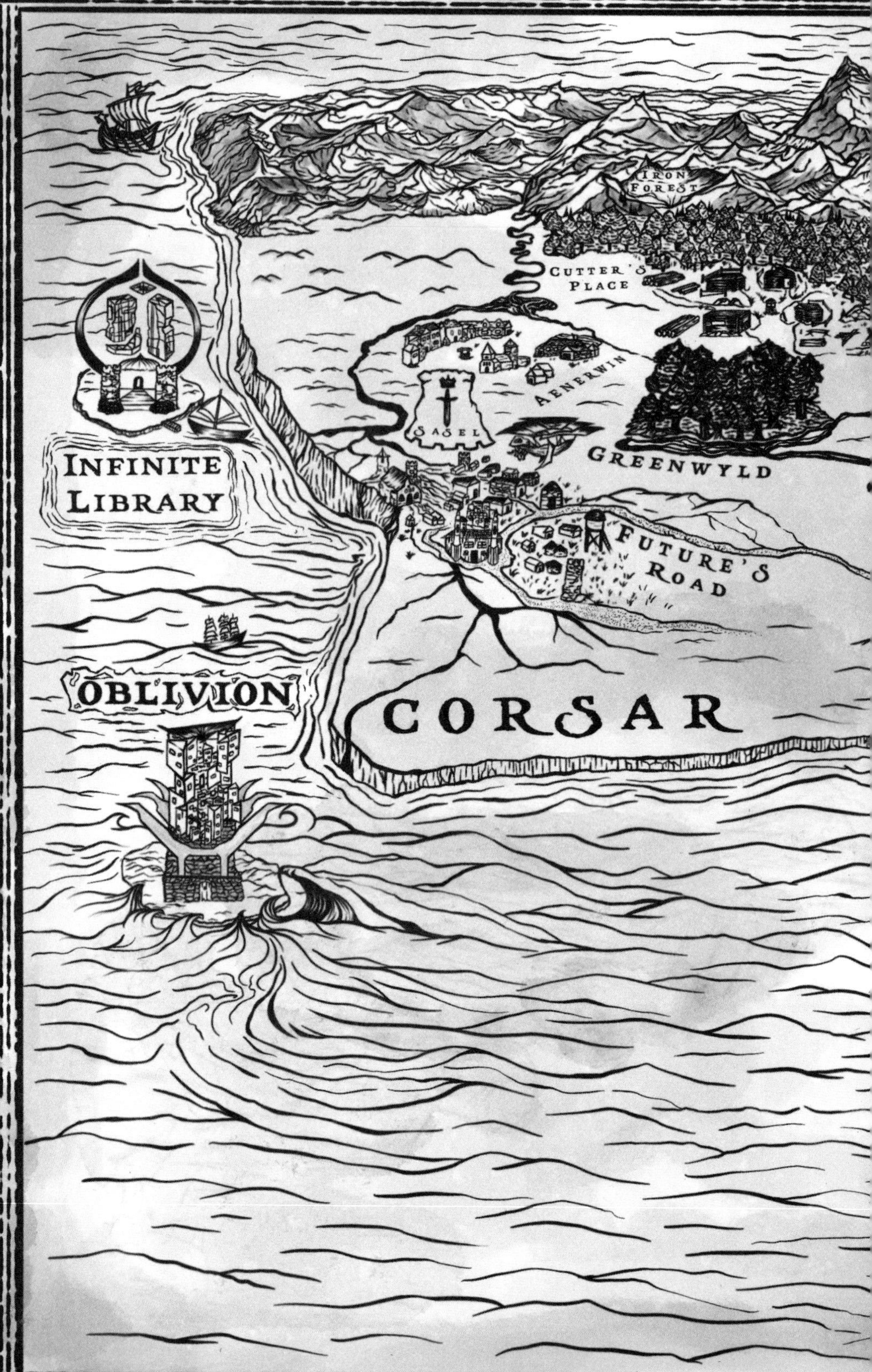

IRON FOREST
CUTTER'S PLACE
AENERWIN
SASEL
INFINITE LIBRARY
GREENWYLD
FUTURE'S ROAD
OBLIVION
CORSAR

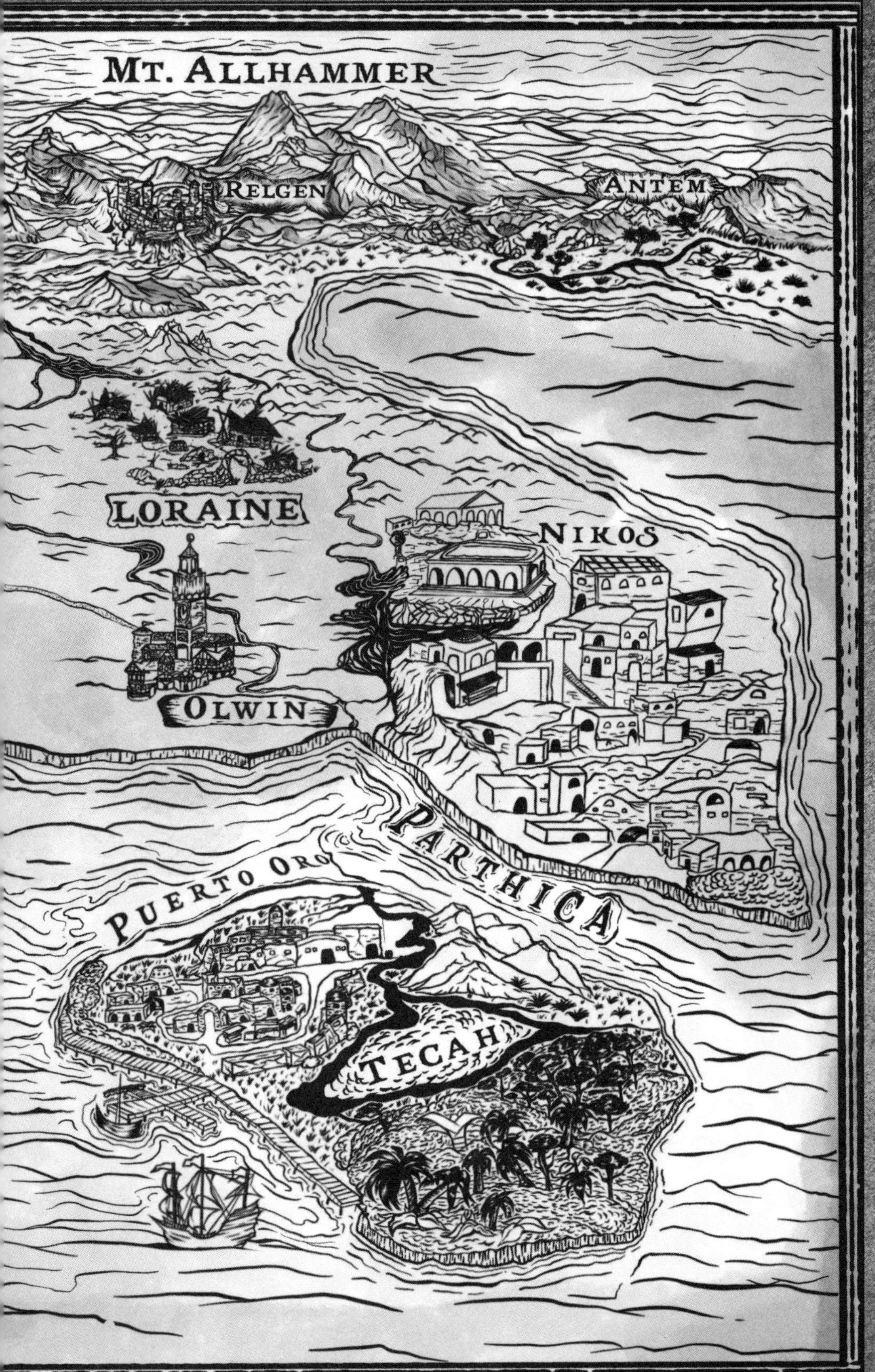

MT. ALLHAMMER
RELGEN
ANTEM
LORAINE
NIKOS
OLWIN
PARTHICA
PUERTO ORO
TECAH

1

AVENGER

As a knight of the Purple Rose, Haegan usually dealt with threats to the kingdom too great for local defenders to handle: necromancer plots, supernatural crime waves, Old World artifacts gone awry. Most recently, the Purple Rose had been tasked with the recovery of the lead engineer of royal skyship maintenance from a band of sky pirates. But that had been months ago, and the city of Relgen and the surrounding lands had been quiet since.

Haegan had taken the opportunity to take a brief sabbatical, his first in years, and left the order and its duties under the care of his lieutenant. He'd gone to visit an old friend, and to see if his friend's son, Silas, was ready to become a squire. Silas was a sandy-haired youth, not yet fifteen, and still in the gangliest stages of puberty. He had never seen the world outside his small village. Today Haegan would get to see his face when Silas saw Relgen for the first time.

They rode side by side, Silas feeding him a constant stream of questions, and Haegan patiently answering without taking his eyes off the road. Silas was an eager prospect, and Haegan could easily see him becoming a dedicated and steadfast knight of the crown. Haegan looked forward to helping him become that knight.

And then, perhaps, retiring. He'd been noticing more and more of his blond hair going gray of late, and sometimes he found himself waking up stiff and sore from sleeping the wrong way. He was getting too old for this life, and sooner or later he would have to leave the kingdom to the next generation. To people like Silas, or that new flying woman from Sasel. He could either retire on his own terms, or at the end of an enemy's blade, and he liked to think he'd outgrown his youthful fantasies of martyrdom. The kingdom's existence didn't hinge on him fighting to his dying breath. If he laid down his hammer and stepped aside, the world would keep turning.

When they rounded the next bend in the road, Silas's questions stopped. They'd reached the outermost terrace farms that decorated the mountains surrounding the city, and the tiers of green spread out before them, interspersed by the homes of the farmers. And beyond the farms was the city of Relgen.

The Bastion of the North stood tall and proud, its walls seeming to grow up out of the mountains themselves. The tallest and oldest of the walls looked perfectly smooth, more impenetrable and immutable than the surrounding terrain. Every layer of them bristled with Old World cannons, constructions of metal and light that gleamed even at this distance, and enormous banners bearing the crest of the city draped down the side.

As they drew closer, a sleek, shining vessel rose up from behind the walls. Rogue Imperia, the largest skyship ever recovered in all the world. Decorative reams of blue and gold streamed from its wings, billowing in the wind as the ship took to the air.

Silas's stunned silence left Haegan smiling and lit a spark of warmth in his chest. Though Haegan traveled the kingdom as a knight, he had called Relgen home all his life. No small part of him derived personal pride in being from the city, and seeing the boy's awe reminded him of why. Relgen was safety. Security. Strength. He was part of that. And now, as a new squire in the Order of the Purple Rose, so was Silas.

"You're lucky," Haegan said, nodding toward the skyship in the distance. "It's not every day you get to see Rogue Imperia take off."

In fact, the crown jewel of the Corsan navy had been grounded since its lead engineer's initial kidnapping, and had remained so even after the Purple Rose rescued her. Haegan's first assumption was that the woman must have finished her inspection and repairs already. Or perhaps this was just a quick test flight, and there was still more work to be done.

But as they drew closer, he noticed something strange. Rogue Imperia was missing her usual escort of flying skiffs. Instead, there were only two craft in the air near the skyship—a single vessel that might have been a flying pleasure barge, and a tiny sky surfer. Then there was a distant, warbling boom, and a bolt of light streaked from the deck of the skyship, missing the pleasure barge by what must have been only dozens of feet. Rogue Imperia was firing its weapons.

"Sir?" Silas asked hesitantly. "What's going on?"

Haegan's grip on the reins of his horse tightened. "Come on."

They rode faster for the city, with Haegan never taking his eyes off the skyship and its two much smaller pursuers. The ship's guns cracked off a few more times before an explosion bloomed on the hull, exactly where the cannon had been. The pleasure barge, billowing smoke, skidded across Rogue Imperia's top deck, and the sky surfer followed.

Haegan and Silas were not the only ones to notice. In the fields and on their porches, people stopped what they were doing, pointing up to the commotion in the sky. When Rogue Imperia itself began to list in the air, someone working on a nearby farm shouted loud enough for Haegan to hear. The knight commander's head whipped to the voice on instinct.

Up ahead, a carriage had pulled just off the road, and a young woman now stood outside it next to where the driver was seated, both of them pointing up at the skyship. The woman had a hand to her mouth in shock.

Then, all at once, there was an earsplitting shriek in the air itself, and the world was swallowed in white. Haegan tried to jerk his horse to a stop as he went blind, but the animal went wild, spooked by whatever had just happened, and he was thrown from the saddle. For a few agonizing moments after he hit the ground, he saw nothing, and heard only a ringing in his ears.

Too slowly, the world faded back into existence.

Silas was on the ground not far from Haegan, one stirrup still on his boot, the end of its strap dangling off his foot after clearly being slashed with a blade. The boy groaned when Haegan prodded him, but nothing looked broken. He'd cut himself free in time. Good instincts, quick thinking, and lucky. Silas was going to go far in this world.

"What happened?"

Haegan started to say, "I don't know," but the words got stuck in his throat. It was as though someone had drawn a line across the world, maybe fifteen feet away from them. On their side, everything was exactly as it had been. But on the other side, the fields of the surrounding farms had all died. Everything was wilted and dried out, turned to unnatural burnt umber. Dead leaves and needles drifted off the trees. The delineation was startlingly clear, and healthy plant life touched dead in a straight, even line that cut right across the road, separating Haegan and Silas from Relgen and its outlying territory.

The carriage Haegan had spotted up the road was on the other side of the line. The woman that had been standing next to it was now lying motionless in the dirt. And so were the horses that had been pulling the carriage. The driver was still in his seat, but slumped backward. All around, the world had gone unnaturally still, and deafening silence gripped the air.

"Don't move," Haegan ordered Silas.

Without hesitation, he ran across the line to the woman, turning her over and brushing her hair from her face. Her eyes were still open, but there was no life or movement in them. He removed a glove to check for a pulse.

Nothing.

He climbed onto the carriage, finding the driver in a similar state. Eyes still open, body limp, mouth slightly agape. From his vantage point on the carriage, Haegan could look out over the dead farms, and see dozens of bodies, all fallen to the ground. Unmoving. Lifeless.

A sudden fluttering sound cut the silence, followed by a soft thud and a small, wet crunch. He whirled to see a crumpled black shape in the ground, framed in a red splatter. Another thud and crunch followed somewhere nearby. When he looked to the sky, what he saw left his stomach twisted with sickening horror. All around him, dead birds fell from the sky.

He looked around, trying to gauge the extent of the field of death. Aside from its border with the still living world, he couldn't see the end. As far as he could tell, it completely encircled the city, and miles of land around it, all the way out to where he now stood.

In the city itself, Rogue Imperia finished its listing descent, crashing into the walls of the city and detonating in an explosion Haegan felt from where he was standing, and his whole body jerked. He staggered backward, off the carriage, away from the city. A pervasive wrongness filled his every sense. Nothing was right. Nothing made sense. His heart pounded, and his stomach lurched. When he caught the lifeless eyes of the dead woman in the road again, he finally lost all control, fell to his hands and knees, and retched.

Haegan walked alone through the corpse of his home. Everywhere he went, there was no sound but his footsteps. Not so much as a breeze disturbed Relgen's deathly quiet. No motion drew his eye. He walked in and out of businesses and homes freely, the lone living thing in the city. He found the same scene everywhere he went.

Bodies littered the streets. Slouched forward in seats. Lay cold and motionless in beds. Everywhere, tasks lay half-finished, meals half-eaten, games half-played. People had fallen over dead in the middle of every activity Haegan could imagine. Taking a bath. Painting a fence. Making love. The few times he saw motion, it was from fires that had been left unattended or sparked by a dropped lantern or candle.

Animals were not spared. There were the dead birds of course, the larger ones having splattered on the ground, the little ones unbloodied but still broken and crumpled from their falls. But he also found cats, slumped in alleyways, dead as the rats still clutched in their mouths. Dogs lay motionless atop the children they had been playing with. Horses, sometimes still harnessed to the vehicles they'd been pulling when they'd collapsed.

By now, everything and everyone were many hours dead, but some unnatural force or phenomenon had preserved them. If he didn't look too closely, he could delude himself into thinking everyone in the city had simply fallen asleep at the same time. But when he did, he would see the discoloration in the skin, just enough to be noticeable. And constant dead, unblinking eyes. They were all around him, staring at him. Pleading with him. They begged for answers, for understanding, for someone to make sense of all this.

Time had vanished from his awareness. His mind and body were numb, save a constant, twisting nausea in the pit of his stomach. He walked without purpose or even conscious thought, letting the horror that gripped his soul drag him along. At some point, it grew dark, and the sun was replaced by distant fires, unattended lanterns, and scattered fixtures of automated lightstone. Fire and light streaked across the night sky as stars fell and burned.

Haegan walked until his legs ached and his eyes burned. His mouth had long ago turned to cotton, dried out from constantly hanging open in shock. His next step faltered underneath him, and he fell to his knees. The shock of pain that followed was like a splash of ice water, returning him to his body. When he looked around, he found that he recognized where he was. From the purple banners that decorated the walls to the oversized painting of the Baroness of Relgen, he knew this building. He knew this room. He knew the armored bodies that lay scattered around him.

This was the headquarters of the Knights of the Purple Rose. And the corpses surrounding him were fellow knights. His brothers and sisters. For so many of them to be here, in armor, their weapons fallen around them, they must have been about to leave on a mission. Maybe to deal with whatever had been going on with Rogue Imperia.

Now, finally, Haegan wept.

Over the course of an hour, his shuddering sobs turned to anguished screams, to desperate shrieks, and then finally to keening whimpers. Haegan was hollowed out, as if he'd wrung out every drop of his being into his tears, and now there was nothing left but a brittle shell. He knelt among his fallen comrades, waiting for that shell to break into pieces.

Instead, he found himself staring down into the dead face of one of the knights. Thadeus, his name was. The boy was only a few years older than Silas. He'd been inducted into the order only half a year ago. Haegan had privately suspected during his journey back that the two young men would become good friends.

Silas—who was now staying with farmers, recovering from his fall and learning what he could from those who had been outside the city—and Haegan had been less than two dozen feet from the edge. A few seconds' delay in their approach was all that had separated them from joining the fallen city in sudden, senseless death.

The precariousness of that shook Haegan, but it also steeled him. Fire filled the hollowness the tears had left behind, filled every inch of his body. The brittle shell he had been only seconds ago calcified, and his whole being redirected itself.

If he had been here, he would be dead. But he was alive now, and there was a world outside this mass tomb that had once been his home. A world where people still lived. A world that had just lost its bastion.

The people of that world needed a knight. Silas needed a mentor. And his fallen brothers and sisters needed justice. Something had killed them, had killed all of Relgen. Something was deeply wrong in the world. And as dark, angry pain kindled inside him, Haegan swore that he would not rest until he made it right.

2
QUARRY

Everyone always looked unhappy when it was hot. That was the only way Snow could tell the difference between a normal sunny day and sweltering heat anymore. When the sun was high overhead on a cloudless day, she checked people's faces for the beleaguered expressions and profuse sweating, because she couldn't feel the difference herself.

Today must have been scalding.

People languished through the ruintown's dirt avenues, scowling and staring at the ground as they stomped through a haze of dust to begin the day's work of stripping down the Old World remnants the town had sprung up around—or rather, in.

In another time, this place had been some kind of coliseum, built into a recess in the surrounding plains. Or maybe it used to tower over the surrounding land and had just been buried by time. She wasn't an archeologist. Either way, now it was a massive half-buried hole in the ground, surrounded by carts and filled with dozens of scattered work tarps and haphazardly erected buildings. People moved through it like an ant colony, milling between work sites, excavating, and carrying materials, all while foremen watched from a flying skiff hovering overhead.

The pub at the center of town was a decent size considering it was probably built out of wood from a few dozen carts and whatever support beams could be bought off excavation teams. She counted the exits—three not including windows—gave the surroundings a once over for any security, and went inside.

A chill swept through the pub as she opened the doors, and every head turned her way. She was a lean, dark-haired woman, clad in a long-sleeved shirt and a dark leather jerkin without a bead of sweat on her face. Even after the doors closed behind her, cold lingered in the air, and the people closest to her shivered.

The patrons were an even mix of dirt-caked locals and out-of-towners overladen with bags and traveling equipment, save for a man and woman at a corner table who were sporting swords and underlayers for armor. Those two were amateurs, or else dregs. No other kind of glintchaser would stick around a ruintown after all the best loot had been scooped up.

They wouldn't be a problem.

Ignoring the stares, Snow scanned the bar for a stool that looked stable and took a seat. The bartender's eyes locked on to her as a visible lump formed in his throat.

Snow was pale. Too pale to be breathing, and yet there she sat, drumming her fingers and staring with ice blue eyes that cut through him. A man didn't work in a ruintown without seeing some strange things, but uncertainty was still plain on his face. People had lots of guesses over the years about what Snow was. Ghost. Winter Spirit. Demon. Whatever the bartender's guess was, it wasn't enough to make him run, but he was still unsettled.

He swallowed. "Get you anything?"

"Beer."

The mundanity of the order was a clear relief, and the man latched on to it like a lifeline. Maybe he didn't know what Snow was, but he knew how to serve a beer.

"Two glint."

Snow set a coin worth five times that on the table. Her eyes made it clear she didn't expect change.

"Anything else you needed?"

"Depends." Snow traced a finger across the surface of the metal tankard she'd been given, and a thin film of frost formed across its surface before she brought it to her lips and took a long drink. The cheap stuff always tasted better cold. "Are you the man to see about getting a new axle for a cart?"

The bartender looked back at the coin, and hesitantly nodded an understanding as he pocketed it.

"Planning on traveling?"

That was the confirmation Snow needed. She had her man. "Actually, I wanted to ask you some questions about your last customer."

"I'm not sure who you mean," the man lied.

"Ex-knight and a set of twins, moving heavy cargo," Snow said. "I want to know the details."

Snow recognized the look on the man's face. Whether it was money, fear, or professionalism, he was intent on keeping his mouth shut. She braced herself for the worst, even as she reached into her coin purse. It didn't hurt to at least try the easy way first.

She set down enough coins to renovate the place into a real bar. "Does this jog your memory?"

The man firmly pushed the stack back toward her. "I think you have me confused with somebody else."

The color drained from Snow's eyes as they shifted from blue to white, and the last dregs of beer at the bottom of her tankard froze solid. Heads turned toward her again as the temperature of the entire room dropped to the point that people could see their breath.

"I really don't think I do," Snow said. Her voice was a warning.

The two glintchasers in the back were standing up now, hands on their weapons. Snow's eyes did another sweep of the tavern, double-checking everyone's position in the room, who had access to anything that could be used as a weapon, and who looked like they'd actually try.

"Last chance," she warned. "Silas Lamark came to you to smuggle weapons. Tell me where they came from, and where they were going, and there won't be any trouble."

Instead of answering like a sensible person, the bartender whistled, and the two glintchasers drew their swords. A few other people stood up from their tables, ready to back them up against the outsider.

"It's time to leave," one of the amateurs warned Snow.

"Okay," she sighed, getting up. "I tried."

Snow kicked her stool backward, and then, in the blink of an eye, vanished, reappearing an instant later behind the hired swords with her dagger already drawn. The man was fast enough to take a swing at her, but it only found air as she ducked, sidestepped, and grabbed his wrist. It went numb as ice spread out from her hand, and he dropped his sword.

By now, the bartender was making a run for the back, but no sooner had he reached for a door handle than a dagger sailed through the air, piercing his hand and pinning him to the doorframe.

The armed woman finally managed to bring her sword around to swing at Snow, only for the assassin to disappear. Having seen that trick before, the woman tried to spin around, and found herself slipping on ice that had formed beneath her feet. Snow reappeared, gave her a firm kick to topple her, and then neatly vaulted over the bar to land next to a still-screaming bartender.

It was over in a second.

The bartender stared at her with the eyes of a cornered animal as she casually rested her hand on the dagger pinning his hand. At her touch, burning cold spread through the blade into his flesh.

"In about a minute, you're going to start losing fingers to frostbite," Snow explained. "Then the hand. Then the arm."

Snow paused, hearing someone approach. Keeping one hand on the dagger, she grabbed a bottle off a shelf, froze its contents solid, and hurled it directly into the forehead of a man rushing the bar. He dropped on the spot, and nobody else moved. The only sound in the room was the bottle rolling across the floor.

For a moment, everyone stared, processing the display of brutal efficiency. Eventually, they came to the conclusion that this was none of their business, and everyone still standing quickly cleared out.

The bartender's eyes fixated on Snow as she leaned in. Her breath had the bite of wind in deep winter.

"What are you?" the man gasped.

If he didn't already know the answer to that question, she really was in the backcountry. Even if only an unlucky few had ever met her, the Cold-Blooded Killer had a reputation that few in Corsar could match. It was honestly a little refreshing to not be recognized, and it put her in a charitable mood.

"Unless you really want to find out," she warned, "you'll start talking."

After the initial scuffle, nobody in the bar tried to get in Snow's way. On one hand, she appreciated the privacy and room to work. It sped the process along when she didn't have to worry about other people trying something stupid.

On the other hand, the odds were that someone had run to get help.

At her encouragement, the bartender gave her what she wanted fairly quickly. He still probably wasn't going to keep that hand, but he was brief enough to give her time to get out of town before the cavalry arrived.

She slipped out a window in the back of the kitchen just as she could hear the beginnings of an angry mob descending on the bar. Staying off the streets bought her a few blocks without eyes on her, and when she finally did step out into them, it was to vanish into a sea of faces walking in a dozen different directions.

Within minutes, the shouts of people searching for her were far behind. If she'd waited until nightfall, it would have been even easier to lose them. But she was well past needing the help of darkness to disappear.

As she made her escape, she considered what she'd learned. She'd spent the last few months trying to track down Silas Lamark, a man who'd crossed her and her company too many times to be allowed to live. It had started with him putting out a contract on all of their heads, and nearly getting them all killed by bounty hunters. Then, with the help of the Cult of Stars, Silas had slipped right through Snow's fingers, and gotten away with a pile of Old

World weapons. Now, finally, she had more than a heading for tracking him. She had a location.

Silas was in Sasel, capital city of the kingdom. And now that she knew that, she would see him dead by the end of the month, and finally put this mess behind her. After that . . .

After that, she wasn't sure.

She could go back to work as a contract killer, which she hadn't done for nearly a year now. That job had been her life for the last eight years, ever since the fall of Relgen. But lately, thinking of going back to the work had felt wrong, in a way it hadn't ever before. Not morally wrong—she'd been killing for a living since she was seventeen, and long since stopped being bothered by it—but pragmatically. Assassin had been the obvious career move after the Starbreakers broke up, but now, maybe, the Starbreakers were back. And even if they weren't back, they were still around, in her life. The job didn't feel as necessary as it had when she was alone.

That still left her with the question of what in the seven hells she was supposed to do instead. She was still thinking about it when she rounded the corner to the scaffolding that would let her leave the ruintown, and had to come to a stop. Standing between it and her was a girl, probably not even twenty, dressed in ill-fitting armor hastily strapped over a rough tunic and pants.

As soon as the girl locked eyes with Snow, she put two fingers to her mouth, and gave the loudest whistle Snow had ever heard. It echoed through the stone streets of the town, and the girl took up a fighting stance.

"Don't move," the girl warned.

Another rookie freelancer. Maybe even in the same company as the ones from the bar. There was fear in her eyes, but her hands were completely still. She had guts, Snow would give her that. But she was in for a rude awakening.

"You really don't want to do this," Snow warned the girl.

As she exhaled, she let the cold take over. The blue of her eyes became paler by the second, and frost spread across her cheekbones and fingertips. At the same time, she felt a numbness take hold, dulling her every sensation and emotion, and sweeping away any pity she felt for the rookie in front of her.

She was an obstacle. Nothing more.

The girl responded by rushing forward. At first, Snow expected a punch, but the girl's hands moved in a quick, swirling pattern before swiping across the air to summon a blade of fire. Snow ducked out of the way but cursed herself. Getting spotted by an amateur was sloppy enough. She should have seen the telltale scars on her opponent's hands sooner. The girl was a wizard.

That whistle had to be a signal, which meant more obstacles were coming. She needed to end this quickly.

She sidestepped the girl's next spell, a burning whip that left scores in the ground, and threw a knife into the rookie's palm. It broke her concentration, and the flames vanished. Snow closed the distance before the girl could even finish screaming. In one motion, she yanked the knife free, jammed it into the girl's shoulder, and twisted until she heard a pop.

With her other hand, she grabbed both the girl's wrists and froze them together before shoving her to the ground. The girl lay there, gritting her teeth and failing to hold back tears. After a second, the knife tore itself free from the girl's shoulder and flew back to Snow's waiting hand, propelled by an invisible force. More footsteps came sprinting up behind her. They'd been closer than Snow would have expected. Before she could turn to face them, a peal of thunder rattled the sky.

The *cloudless* sky.

Snow didn't sheathe her weapon, but she did relax her stance. The fight was over.

Two more rookies arrived with their weapons drawn. And then a gleaming, emerald green blur dove from the sky, too fast to track with the eye. In a blink, the blur materialized as a light-skinned woman in dark green leathers standing right beside Snow, ethereal wings of green light splayed out wide behind her. Her landing was so fast it sent a curtain of wind rippling out in all directions, tossing back her light brown hair, and stopping the advancing glintchasers in their tracks. Snow's own hair was whipped into a wild frenzy, and it was only thanks to flash freezing her feet to the ground that she hadn't lost her footing. The new arrival's wings dissolved to nothing as she stood straight, but her eyes continued to swirl as orbs of solid green thunderclouds. Elizabeth Meshar, the Winged Lady of Sasel, had arrived.

"Wings," Snow greeted.

The Winged Lady took in the situation, the bleeding rookie on the ground and her two stunned friends, and Snow's own bloodied knife, and shook her head.

"You three, clear out," she said, with an even mixture of authority and fraying patience. "I've got business with this one."

"The Winged Lady . . ." one of them let out an awestruck breath. It took the last of Wings's patience with it.

"Now!" she snapped. The wind picked up with her voice, and the gust blew them all back another half step.

This time, the rookies listened. The two late arrivals helped their friend to her feet, and immediately began hauling her away in the opposite direction, casting constant glances back over their shoulders and furiously whispering between them. Only when they were gone did the swirls of Wings's eyes fade back into her ordinary, human eyes with bright green irises.

Beneath the power, Wings looked like she hadn't slept in days. The beginnings of dark circles had formed under her eyes, and there was a dimness to her gaze, as if she couldn't quite focus on what was in front of her. Her mouth was set in a hard line, her jaw was tense, and the fingers she normally used to draw a bowstring were twitching furiously. The irritation hadn't just been an act to get the rookies to leave.

"What's wrong?" Snow asked, and was surprised to find genuine concern creep into her chest. Without her even pushing against it, the cold had receded, letting a bit of feeling back in.

Snow had never seen Wings look so desperate. "Arman's been missing for two weeks, and you were the last one to see him. Tell me you know where he is."

In an instant, Snow's eyes changed color, snapping from pale ice to bright blue. The buzz of emotional numbing from the Heart of Ice retreated enough for her to feel a twinge of fear in her chest.

The assassin's throat tightened. "What?"

3
WITNESS

Two weeks before, Snow was ducking beneath the swipe of a sword that could have taken her head off, and found herself actually annoyed that she was being put on the defensive by a complete nobody. She consoled her ego with the knowledge it was her opponent's sword, and only the sword, that made it possible.

The blade was a silver so bright as to be nearly white, with arcane etchings running its length. The edge gave off a crackling blue glow and left a trail of light in the air with every swing, giving the appearance that Snow was dancing to avoid a flying snake of blue light. The sword was an Old World weapon, forged and enchanted in a time when the secret for doing so wasn't a secret at all, but common science. It would cut through steel like an ordinary blade through wood, and withstand wear far better as well.

It was, as far as enchanted weapons went, bargain-bin quality. It had no special properties beyond its own enhanced durability and lethality, and even that was only noteworthy for how it eclipsed the modern standard. The armies of the Old World had issued weapons like it to every soldier. *Real* Old World weapons could call lightning or blow apart castle walls. Even Snow's own enchanted dagger Companion Piece had more tricks up its sleeve than her adversary's sword. But as basic as the weapon was, it was still dangerous enough to force Snow to be careful.

For about two breaths. Then her opponent stepped too far forward, ruining his footing, and Snow pounced. She vanished from sight right in front of her enemy's eyes in a blink, and reappeared behind him already driving her foot into his back ankle. He crumpled to the floor, and she lunged down over him, driving her dagger into his chest. His eyes widened for a split second, staring up into her cold, unfeeling gaze. Then his eyes rolled back, and he gave a final gasp before dying on her knife.

She stood, wiped the blood on her opponent's shirt, and checked to see how Phoenix was doing.

Phoenix was a man with caramel skin, dark eyes, and even darker hair. It and his beard were on the scruffy side of short, clean but unkempt. Though recent months had seen him more active and out of the house than he'd been in years, he still hadn't shed the extra padding civilian life had given him. His dark leather armor and red overcoat, both enchanted with a dozen different functions, still fit, but where Snow was lithe and lethal, Phoenix looked—well, like what he was. A shabby, slightly out-of-shape, stay-at-home father still shaking the rust off his old freelancing days. Easily perceived as a weakness in a fight.

The spellforger had been backed into a corner by his own opponent, who was wielding a sword identical to the one Snow had, save for one key difference: the glow of the sword Phoenix was facing kept sputtering in and out. Its wielder was a woman at least half a foot taller than Phoenix, with muscled arms exposed by the piecemeal armor she wore. With the skill and strength she moved with, she probably could have taken Phoenix in a straight fight even with her weapon malfunctioning.

But Phoenix didn't do straight fights.

He brought his arm up, and his bracer produced a shield of arcane force that took a sword strike for him. The shield and blade let out a high-pitched, sizzling whine as they connected, and sparks flew from the point of contact. Then, with a flex of Phoenix's hand, the shield rushed out, expanding until it was the size of his opponent. It engulfed her like a net, and her whole body locked up, held still by the force of the magical barrier.

While she was trapped, Phoenix brought his wand up like a club. The cylindrical chamber just above the handle rotated, locking a new power cell into place, and the wand's tip crackled with conjured electricity. When he brought it down on the woman, the power of the shield holding her detonated, and her body convulsed as lightning raced through her nerves. She fell to the ground, still twitching, and smelling faintly of ozone.

"Is that the last of them?" Phoenix asked.

Snow nodded. "It looks that way."

"Good."

A silence fell over the warehouse they had been battling in, and the two of them surveyed the damage they'd done. Six prone figures wearing mismatched armor were scattered among the boxes and shelves, ranging from dead, to concussed, to held in place by layers of ice.

The Old World weapons they'd been carrying littered the floor, some still bright and functioning, but most with light flickering or faded entirely. One sword in particular had been broken in two by a low-powered blast from Phoenix's wand.

"I thought you said these people were willing to talk to us," Phoenix said.

"They were," Snow countered, "until you brought up confiscating their weapons."

"I feel like there should be a bigger gap between 'you can't have my stuff' and 'now you die.'"

"They were quick to fight, I'll give you that," Snow said. Her eyes shifted in color, slowly becoming brighter. Feeling returned not just physically, but emotionally, as the power of the Heart of Ice receded from her, and the twinge of annoyance she'd felt during the fight grew into contempt. This crew really had been nothing but a bunch of overly ambitious, bloodthirsty idiots. "We probably did Harbin a favor taking them down."

"Oh, he'll love that. Glintchasers policing his town for him."

"If he wants, we can let the ones who are still alive go, and he can catch them himself."

"Don't be petty."

"Don't tell me what to do."

Phoenix gave her a hesitant half smile, which only grew more nervous and uncertain when she met it with her usual flat expression. Somewhere distantly, it occurred to her that between his brain and her delivery, he would have a hard time deciphering whether or not that had been sardonic banter or genuine malice she'd just thrown his way.

But she found she couldn't be bothered to clarify, or apologize for making him uncomfortable.

She did briefly wonder if calling him in for an assist without someone else to play buffer between them might have been a bad idea, but she swept that aside. They were adults. They could handle being alone on a job together.

"Well," Phoenix said just as the silence threatened to reach even more awkward lengths. "Harbin aside, at least we've got something to work with." He bent down to the closest fallen Old World weapon to examine it. After taking a closer look at the arcane circuitry—ruined enough to explain the sputtering power output—he stuffed the entire thing into a bottomless pouch on his belt that, on the outside, was no bigger than his fist. "I'll see what I can learn from these things, but if Silas is selling off parts of his new arsenal, it looks like he's only selling the dregs."

Snow nodded. "You look into that, I'll follow up and see what I can get out of these amateurs. They won't be able to give me Silas, but they'll have the next link in the chain."

"Are you planning on questioning them before turning them over to Harbin?"

Snow shrugged. "I can get to them whether they're in jail or not. Might as well let Harbin do the work to hold them."

"Ah, there's that famous glintchaser contempt for authority. It really is part of the charm, isn't it?"

Phoenix and Snow drew their weapons on reflex, even as they both recognized the voice. Materializing out of thin air came a woman with beige skin and bright blue hair and eyes that matched the short, layered silk robes she wore. Arcania script decorated one of her sleeves, marking her as the High Inquisitive of Tarsim Arcane Academy. To most of her professional colleagues, she was Kira Arakawa. But to anyone who actually knew her, she would always be—

"Ink," Phoenix said. "What are you doing here?"

The wizard looked between the two Starbreakers before focusing in on Phoenix. "I need to borrow you for a consultation. I've got an artifact my people can't make sense of, and I need to know what to do with it."

Phoenix's brow furrowed. "Now?"

"No, I teleported halfway across the kingdom to see if you could pencil me into your busy schedule for sometime next week," Ink said, dripping refined sarcasm. She gestured to their surroundings and the enemies that had already been taken care of. "Yes, now. It's not as if you're busy."

"I was going to go home after this."

Ink rolled her eyes. "I will have you back home before supper, if that's what you're worried about. Now come along."

Phoenix glared. He hated being ordered around by anyone, especially Ink, and Snow knew he would say no on principle. But Ink seemed to anticipate that as well, and kept talking.

"I could let my artifact experts keep whittling away at it, but their progress is slow, and everything else I'm working on is being held up by this. You'll be better and faster, and I need better and faster. So please, will you come along?"

She pushed out the last words like it physically pained her.

Snow probably still would have given Ink the finger and been on her way, but Phoenix could be a pushover, if you knew the buttons to push, and wounded and subdued as it had been over the years, his ego was still one of them, especially when it came to Ink.

He let out a long suffering sigh. "Fine."

"Thank you," Ink said, sounding as if the words were poison on her tongue. With Phoenix's assent secured, she began weaving a teleportation spell. The air around her and Phoenix shimmered, then began to break into a fractal pattern.

"Let me know if you find anything," Phoenix said to Snow. "I'll talk to you later."

And then, with a crash and a flash of light, he and Ink were gone.

Phoenix reappeared alongside Ink in what first impression identified as underground Old World ruins. There were no windows, the air had a cool stillness to it, and the architecture was several centuries removed from modern construction. Going off the exact style, he'd put them somewhere on the western coast of Corsar, where the ruins were most often the buried or sunken remains of Old World cities built long before the Collapse. The lightstone had long since been stripped from the grooves in the walls, but new fixtures were bolted in their places. A stripped and renovated ruin, then.

Several worktables had been brought into this room, all of them covered in books, papers, and inks. The walls were taken up almost entirely by chalk and pinboards, and the scrawl of notes and diagrams that filled them was dense to the point of being incoherent. All that, Phoenix considered normal enough. His own workshop back home had looked worse. He'd expected an office of some kind somewhere in the Academy, but then again Sasel was built on Old World ruins. Why couldn't the Academy use some for artifact storage and study?

The thing that tripped him up and got his attention was what all of the worktables and notations were centered around. Mounted on a rack, partially supported by cables affixed to the vaulted ceiling, was an unmistakable, bronze-colored bulk. It was in pieces, and much of its interior workings had been extracted or set aside on nearby work surfaces, but reassembled it would have been a twelve-foot-tall, broad, bipedal metal construct with long arms, a riveted metal exterior, and a central orb in the center of its chest instead of a head.

It was the remains of the Servitor, the Old World machine that had threatened to destroy Corsar. Even *one* of its Hearts could power unparalleled weapons, or turn people into them. Phoenix had fought the Servitor himself, ten years ago, in the ruins outside Loraine. It had choked the air with the dust from its swath of destruction. Hundreds of soldiers, knights, and glintchasers had died bringing it down, his own wife nearly among them.

That was what the Academy was working on. To imitate it, or bring it back, or something else entirely, it almost didn't matter. This was everything he had ever been afraid of since he'd first learned the secrets of spellforging, and had his eyes truly opened to the devastation the elves had brought upon themselves with all their mastery of magic.

"What is this?" Phoenix demanded.

Ink didn't seem to register the distress in Phoenix's voice or the fear and anger that accompanied the sudden racing in his chest.

"What does it look like?" she asked. "We're working to create our own artifacts based on the Servitor so we can actually use the Hearts we find. Without having to shatter them and fuse the energy into a person."

That was the thing about Servitor Hearts. They were incredibly powerful stores of arcane energies, but they were made to work together to power the Servitor, not be used individually by humans. Snow and Wings had gotten power from the Hearts of Ice and Sky, but in both cases, the original housing of the Heart had been destroyed, and the released energy had been infused into their bodies.

It came with physical and mental changes, and they'd needed surgical intervention to withstand the strain of it long-term. There were some people with the power to let them control the Hearts, like Kurien the Prince Killer, but most people could do nothing with an intact Heart beyond exploiting the passive effects of its presence.

"*This* is what you want my help with?" Phoenix asked.

"You're the authority on Servitor Hearts, as you love to remind us all. As well as the only spellforger on the continent," Ink said. "It could take my people decades to work out the principles to even let them get properly started on this project. With your knowledge, with spellforging, we could be prototyping designs tomorrow."

"No." Phoenix shook his head in disbelief. "You had to know I'd say no. I've said no a thousand times. This isn't just a consult to help you understand what you're dealing with, this— I'm *not* giving you spellforging. You know I won't."

Ink frowned. "Really? You're still on that, after all these years?"

"I've seen what spellforging let the elves do to themselves," Phoenix said. "I'm not going to let us end up like them."

"Powerful? Dominant? Spread across the stars?"

"Dead."

Ink's frown deepened, and she gave a frustrated shake of her head. "It's inevitable, you know. Someday, someone is going to unlock it, with or without your vow of silence. You can't keep all of humanity from spellforging forever."

"Maybe," Phoenix said. "But it won't be on me."

"Oh, but it will," Ink countered, raising a finger in a gesture that was oddly lecturing for her. "Choosing inaction is still a choice. You are the spellforger. The one man in all of Corsar, all of Costera, maybe all of Asher with the secret of the art. You have power, and you choose to do nothing with it. You forfeited your opportunity to decide the future, and now whatever shape it takes, it will take because you did nothing."

"This isn't about the future," Phoenix spat. "This is about *power*, and about how it *kills* you that someone else has it instead of you. That's what this has always been about. You, Targan, the whole Academy. You're all the same."

Ink gave a sharp, humorless laugh. It was a short and bitter sound, and it half sounded like her lungs tried to escape out her throat when she made it. Distracted as he was by his own anger, Phoenix might not have registered how out of character it was for Ink, if her face hadn't flickered at the same time. If, for just an instant, her features had looked subtly different. Subtly wrong. It passed with her laugh, but even with Ink's face stable once again, Phoenix couldn't unsee it. There was a shift in his brain, as it set aside arguments of ethics and started picking through the conversation with a new lens, a new goal.

"You knew I would say no," Phoenix said softly, more to himself than Ink.

Ink shrugged. "Perhaps. But one can still hope."

"You weren't hoping."

Now that he was looking with intentional scrutiny, the gesture was all wrong for her. There was no coy playfulness to her shrug, no grace. In fact, all her movements were stiff and tired. He played the entire conversation back in his head, played every conversation he'd ever had with Ink, and as the inconsistencies piled up, his hand drifted toward the holster of his wand.

This wasn't Ink, but that teleport spell had been real. These ruins were real. The Servitor was real. And whoever this really was, they had *known* Phoenix would say no to helping with this. Known, and brought him anyway.

In a single motion, Phoenix drew his wand and fired a blast of force at Ink's face. At the same time, his other hand drew the strongest fire sphere he had in his belt, and hurled it at the Servitor and all the scattered materials in the workshop. He was taking down whoever this really was, and he was turning this whole project to slag and ashes.

Except, without the imposter moving so much as a muscle, Phoenix's attack splashed harmlessly against a shimmering barrier of violet energy six inches from Ink's face. Without looking, she casually raised a hand toward the fire sphere he'd thrown. It froze in midair, and when it detonated, the explosion froze before it could expand beyond the size of a fist. It held in place, a quivering, half-finished combustion, straining against invisible bonds to be let free and fill the room in a superheated conflagration.

If there was any doubt left in Phoenix's mind that this wasn't Ink, it was gone now. Ink had never done anything like *that*.

"One minor benefit to you hoarding your secrets," Not-Ink said. "Without spellforging, we mortals have had little choice but to improve our direct spellcasting."

One of her fingers lifted, and the roar of flames filled the room as the explosion from the fire sphere that Not-Ink had contained erupted in a concentrated beam aimed directly at Phoenix. He threw up a force shield on instinct, and it was the only thing that saved him from being incinerated. The sheer force of the blast still took him off his feet and sent him careening out of the workroom and into the next chamber, this one larger, and dominated by a long meeting table surrounded by chairs. Phoenix's landing cracked the table in half. A groan escaped him as he rolled onto his stomach, then forced himself to his feet. Not-Ink strolled into the room after him with a stiff but unbothered gait, her face flickering again. Phoenix got the briefest look at whatever was under the illusion, lines and wrinkles mostly, but on the forehead, he swore he caught something more deliberate and unnatural. A symbol he hadn't had time to make the details of.

Then his stomach lurched, and he was falling—across the floor, and into one of the walls. His head spun with vertigo as he struggled to adjust to what he was seeing. The broken table, the scattered chairs, the Ink imposter were all exactly where they had been. But now his back was pinned to the wall, and the whole world looked like it had gone sideways. As if for him, and him alone, the concept of "down" had been shifted.

Flung around as much as he had been, Phoenix had lost his wand. He summoned it back to his waiting palm with a thought. It flew across the room to meet him, and the second it touched his hand, he was unloading everything the weapon had into Not-Ink. She extended two fingers toward him, and a beam of sizzling green energy met his wand's stark white. When the powers clashed, Phoenix's blast was instantly evaporated, as if it had been water and suddenly turned to mist. For a second, the dissipated energy hung in the air like a cloud of fog. Then, with a flick of Not-Ink's wrist, it all coalesced into a single point—inside the chamber of Phoenix's wand. He barely had time to widen his eyes in surprise before the weapon exploded in his hand.

Every cell in the wand detonated at once, creating a ball of smoke, flame, webbing, and pure energy that completely swallowed Phoenix. All he saw was white. All he heard was a ringing in his ears. His enchanted armor saved his life, but he felt its protections buckle under the assault. His coat was shredded, his leathers torn, and the flesh of his hand was slashed and burned.

Slowly, painfully, the world came back into focus. Rapidly dying flames licked the remnants of the table and chairs. Thick, massive cobwebs of spider silk clung to everything. Smoke hung thick in the air. And the fragments of his weapon laid scattered around him.

Not-Ink stood completely unscathed, along with a circle of floor around her that stood out stark against the scorched surface beyond it. She looked unimpressed.

"I should have done this years ago," she said. "If only I'd known it would be so easy."

She gestured, and Phoenix was falling again, this time toward the ceiling. Vaulted as they were, it would be a harsh landing. But even battered, even down his preferred weapon, his mind raced to keep up, to keep fighting. He dug a gravity disc out of his belt, activated it to slow his fall, and landed on his feet on the ceiling.

Not-Ink made a *tsk* sound, and a moment later, all of the furniture in the room followed Phoenix's lead, and fell up. Even throwing up a shield, he was battered under a rain of chairs, and when the halves of the tables hit, he crumpled beneath them.

Not-Ink snapped her fingers, and he and all the furniture fell back to the floor. This time, he was too slow to catch himself. He landed with a resounding thud, hard enough to bounce off the floor a few inches on the first impact. The wind was knocked from him, and chairs rained down on top of him until he was buried.

He tried to groan, but it came out as a wheeze as he struggled to get air back into his lungs.

Everything hurt. He was certain he had broken bones, and one of his arms was caught on something. He couldn't get a good look at Not-Ink, just her feet and the skirt of her robes, but it was enough to see as the illusion of her appearance dropped, replaced by long, unflatteringly loose Academy robes. He heard doors open, and more footsteps approach.

"Take him to the Prisoner," an old man's voice said. It was familiar, but Phoenix was fighting to remember it through what felt like a concussion. "Let us see if the madman is as good as his word."

"I still don't like this," a different, younger voice said, and Phoenix thought distantly that he recognized this one too. "His companions will come for him. If they find us—"

“They will be dealt with,” the old man insisted. “We have not come this far to be stopped by a disbanded glintchaser company. Now go. The sooner he’s put to work, the sooner we can move forward.”

Phoenix’s head throbbed, still spinning from being tossed around. Every breath sent a stab of pain raking through his ribcage. His right hand was trembling as it dribbled blood all over the floor, and beneath the shredded and crisped remains of his glove, he could see flesh burned black. He tried to force himself to get up. To fight. He needed to get away, to warn his friends and family.

That was his last thought before he blacked out.

4

STUDENTS

Brass braced his back against the dusty bulk of an old wardrobe and shoved as hard as he could. It scraped across the floor for a few feet, until it caught on an uneven patch on the floor and tumbled onto its side. It managed to land close enough to the door to barricade it, so he called that a win.

"Right. That ought to buy us a second."

Brass was a wiry man, styled as always to the nines in subtle eyeliner, smart riding boots, and a sharp, slim-fitting outfit befitting a fashionable man on a ride through the country, most of which was marred by scuffs and other people's blood. He combed his fingers through his short, dark curls and smoothed out his coat, trying in vain to restore a semblance of presentability to his ensemble. One of the downsides of wearing purple—it got dirty so easily. Realizing he was fighting a losing battle, he checked on his two tagalongs. "Does everyone still have all their limbs?"

Doubled over, shoulders heaving, Ruby nodded. Her shirt had come untucked, her sleeves were torn, and her bright red hair was rapidly coming out of its bun, but otherwise she was okay. For someone who'd been an escort less than a year ago, she took to mortal danger remarkably well.

Bart was more of a mixed bag. Even though none of the blood that splattered the blond paladin's armor was his, his face was just shy of total panic. Brass didn't know why the kid was so scared. He'd been doing great.

"I lost my mace."

Oh.

"That's fine," Brass said. "We'll get you another one. Besides, your body's a temple and temples are weapons. Or something. Right?"

The boy opened his mouth, but didn't find the words to respond.

"What are we supposed to do now?" Ruby asked.

"Excellent question."

It was supposed to be a simple gig. Rescue some hostages, report the numbers of the marauders who took them to the sheriff, and don't die. Classic call for help. Not much of a reward, but good fun and a high likelihood of some heartfelt thank yous. They'd find a collection of tents and campfires in the hills, sneak past a few idiots with repurposed farming equipment, unlock a cage or two, and make off like heroes. Brass had pulled off similar operations a dozen times in his younger days.

That was how he had pitched things to the two rookies.

A collection of tents and campfires turned out to be a partially refurbished Old World fortress, a few idiots turned into a hundred-strong warband, and unlocking cages turned into dueling the band's leader for the fate of the hostages. Thank the gods orc warleaders were all about duels, or the situation might have been hopeless.

Brass won the duel—obviously—but there were still several dozen sore losers in the fort out for their blood. Giving them the runaround in their own castle had worked up to a point, but now they were at a dead end.

The stairwell they'd taken had led them to a single room at the top of an observation tower with window slits wide enough to shoot out of but too narrow to squeeze through, and no other way in or out. Even now, the muffled sounds of shouts and footsteps were coming from the other side of the door.

"That's not going to hold," Bart said, staring at the barricade.

"No, it won't," Brass agreed.

He tried to ballpark the odds of them being able to just kill every marauder in the place, and decided that probably wouldn't go their way. The windows were out, since the only way through them involved grievous bodily harm. If Bart still had some god-juice left in him, they could try blowing a hole in the wall, but he seemed tapped.

"Brass?" Ruby pressed.

"I'm thinking!"

The footsteps from outside the door were getting louder, but most concerning of all were the repeated, lumbering thuds that were beginning to reverberate through the floor. Then came the bellowing growl. Something was coming. Something big. It occurred to him that, during his duel with the warchief, Brass had spotted quite a number of footprints that didn't look particularly humanlike.

"Think faster!"

Brass drummed his fingers on the wall, trying to do that. The growing sense of impending doom was certainly an excellent motivator, but he was beginning to remember why, in the most successful periods of his career, it was generally someone else doing the planning.

Something banged on the door hard enough to rattle the wardrobe and crack the door itself.

"Brass!"

For a moment, Brass considered whether or not this would be a good way to go. Even if they didn't get out, they were sure to take a few dozen of the assholes with them. As heroic last stands went, it was almost perfect. Except no one would live to tell about it. And he couldn't have that.

Finally, his long-suffering brain struck upon an idea.

He rummaged through his jacket pockets, searching for the one thing that could get them out of this, assuming he hadn't gotten high and sold it at some point. *Spare change. Dagger. Healing vial. Messaging paper. Cordon's keys. Birth control. Another dagger. Where's the—*

His search was cut off as another impact turned part of the door to splinters, and the wardrobe was shoved aside. Hunched to avoid scraping the ceiling, with swollen limbs, a wide jaw, and a club the size of a man, was an ogre. With the warband's claw mark insignia scrawled on its jaundice-colored face and murder in its eyes, it let out a roar that shook dust from the ceiling. At that moment, hands still buried in his pockets and horribly mispositioned to get between his sidekicks and the monster, Brass thought they were dead.

And then Ruby stepped forward.

Her skin turned deathly pale, bringing her veins into sharp focus. Her irises shined with an unnatural red glint, and her features seemed to sharpen.

Staring down the creature twice her size, she pointed a finger and shouted, "Stop!"

The ogre's body froze, and it stared down at Ruby, transfixed. The woman's command held the creature in place. It could not disobey, and so it stood, motionless.

To the young man's credit, Bart didn't hesitate. Even before Ruby had frozen the thing in place, he'd been rushing forward, and now, he had a clear opening. The strength of the god Renalt and the will of his saint, Beneger, flowed into the paladin's body. With a cry that tore from his lungs and force beyond anything a normal man could muster, he smashed his fist into the ogre's chest, caving it in with a single blow. The beast gurgled, sputtered, and toppled backward.

The color drained from Bart's face, and he nearly fell over himself. But he bought them precious seconds as marauders behind the ogre retreated to avoid being crushed by its bulk.

Brass's fingers finally found what they were looking for, and he rushed to pull Ruby and Bart to him.

"All right, children, final lesson of the day. Never pick a fight you can't run away from!"

From inside his coat, Brass produced a single, sea green glass orb, and threw it against the floor. Water splashed out as the orb shattered, rapidly expanding from a puddle into an impossibly deep, black pool that took up most of the room. The two rookies stared, transfixed by the sudden display of magic, while Brass merely smiled. He hadn't been sure whether or not the orb would actually work. He still wasn't completely sure, but this was promising.

From the depths of the pool, six enormous, sucker-covered tentacles reached out, breaching the water. An overpowering stench of salt water and mucus filled the room as the tentacles groped the air in all directions, searching. One of them found Brass, wrapping around his waist and lifting him off his feet. In another second, Ruby and Bart were scooped up as well.

"Everybody hold your breath!" Brass shouted.

"What?" Ruby screamed, before all of them were pulled beneath the surface, and the water vanished.

5
TEACHERS

Arno let out a sigh of relief as he sank into the waiting warm waters of Loraine's public baths. Where the water touched, he felt his muscles practically unravel as their tension dissolved. The heat carried away the weight of the day, letting his whole body unwind. He hadn't realized how badly he'd needed this until now.

Arno was a young man, only recently turned thirty, with short auburn hair, fair skin, and a smooth, cherubic face that was good at not showing the layers of stress he regularly operated under as both the leader of Saint Beneger's church in Corsar and a semiretired glintchaser who still spent too many days stopping his friends from bleeding to death.

The last few months had been a mountain of work. As the vicar of the Church of the Guiding Saint, he'd been leading a contingent of his fellows to help with reconstruction efforts in Loraine after the devastation wrought by an attacking army of undead. But today, for a few blissful moments, Arno was able to relax. Nobody needed him, he didn't have anything urgent to do, and he could simply breathe.

Thank you, Renalt.

He managed to do nothing but relax for almost five minutes. And then he felt a cold spot at the bottom of the bath. It started small, but it got bigger, until the entire bath was cold and much deeper than it was supposed to be.

Arno looked down into the water, wondering what had happened, only to see a face rapidly rising up from the water.

The priest's eyes widened, and he scrambled to get out of the way as Brass broke the surface, gasping for air. A moment later, Ruby and Bart followed, both out of breath and thoroughly soaked.

Bart coughed violently as he clung to the side of the bath. By the look of him, it was taking everything he had just to hang on to the edge.

Brass gave a victorious cackle. "Great job, everyone! Top marks all around."

Arno finally found his voice. "Brass?"

"Church!" Brass splashed over, throwing his arms around the priest. "Seven hells, am I glad to see you! Hey, where are we anyway?"

"The baths at Loraine," Arno said, trying to gently pry himself free.

Brass looked around, recognition finally coming to him. "Oh. So we are."

"What happened? How did you get here?"

"And what *was* that thing?" Ruby added.

"We finished up that job I mentioned, I used a kraken token I won from a sailor in a card game to get us out, and it was a kraken," Brass answered sequentially.

Before Arno could ask any more questions, he realized there was blood in the water, most of it surrounding the young acolyte of the church. "Bart, you're bleeding!"

"No, it's all right, Vicar." He tried to wave Arno off. "It's not mine. I just—"

The paladin tried again to pull himself out of the water to no avail. The swim to the surface had used up what little he had left in him, and now his arms refused to cooperate. His head slumped against the edge of the bath. "I am so tired."

"I've got you," Ruby offered.

She grabbed on to his forearms, and between the two of them, they managed to drag him out, where he promptly collapsed onto the floor in a sopping wet heap. Ruby meekly patted his breastplate in a comforting gesture, though she looked almost as spent as Bart.

Arno immediately looked to Brass for an explanation. "What happened?"

"It worked out fine."

"That isn't what I asked."

Brass threw up his hands. "Some of the townspeople got nabbed by a few bandits, and we went to rescue them."

"A few bandits?"

"Maybe a few more than a few."

Arno looked at Ruby. Deliberately avoiding eye contact with the vicar, she dragged Bart onto his feet. "Come on, Soap, let's get you dried off."

Bart gave an exhausted mumble, protesting that that wasn't his freelancer name anymore, but he let Ruby haul him up and out of the room, leaving Brass on his own to deal with his old companion.

Arno scowled. "Brass."

Brass stopped partway through climbing out of the bath, throwing his hands up in the air. "What? They're fine!"

"What. Happened?"

"Well, there were more bandits than we thought, and they had some surprise muscle, but everybody got out fine, and I finally got a use out of that damn marble," Brass said. "You should have seen the kid out there, he's a natural. Both of them, actually. I don't see what the problem is."

"You're endangering their lives, maybe worse. And why did Ruby call him Soap? He's not a freelancer, he shouldn't have a freelancer name!"

"Little late on that caravan, your Holiness," Brass said. "They can take care of themselves. Honestly, I haven't seen talent like them since . . . well, since us. And we got in over our heads all the time at their age."

"We aren't what I would consider an example to follow."

"Oh, so you're one of those 'do as I say, not as I do' priests," Brass said. "I'm almost disappointed. I thought you were better than that."

"This isn't even the important part," Arno groaned. "Ruby should not be using her powers, and you know it."

"I do?" Brass asked. "Because I thought they were really handy. Stopped an ogre dead in its tracks and everything."

"There was an ogre?"

". . . no."

"Could you take this seriously for five minutes?"

"If there's something to be serious about."

"Every time Ruby uses her powers, she ends up more in debt to whatever demon gave them to her. And if it gets to be too much, that's her soul, gone," Arno warned. "Is that serious enough for you?"

Brass rolled his neck, mercifully not snarking back at him. "Well . . . yeah, obviously. But you're cooking up a fix for that, so what's the problem?"

"There is a limit to how much a mortal can interfere with cosmic law," Arno chastised. "She might already be beyond anything I can do."

"Well if she's *already* fucked, no sense in not getting some use out of them before she kicks the bucket."

Arno tried one last time to get Brass to stop dismissing the problem. "Brass, do you have any idea what kind of a fate losing your soul is?"

"I imagine it's unpleasant?"

For once in his life, Arno wished he could channel some of the fire and ill-omened spouting that tended to come from the followers of Saint Ricard. They were good at getting these kinds of messages across, usually in uncomfortably vivid detail. The best he could muster was, "It's very unpleasant. Forever."

"Can you help her or not?"

He shouldn't have let Brass turn it back around on him, but he couldn't help it. There was something about him that couldn't ignore a call for help. Even from Brass.

"I think so. Angel and I have an idea, but we're missing a few pieces, and for our best shot, I'd want to work with the Church of Avelina," Arno said. Before Brass could say anything though, he hastened to add, "And I need Ruby *here*, not out making the problem worse."

"Fine, no more adventures or fun for them," Brass said. "I was just trying to give her a chance to stretch her legs. She's going crazy just sitting around all day."

"She is?" Arno asked. "Or you are?"

For a moment, Brass didn't say anything, and Arno wondered if he had accidentally caused a miracle. He even thought he saw a semblance of shame on the glintchaser's face.

After failing to think of a comeback, Brass gave in. He hauled himself out of the bath and grabbed a nearby towel. "Well. I suppose I'll get out of your hair."

"Brass, wait," Arno said, and was ignored.

Without another word, Brass left the room, leaving Arno alone. The vicar sighed, and sank lower into the water.

"That was my towel."

6

NEW BLOOD

Loraine had come a long way in the short time since it had been attacked by the Dread Knight. Though some people had taken the attack as a sign that it was time to leave for new pastures, much of the evacuated populace had returned once the danger had passed. Thanks to the repair efforts, you couldn't even tell that only a few months ago the town had battled an army of undead—unless you remembered that the crumbled Old World ruins surrounding it used to be a lot taller.

Ruby liked Loraine. She liked what it stood for, as one of the rare ruin-towns that outlived the typical economies of opportunity that created such places. Something about people building a real home out of the broken bits and pieces of the Old World filled her with a sense of almost hereditary pride, like Loraine was a victory for humanity itself. She liked the people, who had the kind of stubborn resilience to keep coming back and rebuilding their home no matter how many times an apocalyptic battle was waged on their doorstep. She liked how *interesting* the town was. Something new was always happening, whether it was a local priest making contact with the ghosts of star-crossed lovers, a merchant coming in with potions and devices she'd never heard of, or, yes, a warband kidnapping locals and holding them up in a restored keep to the east. But more than any of that, Ruby just liked how people treated her here. In the small town of Aenerwin, everyone knew her as the girl whose soul was in the grip of a demon. Everyone there either feared or pitied her. In Loraine, if anyone recognized her at all, it was as one of the heroes who had defended the town from the Dread Knight's army. Or, more commonly, as just another glintchaser passing through the ruintown looking for work.

She scoffed. Never would she have thought that being seen as a glintchaser would make her feel normal, but that was her life these days.

Freshly toweled off, changed, and still aching with exhaustion from the job with Brass, Ruby and Bart staggered through the doors of Loraine's new most popular tavern, a long, two-story building made mostly of stone with a rusted sign depicting a star hanging out front. Inside, the dinner crowd of merchants, mercenaries, prospectors, and reconstruction workers filled the tables and stools.

The new staff, all of them young citizens of Loraine who had lost something in the battle against the Dread Knight, were darting in the gaps between tables, handing out tankards of beer and bowls of chicken soup. Behind the counter, the bartender smiled as she saw Ruby and Bart come in, and her dark curls bounced as she waved to them.

"Hey you two!" Thalia greeted. "The usual, Ruby?"

"Make it two," Ruby said, glancing at Bart.

"Oh, no, that's fine," Bart said. "I don't drink."

Ruby cocked her head. "Is this like a religious thing?"

"No. Well." Bart's head wavered from side to side. "Yes and no? It's a paladin thing. Drink clouds the mind and dulls the senses, and a paladin should always have mastery over himself."

"Oh come on," Ruby prodded. "You're paladin-ed out for the day anyway. And we just fought an army and lived. We deserve to celebrate."

Behind the bar, Thalia finished pouring the first glass, and held up a second with a questioning look. Ruby tilted her head, her eyes asking him, inviting him to join her. Those eyes practically spoke, *Please? For me?*

Those eyes were unfair, Bart thought. A part of him wondered if she was even doing it on purpose, she'd slipped into the look so naturally.

The Tenets of St. Kalvin the Deliverer were very explicit. A paladin was never to allow his mind to be diluted, lest his ability to perform his duty suffer. His resolve must never waver, lest it be broken in the heat of battle.

But that book had been written two hundred years ago, and Saint Kalvin had never had to say no to Ruby. Besides, Vicar Arno drank when he was a freelancer.

"All right."

"That's the spirit!"

Thalia poured the second drink, a short glass of Antemer whiskey, and passed it off to Bart. Gingerly, he took the glass, staring at its contents. After bracing himself, and watching Ruby take a sip of her own glass, he tried to drink his.

He knew it would burn, but how much still surprised him, and then his nostrils started burning too. He fought back the urge to cough, and ended up just clearing his throat several times and rapidly exhaling through his nose. He was worried his eyes had gone red.

Ruby laughed. "Oh saints. That's—" She stopped to laugh again. "Sorry. Breathe in, drink, then breathe out. Helps."

"Good to know." Bart cleared his throat again. It still burned, but he was doing his best to keep signs of it off his face. He did a poor job.

Ruby smiled anyway, appreciating the effort. "You don't have to keep drinking it."

Bart shook his head to indicate he was fine. Trying to put on a brave face, he raised his glass. "To trying new things."

"And not getting killed," Ruby added, clinking her glass against his.

Sure enough, the second sip wasn't nearly as bad as the first. And when Bart got past the initial shock of the burn, he supposed the taste wasn't actually that bad. What he could taste of it, anyway. He still wondered about the actual appeal of drinking, but he reckoned he could finish his glass.

"So what's this about an army trying to kill you?" Thalia asked.

Ruby's eyes lit up, and she hurriedly finished her drink. "Oh, that's a story."

And for the next hour as the dinner rush wound down, Ruby and Bart told it. From Brass asking them to come with him on a "field trip," to using themselves as bait in an ambush, to the duel with the warchief and the subsequent all-out brawl through the keep.

Although, partly from excitement and partly from the drinks Ruby kept ordering, they didn't exactly tell it in order. They interrupted each other, skipped around in the order of events, and more than once seemed to get confused about what actually happened.

Which didn't make it any less fun to listen to.

"And so then it breaks down the door, and the ogre is in the room, screaming bloody murder." Ruby pointed at Bart. "And *this* madman decided to *punch it*. It's as big as five of him, and he's got no weapon, so he *punches* it. And it drops like a sack of rocks!"

"A paladin's body is his weapon," Bart said, setting down another empty glass. "That's why I can't drink. I have to keep it in perfect shape."

"You're drinking right now."

"I'm not paladin-ing right now."

They both laughed, and even when they finally stopped, Bart couldn't get the grin off his face. It felt good to laugh. To be alive. He hadn't even realized until now, talking through the whole thing, how close they'd all come to dying very violent deaths. He was sure that should terrify him. But it just made him laugh again. They lived. They won.

He thought he was beginning to understand drinking.

"I think I could get used to this," he mused. Not just about the whiskey. But about everything their lives had become.

Ruby shook her head. "Okay, but for real. If you're actually gonna be a freelancer, you need a better name."

Thalia cocked her head. "What's his name now?"

The two young people exchanged a glance.

"Soap," Bart said.

"Soap?"

"You know. It's like . . . clean. But morally," Bart tried to explain.

"It's not a very good name," Ruby said. "And neither were the last three he tried."

"I'm working on it."

"Don't let Church hear you say that," a new woman's voice warned.

Angel sauntered into the Rusted Star, flour dusting her dark skin and curly hair as she carried bags of provisions for the tavern tucked under her arms. As the owner of the Rusted Star, she did most of the shopping to keep the tavern stocked and operational. And as the one with six feet of solid muscle to work with, she was the one who did most of the heavy lifting too. Unless she deliberately chose otherwise, Angel was the Starbreaker most likely to pass for a normal person in her day-to-day life. She didn't wear magical or flamboyant clothes or a priest's vestments, or even armor—she got by with a simple tunic and pants, the bright red sash around her waist the only real color to her ensemble. She was strong, but almost never showed just *how* strong. She looked the part of a simple, salt-of-the-earth tavern owner, and for the most part, that was how she liked it.

She gave the pair of young, burgeoning freelancers a questioning look. Ruby wasn't an unusual sight in the Star, but Bart was, and both of them looked like they'd had more than a casual glass to end the day.

"We went on a job with Brass and didn't die!" Ruby said.

"And I'm learning how to drink!" Bart added.

Angel imagined Arno's reaction to the scene, could almost hear the cleric having a fit and worrying over the corrupting influence Brass was having on his protégé, and the thought made her smirk. She turned her attention to Ruby.

"You feeling all right?" she asked.

"Never better," Ruby said. "Why?"

"Church says you've been using your powers. Just wanted to know if anything felt different."

Ruby was quick to shake her head. "Nope."

Angel's stomach twisted into a knot as she watched the girl. Maybe when Ruby was sober, she had a good poker face. But a couple of drinks in, it started to crumble. She didn't make eye contact. Went back to her drink in a hurry.

She was lying.

Angel kept her face neutral as she left to drop off the supplies. The lying wasn't malicious, as far as she could tell. The kid was scared. Six months ago, Ruby had been a high-class escort in a fancy hotel. Now she was living with a bunch of former freelancers while they tried to figure out how to get her out of the demon pact she'd stumbled into during a near-death experience. That was a lot to deal with, and Arno's constant doomspeak about how badly these pacts ended for people probably didn't help.

So, instead of saying anything, when Angel got back, she just patted both of the kids on the shoulder and jerked her head toward Bart. "I think he's had enough for tonight. Can you get him upstairs?"

"I'm fine," Bart said. Unfortunately, he emphasized the point by leaning back in his seat as he waved away her concerns, and whatever precarious balance he still had failed him. He and his stool pitched over, and he ended up sprawled face down on the floor, groaning.

Ruby gave him a sympathetic smile before nodding to Angel. "I got him. Come on, Soap. Let's go."

Thalia was about to say that they still needed to pay, but Angel discreetly held up a hand to stop her. The bartender shot her boss a questioning look, but kept her mouth shut as Ruby hauled Bart to his feet, and, leaning on each other, the two of them staggered upstairs to their rooms.

"Since when do you let anyone drink on the house?" Thalia asked.

"I'll bill Church for it later."

"What's bothering you?"

Angel wondered if Thalia was that good at reading her, or if she was just that obvious. "Ruby. She's getting worse, but she's keeping it to herself."

"She seemed fine to me."

"She's not."

"Is this a Sentinel thing?"

"Not exactly," Angel said. "It's not like a sixth sense or anything. I just know what it's like to have a power inside of you, eating at you while it makes you stronger."

"Right."

"I can be careful with it," Angel said. "Control it, so it doesn't kill me. *Usually*. She can't."

"Is she gonna be okay?"

Angel didn't answer immediately, keeping her eyes on the stairs Ruby and Bart had gone up rather than looking at Thalia. "Church has one last idea. But we're going to need a few things. We're leaving tomorrow to start looking for them, so we should pack tonight."

Thalia nodded. "Okay. But, it will work, right?"

Angel frowned. "If we find what we need, yeah. As long as Ruby can hold on until then."

7
NIGHTMARE

Acrid smoke stung Ruby's eyes as flames roared on all sides. With every breath, embers clung to the inside of her airway. There was no air, only choking black smoke and ash. Fire lashed out at her, drawing ever nearer. Her clothes caught fire. She caught fire. She couldn't draw in the breath to scream.

There was nothing left of the world, just the blaze and the pain. And then, just before she was consumed, it stopped. The pain vanished. A cool sensation slid down her throat and filled her lungs. All around her, fire continued to rage, but she could breathe. There were no burns on her skin.

The fire will not hurt you.

The words reverberated through Ruby. She did not hear them in her mind so much as feel them in her bones. The voice enveloped her, wrapping around her like a thick cloak as the smoke and flames did the same. They merged, becoming a warm breath surrounding her body. In her ear. Down her neck. Across her skin.

Nothing will ever hurt you again.

Flames parted before her, revealing a face Ruby couldn't forget. Tall and thin, narrow orange eyes glowering back at her as his face twisted into a sadistic grin. Pitch.

Her blood boiled at the sight of him. Of his smile. It was the one he'd worn when he'd burned down her life.

I will give you revenge.

Without thinking or knowing why, Ruby extended a hand toward him. From her wrist, a twisted black vine of thorns shot forward, wrapping itself around Pitch's arm and biting into his flesh. His smile vanished, and Ruby felt a rush of satisfaction.

She extended her other hand, and another vine shot forward, finding his other arm and coiling up to reach around his neck. The vines tightened, digging the thorns in deeper and wringing blood from Pitch's flesh like a rag while he screamed.

Let him know what it felt like to be powerless. To suffer more pain than he knew was possible. To be afraid and hate himself for letting someone else make him feel that way.

With a yank on the vines, he was on his knees at her feet, and her hands latched on to his head. His skull cracked and gave like an eggshell under her fingers. He screamed again, and she found herself drinking it in.

I will give you power.

Her wrists flared in pain, and she watched as the very same thorns she'd wrapped around Pitch wrapped around her own arms. And they grew, trailing off into the void around her. The vines tugged, and her hands moved without her consent, pressing on Pitch's head until it burst. Wet gore exploded out, splashing her face and coating her hands.

The flames vanished.

In their absence, Ruby was left in a hazy, smoke-filled void, charred ground beneath her feet. The thorns still wrapped around Pitch's body and hers, linking them in a chain that continued into the smoke. Her heart was pounding in her chest as she stared at what her hands had been made to do. She tried to back away, but the thorns held her in place. She tried to scream, but the sound stuck in her throat.

Something stirred behind Ruby. Suffering came off of it like heat from a flame, and she felt its breath again, washing her in a stench of sulfur that made her sputter and gag. Her legs gave out from underneath her, but the thorns held her up.

You will give me everything.

From somewhere behind her, a long, sinuous tongue unfurled. Its slick, slime-covered surface ran up her cheek, lapping away the blood still there. Finally, the scream Ruby had been struggling to get out tore itself free, and she sat up in bed. There were no flames. No smoke. Only the room she'd been given in the Rusted Star.

Ruby sat in the dark, shaking. Her heart still pounded, and her whole body was covered in a cold sweat that had soaked her bedding. Instinctively, she curled into a ball, hugging her knees as she tried to steady herself.

Breathe. Ruby was no stranger to nightmares. Not for the last several months. *I'm okay. Everything is okay.*

Surely with enough repetition, she could convince herself it was true.

The lie broke down the second she heard a knock at her door, and almost jumped out of her skin.

"Ruby?" Bart's voice came from the other side, laced with concern.

"I'm fine."

Her voice cracking didn't make it sound particularly convincing. She took a slow, deep breath, and brushed her hair from her face. Composed as she could manage, she answered the door.

Candlelight flooded the doorway, revealing Bart's worried face. His eyes were wide and alert, but his hair was still tousled from sleep.

"I heard you scream," Bart explained.

"I'm all right," she stressed, much more evenly this time. She almost believed it herself. "Just a bad dream."

"You have those a lot."

"Yeah."

He wasn't wrong. And he knew better than anyone, given their rooms shared a wall. She didn't always make enough noise for someone else to hear. But when she did, he always heard. And he always came.

"Maybe we should tell—"

"No!" Ruby surprised even herself with how fast she cut him off. She couldn't even place why she didn't want to tell Church or any of the other

Starbreakers. She only knew that she didn't want them to know, and that she had to convince Bart not to say anything.

She could just make him stay quiet. A few silvered words, and she could compel him to secrecy. Compel him to do anything.

No.

Ruby found herself thinking like that more and more. About how much easier her powers could make whatever situation she was in, whether it was dangerous or not. How it wouldn't hurt to use them just a little more.

Bart looked unsure. He was afraid for her.

"Church said everything would be fine soon," she reminded him. "There's no reason to get everybody worked up."

On an impulse, she took his hand. Her hand was steady by now, and she hoped it would be enough to prove she was all right. But then he surprised her as his grip on her tightened.

"I'm okay," she repeated.

"If you're ever not—"

"You'll be the first to know."

He nodded, accepting this for now. He squeezed her hand once before finally letting go. "Renalt watch over you."

She smiled, even as she felt her ears prickle at the god's name. Hearing a god's name had never bothered her before. But it did now. "Goodnight."

Gently, she closed the door to her room, and as quietly as she could, leaned against it until she slid down to the floor.

He'll never accept what you've become.

The voice was weaker when she was awake. A whisper in the back of her mind. Sometimes it even sounded like her. But as long as she could separate it out from her own thoughts, she could ignore it. Ignore it, and endure it.

She'd gotten enough sleep for the night anyway.

8

THE ACADEMY

Ink was upset.

By any reasonable metric, she was one of the smartest people in Corsar, if not the world. There was very little she didn't know or understand, and when she encountered something that fit that description, it never stayed that way for long.

But the Oblivion breakout was proving difficult.

She stared at the illusory replica of what had, until a few months ago, been the most secure prison in Asher. It was a near-perfect replica, complete with the positions of every guard and inmate as best could be approximated. At a gesture, she could make it translucent, change colors, and even advance and reverse the timeline of events within it.

As rough a timeline as she had to work with, anyway. The guard and inmate positions in the illusion were based on extensive interviews, on-scene investigation, and her own assumptions, which left gaps. Inmates especially were hard to track, even though this model alone had helped the guards recapture three that had been hiding on the island itself.

She had the epicenter of the breakout. Everything had started outside the cell of Kurien, the Prince Killer. According to the killer herself, someone approached her, and offered her freedom in exchange for her securing a shipment of Old World weaponry and delivering it to a handoff in Parthica.

Kurien's cell had been torn open with nothing but sheer, blunt force, and from there dozens more cells were open until enough inmates had been free to perpetuate the chaos themselves.

The problem was that, whoever Kurien's benefactor was, they'd gotten into the prison without leaving any sign of forced entry anywhere in the prison. Since Oblivion was warded against every form of teleportation and dimension travel known to man, there were only two possibilities. Either someone had found a physical way into the prison that bypassed all security and left no trace, or someone had found a way to do the impossible, and teleport into Oblivion through every ward and contingency the combined power of the Academy could muster.

Ink had spent most of her efforts on trying to definitively disprove that second option, because it would make her life so much simpler if she were only dealing with an immaculate infiltration. If someone had actually teleported in—

"Impossible" was always a shaky word when dealing with magic. Human understanding and capability in the field were growing every day, and the next major breakthrough was always around the corner when any provincial deer hunter might stumble on an Old World portal generator on a trip into the backwoods.

But there was a simpler explanation than the rules of magic being broken. It was one she dreaded, which was also why she held it as the most likely explanation. When it came to the kind of problems she dealt with, things tended to default to the worst-case scenario.

And it would have been easy to teleport into Oblivion if somebody on the inside had turned the wards off.

"High Inquisitive?" a metallic voice interrupted her thinking.

Gamma was an autostruct, a seven-foot-tall Old World construct made out of polished dark wood and silver metals. His body was a conglomerate of the remains of several autostructs, each with a different aesthetic sense to it. His right arm was the most ornate, with engraved marble accents inlaid across it. The disparate pieces had been a necessary work-around after a battle cost him his original body, but Ink actually liked the new look better. It had an improvised charm.

"What is it?"

"The reports from your requested resurrections of the Oblivion guards have been completed."

The autostruct held up a scroll case, and Ink immediately teleported it from its hand into hers with a snap of her fingers.

"Additionally, accounting has flagged the expense of the resurrections for review. You are now thirty-five percent over budget for the quarter."

"Tell accounting I'm thirty-five percent over their whining."

Fifteen guards had been at the scene of the epicenter of the breakout, and would have been right next to Kurien's cell when whoever freed her showed up. But all of them were killed in the breakout, and gravespeaking had been unusually unreliable for years now, as if there were some kind of interference between this life and the next.

So Ink had ordered for every single guard to be sent to the Church of Avelina for resurrection. Expensive, and probably a waste for some of them, given the state of a few of the bodies, but they needed eyes on the start of the breakout if she was going to make sense of this.

Of the fifteen, the church had outright refused to perform two of the resurrections, citing "excessive cruelty to the deceased." Another eight of the attempts failed. Of the five that actually came back, all had needed time to adjust to the trauma of coming back from the dead enough that they could actually be interviewed. Now, she finally had the results of those interviews in her hands. Three hadn't seen or couldn't remember anything useful. But the final two were where she struck gold.

Two accounts, in agreement. The breakout began with a man in golden armor teleporting into the middle of the cellblock in a cloud of silver smoke. He slaughtered the guards and ripped open Kurien's cell door, all without physically touching anything. The man wore a helmet that had stopped either of the guards from getting a good look at his face, so a proper description was out. But that almost wasn't necessary.

Silver smoke teleportation. Golden armor. Telekinesis.

On its own, it might not have been enough. But there was another piece to the puzzle: Pitch, the one escapee they'd never found, because the only thing the Oracle had told them was that he was already dead. Pitch, whose cell she'd personally found with a giant hole in the wall not made by fire. Pitch, who had been infused with the Servitor Heart of Flames.

There was only one person Ink could think of that fit the description of Oblivion's intruder and had a known interest in collecting the Servitor Hearts.

Sir Haegan of Whiteborough.

Except he was supposed to be dead. She'd read the autopsy report herself, after the Academy had recovered his remains from the ruins of his base. Killed by a sword to the throat, body incinerated, armor moved to an Academy vault for later study.

Then again, she hadn't seen the cremation herself. There was no doubt in her mind now.

She was dealing with the worst-case scenario.

There was a mole in the Academy.

"I'm sorry, what?"

Headmaster Targan glared at Ink, and his bony grip on the edges of his desk tightened. "I said: Drop. It."

As the High Inquisitive of the Academy, Ink's official role was to oversee the Academy's search for and acquisition of knowledge, and undertake whatever actions she deemed necessary in pursuit of that role. The inherent flexibility in that mission statement had always given past High Inquisitives a great deal of power and influence in the Academy's operations, but Ink had shaped the position into something even more than that. There were very few people within the Academy who didn't explicitly take their orders from her, and no one who gave them to her.

No one except for the Headmaster.

Targan was only fifty years old, but he looked eighty. His pale skin was speckled with sunspots, and set with deep wrinkles that left his face in a permanent frown. His hair had gone snow white, and was completely gone from the top of his head, having mostly migrated to his long beard. His fingers—his whole body, really, but especially his fingers—were gnarled and bony.

That was what happened to a human who used arcane magic without having their body altered to handle it. Across the sea in Hidora, mages had been undergoing a surgery to prepare their bodies to handle spellcasting for centuries, but the practice had been a closely guarded secret, and mages everywhere else in the world had to bear the burden of a lifespan slashed in half. Until a young Ink had stolen the secrets of the alteration, and fled to Corsar to escape service as an indentured court mage.

The alteration was standard practice in the Academy now, but by the time Ink had brought it over, Targan had already lost thirty years of his life to casting. Usually, Ink felt a small degree of pity for his situation. She'd been altered at the ripe old age of fifteen, before she'd cast so much as a cantrip. She was only just into her thirties, and she looked even younger than that. Targan was going to die decades before his time.

That usual pity was currently dried up, and replaced with seething, dumbfounded irritation.

"A dead man breaks into our prison, possibly makes off with the power of one of the artifacts we've been chasing for almost a decade, very likely supported by one of our own, and you want me to *drop it*?"

"Yes!"

Targan's voice boomed with supernatural volume, and the office itself shook. On the ceiling, an illusory rendition of the city of Sasel flickered as the Headmaster's concentration wavered, while every lightstone in the room flared up in response to his outburst.

Ink fell silent. It was easy to look at the Headmaster of the Academy and see only an aged man with a body ravaged by a lifetime of arcane practice. But he was also the most seasoned, and likely most powerful, mage in Corsar. And that, she begrudgingly admitted, was even counting her.

In a much more measured voice, she asked, "May I know why?"

"There are other forms of telekinesis besides the Heart of Force. Neither the teleportation method nor golden armor are exclusive to Sir Haegan, and more to the point, the man is *dead*!" the Headmaster snapped. "The Oblivion crisis is resolved, and we have already appointed a committee to review its security and close the gaps that were exposed. There are too many other, more pressing concerns that require our attention for you to waste time and resources chasing a man who is already ashes."

Targan rubbed his temple before picking up a glass of half-drunk tonic from his desk, and finishing it with a hard swallow. He slammed his now empty glass down. "Am I clear?"

"I will keep your priorities at the forefront of my mind," Ink said, choosing her words carefully.

All the pleasantry of agreeing to follow orders without any of the commitment. Her way of acknowledging that he was in charge while still tacitly admitting that she would be bending his wishes behind his back. This was how their dance had gone for almost a decade now.

But today, the Headmaster didn't stand for it. "This is not a request, Kira. I—"

"Arakawa." Ink cut him off, glaring daggers.

The Headmaster blinked.

"You may call me Arakawa. Or Ms. Arakawa, if you want to be formal about it. You may call me High Inquisitive, if you're feeling professional. You can even call me *Ink*, if you're feeling emasculated by glintchasers again and want to talk down to one to make yourself feel better," Ink said. "You may not, and will not, call me by my personal name. Am *I* clear, Headmaster?"

Targan had overestimated the leeway his position gave him when speaking to her, and her sympathy for the pressures on him. He knew damn well what a personal name meant to a Hidoran. Between two colleagues, it could have been an overstepping of personal and professional boundaries. But for it to come from a superior was the belittling equivalent of talking to her like a child. And that, she would not allow.

He met her glare and matched it. For a few seconds, they were silent as they each dared the other to speak another word.

He broke first. "I will be informing the other department heads. There will be no further resources directed to this, and I am to be informed if you attempt to access anything pertaining to Oblivion or Haegan. I have several other matters requiring your attention, which I expect you to devote yourself to. If you do not, there will be consequences. So for the final time, Ms. Arakawa, drop it."

He didn't apologize for the earlier slight, not that she expected him to.

In truth, calling him out on it had been more about principle and maintaining respect than any actual offense felt on her part. She didn't have time to be truly offended by the Headmaster's cultural insensitivity. She was too busy pondering a new avenue in her mole theory, one she would need to be *very* cautious in pursuing.

Ink gave Targan a stiff nod. "Yes, Headmaster."

The rest of their meeting was terse and brief as he laid out a laundry list of projects and lines of inquiry to bury her in, and she quietly and calmly accepted them. She maintained her composure all the way back to her office, even as her heart raced.

"High Inquisitive," Gamma greeted her at her office doors. "You have received an urgent meeting request."

"Tell them I'm busy, Gamma," Ink said.

"The request comes from—"

She held up a hand, and by preprogrammed directive, he silenced himself. "Busy."

Targan was an arrogant and bitter old man, and no one would mourn him when he was dead, but he had always been tolerable as employers went. His expectations were reasonable, his compensation to her was generous, and more to the point, he stayed out of her way. In her near decade working for the Academy, she had only been told to drop a line of inquiry twice. The first time had turned out to be because she was unknowingly poking into King Roland II's love life. The second had been Targan's plans to negotiate a cessation of hostilities with the Imperial Hall of Sorcery in Hidora, which he hadn't trusted her to be objective with on account of them wanting her dead. That was it. Targan trusted her instincts as High Inquisitive. If she thought something was worth pursuing, he let her pursue it.

So if he was blocking her now, she could only assume he was keeping her away from something. She suspected Haegan—and by now she was working off the assumption that Haegan had been the one behind the Oblivion breakout—had inside help with getting into the prison. And when it came to the sort of problems she dealt with, things tended to default to the worst-case scenario.

What could be a worse scenario than the Headmaster of the Academy himself helping to cause the largest breach in security in the Academy's history?

She'd have to be very careful looking into it, especially with him looking over her shoulder and constraining her resources. It was a problem. A puzzle, so engrossing that when she entered her office, she made it all the way to her desk before she realized she wasn't alone.

A gust of wind whipped through the room, slamming the doors shut behind Ink, and in the blink of an eye, there was a blade as cold as ice held to her throat. Wings stood by the open window of Ink's office, bow out, arrow drawn back. With the chill running down her back, Ink didn't need to turn around to know it was Snow holding the knife to her neck.

"Ink," Wings asked with barely restrained violence in her voice, "Where is my husband?"

Urgent meeting request indeed.

Ink smiled. "Ladies. Would you like to sit down?"

9

CONFIDANTS

Ten minutes of tense negotiations and a teleport spell later, Snow, Wings, and Ink were all sitting at a table in Ink's second favorite restaurant in Sasel: a rooftop steak and seafood spot that overlooked the harbor and sat just off the skyship *Cielsereno*'s patrol path. From their table, they had a clear view of the multicolored tapestry of hulls and sails in the harbor, the glittering towers of stone and glass that made up the city skyline, and even the great architectural marvels of the First Church of Avelina and the Pearl Palace. It was the sort of place most people in the city needed a reservation a month in advance to visit. Ink had teleported them all into the foyer, been instantly recognized by the staff, and seated within seconds.

Wings barely registered any of it, her attention fixated on the wizard in front of her. Her fingers were twitching, a nervous tick she'd developed after too many years finding comfort in the pull of a bowstring, and one of her legs wouldn't stop bouncing. She chewed her bottom lip, and fought down the urge to get out of her seat, fly around the city, and shoot the first thing she found that looked like it deserved it. The Heart of the Sky demanded freedom, motion, action, and that demand always grew stronger when she was stressed. It gave her incredible instincts and reaction time in fights, and made flying feel better than sex, but it also made moments like this, where she was stressed and had to stay put, absolute hell.

"Why did we have to come here?" she demanded.

"Because, for a variety of reasons, this is a conversation I'd like to have outside of the Academy's walls. There are eyes and ears I don't trust in that place right now, me throwing up an obfuscation spell isn't nearly as suspicious in public as it would be in my office, and neutral ground with lots of witnesses tends to help people behave," Ink said. "Also, it's past three o'clock, and I still haven't had lunch."

A waiter came by, and Ink put in an order for three of her usual.

Wings nearly exploded into a half-coherent flurry of shouts and demands for the wizard to take things seriously, and only just restrained herself. Sitting next to her, Snow couldn't have been a sharper contrast. The assassin sat motionless, face frozen in a flat expression, staring at Ink as if she were prepared to wait all day.

"What's got you so paranoid?" she asked.

"Maybe we should circle back to that," Ink said. "Although apparently I can add 'someone is impersonating me to kidnap glintchasers' to the list."

"If it wasn't you, then who took Arman?" Wings asked. There was no accusation in her tone. They'd gotten that out of the way back in Ink's office, and Wings's own knack for catching lies left her certain of Ink's sincerity when she said in no uncertain terms that she had no idea what they were talking about, and that she hadn't seen Phoenix in months.

"Well, that's the million-glint question," Ink said. "You're looking for someone with access to illusory disguises, teleportation, and a way of pinpointing the location of either a shadow thief, or a man who literally wraps himself in antiscrying wards."

"Which still describes you," Snow pointed out. Wings might have been convinced that Ink was telling the truth, but Snow preferred to keep a healthy distrust of everyone, even in the most exonerating of circumstances.

"Oh gods and spirits, I didn't take him," Ink said. "What would I even *do* with him? If I wanted an egotistical man with expertise in arcane theory, I've got my pick of them back at work."

"None of them are spellforgers," Snow said.

"Have you ever heard of the Tarsim Definition of Insanity? About trying the same thing over and over again? Phoenix has said no to working with the Academy more than enough times to make himself clear, and even if I wanted to coerce him into doing it, I wouldn't kidnap *him*. I'd kidnap her." Ink gestured to Wings, whose eyebrows shot up. "Or maybe the baby." The eyebrows rose even higher.

Snow gave an acquiescing shrug of her head, acknowledging one cutthroat to another that that probably would be the best way to coerce Phoenix into service, short of outright mind control.

"Where is the little bundle of chaos anyway?" Ink asked nonchalantly.

Wings stared at the both of them in utter disbelief. In fact, Wings had moved Robyn and the rest of Phoenix's family to a warded safe house as soon as she'd suspected something had happened. But Ink didn't need to know that, and given her attitude, didn't deserve to.

"Can we stay on topic?" Elizabeth asked.

"Fair enough. If I had to make an educated guess—" Ink said, and hesitated. Cold calculus and tactical evaluation were written across her face as she stared at her two lunch companions. "I would wager it was someone inside the Academy behind this."

Wings's eyes were already as wide as they were going to get, and the intensity of her stare hadn't dropped since leaving Ink's office, but now Snow looked intrigued as well.

"Circle back to you not trusting the Academy," Snow said.

Ink nodded. "I've come to the conclusion Oblivion was partially an inside job. I think there's a mole in the Academy who worked with Haegan and his lot to orchestrate it. And I think it's Targan."

"You mean Silas," Snow corrected. "Haegan was his boss."

Ink gave a tight-lipped smile. "About that."

She told them everything she'd learned and now suspected about the Oblivion breakout. The eyewitness descriptions of the perpetrator that eerily matched the deceased Sir Haegan of Whiteborough. The way Targan had shut down her inquiry into the subject.

“If he is working with Haegan, Silas, whomever,” Ink said. “It would explain how Silas’s lackeys were able to teleport out of Nikos.” She nodded to Snow, who had seen Silas’s lieutenants, René and Rosa, vanish along with an entire shipment of stolen arcane weapons. “You described the device they used as a beacon, but we were sure it had to be a teleporter of some kind, because a beacon shouldn’t have let them teleport out. But, it’s not that it’s impossible for a mage to reach out across a continent and teleport something thousands of miles away. It’s just that doing it, even with a beacon to help aim, would require said mage to be exceptionally powerful. As powerful as the Headmaster.”

Snow nodded, slow and thoughtful. “Silas and Haegan have been after the Servitor Hearts for years. Anyone looking into those has to know Phoenix is the biggest expert there is on them. The contract didn’t work, but they still need what he knows. If they’re working with the Headmaster, and they were desperate enough . . .”

Wings tensed in her seat, her whole body suddenly like a loaded spring. Ink hadn’t just given her a lead, she’d given her a name. A target to shake down for answers. The wind picked up, blowing several surrounding tables’ napkins away, and Wings’s irises swirled and crackled like the clouds of an oncoming storm.

“I hasten to clarify that I don’t have any real proof,” Ink said. “Certainly not enough for you to go storming the office of the most powerful man in Corsar.”

Wings drew in a deep breath, knowing Ink was right even as her bones screamed for her to take to the skies, fly straight to the Academy, and have an informal meeting with the Headmaster. That would be impulsive, and stupid, and liable to get her arrested at best, killed at worst.

“Do you think he did it or not?” she asked.

“I don’t know, and I can’t look into it at this point without him knowing,” Ink said. “If he’s watching everything I do at the Academy, then someone else might be able to do some digging without being noticed. Especially if that someone could claim to be working on official business for the Crown?”

Wings took Ink's meaning. "Where should we start looking?"

"Haegan being dead and at Oblivion is a rather glaring discrepancy that Targan doesn't seem to want me poking around at. Start there. Ask for the head of Cataloguing and Collections. She'll be able to help."

Wings nodded, before glancing to Snow. "You know, you might be better off doing some off-the-books snooping. I go through the front door, you rifle through their drawers, that sort of deal?"

Snow shook her head. "I want to come at this from the other side. If we think Targan's working with Silas, then I might be able to dig something up by sticking with tracking him down. I already know he's somewhere in this city, and if he's moving the weapons he got from Nikos through here, I know someone who can find him."

"Sound strategy," Ink said. "I daresay we have a plan. And just in time for the salad course."

Wings nodded, even though she wasn't hungry. Because they had a plan now. She had something she could do besides flying around the kingdom, frantically checking all of her husband's old haunts and reaching out to everyone she knew for answers they didn't have. She was going to find Arman. She just had to pray that wherever he was, he was all right, and would stay that way until she found him.

10
THE SERVITOR

Her Royal Majesty Queen Katherine and her husband King Roland I had put out a call for aid, and by the gods and saints had they gotten a response. Dozens of faces were crammed into a war room normally meant for a council of seven. Outside, in the courtyard and outside the gates, hundreds more waited.

Everyone the monarchs normally depended on was here: their general, their castellans, the Headmaster of the Academy. So were representatives of the knightly orders sworn to protect the kingdom. The Order of Saint Ricard from the mountains. The Seven Gates from Sasel. The Purple Rose from Relgen. But most of the people in attendance were freelancers. The most renowned companies from across the country were here, brought together to fight a single threat, and hand picked by the people running the meeting.

The Starbreakers.

Roland had just finished his speech, thanking everyone for coming and warning them that the threat they faced was impossibly dire.

Gray, the current leader of the Cord of Aenwyn, spoke up. "Since no one else is getting to it, what—exactly—are we dealing with here?"

Phoenix cleared his throat, scratching at the stubble on his chin. Herding four other freelancers through ruins was one thing. Addressing a room of this many important people was more authority than he had ever felt prepared to wield. But it was too late to worry about that now.

"Well, the full explanation is a bit of a history lesson, so I'll go with the Cliff's Notes."

He turned to the Cord's wizard, usually one of his least favorite people. "Ink, would you be so kind as to provide visuals?"

The young woman smiled, steepling her fingers as wisps of light began to gather in her hands.

"But of course. Care to give me something to work with?"

Phoenix gestured for Church to step forward.

"Don't worry. I won't bite," she teased with a smile.

"Why would you?" Church asked, confused.

Ink sighed, before placing her hands on either side of the boy's head. She closed her eyes, and reached into Church's mind, searching through his memories to find an image. After getting what she needed, she traced a quick arcane pattern in the air, and an image of what they were up against shimmered into being in the center of the room. It was vaguely humanoid in shape, with broad shoulders, long arms, and a central orb of some kind in the center of its chest instead of a head. The creature looked to be made of thick, riveted bronze with pegs jutting out from its back.

"It's called the Servitor," Phoenix explained. "It's an Old World weapon. The biggest, most powerful we've ever seen. And it's on a rampage. It carved a canyon through the mining town where they dug it up, and every village it's found has been wiped off the map. Given its current path, it'll hit Olwin in just under two weeks, and do a lot of damage on the way there."

"What kind of power does this weapon possess?" Headmaster Targan asked.

"They're called Hearts. Magical power sources. Some of them are keyed to elemental magic, others are for more complicated things. One Heart is almost impossibly powerful. This thing—" Phoenix pointed to the things protruding from the Servitor's back "—has four. The Heart of the Sky, the Heart of Life, the Heart of Shadows, and the Heart of Force."

"And how is it that you could be so knowledgeable about them while the Academy knows nothing?" the Headmaster inquired.

"We found the Heart of Ice," Snow stated, deadpan. To drive the point home, she let frost creep across her features. "It was an educational experience."

"With all due respect, Headmaster," Ink offered, "there's only so much staying in school will teach you. Digging up Old World secrets is just what we freelancers do."

"Your Majesty, why are glintchasers in charge of the defense of the kingdom?" the knight commander from the Purple Rose asked. A tall, thickly built light-skinned man, with closely sheared blond hair. His eyes narrowed as he glanced to Phoenix, whom he was at least a decade older than. "Their ilk have caused dozens of problems like this."

"First off," Brass declared, pointing an admonishing finger at the knight, "'glintchasers' is our word. You can call us 'sword sluts.' Second, we're in charge because we've got a Sentinel, the Heart of Ice, and the only spellforger on this side of the world. And also Church, I guess. We are literally the best bet anyone has of stopping this thing."

"I also have a plan," Phoenix was quick to add. "I've got a way to drain the Hearts out of the Servitor and into artifacts that can contain them. But, we're going to have to keep the Servitor in one place long enough for them to work. And I'm going to need materials from the Academy to make more."

The Headmaster turned to the king and queen, to see whether he was expected to obey this young upstart.

"Get him whatever he needs," Queen Katherine ordered.

The Headmaster grimaced, but nodded. "Of course, Your Majesty. It will be done."

"Everything we know about this thing says it'll hit the town of Loraine in a week. Just outside the town are mostly intact ruins that'll give us the advantage and make it easy to box the thing in. We lure it there, pin it down, and drain it until it can't fight back," Phoenix concluded.

"We're engaging the weapon near the people?" the Rose's commander asked, appalled.

"The ruins outside Loraine are our best shot. If we pull this off, the people will be safe," Phoenix said, rubbing the back of his neck. "If we don't . . . well, they're in trouble anyway, no matter where we fight it."

"We will be following the Starbreakers' plan," Roland announced, his tone implying he would hear no protest on the matter. "My wife will command all orders and companies at the site of the battle."

The commander of the Purple Rose yielded. "Yes, Your Majesty."

The meeting broke up soon after, and everyone started leaving to prepare their various roles in the coming fight. Phoenix tried to flag down Snow to talk strategy, but she very pointedly ignored him, and walked out.

"Everything okay with you two?"

Sable, the warden from the Broken Spear, sauntered over, a curious expression on her face. Very little about people ever seemed to get past her, and the tension between Phoenix and Snow had caught her eye.

The Spear were the closest thing the Starbreakers had to a sister company. While they weren't actually the most accomplished, they were trusted friends, which was more than welcome right now. But it had been a while since the two companies had crossed paths, which was probably why Sable didn't know what was going on.

"Actually, we, uh . . . you know, we stopped—"

"Oh."

"Yeah," Phoenix said. "It's . . . been awkward working together since."

"Right." Sable was silent for a long moment before clearing her throat. "Well, I just wanted to . . . say good luck. And thanks for asking for our help."

He seemed to buy that, nodding.

Sable immediately turned to go. "Anyway, I'll see you in Loraine, I guess."

"Elizabeth?"

Sable stopped, surprised he used her real name. "Yeah?"

". . . be careful out there."

She gave him a smile, easy and genuine. "You know, between the two of us, I'm pretty sure you're the one with the bigger penchant for getting into trouble."

11
PAWNS

Phoenix was fine, and that worried him. The last thing he remembered, he'd been blasted, tossed around like a rag doll, and battered by furniture. He'd had cuts, bruises, burns, and broken bones.

And now, he was fine. Locked in a too-bright, windowless cell with iron bars and stone walls, stripped of his armor and tools, with no clear sense of where he was or how long he'd been there. But physically, he was fine. If he'd been rescued, he'd expect to wake up at home, in the Rusted Star, or maybe a church, not a prison. But if he hadn't been rescued, that could only mean his captors had healed him.

He could only think of so many reasons why his kidnappers would decide to heal the injuries they'd caused. None of them were pleasant.

There was a cot in his cell with a thin pillow for cushion, and a toilet in the opposite corner. Beyond that, and lightstone embedded in the walls where they met the ceiling, it was empty and gray. There were no other voices, no sounds of anyone else stirring in this place, and as best he could tell, the two other cells in this hallway were both empty.

The silence gave his mind plenty of opportunity to run out of control. A dozen questions, facts, and suppositions darted around, demanding his attention. Where was he now? It felt strangely familiar, but that didn't make any sense, because he'd never been jailed in a place like this. Different construction to the ruins from before, still probably underground by the air. But not as deep. Maybe just a basement.

He'd been targeted. Taken. Why? By whom? Were the others targets? He didn't have enough to information to know. Images of his friends, his family, being duped and ambushed like he had, appeared in his mind. Someone wearing his face, asking them to come with him.

Would they buy it? Did they know what had happened to him?

Snow had seen him leave with Ink by choice, but sooner or later, Elizabeth would wonder where he was. He was supposed to have come home once he was done helping Snow. He hadn't set a hard date and time for when he'd be back, and he easily forgot things like messaging to check in when he was distracted, but that would only excuse a few days at most. If she tried to reach *him* through the messenger coils and he didn't answer, she'd know something was wrong immediately.

And there was still the question of the healing. Why go out of their way to fix him after hurting him? Was it a warning? That they could hurt him as much as they wanted, heal him, and start over?

As threats went, it was . . . actually not that original. It was a favorite of black priests and any other sadistic bastard with access to healing magic. But still, unpleasant. Without meaning to, he recalled the state he and the others had found Brass in when he'd been captured and interrogated by the enemy. He swallowed down the lump of fear that formed in his throat.

A door opened somewhere down the hall, and he jumped. Footsteps, the clink of chain mail, the rustle of clothing. Phoenix hadn't realized how quiet it had been until these sounds were suddenly deafening.

Three figures arrived in front of the bars of his cell. One hung back, hooded and off to the side, too obscure to identify. But the other two, he recognized immediately. There was Silas Lamark, who Phoenix had never actually seen in person, only through images pulled from Brass's and Snow's memories. He was short, light-skinned, with sand-colored hair shorn close on top and shaved on the sides. He wore sleeveless chain mail, and a pair of shortswords joined by a quicksilver cord hung from his belt. And then there was a much,

much older man. Thin, his robes hanging off him, with a long beard and deep-set wrinkles that left his mouth in a permanent, arrogant scowl. Targan, Headmaster of the Tarsim Arcane Academy.

Suddenly, the duel with "Ink" made so much more sense.

"Headmaster."

"Phoenix."

"Honestly," Phoenix said, "I'm amazed it took you this long to try something like this. Even more amazed you actually did it yourself."

Targan's mouth pressed into a tight line. "Quite. But you did a reasonable job making yourself difficult to reach all these years. In the crown's favor. In hiding. But my patience only extends so far. When an opportunity arose, even one as crassly blunt as this, I decided to seize it."

"You've got a half-decent Ink impersonation."

"I had ample examples to draw from. The woman loves to hear herself speak."

Says the pot about the kettle. Out loud, Phoenix said, "So what, you're working with him now?" He jerked his head toward Silas. "And you two are going to torture me until I agree to work for you?"

"Satisfying as that would be after all these years," Targan said, "No."

"I tortured Brass because it was the best means I had to get what we needed from him. At least, the best I believed," Silas said, frowning. "We have since found a better way to obtain cooperation."

Targan smirked, and both men finally acknowledged the presence of the third that had come with them. The figure wore simple, dark wool robes that looked as if they'd been worn too long without a wash, but didn't smell nearly as bad as they looked. Though he moved forward, his footsteps were whisper quiet, and he did not walk so much as glide. When he pulled back his hood, he revealed the twelve-pointed star carved deep into his forehead.

Phoenix's blood turned to ice. Even having been told by Snow, even having seen the images of her memories, he was not prepared for what it would feel like to see the Cult of Stars back in the flesh.

"Arman Meshar," the cultist greeted. "Hello again."

Phoenix knew he had never seen this man in his life. But what one cultist knew, they all knew. They weren't a hive mind. It was more as if every one of them was another iteration of the same person. Different face, but always the same behind the eyes. He didn't know exactly how it worked, and he didn't want to.

All questions that had been dancing in Phoenix's mind went silent, replaced by one single thought.

"How?" he asked. "How are you still here?"

"I can never die. When man looks up into the night sky, and he knows he is small and nothing, that is his fear of his own insignificance. His acknowledgement of things greater and beyond him. That is what I am. So long as there are those who search into that abyss, I will be there to show them what they know they must do."

The cultist spoke with a zeal that bordered on ecstasy.

"The time draws near, Starbreaker," the cultist intoned. "This world shall have its reckoning. Humanity shall finish the call that I started. It will demand this world, demand the right to exist, and the Stars shall deliver their answer in judgment. And you will help us make that demand."

"Die in a hole."

"Oh, but I have. Let me show you what it's like."

The cultist's eyes clouded with silver smoke, and Phoenix braced himself, though he could only guess what he was bracing for. An illusion, probably.

Except then, something strange happened. The Headmaster's eyes also clouded with silver smoke. A weight, unfathomably deep and never ending, settled into Phoenix's mind, and his vision doubled. He was in the cell, struggling to keep standing. He was outside the cell, watching himself writhe and clutching his forehead. He was and wasn't Phoenix. Arman. He was and wasn't Targan, the Headmaster. He was and wasn't—

Stars.

There were so many stars. They spun and burned and piled atop him, one after the other. They buried him. Smothered him. Fire and light and fire and life and darkness and death and music and silence. It came to him in layers.

He bent. He buckled. He broke.

He was and wasn't. The universe spun, and for a moment he was shaken loose from it. Unmoored, directionless, he pinwheeled through creation and begged to be reoriented. To understand where he was, who he was, what was happening.

What *was* happening?

All at once, it stopped. Phoenix was standing in his cell, and he could breathe again, see again, and the world made *sense* again. He was still in the cell, but that didn't bother him anymore. The walls did not feel constraining. He knew this was where he was supposed to be right now. Targan, Silas, and the cultist were all still outside the cell. It hadn't been long then. It didn't look as though they'd moved.

"Did it work?" Silas asked.

The cultist said nothing, instead simply stepping back. Targan addressed Phoenix. "I'm going to open this cell. Stay where you are, and do not try to escape."

Phoenix nodded, and with a wave of Targan's hand, the cell door opened. Phoenix stood still, as instructed. As he was supposed to. In the back of his mind, it occurred to him that only a few seconds ago, he'd been desperate to get out of this cell, and now he wasn't, and that wasn't natural. But it didn't bother him.

"I believe it worked," Targan said.

"What did you do?" Phoenix asked out of pure curiosity.

"Mental domination is not new spellcraft," Targan said. "But it's essentially brute force overriding a person's thoughts. It makes good puppets, or stupid and obedient slaves, but it's useless for compelling someone and keeping their full faculties intact. So, we innovated. A brief overwhelming of the psyche combining spatial and temporal distortion, mental assault, and the esoterica of the Cult's powers that leaves a mind vulnerable to . . . adjustment of personal reality. I devised it myself. You are yourself. Only now, a version of yourself that believes with absolute certainty that you are obedient to us."

Phoenix nodded, trying to wrap his head around it. There had been a moment, in the mental assault, that he'd felt desperate, confused. It would be the perfect time to insert new understanding. It was brilliant, and horrifying, and it had been done to him and he couldn't find it in himself to be upset about it. Still, it had been so . . . quick. Was that due to the spell efficacy, or his long history of being absolutely terrible at resisting charms and dominations?

Something to look into later, he reasoned absently.

"This is awful," he said in a simple, matter-of-fact tone. He knew it was true, but didn't feel it, believe it.

"And effective. The possibilities for this spell are . . . intriguing." Targan smiled, and Phoenix imagined the possibilities for a spell like this, that dominated so . . . cleanly. He felt fully in control of himself. If he wanted to, he could swing and punch Targan in the face. But he didn't. He wanted to *listen* to Targan.

The Headmaster waved his hand. "But for now, there is work to be done. Come."

The Headmaster beckoned, and Phoenix followed. The cultist broke off from their group to step into the open cell next to Phoenix's and shut the door behind him, smiling the whole time. Phoenix wondered what that was about, but kept following the Headmaster and Silas. Through a door, into another bare room, and then down an elevator, but not one built during the Old World. It was based on the same design principles, functioned the same, but the materials and style were all wrong. In fact, it looked like something *he* would have built.

"Where are we?" Phoenix asked.

"Somewhere you will have what you need to work," Targan said, "and be able to do so uninterrupted."

"But, where?"

"You don't need to know," Targan said, and Phoenix stopped asking.

The elevator opened up into the ruins Phoenix remembered fighting in. Where he'd fought Targan. The table and chairs had all been repaired or replaced. He wondered if Targan had done it himself, or had some Academy people do it for him. They reached the workshop that housed the Servitor's remains, and Phoenix noticed that now, tools had been brought in. Spellforging tools that he recognized, because they were *his*.

"Everything in here was taken from your workshop in Sasel after you were banished and your assets were seized by the crown or recovered from the bottomless pockets we found on your person," Targan said. "You will be provided with additional support staff, and any materials you may require. You will document everything you do in detail with explanations as to the theory and technique."

Phoenix nodded, staring at the Servitor remains that were to be his starting point. "Alright. What am I making, exactly?"

It was Silas's turn to speak up. "We need something that will allow a person to wield the power of multiple Servitor Hearts without having to infuse them into themselves."

"I don't even know if a person could infuse themselves with more than one," Phoenix said. "But I can do that, especially with the Servitor to work with. If we're talking multiple Hearts, it's going to need a pretty heavy chassis to take the strain; it would need to be armor, at least. Do you have any Servitor Hearts for me to work with?"

"We have the Hearts of Flames and Shadows," Silas said. "They'll be delivered soon, along with your staff. We'll be collecting more shortly."

"Which reminds me," Targan said. "You will also need to construct new extractors. We have already used the one previously left to us."

Kurien the Prince Killer had said the Heart of Shadows had been taken from her when she'd fallen into the fog of the Cult of Stars. If Targan and Silas were working with the cult, that explained how they had the Heart of Shadows. But the Heart of Flames had been infused into the assassin Pitch after a blundered mission. If they had that one too, and needed new extractors . . .

"Did Pitch survive having the Heart extracted?" Phoenix asked.

Silas's frown deepened. "He did not."

Phoenix felt his stomach twist into a knot. He'd spent years trying to figure out how to get a Servitor Heart's power out of a person—after Snow's transformation. But she'd *liked* the new her, even if he hadn't. She told him to stop. He hadn't listened. And the fight they had when she found out had gotten ugly enough that they'd broken things off between them. The furthest he'd ever gotten into the research was the prototype extractors, which he knew weren't safe enough to use on a human, but had been perfect for bringing down the rampaging Servitor itself. When he used the Heart of the Sky to save Elizabeth's life, he asked if she wanted him to try to remove it. He'd learned his lesson though, and when she said no, he hadn't looked further into the possibility.

Now though, Silas and Targan were going to be using extractors on people. On Snow, certainly. Maybe on Elizabeth, if they knew she had a Heart too. His heart wrenched at the thought.

"Noted," Phoenix said simply. "That just leaves the question of who's going to be wearing the armor. I can make it adjustable, but it's still good to have some base measurements to start."

"That would be me," a new, deep baritone announced.

The man who spoke was tall, with short blond hair streaked gray at his temples, and steel blue eyes. Scars like deep purple veins ran along his flesh, and there was a clean, bright scar going across his neck, as if his throat had been slit and then healed shut. He carried himself with a tall and proud posture, like a king striding onto a battlefield to command his armies. With every step, he radiated power and authority.

Considering the knight had been dead the last time Phoenix had seen him, Sir Haegan of Whiteborough looked good.

12

THE RETURN

The last thing Haegan saw before he died was the face of the Starbreakers' priest. Haegan didn't hear his voice, but he could still make out the words as the priest whispered, "I'm sorry."

There was a flash of divine light as an angelic blade sliced through his throat.

And then there was nothing.

The nothing didn't last forever. But then again, maybe it did. Any sense of time was gone from his awareness, along with a sense of most everything else. He had no body. No position in space. But something did eventually cut through the void of death—weight.

That was his only word to attempt to describe the sense of pressure that seemed to slowly descend on his awareness. The weight of something looming and endless, pressing down on his existence, and the existence of everything else.

He became more aware of it with each passing moment, and with each passing moment, the sensation of that weight grounded him, letting him perceive things that much easier. It was like being in pitch blackness, brushing his fingers against objects in the dark to slowly gain an understanding of the shape of the room he was in.

He didn't see anything, exactly. He didn't have eyes, wherever and whatever he was now. Rather, an innate understanding of what surrounded him filled his perception, such that he could picture it perfectly in what was left of his mind. The void was not a void, but an endless violet ocean full of stars. Those stars buzzed with energy and life, and their distant twinkling was like an indecipherable, structureless song.

One star shone brighter and closer than any other in his mind, and he understood it at once for what it was. Asher. His world.

Home.

That was where he was from, where he belonged, but he couldn't enjoy the sight of it because of what else was there.

Something else swam through the endless violet ocean. Its body was a void, a massive encroaching blackness that silenced everything around it. It radiated a cold, dispassionate malice that chilled Haegan's soul. And it was looming over Asher like the hand of a god of judgment.

The thing's intentions were so potent Haegan understood them instantly. It had heard the sudden end of hundreds of thousands of lives coming from this world, and it had been intrigued. It had heard the fall of Relgen, and it had come to investigate. This thing, it was displeased by the continued existence of living things. And it was always looking for opportunities to wipe them out.

Haegan knew at once what it was. This thing that lived among these stars but was so clearly not of them, that viewed his world and everything on it with displeasure. This was one of the beings the Cult of Stars worshiped. One of the entities that predated gods and existence, and had not taken kindly to the emergence of either. This was a Starborn, and it was bearing down on his home.

Haegan had known his world was on the brink, but even in his darkest moments, he'd never dared to imagine the situation was this dire. All his plans, all his preparations and ambitions, suddenly felt so insignificant. So insufficient. He had sworn once, when facing down a Cult of Stars cultist, that even if the stars themselves threatened his home, he would find a way to fight back. But none of the work he'd done so far would be enough to stop this.

The work wasn't done. This couldn't be how his existence ended—drifting away, watching a threat he'd failed to prepare his followers for consume his world. He had to do more. Something. Anything. The fight wasn't finished. He wasn't finished.

He had to . . .

Had to . . .

Had . . .

Something latched on to Haegan's being, anchoring him. The slow, inevitable drifting that had been carrying him away from his world came to a sudden halt, and he could feel again. His body was distant and tingling with stiff numbness, but it was there. And then in a breath, so was he.

Haegan sat upright, sputtering for air like a drowning man breaking the surface. He was only vaguely aware of his surroundings, of the stone walls around him, the lightstone in his face, the steadying hands on his shoulders. For a full minute, he could focus on nothing but his lungs filling with air and the physical sensation of being in his own body again.

His heart hammered in his chest, and he was rapidly breaking out in a cold sweat. Absolutely everything ached, and moving was an agony of pins and needles. The worst of it faded rapidly, but some of the discomfort lingered. When Haegan stared down at his own body, he found his skin laced with deep purple, veinlike scars. Haegan had seen people resurrected before. None of them had ever looked anything like this.

"Sir?"

Haegan's focus snapped to the source of the voice—Silas, wearing an expression of concern that looked awkward on his hard features. Haegan was suddenly deeply unsure how long he'd been gone. It was impossible to resurrect someone after more than a few days had passed. But Silas looked so much older now than he had the last time Haegan had seen him. Older, and tired.

"Are you—?" Silas asked, but he didn't finish the question.

Resurrection wasn't infallible. Even beyond the time limit, there were other factors. The condition of the body. The strength of the soul. It could fail to bring someone back, or it could bring someone back . . . wrong. Silas clearly wanted to know if Haegan was still Haegan, but was also afraid to ask.

Haegan supposed that if he wasn't, he wouldn't have any way to know. He was hurting. His body throbbed dully in time with his heartbeat—he felt it in his muscles, his veins, behind his eyes. But he could barely bring himself to care. He had more pressing concerns.

"How long?" Haegan croaked.

"Just shy of three days," Silas reported. "We were able to get you out of the Academy and to Rita."

"Vicar Rita, boy" the priest corrected. "Show some respect to your resident miracle worker."

The woman was sitting in a chair to Silas's left, looking pale and holding a damp cloth to her head. The resurrection had been strenuous on her, it seemed. But she was still alive, had done her job, and would continue to be able to do so. Haegan didn't spare her another thought.

"What's our status?" Haegan asked.

"Our forces evacuated the mansion and are still falling back to our reserve strongholds in the rest of the kingdom," Silas reported. "There is at least one army patrol searching for us, and we've likely piqued the interest of the High Inquisitive, but Targan believes she won't be a problem. He, Guerron, and the baron all have concerns about how this will affect our timetable."

The timetable to seize control of Corsar. That was the mission Haegan had eventually set himself toward. As one man, he wasn't enough to save the kingdom. But in the years since the fall of Relgen, he'd come to the conclusion that he wouldn't be able to do it even with an order of knights like Silas behind him. Corsar needed change from top to bottom.

New, stronger leadership. And so he'd spent the years gathering not just followers, but allies. Friends in high places with similar dissatisfaction with the leadership of Roland II.

It all seemed like such a colossal waste of time now. Literal years of skulking in the shadows and making dark deals to stay hidden, all to topple one man, one crown, one kingdom. What did it matter who was sitting on the throne of Corsar when there was a Starborn coming for them all?

Something had to be done about it. But what? How? The place he had seen it was beyond the physical world, beyond this plane of existence. It couldn't reach them itself—yet—but by the time it found a way to, it would be too late for all of them. They needed to find a way to bring the fight to it, but even if they did, what would they fight it with?

"We have the Heart of Flames nearly within our grasp," Silas continued. "Getting it and its current host out of Oblivion will be a challenge, but at least now we know where it is, and that it isn't going anywhere."

Haegan stared at Silas with such a sudden, desperate hunger that the younger man took an instinctive step back.

Yes. The Hearts. Haegan and his allies had gravitated toward them as a source of power to be used in the coming struggles. They were Old World weapons, used in conflicts that had shaken worlds. If anything in this world had the power to strike back at the Starborn, surely they did. And if they didn't?

No. Even if they didn't, Haegan would rather die fighting than sit and wait for the end. If the Starborn wanted this world, it would take it over Haegan's dead body, and only after he had thrown everything he could muster at it.

"Sir?" Silas asked, and his previous unspoken question leaked into his tone.

He wasn't feeling all right. He was feeling impatient. There was so much to do now.

"Our fight isn't what I thought it was," Haegan said. "We have to meet with our allies, and tell them the plan has changed."

Haegan felt the beginnings of a headache already starting to come on. Targan, Guerron, the baron. Even Vicar Rita. They were all such petty individuals. All of them had bought into Haegan's revolution for such small personal reasons. Pivoting the purpose of their alliance now was going to cause no end of arguments and complaints, because they hadn't seen what Haegan had seen. That had been true even before Haegan had died but now . . . now *not even Haegan could fully grasp what he'd seen.*

It was surprisingly difficult to recall the exact sights and feelings that accompanied his time on the other side of the boundary between life and death. To fully understand what he had seen among the stars. He felt like he could almost reach that understanding, like it was locked away somewhere deep inside himself, and he could access it if only he could just dig a little deeper.

His forehead started to itch.

Silas asked questions, and Haegan brushed them all aside, too consumed by his own plans. Fighting the Starborn was the way forward. But where? There were ways to cross into other planes of existence—rare and difficult to access as they were. He could go to where the Starborn lived. But was that the right course? To fight it in its own element, in a place with physics they'd barely understand? No. Better to fight it here on Asher, but on their terms.

Yes. Don't bring the fight to the Starborn. Bring the Starborn to the fight, before it was ready. That was the answer. That was their salvation. That was the only path forward that made any sense. But where to do it?

The answer presented itself almost immediately. What better place to call forth the Starborn than where its attention had first been grabbed? The dead city. The monument to humanity's fragility. The place where all the troubles had begun.

They would make the stand in Relgen.

Haegan grew animated as the details took shape in his mind. Already, he was working on how to present this new plan to his allies, and how to appease their own ambitions. This would work. This would be perfect. And as he dictated orders and messages for Silas, the itch in his forehead only grew stronger.

13
RELICS

"So, what are we actually looking for?" Thalia asked as the Rusted Star settled back into stillness after its latest trip.

"Back in the day, I had this axe called Daybreaker," Angel said. "Got it . . . well, from Heaven, basically. Magic axe, made to be used by angels, could do all sorts of stuff. Church has a plan worked out to use it on Ruby to purify her soul, but I sold it to a dwarf in exchange for him building this place." She gestured to the surrounding interior of the Rusted Star. "That's why the bar can . . . you know."

"Tunnelport?"

"I still fucking hate that word, but yeah. The whole moving through the ground thing's a dwarf trick, and he built it into this place."

"Why sell the axe in the first place?"

"This was right after Relgen. Between the way things ended with the others, me leaving the country, and the crown seizing most of our stuff, I wasn't very liquid at the time." Angel gave the kind of pause that Thalia had come to recognize meant she was steeling herself to reveal more of herself than she was normally comfortable with. "And I thought I was done fighting."

Thalia heard the past tense in Angel's words, and vividly remembered her choosing to battle the Dread Knight when it threatened Loraine. "What do you think now?"

"Now I think we need that axe," Angel said, dodging the real question. She'd hit her limit for introspective sharing. "The dwarf lives here in Allhammer. If he hasn't moved, we should be in his backyard."

"And he'll just give you the axe back?"

"For what he gave me for it? Probably not. But I used Brass's money to buy some gemstones. Should be enough to convince him to loan it out."

"And if it's not?"

"I can be very persuasive."

As soon as Angel stepped out of the Rusted Star, she was beaned in the skull by a smith's hammer. Had it hit anyone else, they would have been unconscious, if not dead. Angel had a small trickle of blood from her forehead.

"Ow, you fuck! That hurt!" she snarled.

Thalia stepped out from behind her to get a better look outside. "What—"

Her question died in her throat.

The Rusted Star had emerged at the deep end of a long crevasse. Walls of ice and rock towered around them, the sky was a thin crack of light far above. The space was wider than the Rusted Star by about ten feet on either side, and as it stretched out, it grew slowly shallower until at the far end it reached up to the surface. Snow drifted down from the edges in fluffy imitations of waterfalls, blown in by a cross breeze that couldn't be felt this far down.

A few yards away stood a squat stone hut, which had been carved from a single, massive boulder. The glow of fire filled its tiny windows, and smoke billowed out of its chimney, all the way up and out of the crevasse, which was wider around where the smoke was than anywhere else. A circle of bare, dry rock had been cleared around the hut, and it joined with a stone path that went all the way up the crevasse back to the surface. Except for that circle and path, every square inch of the ground was buried under a massive pile of junk. The mound was half as tall as the Rusted Star, made up of scrap metal, rusted weapons, battered armor, pieces of wagons, hunks of statues, old boxes, and cracked barrels.

But none of that was what had stunned Thalia to silence. Instead, she fixated entirely on the dwarf.

It stood only four feet tall, but broad shouldered and squarely built. Its skin was the color of dark granite, full of cracks that glowed like magma. It had a wiry black beard that smoldered with embers, and its eyes were glassy obsidian orbs with rings of fire for irises. Like most people in Corsar, Thalia had never actually seen a dwarf in person, only heard of them in stories. Even after everything she had seen since her fateful first encounter with the Starbreakers, she hadn't been prepared to come face-to-face with a figure straight out of a myth—and watch it angrily shout at Angel and shake its fists like a disgruntled village neighbor.

Thalia didn't understand a word it was saying, but Angel was shouting back at it in what sounded like the same language in between the dwarf grabbing more odds and ends from the surrounding pile and throwing them at her. Angel lost her patience after the third hunk of scrap was hurled at her, and her eyes flashed.

Twin beams of golden light shot out from her, scorching a line in the rock in front of the dwarf's feet. It stopped throwing things, but the two kept arguing. The dwarf pointed to the Rusted Star. Angel thumped her chest and got in its face.

"You speak Dwarf?" Thalia asked.

"No, but I can swear in Erdic, and that's close enough," Angel said. She repeated something a few times to the dwarf, sounding out her words with exaggerated enunciation and pointing at her mouth as she did.

"Corsan, asshole," she said. "I know you speak it."

"You make mess."

The dwarf's voice was a gravelly baritone that echoed in its own chest. It had sounded that way in its other language, but now that Thalia could understand what it was saying, how it said it sounded all the more wrong. This thing might have learned human words, but its throat had never been made to speak them.

Angel looked at the piles of detritus around them. "Seriously?"

The dwarf started shouting again, pointing to the Rusted Star and everything that had been displaced by it. Angel didn't understand the words, but she'd spent a few years living with Phoenix and the mess he insisted was organized, and took the meaning.

"Well there was plenty of room the last time I was here," she said. "How was I supposed to know your shit pile tripled in size?"

"Mess," the dwarf repeated with a grunt.

"Get over it," Angel said. "I need the axe."

"No axe."

"I just need to borrow it for a couple days. I'll bring it back, *and* I'll pay you for it."

"No axe," the dwarf insisted.

"Maybe if you offer to clean up the mess you made," Thalia suggested.

Angel could not have looked more absolutely done with a person than she did in that moment.

"Just saying. You get more bees with nectar than vinegar."

"I hate bees."

"Who hates bees?"

"No axe," the dwarf cut in. Angel was about to yell at him that she got it when he kept talking. "Axe gone."

"The fuck does that mean?"

"I give," the dwarf said, and he jerked his head towards the path that led up and out of the crevasse.

When the Starbreakers had first encountered the dwarf, it was after it had been displaced by the destruction of its home. At a loss for what else to do with it, they'd taken it to Allhammer, a city named for the mountain it was built on. It was constructed and ruled by dwarves, but populated by everything from humans to giants. The dwarf, a different kind than the ones from Allhammer, was an outcast even in the city, though the crevasse it called home was technically within its territory.

The dwarf was saying it had given the axe to someone in the city of Allhammer.

"To who?" Angel asked.

"I give to queen," the dwarf said. "Queen give to gravers."

Angel had only taken Thalia with her on this trip, having told the others it wouldn't be complicated, and wouldn't take her more than an afternoon. The dwarf giving Daybreaker to a queen wasn't much of an obstacle—there was only one woman this far north who could claim that title, and she'd been an ally to the Starbreakers since before she *was* queen. But it was a problem if Queen Astrid had given Daybreaker to "gravers."

That was the name people this far north had for glintchasers.

14

GRAVERS

Silver was doing her best to focus on the little things that were still working out for them. Despair thrived when a person only focused on everything going wrong, and despair was the work of the Betrayers.

The attic of the Horned Tankard was significantly colder than its bar and actual rooms, but it was still better than sleeping on the streets of Allhammer in a tent. Between the walls, some blankets, and her traveling vestments, she hardly even shivered. They were out of money, but staying in the attic was free, and as long as the kitchen made more beef stew than they sold and the cook didn't forget about them, they weren't going to starve either.

She pulled her blanket tighter around her as another chilling breeze swept through the draft they'd been unable to locate for the last three days. Across from her, Gamble swore and threw a knife into the wall.

"Fuck this shithole," he said. "We can't stay here."

"Where would we go?" Silver asked. "We've got no money, no food, and the blood rings are still looking for us."

"How about we start by saving Patch?" Gamble demanded. He was pacing the room, as much as the cramped space allowed.

"We can't," Silver protested, the words acid in her mouth. Her eyes fell to the floor, unable to look her only remaining companion in the eye.

"You want to just leave him with them?" Gamble asked.

"No!" Silver said. "I'm just trying to keep things from getting any worse."

"Worse than this?" Gamble threw his arms out, gesturing to their surroundings. To the cold, low-hanging stone roof, the dried gargoyle droppings in the corner, and their missing friend's empty bedroll. "We're freezing our asses off while they bleed him dry!"

"I—" Silver choked on her words as tears welled in her eyes. A lifetime of studying the teachings of Saint Avelina, of upholding the virtues of hope and perseverance, were at their limit.

She missed her friend. She missed warm beds. She missed a good night's sleep uninterrupted by nightmares.

Gamble tried to yank his knife free from the wall, but it was embedded deeper than he'd expected. He tried a different grip, and when his hand slipped, he sliced his finger open.

"Fuck this," Gamble declared. "I'm going to save Patch. Come or don't."

Silver scrambled to stop him, grabbing his arm. "They'll kill you."

"If it were you or me, Patch would try," Gamble said.

"That's what got him caught in the first place!"

"So we leave him to die?"

Gamble had expected Silver to flinch when he snapped at her, or maybe yell back. It was actually hard to gauge how much spine the priestess had at any given moment. He hadn't expected her to grip his arm even tighter and start crying.

"Please," she begged. "I can't lose you too."

Gamble glared at her from underneath his hood, but there was no malice in it. Just desperation and fear. He shook his head, prying himself from her grasp. "I've gotta try, Sil."

Silver's heart broke. She could have tried to stop him. To drain his stamina, or hold his mind. But she couldn't bring herself to form the words of a prayer. Not a priest's prayer, at any rate. All she managed was a desperate whisper of, "Avelina, please. Help us."

There was a knock at the door to the attic, and Silver and Gamble both stiffened. It was too early in the day for the cook to be bringing them food.

"Hello?" A man's voice came from the other side of the door. "Anybody up here?"

A dozen worst-case scenarios played in Silver's head, but before she had time to ask Gamble what they should do, the door opened, and the man came in.

He was a lean and wiry man in a garishly bright purple coat and yellow scarf, and his hand rested casually on an ornate rapier at his side. When he saw the two of them, the stranger's eyes lit up. His smile promised trouble.

"Oh good, you're still alive," Brass said by way of greeting. He pressed his fingers to the messenger coil at his ear. "Hey Angel, guess who owes me ten glint?"

It took some talking on Brass's part—and a truth prayer from Silver—to convince the young freelancers that Brass, Angel, Thalia, Church, Bart, and Ruby were not enforcers sent by the blood rings to kidnap or kill them. It took even longer, and Church's professional link to Silver as a fellow priest, to get them comfortable enough to share their story, and Gamble still didn't seem happy about it.

There had been four of them, all fresh faces, new to freelancing. They'd barely finished their first job and decided on a name when they'd come across a particularly bold gang of thugs trying to shake down a courier. They intervened, and it had turned out the courier had been carrying a lifesaving medicine for a dear friend of Astrid Silverspear, Queen of the Frelheim. She'd been so grateful that, on learning of what they'd done, had offered them their pick from her private armory. Their leader, Patch, had chosen Daybreaker.

They'd all thought it was some kind of sign. That they were on a righteous path, or that maybe there was some grand destiny in store for them. As it turned out, their grand destiny was pissing off a local bloodsmoke operation, being ambushed in the street in the middle of the night, and watching one of their own die and Patch be dragged off. It was only thanks to Silver that she and Gamble got away and hadn't bled to death in an alleyway. That ambush was three days ago, and Silver and Gamble had been hiding in the Horned Tankard ever since, trying to figure out what to do next.

"Your friend," Angel said. "What is he?"

Silver blinked. "What?"

"What is he? Human? Anima? Orcblood?"

Silver was too shaken and confused to say anything right away, but Gamble answered for her. "He's hellborn."

Angel nodded. "He'll still be alive then."

Silver shuddered in equal parts relief and horror. She had been trying not to think about Patch's fate. Gamble's face darkened.

"Do you know where they'd take him?" Angel asked.

"There's a lab on the east side, underneath a brothel," Gamble said. "We tried to get in once, but—"

Brass cut him off. "Church, it seems like these two have been through a lot. Why don't we all go downstairs, get them something to eat, and you and Bart can treat whatever frostnip they got from sleeping up here while me and the ladies talk to some locals about what we're dealing with? I think that's a good plan, let's do that."

He said the last part before Church or Angel could offer any alternative, and even began ushering the closest people to him—Thalia and Bart—toward the stairs to the tavern below. Caught up by his momentum, and genuinely not seeing anything wrong with the idea, Church went along with it. And as the priest went, the others followed.

Gamble protested about not needing charity, but he still took the bread and stew when it was offered, and he and Silver both ate greedily. While they ate, and Church waited patiently, Brass met eyes with Angel and jerked his head to the door.

The two of them stepped outside, and Thalia and Ruby followed. Angel broke the silence, though she didn't look at Brass. "Thanks."

Brass took out a nail from his pocket and lit it with a match. He'd forgotten what he'd made this one with and was looking forward to finding out.

The only thing he knew for sure was that it wasn't bloodsmoke. Never bloodsmoke. "Of course. Have a nice time. Don't stay out too late, and remember what I taught you if you see any strange men."

Angel scoffed. "Never change, asshole."

"Not as long as I live."

Brass blew out his first breath of smoke. It tasted like cherries and burnt shoes, which meant in about five minutes, everything was going to feel just great. Angel walked away without saying another word.

"Where's she going?" Ruby asked.

"To get her axe back," Brass said, waving his nail around in a dismissive gesture. "And their friend, I guess."

"What happened to asking around while Church takes care of those glintchasers?" Thalia asked.

"They actually call them gravers up here, and that was mostly just an excuse to distract Church. Though those kids did look like they could use a nap and a sandwich," Brass said. Thalia and Ruby were confused, so Brass elaborated. "Church fights when he has to, kills when he has to, but he's not usually a fan of it. If he sees an angle to spare the bad guys, to take them in alive, he'll usually go for it. Angel, not so much. They fought about it a lot, back in the day, and Angel deserves not to have that fight today."

The beginnings of understanding dawned on the women's faces, and Thalia cast a look in Angel's direction. She'd already disappeared down the street. Brass took another drag before continuing.

"Angel got taken by a blood ring once." Brass paused after he said it, finding it easy to drift into the memory of the incident as a dreamy disclarity took hold in his head. It took him a while to come back to the present, giving Thalia and Ruby plenty of time to imagine what had happened.

The looks on their faces mirrored the ones Silver and Gamble had worn when talking about Patch.

"It was a long time ago, and we were a lot worse at this. You can make bloodsmoke from anyone in a pinch, but for decent quality, you want to source it from people with real magic in them. Someone like Angel was a gold mine to them, so they didn't kill her. They just kept her, bleeding, barely alive. It took us a month to get her back."

At that, Thalia grew worried. "Then why did you let her go alone? What if something happens?"

Brass waved away her concerns. "Angel doesn't need help with a blood ring anymore. She just needs permission."

15
RETRIBUTION

The streets of Allhammer were full of sights that could never be seen in Corsar. On one street corner, a fifteen-foot-tall giant sat hunched over a brazier, using two fingers to turn a rotisserie of glowing slabs of meat and doling out slices to paying customers. A trio of pointy-eared, big-headed gnomes wearing snow goggles darted between the ankles of the crowd, making grabs at exposed coin purses. A group of muscle-bound orcs marched by, wearing nothing but silk skirts and carrying an ornate gold-and-alabaster-shrouded dais. Overhead, tiny winged gargoyles the size and shape of cats flew by, squawking like birds as they circled each other.

Angel marched past it all with a permanent scowl on her face. Of all the people who could have gotten hold of the axe, it had to be a bunch of glint-chasers—gravers—stupid enough to get mixed up with blood rings. When Astrid's people told her Daybreaker had gone to a group calling itself Trade Secret, Angel had imagined a real company. Five or six professionals at least, kitted out, experienced enough to have a name and reputation and a reason to believe they could actually use a weapon like Daybreaker. But the two kids in the attic barely looked old enough to know what bloodsmoke was, let alone try and fight the monsters who made it. They were idiots, in over their heads in an ass-backward city run by little men made of rocks. It was a miracle only one of them had died.

Her face already felt hot by the time she made it to the brothel. There were no bouncers outside—probably because of the cold—but there were two waiting just inside. Up to this point, anyone who had seen Angel and the look on her face had promptly gotten out of her way, but the two men inside were paid to get *in* the way of trouble. Angel couldn't simply scare them off by making her eyes glow. So instead, she shoved them both hard enough to send them hurtling into different corners of the building.

The brothel stank of coppery smoke and sex, with a fog of perfume hanging over it that failed to mask anything. It was lit by red-tinted lightstone and lamps in combination, which always made lighting look uneven and unnatural, and it was full of half-dressed trulls flirting with their marks in cracked-leather booths. In the center of the room, a stage played host to a pair of dancers, who froze in their frantic dancing as Angel made her entrance.

Even the nicest of brothels had never been her scene. This place was a sweaty shithole.

Ignoring the stares of patrons and curses from the bouncers who were getting back to their feet and calling for help, Angel pushed her way forward. Someone grabbed her, so she broke their hand and punched them in the face. More people rushed after her, some of them drawing knives and clubs. None of them lasted longer than a second. The last man standing was half dwarf, going off the stocky frame and pebbly complexion. Angel grabbed his arm as he tried to bring a mallet down on her head, and his stone-hard skin cracked under her fingers. He gaped, too stunned to even scream in pain. She tightened her grip, and the cracks spread all the way to his elbow before she shoved him through a table.

There were still more goons in the fringes of the club, but they were retreating to get help and raise the alarm. Angel paid them no mind, storming for a door she guessed would lead downstairs. She guessed correctly, and when she found the door waiting for her at the bottom of the stairs locked, she yanked off the handle, taking the lock with it.

A little man in a bloody apron and glasses stumbled away from the door as Angel sauntered in, still ignoring the sounds of footsteps furiously pounding down the stairs after her. An evil dog chained in the corner—she knew it was evil from the way its eyes smoldered red and its spit sizzled when it hit the ground—immediately began barking at her and straining on its chain.

Despite what Brass expected of her, Angel's plan had been to storm in, ask where they were keeping the victims, smash all the equipment, grab the hellborn and Daybreaker, and leave, only punching anything that got in her way. The first words of her question had already formed on her lips.

"Where's the—"

Then she saw it. The bloodsmoke lab.

It wasn't even that she'd necessarily forgotten what they were like. She could never do that.

But it had been a long time since she'd actually been standing in one.

An overwhelming smell of copper and piss choked the air. The stone brick walls and floor were bare, save for the dried, half-cleaned bloodstains, the steel worktable of alchemy supplies—and the cages. There were four of them, lining the far wall of the room.

Only one of them was empty. The rest were occupied by people, gagged and hands chained above their head. They had nothing to wear except their own filth and dirty bandages around their arms. Sure enough, one of them was a hellborn boy about the same age as the glintchasers back at the Horned Tankard. His red skin had gone ashen, and his whole face was sunken. The other two looked worse, and going by the tear-streaked makeup on their faces, they used to work upstairs. Almost certainly until they'd upset whoever was in charge.

Just like that, she could feel the needle in her arm again. The cold iron of the shackles that held her. The bone-deep, delirious exhaustion that came with being slowly bled dry over days and days. The feeling that she was wrung out. Used. Discarded.

Her stomach twisted into a knot as the heat that had been steadily building inside her erupted. Searing pain raced through every fiber of her, carrying fury and disgust with it. Her eyes became twin suns, and a burning halo formed over her head.

When Angel drew out her power, it didn't just make her stronger and glow in the dark. It didn't simply burn her and her enemies. It brought clarity. It burned away everything, all the world, until there was nothing but her purpose, and the one truth she knew with everything she was.

There was good, and there was evil. Where there was good, it must be protected. And where there was evil, it must be destroyed.

Light radiated from her skin and poured out her eyes and mouth as righteous fury literally began to spill out of her. In the corner, the evil dog had stopped growling, and started whimpering. The man in the apron, who'd been backing away the entire time, tripped over his own feet and fell ass-first to the floor. She stalked toward him, glowing like a beacon. When she spoke, her voice was doubled, as if there were two of her speaking in unison.

"You will never do this again."

"Okay!" the man whimpered, trying to use his arms to shield himself from the heat coming off Angel. "Whatever you want! I swear! I'm done!"

He misunderstood.

Her glowing hands grabbed him by the straps of his apron, smoke curling off where she touched, and lifted him off his feet.

"W-wait! Don't—"

Skull met tile with a crunch as Angel slammed him headfirst into the wall, and his limp body crumpled to the floor. Behind her, the door flew open again as a trio of bouncers from upstairs ran into the room, only to stop dead in their tracks. By now, the light coming off her was almost blinding. The edges of her own vision were going white, and her nerves were on fire. But she could make out the bouncers.

"Did you know this was here?" she asked.

The bouncer at the head of the pack came up short, frozen in sudden, awestruck terror.

"Did you know?" she demanded.

All of them began hurriedly backing away, the furthest already running for the stairs. None of them had answered, but the power of Renalt was flooding her veins. There was no hiding anything in the god of truth's presence.

They knew. They'd protected it. Profited off it. Collected victims for it.

She lunged.

Two of them were dead before either hit the ground, and the third only reached the first step before beams of light fired from her eyes, dropping him. Blood still boiling, she stomped upstairs, her every step leaving a scorched boot print.

She would come back for the victims when she was finished with the monsters upstairs.

Thalia sat at the bar of the Horned Tankard, nursing a warm mug of a drink whose name she couldn't pronounce. Church was having a one-sided argument with Brass, who was too high to understand why he was in trouble or care in the first place. As newly minted glintchasers themselves, Bart and Ruby were closer in age and life experience to Silver and Gamble and were trying to put on a relatable and reassuring front. They were surprisingly good at it, even if Gamble hadn't stopped pacing since finishing his meal.

"I can't," Gamble said, loud enough to draw the attention of the rest of the group. "I can't. I have to go."

"Gamble—" Bart tried, only to be cut off.

"No! All right? Patch is our friend. We should have gone to save him, not have some stranger do it. We should have at least gone with her."

"Trust me, kid, you'd only have gotten in her way," Brass called out.

"Screw you!" Gamble shot back. "Who is she anyway? Who are any of you?"

"Ask her yourself," Thalia said.

Two people staggered into the tavern. Angel was one. The other was a young, red-skinned hellborn boy, wearing Angel's coat over ill-fitting clothing. His legs shook with every step he took, and his entire face was unnaturally sunken. As soon as they saw him, Gamble and Silver both went silent. Tears welled in Silver's eyes.

"Patch?"

"Hey, Sil." The hellborn's voice came out weak and raspy, but he forced a smile onto his face.

His companions sprinted into him, enveloping him in their arms just as his legs finally gave out from under him. In seconds, the three of them collapsed into a group hug on the ground, tears flowing from all of them.

Angel walked around them, joining Thalia at the bar. Thalia noticed the new, milky white belt that hung around Angel's waist, and the gleaming gold-and-pearl white axe that hung from it. Even indoors, at night, it glinted like the sun itself was shining off it. Thalia had never seen it before, but she knew at once that this was Daybreaker.

"You got it."

"I got it."

She said it like it was an afterthought, and not their entire reason for coming here. Her eyes held a distant stare, watching the three glintchasers on the floor and at the same time looking through them. Angel's clothes were covered in blood that wasn't hers. Thalia had some clean ones set aside for her on the barstool next to her. They had been the last sober idea Brass had after Angel had left.

"Are you okay?" Thalia asked.

"Yeah. I just . . ." Angel paused. "I forgot what this part felt like."

There was a wistfulness to Angel's voice that Thalia didn't think she'd ever heard from Angel before, and at once, she knew the answer to the question she had asked Angel before, about whether or not she was still done fighting. It should have been obvious to both of them months ago, after Loraine. But those had been extreme circumstances. This was smaller. Mundane. And it had left Angel profoundly satisfied in a way Thalia knew at once nothing else ever could.

Thalia gave a nod of understanding and handed Angel the clean set of clothes.

16
THE GUERRONS

The Guerron estate was a fortress. Three guards at the gates, with a dozen more in a nearby watchtower. Every door and window was sealed, save the front door, which was manned by more guards and an Academy-trained butler who could root out any magic before it was smuggled inside.

The house itself was more castle than mansion. Built like a citadel with wide sight lines in all directions immediately surrounding it, and watchtowers on every corner. At the command of the owner, every potential exit down to the sewage line could be barred and locked with iron shutters.

Still, Snow was confident that, if dinner really went that poorly, she could escape.

Her stomach twisted in knots as she made sure none of the knives hidden on her person were visible. She wasn't sure how exactly to feel about what she was doing, whether to dread it or simply be annoyed by it. But whatever the feeling in her gut was, it was awkward and unpleasant, and a distraction.

The assassin let out a long sigh, and the air around her cooled as she let the Heart of Ice spread through her. Just a little, to take the edge off the night. Her heart rate, already unnaturally slow, dropped to a crawl, and the space between beats became seconds. Her eyes faded from bright blue to a pale, near white. When she opened the door in front of her, she left a trace of frost on the handle.

The dining hall was built to serve hundreds, with enough space for several long tables and a small company of servers and guards. In this massive room, there were only two people seated. One of them was Amelia Guerron, lady of the house.

She was a woman born to be wealthy, from her poise to her fashion sense to the meticulous perfection of her hair and makeup. The pearls around her neck were worth more than most people would see in a lifetime.

The other person, sitting at the head of the table, was her husband. Sebastian Guerron was a silver-haired man in his sixties, but still boasted a broad physique that filled out his finely tailored clothes.

As ever, a white carnation adorned the breast of his jacket, just beside the pin of a hawk. He was the master of this house, patron of his own personal freelancer company, and the single wealthiest collector of Old World artifacts in Corsar.

The hinges of the door weren't especially loud, but in the silence of the room, their echoing sound was almost deafening. Both pairs of eyes descended onto Snow, and for the briefest instant, she was sixteen again, trapped in this place, and under those eyes. She let the Heart of Ice bury those feelings.

"Hi Dad."

Sebastian sat up taller in his seat. His face tightened in a measured expression. "Chloe. Welcome home."

Snow's father gestured to the seat next to him and across from her mother, where a place had already been set. As long as the table was, it felt a hundred times longer as she walked its length, both her parents watching her while her footsteps made the sole sound in the room. A servant dutifully pulled out her chair and helped her into her seat, before excusing themselves to check on dinner.

"Your letter took us by surprise," Sebastian said. "We haven't heard from you for a while now."

"I need a favor," Snow said, cutting to the chase.

"Hello to you too," her mother chided.

"What?"

"Some of the glintchasers your father employs grew up in the hills, and even they have the manners to at least wait for food to be served before trying to talk business," Amelia said. "I did not raise you to be this crude."

Snow did her best to let the words bounce off her.

"Sure."

"And it's always favors with you. Do you know the last time we heard from you without you asking for something?"

"I'm sure you'll tell me."

"Eight years, right after Relgen. You sent one letter to tell us you were alive and weren't coming back to the city."

"I figured you should know."

"Eight words!" Amelia snapped, raising her voice.

No sooner had she done it than she stopped herself, withdrawing her hands and pushing back the strands of her hair that had fallen out of place from the outburst.

"I got eight words scribbled on a scrap of paper while the whole city watched my daughter's mass murder trial. A trial that she wasn't even there for," Amelia said, her voice once again restrained even as her distaste came through even clearer.

"Sorry I embarrassed you," Snow said, voice hollow and monotone.

"Amelia."

Sebastian's deep, firm voice cut his wife off before she had a chance to retort. With his eyes, he pointed out the servants arriving with the first course of the evening. With an audience now in the room, Amelia silenced herself. For a few moments, the only sounds from the table were the clinks of silverware, until Amelia took the first sip of soup from her spoon and winced.

"Jacque, why is the soup freezing cold?"

The color drained from the butler's mortified face, and his jaw went slack as he frantically looked from the lady of the house to the soup to the doors that led to the kitchen. As he desperately stammered out an apology, Snow cleared her throat. Realization dawned on her mother's face, and at once her indignation vanished. Jacque visibly relaxed.

Amelia nodded her apology to the butler. "Right. Of course."

"Jacque, could you ask the kitchen to prepare something best served cold? Gazpacho, maybe?" Sebastian requested. "And something suitable for the other courses as well."

The butler needed no more excuse to quickly hurry out of the room.

Snow stared at her own bowl of soup. She'd long since gotten used to eating everything cold.

"That was an accident," Snow stated.

"I'm sure it was," her mother said.

"I should have remembered." Her father's face softened, and his voice lost its commanding edge. It was a weakening of his outer facade that might have been his own form of an apology. When Snow met his eyes, she felt the cold in her chest falter, and some of the blue color returned to her pale irises.

She went back to staring at the soup.

"It's fine."

Something about her excusing something he did felt wrong and out of place, but only just. The cold was doing its job almost too well, keeping her numbed to the whole affair.

When the new, cold soups arrived, her father finally broke the silence. "What did you need?"

"I'm looking for someone here in the city."

"Do I want to know why?"

"He tried to kill me. I want to kill him," Snow stated.

Amelia stared at her daughter in abject horror, which Snow ignored.

"Silas Lamark. He's here in the city somewhere, and he's been selling Old World weapons on the black market. Nobody can move Old World tech in the city without you knowing about it."

Sebastian's face hardened as he listened and nodded. He stared down at his own food for a few moments, weighing something in his mind. While Snow waited, Amelia shook her head in disdain. If Sebastian saw it, he ignored it.

"I'll see what I can find out."

Snow nodded. "You can send word to the Broken Cask."

"Is that where you're staying?"

"It's where I can get the message."

"You could stay here while I look into things," Sebastian offered. "If you wanted."

Snow glanced across the table at her mother and saw the judgment and contempt in her eyes. For the first time that night, she felt well and truly angry, even through the cold.

Sebastian's face fell, but he nodded. "I'll send word to the Cask."

"Are you out of your mind?!" Amelia shouted.

"I doubt I'd know if I was. But I'm assuming that question was rhetorical."

Sebastian and Amelia stood at opposite ends of the sitting room, separated by an unlit fireplace and an imported carpet. Though they hovered near their respective plush cushioned chairs, neither of them sat down. Sebastian refused to look at his wife, his eyes instead on a glass of brandy. She was glaring daggers into his back.

"Why would you agree to this?" she demanded.

"She's our daughter."

"Our daughter is dead," Amelia spat. "That is a frozen corpse that still moves."

Her husband grunted into his glass before taking another sip, and Amelia's hands trembled from her desperate attempts to retain composure. She wanted to knock that glass out of his hand. But even though they were alone in the room, it was never a good idea to assume no one was watching or listening. Not in a house with so many servants. And it would not do for the lady of the estate to lose control of herself.

Even still, Sebastian's refusal to so much as look at her was testing her limits.

"This is your fault," she cried, a combination of anguish and condescension. "She never would have ended up like this if you hadn't filled her head with your stories. If she had stayed here, she would still be our daughter, and not that thing she turned into."

Her goading had the desired effect, as Sebastian finally met her eyes. "We lost her long before she ran away. Her staying wouldn't have made a single difference."

"Well, how could she ever turn out any differently when you always make excuses for her?" Amelia retorted. She threw her hands in the air. "You blamed me when she acted out. You blamed me when she ran. And now you're blaming me that she won't come home. Always me. When is it ever going to be her fault? When is she ever going to be responsible for herself?"

"I thought this was supposed to be all my fault?"

"It is!" she hissed. "You spent her whole life shielding her from any kind of consequences, so of course she thought she could run off and be a glintchaser just to spite her family and nothing would happen, and of course that got her killed."

She jabbed a finger at him.

"We saw her before it happened. She was . . ." Amelia paused, recalling the image of her daughter, the glintchaser, parading through the streets of the city with the band of ruffians she called a company. She shuddered, but bit her tongue. ". . . she was many things, but she was *alive*." Amelia's whole body was shaking now. "She smiled. She laughed. She was in love."

"You hated that boy."

"I hated everything about her life, because I knew what it would do to her! You would be buried dead in a ruin by now if I hadn't gotten you out of that world, and you know it. We built this place so we wouldn't have to live like that anymore!" Amelia shouted. "I loved my daughter enough to hate what she was doing, but you just let her go. You let her live that life, and look at what happened!"

Her voice broke until she managed to sound like she was sobbing without a single tear rolling down her face. Her husband was her opposite, closing up into a stoic fortress as they fought. His sentences shortened. His eyes narrowed. His jaw set. He weathered her every word like a stone wall. She always hated it, the way he refused to react to her. As if he thought ignoring her enough would make her give up being angry. If anything, it had the opposite effect.

Amelia Guerron's carefully crafted composure shattered, and she swung a hand for her husband's face. He caught her wrist before she could even come close, and held it like a vice. He was an older man, but for as much as he had slowed and shrunk over the years, there was still strength in his hands enough to hold her still.

"You never blamed her for anything," she said. He could stop her hand, but not her words. "So I blame you for everything."

"She came to us," Sebastian stated. "If I don't step in, she'll pursue this on her own. And it will be worse."

"Am I supposed to be happy about that?" Amelia asked. "Am I supposed to be grateful for what you're doing?"

"You don't have to be grateful," Sebastian said. "You just have to let me—"

The two of them were interrupted by a rolling, hollow crackle on the window as frost spread across the glass. Sebastian set his drink down and raced to the window, but by the time he undid the latch, there was no one outside. All he found was a layer of ice on the windowsill, and a few frozen droplets he couldn't have known were tears.

17
THE ACADEMICS

Sasel was a tall city, made of spires and towers, overlapping bridges and flying buttresses. Between that and the crisscrossing traffic of flying skiffs, most people in the city tended to avoid looking up just to not get lost in the congested mess overhead. But the Academy was different.

It was situated northwest of the palace—not on the shore, but close to it. Unlike most of the city, which climbed up, the Academy sprawled out. Few of its smooth, white granite buildings reached higher than two stories, but they were spread out across the landscape, contained within a circular plot of land. Which made its central structure, the Headmaster's tower, stand out all the more.

The hexagonal base of the Headmaster's tower stood a full twenty stories tall, with long, narrow window slits along its sides at regular intervals. Floating directly above it, anchored to the ground by a series of gargantuan tethers that formed a tentlike structure around the base, was a massive, diamond-shaped citadel of solid granite the size of a house. Fifty-foot cobalt banners draped off the sides of a balcony that encircled the entire floating structure, gently undulating in the breeze and displaying the Academy's motto in massive Arcania lettering.

"You're sure you can't make it?" Elizabeth asked. "You're a lot better at this whole snooping thing than I am."

"My contact has some leads on Silas he wants to go over today," Snow's voice came through on the messenger coil in Elizabeth's ear. *"If it's quick, I'll try to head your way. No promises."*

"Chloe?" Elizabeth made deliberate use of Snow's real name, trying to reach whatever bond of familiarity there was between them. Elizabeth had an idea of what avenues Snow might be pursuing to find Silas, and this seemed as good a time as any to bring it up. She was curious, a little worried, and more to the point, she needed something to distract herself from how *she* was feeling.

"That contact you're working with? Is it your dad?"

"I'm fine."

So she'd been right.

"I know you have a complicated relationship with your parents. If you need—" The other side of the connection abruptly went dead, and Elizabeth frowned. "Good talk."

"Lady Elizabeth," Gamma greeted her in his tinny monotone. "Welcome to the Tarsim Academy of Arcane Arts. The Head of Cataloging and Collections is expecting you."

"Thanks, Gamma," Elizabeth sighed.

She followed the autostruct, feeling alone and out of place. She was a warden, trained to navigate the wilderness and fight whatever dwelled inside. Now she was standing on a stone path lined with sculpted iron lampposts, with blue-and-gray-robed scholars milling about, idly discussing campus gossip and arcane theory, and the only hints of the natural world were a carefully manicured lawn and a few trees cultivated for shade. This was Arman's territory, not hers. She tried not to dwell on the anxiety that rose in her chest from even thinking his name, and found herself whispering a prayer to Avelina. Not just for her husband's sake, but for hers. She needed help. She needed—

"Kaila?"

When Gamma had opened the doors to the Cataloging and Collections office, there had only been one person waiting for them in the cluttered room. She was a petite woman in her late twenties, with light-bronze skin and short, straight dark hair, dressed in a floor-length satin dress. As soon as she saw

Elizabeth, her eyes lit up, and she snapped her fingers, causing a momentary spark of green light to flash in the air in front of her. With a giddy shriek, Elizabeth rushed forward, enveloping the woman in a bear hug.

"Kaila!" Elizabeth repeated. "Renalt above, I missed you!"

Elizabeth squeezed tight, even lifting the little wizard off her feet, and Kaila smiled and squeezed back. When Elizabeth finally released her, neither of them could stop smiling. It had been years since the two of them had seen each other, when Elizabeth had still called herself Sable, and Kaila had gone by Canvas, but sisters of the Broken Spear never forgot each other.

Elizabeth's hands began moving, and she surprised herself by how effortless the motions were as she slipped into Antemer Signspeak.

"What are you doing here? I thought you were back in Antem."

"I have a friend who works in the Bursar's Office, and he let me know about a position that opened up last spring," Kaila signed back. *"It turns out the Academy actually pays pretty well. Not glinchasing well, but I'm also way less likely to get killed."*

"Well, congrats. But why didn't I hear from you?"

"I tried. But apparently the 'Winged Lady of Sasel' is a bit of a recluse. I couldn't find anyone who knew how to get a message to you. And anyway, no one had even seen you in months."

"Give me a break. I was pregnant, and this armor does not stretch like that."

Kaila froze, and Elizabeth had a split second to brace herself before Kaila's hands became a blur of movement. She caught maybe every third word of Kaila's excited questions and congratulations, and when it became clear Elizabeth was lost, Kaila laughed, and held out her hand. A miniature, illusory duplicate of Elizabeth appeared in Kaila's palm, and quickly became covered in a layer of rust. One of the duplicate's arms fell off, and the illusion vanished.

"Someone's signing is rusty."

"Cut me some slack, it's been a while!"

Kaila smiled, and much slower, signed her question. *"So, does that mean you and Phoenix finally got your shit together?"*

Elizabeth's smile vanished. For just a moment, she'd been so excited to see a friendly face that she'd forgotten everything else. But the relief was over. *"Actually, about that . . ."*

Kaila had not been told about the nature of the meeting beforehand, only that the Winged Lady of Sasel would be coming on official business for the crown, but she immediately grew serious as Elizabeth explained the broad strokes of what was going on. Phoenix was missing, Ink suspected foul play from within the Academy, and Elizabeth was trying to find a trail to follow that could lead back to whoever had taken her husband. Kaila agreed to help without a moment's hesitation, and with a quick scrawl onto an enchanted tablet, had her secretary clear her schedule.

Ink had suggested starting by looking into Haegan, and Elizabeth didn't have any better ideas. They had Gamma bring them everything the office had on his body, which, like all the other materials the Academy acquired, came through Kaila's department. There was a record from the field team that recovered the corpse, an examiner's report on the body and its armor, and a copy of the logs of possession. According to everything they dug up, Haegan's body had arrived the day after it had been uncovered, been examined, and then cremated. His armor was officially listed as stored within the Academy vaults.

Kaila asked what they were looking for.

"*Something* . . ." Elizabeth's hands stopped moving, because she wasn't sure.

She wanted something that would tell her where Arman was, or who had taken him, but she knew that was too many steps removed from what she was doing now. She tried to channel her inner Arman, focus on the task right in front of her, to find the next link in the logical chain.

"Something that explains how Haegan could be alive," Elizabeth signed. Technically, they didn't have any proof that Haegan was alive. Ink had insinuated the possibility, and she'd been barred from looking into it. But if that was still uncertain—if that was "just a hypothesis," as Arman would've said—then that was where she had to start. First question: is Haegan actually back from the dead?

Kaila frowned. *"You can't resurrect ashes."*

That was true. Resurrections needed a body, as intact as possible. You could get away with a few missing pieces on occasion, but ashes were out of the question. And yet—

"Ashes are a lot easier to fake than a corpse," Elizabeth signed.

Kaila shrugged, conceding the point. She took another look at the files and fingered a line from the field team's records. Haegan's body had arrived at the Academy the day after it had been found, but everything else from the estate had taken a week or more to arrive. That was about how long it took a flying skiff to get from Sasel to the estate outside of Olwin. They'd teleported Haegan's body back specifically.

It could have been as simple as the Academy wanting to examine the body while it was still fresh. But it meant Haegan had been dead less than three days when he came to the Academy, well within the time window for a resurrection.

It still wasn't proof. But it meant it was possible.

Still, Elizabeth was unsatisfied. Ink would have certainly already known this to even begin to suspect Haegan was alive. She needed more. She needed something Ink couldn't or wouldn't have seen. At her request, Kaila handed her the examiner's notes on the body. Elizabeth still didn't know what she was looking for, only hoping that she'd know it when she saw it. She read and reread the notes, wracked her brain for everything she'd ever heard Arman say about Haegan, about that night, about magic.

"Ugh," she grumbled. "You're the smart one, Arman. I'm supposed to be—"

And then it hit her.

Their old catchphrase, "You're smart, and I'm stubborn." Normally, they meant it purely in their mentality of how they approached problems. Arman thought through them, she tackled them head on and never relented. He was the planning, she was the will. He was the brains, she was the brawn. She wasn't just physically stronger than him, she had more raw power—thanks to the Heart of the Sky.

He'd first infused her with it by destroying its original vessel to allow the power to escape and flow into her. That was how everyone they knew—her, Snow, Pitch—had been infused with a heart. Effectively, their bodies became the new vessel for it. And since she was a vessel, she'd asked once if the Heart would escape and flow into someone else if anything happened to her.

"Maybe if your body was completely destroyed," he'd mused. "But if you just *died* . . . I imagine some would leak out, but most of the power would probably still stay in the body."

If someone with a Servitor Heart inside of them was killed, the bulk of the power would still be in the body after death. But nowhere in the examiner's notes was there any mention that Haegan's body was supercharged with power. Only a brief note of the body "showing minor signs of arcane exposure." That was it.

When Elizabeth read that, she scoffed. *Arman* would show signs of minor arcane exposure. Anyone who made a living dealing with magic and arcane artifacts would. Someone who's had a Servitor Heart should have peaked every test and sensor the Academy had.

But Ink wouldn't have seen this even if she'd read the report. She didn't know what happened to a Servitor Heart if the person it was inside died. She'd never had the chance to study them up close. But Elizabeth and Arman had. And now, she had a real thread to pull.

"We need to talk to this examiner," Elizabeth signed to Kaila. *"Because they lied about what they saw."*

The examiner's name was Kim Ryung, and a request from Kaila had him in a chair in the office in ten minutes. He was young, perhaps not even a full graduate of the Academy yet. The obvious nervousness could have just been from being called in to speak with his boss's boss, but Elizabeth would know for certain soon.

"Director Kaila," Ryung greeted. "How can I help you?"

Kaila signed for him to sit down, but he only stared at her, uncomprehending. Kaila sighed, and a miniature image of Ryung appeared in front of her before falling back into a chair and dissipating. Ryung understood this time, and sat down.

"Is everything all right?" he asked.

Elizabeth ignored him for the moment. Knowing now that he couldn't understand it, she signed, *"You work here. Do you want to be the carrot or the stick?"*

A smile briefly flickered across Kaila's lips before she restrained her anticipation. *"Stick."*

"Um. I'm sorry, I haven't really learned how to read that yet," Ryung apologized. "Usually somebody translates?"

"Don't worry, I can," Elizabeth said. She took out her copy of the examination notes, making a show of reading off of them. "Ryung, is it?"

"That's me," the man nodded. "Who are you, if I can ask?"

"Lady Elizabeth. I'm a friend of Kaila's," Elizabeth introduced.

Ryung's eyes widened in recognition, and for a moment, his nervousness was replaced by awe. "You're . . . you're the Winged Lady!"

"I am," Elizabeth admitted, dipping her head slightly as if embarrassed by the recognition. "And I could use your help."

"O-of course!" Ryung said, standing up. "What can I do for you?"

Kaila folded her arms and glared as a miniature image of Ryung appeared in front of her before falling back into a chair and dissipating. He promptly sat back down, his excited energy quickly subdued.

"Apologies."

Elizabeth pulled up a seat next to him and slid the notes back over. "You were the one who examined Sir Haegan's body, correct?"

Ryung blinked. His tells were subtle and brief, but Elizabeth still caught them. His throat tensed just a little, and his eyes flicked to the papers without reading them, like they were a spider he was afraid was about to jump at him.

"I was."

"I just had some questions about your examination I couldn't find answers to in your notes," Elizabeth explained. "It shouldn't take long."

Kaila narrowed her eyes and signed, *"What did you do?"*

Ryung balked under Kaila's expression. Even if he didn't understand what she signed, he could read her face just fine, and it was angry. "What did she say?"

"I think I might be getting you in trouble." Elizabeth dodged the question with an apologetic tone, knowing that not giving an answer would only make him more unsettled.

"Why?"

"I'm sure it's going to turn out to be nothing," Elizabeth assured him. "Ryung, during your examination of Haegan's body, did you find anything unusual?"

"Well, I suppose the assignment itself was unusual," Ryung said. His eyes kept going back to his notes in her hands. "It's rare that we examine the *recently* dead, but apparently circumstances surrounding his death warranted an arcane evaluation."

Kaila cut in again. *"Are you making excuses already?"*

Ryung looked to Elizabeth for translation, and she made a show of worriedly biting her lip. "I think she's concerned you might have made a mistake. If looking at the recently dead isn't your usual work, do you think maybe you might not have known what you were doing?"

"No! It's not common, but I have done it before. We all have. I'm well-versed in the procedures," Ryung protested. He turned to Kaila specifically, trying to defend himself. "I do good, accurate work."

"Perfect," Elizabeth said. "Then would you mind explaining why you failed to make any note of the massive reserves of arcane power that would have been present in the body."

The color rapidly began to drain from Ryung's face. "What?"

Kaila slammed her hand down on the table to get his attention as she created a new illusion in Ryung's face. This time, it was a miniature knight, who looked around for a moment before being run through the chest by a tiny sword. The image of the miniature warrior fell onto its back, and its corpse began to glow with barely constrained power.

Elizabeth had to bite back a laugh from watching her five-foot-tall friend cartoonishly recreating a violent murder. But Ryung was experiencing just the right amount of anxiety over his job security to actually find the display as aggressive and menacing as Kaila had been going for.

"I-I didn't see anything like that."

Kaila's hands became an angry blur. *"Are you blind? How could you not see it?"*

"I'm sorry!" Ryung apologized on instinct, not even aware of what he was apologizing for. His eyes gave Elizabeth a desperate plea.

Elizabeth shook her head. "She wants to know how you missed something that should have been fairly obvious. And so do I, actually."

"I—"

"You said yourself, you do good, accurate work," Elizabeth reminded him, crossing her hands in front of her. "You weren't lying to save face in front of your boss, were you?"

"I wasn't given time to properly examine him!" Ryung snapped in his defense. As soon as the words left his mouth, his eyes went wide, and his jaw clamped shut.

Elizabeth cocked her head. "Ryung. What do you mean by that?"

"He . . ." Ryung trailed off. "I can't say."

Kaila gave Ryung a stern look, never breaking eye contact as she planted her hand on the table in front of Ryung. An illusory letter of resignation materialized beneath her fingertips.

"Ryung, I think you should probably start talking," Elizabeth noted. She gestured meaningfully toward Kaila's latest illusion. "Assuming you want to keep your job."

"Haegan's body was taken out of the workspace before I could do anything," Ryung admitted. "I had to . . . I was told to write a report based on what I'd already seen. I did the best I could, but I scarcely had more than a look!"

"Who took the body?" Elizabeth asked.

"I . . ." Ryung faltered. "I can't say."

Angry sparks danced across Kaila's fingertips in threat. Her eyes demanded an answer.

"Please," Ryung pleaded. "He said if I said anything, he'd ruin me."

"Hey. You don't have to be the one in trouble here," Elizabeth said. "You were just doing your job. If somebody over you forced you into this, just let the bosses work it out between them. Give us a name."

Ryung looked between Elizabeth's sympathetic eyes and Kaila's looming glare, and his mouth trembled.

"Who was it, Ryung?" Elizabeth pressed. "Who took Haegan's body? Who told you to cover it up? I can't help you if you don't help me."

He finally broke.

"It was the headm—"

His words stuck in his throat, turning into a strangled noise. There was a loud, fleshy pop, and his body went rigid for an instant before he fell face first into Kaila's desk, muscles limp, eyes vacant, and mouth agape. Both women flinched in surprise at the suddenness of it before Elizabeth rushed forward to examine him.

His eyes were so bloodshot as to have gone red, and after a few seconds, fluid began to dribble out of his eyes, nose, and ears. He had no pulse, and he wasn't breathing.

"What just happened?" Kaila signed frantically.

"I don't know," Elizabeth signed. *"But I think I know who did it."*

18

ASPIRATIONS

"All right, kid, come at me."

In a small clearing just outside Aenerwin, Bart and Brass squared off. The young paladin glanced hesitantly between his sword and the veteran freelancer, who stood confidently a few feet away, sidesword resting casually at his hip. Bart wore the gambeson underlayer of his armor, but Brass sported only a loose cotton shirt and leather vest. Ruby sat on a tree stump off to the side, chewing an apple as she eagerly waited for the bout to begin.

After double-checking his stance and footing, Bart tightened his grip on his sword, and swung. Almost too fast to see, Brass's blade reacted, deflecting Bart's and leveling at the paladin's throat before he could even react. Bart froze, and Brass offered an apologetic smirk before lowering his weapon.

"Good try," Brass encouraged. "Your basic form's in real danger of being flawless. But you're still too focused on your own movements. You need to act and react at the same time, and you need to do it without thinking about it. It's harder than it sounds."

"That doesn't sound easy at all," Bart said.

"I know."

With Daybreaker secured, their party had returned to Aenerwin to prepare for freeing Ruby from the demonic influence that had been hanging over her the last several months. The actual ritual would be taking place at Saint

Avelina's Cathedral in Sasel, since their facilities were far beyond those in Aenerwin's own Church of the Guiding Saint. But before they made the trip to the capital, Church had some of his own materials to consecrate, tasks to delegate, and messages to exchange. So everyone else was left waiting.

Already packed for the trip, Brass had offered to train with Bart and Ruby. Even though the latter wasn't in the mood, she did want to watch.

"Come on," Brass prompted Bart. "Try again."

Bart nodded before lunging forward. Each time he attacked, he was parried, with Brass keeping one hand behind his back and barely moving from where he stood.

For the most part, Brass was content to simply defend, but whenever he suspected Bart was getting complacent or sloppy, he countered. For someone who'd only picked up a blade for the first time a few months ago, the young man took to it encouragingly quickly.

Brass punished a sloppy swing from Bart with a quick, precise swipe, leaving a thin stripe of blood across the kid's cheek. Bart backed away, his hand shooting up to touch the stinging wound.

"Ow," he hissed.

"That's what you get for holding back," Brass warned.

"I wasn't."

"Really?" Brass cocked his head. "I've seen you knock an ogre on its ass. Where's that guy?"

Bart's brow furrowed. "That's . . . I don't think that's a good idea."

"Oh come on. Let me have it."

"But . . . what if I hurt you?" Bart asked.

"There's a cleric who can bring back the dead a two-minute walk from where we're standing. I think I'll be okay," Brass chuckled. "Look, you want to get better, or you want to lose your sword every fight? You've gotta practice with everything in your toolbox. Even god-bothering."

"I don't know—"

"It'll be fine," Brass insisted. He gestured with his sword to their lone audience member. "Ruby, tell him it's fine."

By this point, Ruby had set down her apple, too engrossed by what looked to her like a disaster waiting to happen. Her eyes said this was a terrible idea, but out loud she said, "He says it's fine . . ."

It was only a half-hearted endorsement, but even that was enough peer pressure for Bart to cave. After all, Brass was a seasoned freelancer. If he'd lasted as long as he had, surely it was because he had to know what he was doing.

"Okay . . ." he muttered, taking up a fighting stance once again.

Brass grinned ear to ear, and saluted Bart with a flourish of his sword before taking up position himself, with one hand behind his back, feet together, and sword held low.

Bart rolled out his shoulders and drew a deep breath to center himself. In his mind, he reached out to Saint Beneger, servant to the god Renalt and a guide of humanity. For the protection and guidance of all, he asked the Guiding Saint to lend him the power of the god of justice.

The medallion hanging around Bart's neck began to warm as the saint answered his call. Divine might flowed into his body like fire in his veins, spreading like heat into every muscle and fiber of himself. His face and chest grew hot, and his heart raced. A true paladin could hold this state, using divine power to fuel their every movement. For Bart, all he could manage was to channel it for a short burst before it became too much to bear. But that would be all he needed to strike. He met Brass's eyes one final time and saw nothing but naked anticipation in them.

Bart catapulted himself forward into a lunging slash, kicking up earth in his wake as he put his whole body into his strike—only for his blade to cleave through empty air. The foot he'd lunged forward with never touched the ground as Brass kicked it out from under him, and the momentum of his empowered swing sent him tumbling head over heels across the grass until he slammed into a tree with an audible crack.

"See?" Brass said. "You definitely need to practice that more. You may as well have sent a warning by mail for how advanced a notice I got."

For a moment, Bart was too disoriented to make sense of what had just happened or even register anything beyond a spinning sky and a dull ache in his right arm. Then his view became dominated by Ruby's concerned face hovering over his.

"Bart?"

"I'm okay," he said, letting her help him sit up. "I just hit my—"

The words got stuck in his throat as he glanced down to his right arm and became acutely aware that it was bent in a spot that arms weren't supposed to bend. Ruby's eyes widened, and his mouth suddenly felt very dry.

He didn't scream, but he went very pale very quickly, and his voice cracked as he called out, "B-Brass?"

"Oh, shit!" Brass exclaimed, sounding more impressed than concerned. "Hey, whatever you do, don't move that arm!"

"Brass!" Ruby snapped, far less calm. She was fairly certain the only reason she couldn't see Bart's bone was because of his long sleeves.

Bart wasn't speaking, and was barely moving, apart from a slight, terrified tremble that wracked his entire body. He'd seen battle already. He'd hurt, and killed, and been hurt in return. But never something that had left his body so visibly out of its correct shape. His head spun.

"Relax! I've gotten hurt way worse than this sparring!" Brass tried to reassure them. "We're gonna need some sticks, some bandages, and something for him to bite down on."

Before he could say anything else, a very perturbed voice shouted something in the language of the gods. Compelled by the words, Bart's arm snapped itself straight, eliciting a surprised yelp from Bart and Ruby. A warmth similar to what Bart had channeled before, but far gentler, flowed through his arm, melting away any lingering pain. Almost immediately, Bart's heart began to steady itself, and some color came back into his cheeks.

Church marched into the clearing, annoyed and failing to hide it. Both Bart and Ruby shrank under the vicar's gaze, but he only had eyes for his former teammate.

"*Brass*," Church said. "A word?"

Brass nodded. "Well, kids, Mom and Dad need to have a talk, so take five. Ruby, make sure he doesn't go into shock?"

"What?"

Church sighed, but otherwise said nothing, waiting for Brass to saunter over. After making sure they were a reasonable distance from Bart and Ruby while still being close enough to intervene if Bart *did* go into shock, the cleric turned his attention to Brass.

"What did I just walk in on?"

"We were just sparring."

"How did *that* lead to him nearly breaking his arm in two?"

"Oh, I had him take a paladin swing at me, and he launched himself into a tree. I mean, I tripped him, but he did all the real work."

"Brass—" Church raised a finger, before again forcing himself to breathe. He couldn't meet Brass's chaos with his own. He needed to remain calm. Even if Brass was the one person who made it genuinely difficult for him to do so. "If I hadn't been here—"

"You would have been within spitting distance back in town. And if you hadn't, people have been breaking bones since they were invented, and we're all still here," Brass said. "Besides, I didn't force him to do it. He *wanted* to train. And if the kid really wants to be a glintchaser, who am I to stop him?"

"An adult who knows better? My friend who respects my concerns?"

"Neither of those sound anything like me," Brass said. "But if it's any consolation, I don't think either of us could talk him out of it anymore. Not now that he's got a girl to impress."

Church's eyebrows shot up. "What?"

A coy smile slowly spread across Brass's face as he jerked his head back toward Bart and Ruby. The two of them were still sitting together on the tree stump, talking. Any lingering trauma he might have harbored was clearly being overruled by whatever discussion they were having. Bart made some kind of gesture akin to swinging a sword, and Ruby laughed. Bart's eyes shined when she laughed like it was the most amazing sound he'd ever heard. To Church's eye, they looked like they were getting along. But by now, he was well aware of his blind spot to this sort of thing.

"*Really*?"

"Oh, he's got it bad."

"But she's . . ." Church struggled to find the words to explain his incredulity at the pairing, but the best he came up with was, ". . . older."

"By, what? Three, four years?" Brass guessed. "He's a strapping young man. If he's got the game, he might actually pull it off."

"I—" Church was at a loss for words. Somehow, in trying to talk Brass into being responsible, they'd ended up here. Damn it if Brass didn't know how to steer a conversation. "This isn't what we were talking about."

"The way I see it, if he's going to do this, and he is, he may as well be prepared for it. But if you're really worried I'm going to mess him up, then why not teach him how to hack it yourself?" Brass suggested. "After all, I'm not the one he wants to be when he grows up."

Church knew what Brass was implying, and that he was right. Even if the battle in Loraine had been what finally got him started, Bart's desire to be a freelancer had already been there for some time. It had been ever since Brother Michael had first started filling his head with stories of Church's time as one. Before Church could decide whether he should feel proud or guilty about that, Angel arrived.

"What are you all standing around for?" Angel asked. "Are we doing this, or what?"

"Sorry, I was distracted," Church said. "We're ready to move."

"Ruby, Bart, time to get the show on the road!" Brass called.

Bart immediately got to his feet, but Ruby hesitated. Even after she eventually stood, her eyes were fixated on Daybreaker, which now hung from Angel's belt.

"I've been meaning to ask," Ruby said. "What *exactly* is this ritual going to involve? And why does it include an axe?"

The three former Starbreakers in the room all exchanged looks. Brass gave a shake of his head, trying to dissuade Church from being Church. It failed, and the vicar sighed before giving an honest answer.

"Whatever pact you were pulled into is too ironclad to be broken by conventional means, so we're using a work-around," the vicar stated. "Daybreaker is an angelic weapon. If you're killed by it, any hold on your soul will be released. Afterward, I can resurrect you, and—"

"You're going to *kill* me?" Ruby shrieked, immediately taking a step back.

"Painlessly and temporarily!" Church tried to explain. "I'll be resurrecting you immediately after, and between that and everything the church has at its disposal, you'll be completely safe, I promise." Church held up his hands placatingly. "You don't have to do this if you don't want to. But in my opinion as your priest, it's your best option."

Ruby's palms were clammy as her heart pounded in her chest, so intensely she could feel it in her ears. Her mouth went dry. People's mouths were still moving, and yet all she could make out was indistinct din. One word sounded in her mind, over and over again like a drum.

Dead.

These people wanted her dead. They told her so right to her face. They said they'd bring her back, but how was she supposed to trust them? She remembered the Order of Saint Ricard, how set they'd been on killing her. She remembered how terrified of her everyone in Aenerwin had been. They were on the side of the gods, and in their eyes, she was already on the side of the demons. Of course they wanted to kill her.

Next to her, Bart said something she didn't hear, but he looked afraid. And for just a moment, that vulnerable, worried look on his face disarmed her. Then she saw movement on her left.

"Listen to him, kid," Angel stressed, moving toward her. Bringing that axe closer to her. "We're trying—"

"Stay away from me!"

The color drained from Ruby's skin as thorns began to break out across her arm, tearing open her skin as they did. The thorns grew into black, twisted vines that shot out from her in every direction, seeking out everyone around her. In an instant, the others were entangled in writhing cords and pinned to trees or the ground. At first, all of them thrashed and struggled, but the more they moved, the more the thorns in the vines seemed to dig into them. Eventually, everyone but Angel went still.

"Kid, I don't want to hurt you," Angel warned. She was already beginning to pull apart the vines holding her.

Ruby felt the sensation from her dreams, the hot breath running down the back of her neck. But now, it didn't feel like a monster creeping up behind her. It felt like something powerful ready to back her up. With a confidence that wasn't hers, Ruby retorted, "You won't."

The vine holding Angel cracked like a whip, launching her out of the clearing.

Arms pinned awkwardly to his side and thorns biting into his cheek, Brass called out, "Ruby! This isn't you!"

"Shut up!" Ruby ordered. As she shouted, the vines protruding from her arm tightened around everyone. She tasted their blood in her mouth. It sickened her. It excited her. "You don't know me. You don't even know my name!"

"I know what you're like when things get scary," Brass said. "With Pitch, with the Dread Knight, with freelancing—you don't let scary get in the way of what you want. If you don't want to lose your shiny new demon powers, that's fine. But if you're *afraid* to take a risk to cut this shit out of you, that's not you talking. That's the thing squatting in your head!"

Don't listen to him. He's lying.

The voice in her head. It still sounded like her voice. But it felt more distant now. More separate. Other.

Her head started to ache, and she squeezed her eyes shut.

"They want to kill me," Ruby protested. She was so confused. Her arm was screaming in pain.

"We don't!" Bart joined in shouting, even as a thorn snagged his lip. "Ruby, you have to believe me! We would never hurt you."

Ruby met Bart's eyes, and saw he was terrified. But not *of* her. He was afraid *for* her. Suddenly, she was on the front steps of the Church of the Guiding Saint, meeting the first acolyte in the church that treated her like a person. She remembered asking him for help with understanding her powers. Remembered him running away from Aenerwin with her, remembered fighting the army of the Dread Knight alongside him. She remembered Angel fighting to nearly the last breath to keep her *safe* from the Order of Saint Ricard. And in that moment, she felt insane for even thinking that any of these people could ever mean her harm.

With a gasp of pain, Ruby willed the vines to release. Immediately, the vines detached from her and withered to dust. The open wounds left behind on her arm healed themselves shut, leaving only her bloody, tattered sleeve as evidence they had ever been there at all. Her legs gave out from under her, and she collapsed to her knees, suddenly feeling lightheaded. Slowly, everyone got back to their feet, all of them bleeding from multiple places. Hesitantly, Brass checked on her.

". . . Ruby?"

"I'm sorry. I don't . . ." Ruby didn't look up from her arm. She could still feel where the thorns had pierced through her skin. Her heart was still pounding. Swallowing hurt. For a moment, the other voice had been indistinguishable from her own. It had made her forget things she should have known, changed how she felt about others. And she'd been awake. "I'll do it. Whatever we have to do, I'll do it."

19
GUESTS

One of the things Snow hated most about her family's mansion was how *empty* it was. When it was first constructed, Sebastian Guerron had envisioned it not just as his home, but the home of his personal, privately sponsored freelancer company, the White Hawk. The idea was to have all of his employees living under one roof, sharing their spoils and stories when they weren't out collecting rare artifacts for their patron's private collection.

But despite the fact that their escapades paid for her entire lifestyle, Snow's mother never liked freelancers, and disliked them even more once Snow had been born. As a result, Sebastian had to construct an entirely separate headquarters for the White Hawk, leaving the Guerron estate, a mansion built to house hundreds, only actually used by two people and a few dozen personal staff. So many rooms and halls made for scores of people, now empty shells half-heartedly decorated with whatever symbols of wealth the Guerrons picked up.

The only time the mansion seriously threatened to come alive was when her parents threw a party, and even then, with the crowds of refined socialites and old nobility her parents tended to invite, it wasn't by much.

Now, walking its halls again, listening to her footsteps echo louder than they had any right to, Snow remembered why she'd been so eager to leave this place as a child.

She didn't miss it.

"Right this way, Ms. Guerron." Jacque gestured for Snow to follow. "Your father and his contact have already arrived."

Snow said nothing as Jacque led the way, keeping her thumbs tucked into her belt. Jacque hadn't mentioned her mother. Not surprising, after what Snow had heard the last time she was here. Maybe the woman had finally decided to stop pretending to care.

So far, her father seemed determined to keep up his attempts. He could have just sent word to her with everything he'd learned from his contacts, but instead he'd insisted on inviting her back to the house to talk in person with someone he'd tracked down. Even encouraged her to wear something more formal.

Sebastian had included an excuse about only Snow knowing exactly what she wanted to ask, but she suspected the real reason for the invitation was just getting her back in the house. It didn't matter. She'd tolerate a father-daughter lunch if he got her the information she needed. But she wasn't dressing up for it.

Jacque opened the door for her, and she gave a curt nod before entering. Two steps in, before the door had even closed, Snow caught sight of her father and his contact. She hadn't had much in the way of expectations, but maybe the one thing she hadn't expected was to see her father seated directly across from Sir Haegan of Whiteborough.

Sebastian tried to calm his daughter. "Chloe—"

Before a third syllable could leave her father's throat, the temperature in the room plummeted, ice began spreading across the dining table, and Snow had already thrown Companion Piece at Haegan's face.

Snow's knife halted midair, inches from its target, and at the same time Sebastian was hurled from his seat by an invisible force in one direction while the table flew in the other. As his eyes shone bright purple, Haegan lifted off the ground, hovering in the air as Snow rushed to meet him.

In a blink, Snow was inside Haegan's guard with another dagger already in hand, and the knight was only barely able to stop her knife from slipping between his ribs. Everything that wasn't nailed down lifted into the air, before descending on Snow in a shower of debris.

Piece by piece, she nimbly avoided every plate and chair Haegan threw her way. When the dining table itself came hurtling toward her, she leapt into the air and used the table as a springboard to vault out of the way of the assault.

She landed in a low crouch, ice racing out from her fingertips across the floor after Haegan. Just as it began to build itself into a wall of frost to slam into him, Haegan threw out his hands, shattering the entire construct in an instant and showering the room in an impromptu flurry.

Then, before Snow could make another move, a force like an invisible lasso yanked her off of her feet and hurled her into a wall, pinning her. In an instant, the force holding her became all-encompassing, holding down her entire body until she couldn't move a muscle. As Haegan stood with his arm outstretched, the dining table lifted itself off of the floor, preparing to launch itself at Snow. She braced for the impact.

"Stop!" Sebastian shouted.

The dining table held its position in the air, floating, waiting to be thrown. Haegan slowly descended to the floor, but he kept his hand up to keep Snow in place. An instant later, her messenger coil tore itself from her ear and flew into Haegan's waiting palm. He crushed it in his bare fist.

"I'm only being cautious," Haegan assured Sebastian. "We both want her alive."

"You're working with him?" Snow asked, struggling to talk through whatever grip Haegan had her in.

"I'm sorry you had to find out like this," Sebastian apologized. "Sir Haegan is undertaking a mission for the benefit of all Corsar. All mankind. He came to me for help. I know the two of you have . . . history. But you're also your mother's daughter. I thought that if we had enough to show for ourselves, and paid you generously, we'd be able to convince you to work with us, not against us. I was putting together a proper presentation to approach you with. But you coming to me forced our hand."

Snow wasn't sure what made her angrier, the repentant look in her father's eyes, that he was insinuating this was somehow her fault, or the fact that he'd just compared her to her mother.

The doors opened, and the new faces that walked in sent ice through Snow's veins. The first was a nondescript member of the Cult of Stars—though they were all nondescript, so that wasn't saying much. They had the telltale scar on their forehead, and that was all Snow needed to register about them to know they needed to die. Their presence wasn't much of a surprise. The last time she'd fought Haegan's right hand, Silas, it had been the Cult of Stars that had saved him.

The second new arrival was the head of the Academy himself, Headmaster Targan. His presence more or less confirmed basically every theory she, Ink, and Wings had, so it was a shame she would probably never get a chance to tell either of them.

"When this is all over," Sebastian said to his daughter, "I hope you'll understand that I was only doing what was best for all of us."

Snow spat, and it froze solid at his feet. Headmaster Targan and the cultist both turned their attentions toward her while Haegan continued to hold her in place.

At the very least, she thought, she was probably about to find out what had happened to Phoenix.

20 PRISONERS

Snow wasn't sure what she had to thank for being able to keep so much of herself. She knew that was what had been under attack when the Headmaster and the Cult of Stars had joined forces to screw with her head—her very sense of self, of reality. Whether it was the Heart of Ice's protective numbing of her emotions, practice resisting other mental incursions as part of her training as a thief, or pure, brute stubbornness, she had enough of her own will left to keep herself and what she was now compelled to do separate.

She still couldn't refuse the orders of the Headmaster. In her father's dining room, she'd been ordered to stand down and follow, and she had, without a second's hesitation. But the commands did not consume her. They were not her whole world. Instead, she felt them like a set of impenetrable boundaries. She couldn't cross them, but there was still room for her to maneuver inside them, to be herself. She could use that, she was sure.

Haegan had taken her to the headquarters they were using in Sasel. Because they teleported in, she didn't immediately know where they were. She assumed they were still in the city, but even that was only a guess based on the leads she'd gathered up to now. Every window was covered, and the rooms were spartanly furnished. There were no decorations, nothing of artistic or sentimental value, only utilitarian function. Seating and tables for dining, cots for sleeping, crates and racks for storage of weapons and supplies. Even though the place had clearly been cleaned, a sense of musty abandonment clung to the walls. It could have been any abandoned mansion in the capital.

Except that she knew the shape of these halls. It took her a few rooms of walking to register it, but once she did, everything clicked into place, and then she couldn't *not* see it. The places where the paint had been redone after stray house fires. The extensive repair made to a wall after it had been nearly knocked over by an angry punch. The "C+A" carved into a tiny heart in one of the door frames. By the time Haegan led her to a set of stairs, Snow knew exactly where they were.

Years ago, the Starbreakers had saved the life of Roland II, prince of Corsar, and been honored by the Crown for their heroics with a parade, and a tidy reward that they had opted to spend on a mansion in Sasel. It had served as their home and company headquarters for four years, until the fall of Relgen, and the trial that had seen them banished from the city and their assets seized. Now, after all these years, their enemies had moved in.

She expected to be led to the holding cells downstairs—which she was—but she didn't expect to pass the mansion's basement workshop and find it *alive*. There were easily a dozen people in the space, all dressed in smithing clothes, hammering, cutting, engraving, and refining. A multiarmed construct with tools for appendages was taking apart and reassembling pieces of some massive machine. Some rattling, glowing contraption with a dozen hoses coming out of it was making a sound like a metal horse being beaten to death with a thousand hammers. And at the center of it all, wearing heavily stained work clothes, covered in soot and grease, was Phoenix himself, directing everything even as he worked on a mess of gears, wire, and glowing rocks.

Snow stopped in her tracks. It wasn't just seeing Phoenix—though that was a surprise.

She hadn't seen Phoenix at work like this in years, not since Relgen. That would have been nostalgic enough on its own, but to see him working here, in this space, was like suddenly being sent back a decade in time. If not for the disheveled weariness and extra weight he'd since gained and the other people ruining the illusion, she might never have stopped staring, transfixed by the window into the past.

"Phoenix."

At her saying his name, he froze. When he glanced up, she could see at once something was wrong with him. There was a lost expression running under the usual look of focus he had while working, as if he was clinging to his task like a lifeline in a hostile and unfamiliar world. But he was alive, and not only was he not chained up in a cell or being tortured, he was working. Spellforging. With people who worked for Haegan, if not the Academy.

"Snow," he greeted her back, just as surprised. "They got you too?"

Then he went back to work, and she saw herself disappear from his awareness as his task completely reabsorbed him. Any doubt she'd had was gone. The same thing the Headmaster and the Cult of Stars had done to her head, they'd done to him, only it had gotten its hooks even deeper into him. He hadn't bathed or trimmed his beard since she'd seen him last, and his clothes were discolored and rumpled from days of wear. His hands moved with a degree of desperation to them that said he didn't just want to do this, but that he *needed* to.

"Yeah," Snow said. "We're prisoners in our own house."

Phoenix gave a single, breathy chuckle, not looking up. "I'm sure Targan loves the irony."

Snow could sense Haegan's gaze on her. She'd been told to follow him, and instead she'd stopped to talk to Phoenix. He was only just down the hall, close enough that she didn't feel like it counted as not following him yet, but if he ordered her to move on, she'd have no choice.

He didn't though. Haegan was waiting. Watching.

"Can you fight it?" Snow asked.

Phoenix looked at her, and through her, and at nothing at all. "Fight what?"

It really was worse for him. Snow could feel her mental bonds, chafe and strain against them. Phoenix seemed to not even notice they were there. Distantly, she filed this moment away as something to be angry about, but none of it reached the surface for her. With her usual cold dispassion, Snow made note that she wouldn't be able to expect any help from Phoenix getting out of this.

"Nothing," Snow said.

"Snow." Haegan's voice was like a yank on a leash, and Snow turned toward him. Context said he'd lost patience and wanted her to get back to following him. But since he hadn't explicitly said that, she simply stood in the hall, giving him her full attention, along with a look of cold distaste.

Haegan narrowed his eyes. "Follow me."

She did, leaving Phoenix behind.

Haegan finished leading her to the holding cells, and told her to stay put. Smart of him to add that last command. She'd helped Phoenix design these cells, and they hadn't been built to hold anyone as strong or skilled as her in the first place.

"Do I get food?" Snow asked.

"If we wanted you dead, you wouldn't be here," Haegan said, which was and wasn't an answer. "We will find some way for you to be useful. Until then, stay put."

Snow narrowed her eyes. "We're going to kill you. And this time, you're going to stay dead."

Haegan gave a rueful smile that quickly devolved into a frown. "I'm about to become stronger than the Servitor itself was. In a year's time, this kingdom will be mine, and you and everyone else will enjoy a long life under my protection."

"Except for everyone you murder for your new friends' space god," Snow said. "You know that's how the Cult of Stars works, right? They kill as many people as they can so they can talk to the sky. That's who you're 'saving the world' with."

"You already helped them kill all the people they needed to!" Haegan snapped as he slammed his fist against the cell door. His expression, which had been stoic and impassive, cracked into something manic. His eyes bulged, and his lips curled back into a snarl. For a moment, he was a completely different person. A man on the edge, unraveling at the seams in front of her. Someone who had seen and done and been through too much to keep a grip on reality, or even his sense of self. Outwardly, Snow didn't so much as flinch. Internally, the first stirrings of dread fluttered in her stomach. "All of Relgen died, and the Stars heard it. Your last act was to bring the Starborn to us. So my first will be to rid us of them once and for all."

"You think the Cult's going to like that?"

"The Cult wants a confrontation between humanity and Starborn. They do not care who wins," Haegan spat.

"And you think you can?"

Haegan pulled away from the cell door, straightening back into the image he'd presented before. Snow watched the transition happen, could pinpoint the exact moment he went from the broken man mad with grief to the controlled, immovable knight commander.

"I *will*."

He made the change so smoothly. But that first break in his cool demeanor was like watching a vase get smashed. Even now that he'd glued it back together, she could still see the cracks. She'd seen Haegan at his limit before, the day they'd killed him. He'd been proud, defiant, and determined to the bitter end. That was not what she'd just seen.

The Starborn were older than the gods, and had so thoroughly beaten the elves at the height of their power they'd ushered in the Old World's Collapse. It didn't matter what Phoenix was building for him. That wasn't a fight anyone could win. He was going to get them all killed. The indomitable knight standing before her now might believe it wasn't impossible. But the face Snow had seen behind that facade didn't care.

She resisted the urge to tell him he was insane. She suspected, somewhere in the recesses of what was left of the man he'd been, he already knew.

Haegan took her silence as his cue to leave. She kept her face placid, but the ice blue of her eyes was brighter than usual as he walked away. More than being captured and brainwashed, more than the betrayal from her father or the frustration of learning an enemy hadn't stayed dead, Snow didn't like the look in Haegan's eyes when his composure had slipped. It reminded her too much of a look she'd seen too many times before.

As if summoned by the thought, a voice cut through the silence of the dungeon, coming from just next door.

"He is telling the truth, you know."

She couldn't see the face of whoever it was from her angle, only the bars of the cell, but the haughty emptiness of their delivery was unmistakable. A shiver that had nothing to do with cold ran down Snow's spine.

"I thought Haegan made nice with you," Snow said.

"Hello, Chloe Guerron," the Prisoner said. "We are two of the same, you and I. We are useful to the Knights in Exile. They consider us tamed. But they do not trust us. Safer for them to keep us in cages until they need us."

"What does Haegan need you for?"

"The man seeks to go to war with the Stars themselves. What do you think he needs?" Snow didn't answer, not that it would stop the Prisoner from talking. Nothing short of a knife to the throat stopped the Cult of Stars once they got started. "Power. To go where he pleases. To hide his movements. To bend space and thought and time to his will, and more. And he needs insight, into the nature of his foe."

"So you really want to help him fight the Starborn?"

There was a slam on the bars of the cell next to hers as the Prisoner threw their whole body into them. Shaking hands grasped the bars in a white-knuckle grip.

"I *am* him," the Prisoner hissed, face pressed close enough to the bars for Snow to catch a sliver of wet lips. "I am the terror of every man in the face of the uncaring infinity. I am the knowledge that we are nothing but the frail parasites that fell off of a giant when it died. I am the fear that our struggles and ambitions are nothing but an echo of what came before, and that we can do nothing but follow our forebears into oblivion. The Starborn are the inevitable and the real made manifest. Why delay our reckoning with it? Why not face it? With open arms or with a spear, it doesn't matter. The result will be the same.

"You and your company have long been thorns in my side," the Prisoner said. "But in the end, I must thank you. Without you, I never would have been able to use the Ending. I never would have been able to send a message loud enough for the Stars to hear. They are close now. I have only to pull them across the final threshold. And as a tribute to all you've done for me, I will do it in the same place where you helped me make the call. In the dead city of the northern mountains, humanity will be shown its destiny."

Snow could hear the Prisoner's entire body shaking in religious ecstasy. Unconsciously, she'd taken a step away from the bars of her own cell. She had been fighting the Cult of Stars off and on since she was eighteen years old, but this was the first time she thought she might truly understand what was going on inside their crazed heads.

To them, the coming of the Starborn would be an answer to the cosmic question of humanity's place in the universe. It didn't matter whether humanity fought the Starborn or bent its collective head and accepted extinction. All that mattered was the Starborn came. Because once it did, the outcome was a foregone conclusion.

And if the Cult of Stars really was just a bunch of existentially terrified lunatics, then it was no wonder they were helping Haegan. No wonder they lent him their powers and secrets. They were driven by the same underlying fear. Fear of uncertainty. Of instability. Of insignificance and impending doom. Haegan had seen it just like they had, and decided to run straight at it with the biggest sword he could get.

His reasoning was almost irrelevant. Haegan was going to summon a Starborn and get them all killed. Without ever realizing it, he and his followers had *become* the Cult of Stars.

21

HAEGAN

With a swing of his hammer, Haegan took a man's head clean off. Gore splattered his face and weapon as his enemy's remains crumpled before him, and he sagged with relief and exhaustion as the forest clearing finally went silent.

Half-dried mud clung to his face and hair, and a fresh trickle of his own blood was running down the armor of his gauntlets from a wound near his armpit. His legs shook. His body ached. It had been too long since he'd slept or eaten. But even now, in this brief moment of catching his breath, he felt he couldn't afford to rest.

Six months.

It had been six months since the fall of Relgen. Since the kingdom he called home, had sworn to serve and protect, had fallen to chaos.

Two dozen corpses lay scattered around him, along with the torn and collapsed remnants of the camp they had made. They had started out as bandits raiding a defenseless countryside, stealing food, weapons, valuables, and even people from villages that had once been protected by Relgen's garrisons. Somewhere along the way, they'd gone mad, morphing into a death cult that sought to appease whatever had killed Relgen through ritual sacrifice.

Haegan had been following their trail of murders for weeks. He hadn't found them fast enough to save their most recent victims. Only to avenge them. Now there was one less threat to the people of Corsar.

And so many more still out there.

Relgen was more than a city. It had been the heart and soul of Corsar's military strength. The soldiers that patrolled the roads, that guarded villages, that dealt with monsters and madmen, and watched the borders, were all trained, outfitted, and deployed from the city. When Relgen fell, it had taken nearly half the kingdom's strength with it, to say nothing of its economy. Entire industries had lost their central hub overnight.

Raiders from the north, human and otherwise, were pouring over the border. Unpaid and unprotected citizens and soldiers turned to banditry or worse. And the two remaining cities were in the throes of a sudden and massive refugee crisis as people who had lived near and depended on Relgen sought new shelter.

It was all the remaining crown forces could do to keep the major cities safe. Beyond their walls, out here in the country, the people of Corsar were exposed, little more than prey for an endless horde of predators.

Haegan had spent the last six months fighting, trying to stem the tide, to make a difference. To somehow, someway, put right everything that had gone wrong when Relgen fell.

It wasn't working.

Every ache in his body drove it more home. He wasn't enough. He wasn't strong enough. He wasn't smart enough. He couldn't be in enough places at once.

That was a large part of why he was so tired. Why he'd run himself so ragged. It was never enough, so he always had to keep going. Keep fighting. Keep trying to do more. Somewhere underneath the haze of his exhaustion, Haegan knew it would never be enough. But he had stood in the hollow husk of his home and resolved to fight. No one else had seen what he had, understood the true stakes like he did. He would rather die than stop. And he was not dead yet.

Though, when his legs gave out from underneath him after only two steps, he conceded he was closer to it than he'd been willing to admit.

Haegan collapsed face first into the mud, still at the center of a ring of bodies.

It started to rain.

He lost track of how long he had lain there, listening to the rain ping off his armor and his own labored breathing. Long enough that he started to become aware of the real possibility of drowning in a puddle if he didn't move. Standing up or even pulling himself into a seated position felt like too much, so he settled for rolling onto his back with a grunt, telling himself all the while that he would rest just a little while longer, and then get back to work.

Just.

A little.

Longer.

"And so another good knight falls to their own crusade."

The sudden intrusion of another voice did what the rain hadn't been able to, and woke Haegan from his exhaustion. His eyes snapped open, and he even managed to sit up. His gaze swept his surroundings, and found no one. Only trees, and the first streams of fog rolling across the ground.

No, not fog. Silver smoke.

It crawled forward, and in seconds was so thick Haegan couldn't see his own hands braced against the muddy ground. His skin prickled and itched under his armor, and a deep wrongness settled into his stomach.

And then he was there—a man in a tattered, moth-ridden cloak, dry despite the rain, with a smooth face that clashed with something much older and wilder in his eyes. He was tall, but hunched forward, and there was a mark on his forehead peeking out from behind a curtain of greasy dark hair that came down to his eyes.

Haegan had just dispatched an entire sect of delusional madmen, and this man could have easily been mistaken for one of them. But Haegan knew he was a different breed altogether. Even with the forehead marking partially obscured, Haegan had been a knight long enough to recognize a member of the Cult of Stars when he saw one.

Everything he knew about the Cult told him he was in danger, but despite the obvious madness in the man's eyes, Haegan saw no malice in them. Only curiosity. The cultist had yet to attack, and even alert, Haegan was still too exhausted to make the first move.

"I am Sir Haegan of Whiteborough," he panted. "Sworn knight of the Crown. Who are you, and what are you doing here?"

"I am what all become after they see the other side of the veil. I am a prisoner of fate, and an instrument of the stars," the cultist said. "And I am here for you."

He approached Haegan with every word, and as he drew closer, he knelt down to Haegan's eye level, crawling forward the last bit of distance on hands and knees like an advancing predator. Haegan tensed.

"I can sense when people are close to the truth of the world. Some can pull back the curtain for themselves and see it. But some need help to draw it out. Some like you."

Haegan threw a punch. It was wide and sloppy, and the cultist easily scrambled backward and out of the way, letting the beleaguered knight collapse into the mud he could no longer see through the blanket of silver smoke.

"Fighting even now?" the cultist asked.

"You," Haegan seethed. "And yours. You killed Relgen."

"I sent a call to the Stars, and I was heard," the cultist shot back. For a moment, his body shook with religious fervor, but it died out just as quickly, and the ragged man practically deflated. "But I was not answered. And there is so little left of what I was." His gaze had drifted sadly downward, but now it snapped back up to Haegan. "But not for long." He crept forward again, only slightly wary of Haegan's fists. "You've done so much fighting. But do you know, even, what it is you are fighting against?"

Haegan wanted to stay furious. He wanted to attack this madman, and kill him before he could do any more damage to the world. But there was no power left in him for explosive movement. And more to the point, the cultist's question pulled at him, drew him in like a warm fire and dry shelter would any person lost in a rainstorm. Even with Silas following him, Haegan's crusade had been a lonely one. There was no one he had been able to properly explain himself to. What he had seen. What he was doing now.

"Everything," Haegan said. "This kingdom . . . it's under attack. Every day, from every side."

The cultist looked excited. "Yes. There it is. You're so close. You almost have it."

"What do mean?" Haegan snapped. "What do you think I have?"

"It's not the kingdom that's under attack," the cultist said. "Do you think Corsar's problems are unique in the world? Do you think the Ending was the only calamity buried beneath the thin shell of civilization?

"Everywhere, every day, on every side, humanity is under attack. This world was not always ours, and destiny itself conspires to send instruments of the past to wipe us from the present. We are not meant to be here. The world itself knows it, and it will not rest until we are gone. The Dreadnought in Tipal. The Dragon and the Servitor, here. The Tower in Iandra. The natural order of things, our own insatiable desire to dig up that which is buried, the stars and that which rules them, it's all arrayed against us. It's all aimed at our hearts and driving toward our extinction."

Memories of the bodies lining the streets of Relgen came to Haegan's mind. Hundreds of thousands of lives, wiped out in a blink. One of the greatest strongholds of safety and power in the kingdom, in perhaps the world, and in the end, it had been so fragile. Centuries of work, of struggle, of collaboration and love and loss, undone in an instant.

It had taken only a single weapon, dug up by one company, set off by one cult. And there were so many more weapons. So many more companies. So many more cults. In that moment, as the rain beat down on him and he struggled to stay upright crouched in the mud, Haegan saw it. The true fragility of humanity was laid bare before him. He hadn't realized in Relgen that was what he was really seeing, but now he did.

"Do you understand? Against the inevitable and the endless, humanity is nothing. We are doomed. And the more we struggle against that truth, the more we suffer."

When he'd first seen Relgen, it had been grief and righteous anger that had swelled up inside him. But now, something very different kindled in his chest. And the knight said, "No."

Haegan's arm flashed forward again, faster this time, and his armored fingers wrapped around the cultist's throat. The madman's eyes bulged in surprise as Haegan slowly rose to his feet. It was not righteous fury or grief or revenge that fueled his body in that moment, but sheer defiance.

Haegan understood the Cult of Stars perfectly, and he even suspected this cultist understood him better than anyone else still alive. After all, they had both seen the same thing—the frailty of life, of the future. They had just come to very different conclusions.

"The Dragon was slain," Haegan spat. "The Servitor was destroyed. The Tower fell. If the natural order wants humanity dead, it will have to try harder. If it can be dug up, it can be buried. If the stars are against us, then I will paint the sky black. I do not care what comes. I do not care how many threats there are. I refuse to die simply because something else wills it."

Only minutes ago, Haegan had thought himself out of strength to carry on, to even stand. But from his very first days as a squire, there had been one simple fact about him that had seen him through countless struggles—the more impossible the task, the more determined he was to face it.

If this single man had come simply to kill Haegan, he could have. It would have been too simple, too real, and Haegan likely wouldn't have been able to find the will to resist. But if an army had marched on him and declared him dead to rights, Haegan would have stood and fought like a man possessed. And this cultist had made Haegan believe that the universe itself was seeking to crush him, to decree him and all humanity with him null and void.

Against odds like that, there was no end to the reserves Haegan could draw on.

And he'd come to another revelation. All those great threats he'd listed off that humanity had defeated, none of them had been defeated by one man, or even a small team. Each of them had been met by a massive undertaking of men and women from across regions all coming together under a common cause. Haegan had felt so alone after losing the rest of the Order of the Purple Rose. But if he was going to save the world, he would need a new order. New allies, new followers, who saw the problems that he did, and who shared his desire to do something about it.

The cultist choked out sounds that might have been an attempt at speech, and reached out a shaking hand to press his thumb into Haegan's forehead. The knight's grip on the man's throat tightened, threatening to break his neck in his grip.

The cultist tried again, and against all odds, forced the words out in a dying man's rasp.

"You. Will be. Perfect."

In the same instant that Haegan snapped the man's neck, everything around Haegan was erased, replaced only by the sensation of a white hot spike driving through his forehead, and the sound of his own screams.

"Sir?"

Haegan was snapped from sleep by the sound of Silas's voice outside his quarters. Quarters, he noted with irony, that had once belonged to the two glintchasers who were now his obedient servants.

Haegan didn't need to ask why Silas had come. "I'll be down for the meeting shortly. See to it Phoenix is in attendance as well. I want his progress report with that of the others."

"Yes sir."

Muffled, precise footsteps signaled Silas's departure from the other side of the door, and Haegan took the moment of solitude to indulge in a grunt of discomfort as he rose from his bed. His body, as usual, protested heavily.

Some factor in Haegan's resurrection had gone wrong. It wasn't time—he'd been dead less than three days. Though his wounds had cost him blood, they'd left him essentially in one piece.

He suspected it had something to do with the Servitor Heart of Force he had fused into his body. While he'd been dead, there had been no will to stop it from going rampant inside him. But whatever the ultimate cause, the result was that it hurt to be alive.

It had from the moment he'd woken up, but at first, he'd dismissed that as symptoms of resurrection exhaustion that would go away in time. They hadn't.

His body throbbed with every beat of his heart. He felt it in his muscles, his veins, behind his eyes. His joints ached constantly, and his skin itched at the edges of the purple veins that now decorated his body. Sometimes, when he looked in the mirror, he didn't see a man so much as flesh that contained power. Of the Servitor, and the Stars. And that flesh was tearing at its worn-down seams. He'd felt like he was getting older, before the fall of Relgen. These days, he felt as if he were falling apart.

But he would endure, and cling to the one thought that had allowed him to hold on in the black void between life and death, when the visage of the Starborn had threatened to drown his consciousness: the work was not done.

With indelicate hands, he fastened the straps and buckles of his uniform, the loose, gray clothes he wore whenever not in full armor—which he hadn't been in since Oblivion. His clothes were fashioned after a soldier's uniform, but absent any adornments like what he'd known in the Purple Rose. He was a knight without a kingdom now. An exile, bound only by purpose. It was a grounding thought, whenever he felt adrift.

He'd been feeling adrift more and more lately. Another side effect of an imperfect resurrection, he was sure.

Ever since dying and being brought back, his order's original goal of taking control of Corsar had rung hollow to him. It had seemed like the right way forward once. When he'd thought failing systems and inadequate leadership were all that plagued Corsar. But what did it matter who was running the kingdom when there was a Starborn waiting in the beyond to snuff out the entire world at the first opportunity? That was the true threat his home faced, and the need to eradicate it gave him the strength to stand under the new strain of his body.

He finished dressing, ignoring the throbs and aches of pain that had become his constant, chronic companions, and made his way to the elevator, and the meeting room where his collaborators would be waiting for him. He took his seat at the head of the table, Silas to his right, and the twins René and Rosa down the line from him. They had not always warranted presence at these meetings, even as the most skilled fighters in the Exile Order apart from Silas, but their recent efforts and successes had won them a seat at the table. Phoenix had taken the seat to his left, and though he wasn't pleased to see Haegan, or to be in the room, he said nothing, and did not so much as twitch in protest.

The rest of the seats were taken up by illusory projections of individuals coming from a tiny, pyramid-shaped artifact at the center of the table. Each face represented an individual who had their own reasons to be dissatisfied with the state of affairs in Corsar, and who had been won over by Haegan's original proposed vision of a safer, more secure kingdom, with himself at the head, and all of them in prime position to benefit. Patrick Hitzkoff, the Baron of Loraine. Rita Salvione, a vicar of Saint Avelina. Sebastian Guerron, owner and proprietor of the White Hawk freelancer company. And Targan, Headmaster of the Academy.

They had predictably all balked at the redirection Haegan had undertaken after coming back from the dead. He understood what the true stakes they faced were, but once again, others had not seen what he had. They thought too small. They did not understand. There had been no end of arguments and complaints, and he had to make concessions to retain their loyalty and commitment. Petty. Blind. Insufferable.

But he still needed them.

Targan's projection was the last to flicker into existence, not arriving until even after Haegan. And as soon as his face materialized, everyone at the table save Haegan sucked in a breath. Carved into the Headmaster's forehead, still pink and angry around the edges, was the twelve-pointed symbol of the Cult of Stars.

"What have you done?" Silas demanded.

"Don't be so closed-minded, boy." Targan's voice was distorted as a projection, but his dismissive disdain was perfectly preserved. "Your master already uses the cult's powers. I've simply taken the next step to explore the possibilities they've offered us. Concealing it will be trivial."

Silas was openly disgusted, and everyone else shifted uncomfortably, but Haegan's expression remained stoic. His eyes locked on the freshly carved symbol on Targan's forehead, transfixed.

There were almost countless scourges that threatened the kingdom of Corsar, but the Cult would always spark a special hatred in Haegan's heart for what they had done to the city of Relgen, and to him. The night they'd first found him and forced their power onto him, he'd spent hours scrubbing himself in a river, trying to remove the feeling of being tainted, and for weeks afterward, he'd been sick to his stomach. Only then had he started learning to use it. To move like they did. To obscure himself like they did.

It was horrendously useful magic. In time, he'd let himself forget where it came from and focus on its utility. It was a tool, like the alliances he'd forged, the resources and followers he'd collected. One more weapon in the arsenal of his Exile Order, as it sought to reclaim and restore the world.

Now, looking at Targan marking himself with the mark of the Cult of Stars, Haegan felt a strange connection to the symbol, as if on some level, he understood what it *meant* in a way that went beyond basic iconography. He found he couldn't look away from it. His own forehead itched.

"Results?" he asked. Targan was not the sort of man to risk his sanity on a whim. If he'd marked himself like this, he'd done it because he'd believed there to be a real, tangible benefit. Haegan wanted to know if he was right.

"I have grasped the principles behind the cult's most common powers. I'll no longer need the Prisoner's help to perform and maintain the psychic overwrite spell," Targan said. "The mark itself is largely symbolic, though like somatic casting, it helps to guide the mind. The important factor is the insight into the Starborn itself. That is where the power comes from. Our forces should be able to utilize it easily enough, with guidance."

"You want our men and women marking themselves like the Cult of Stars?" Silas asked.

"I want our forces armed," Targan said. "And this is a way to arm them."

Haegan saw the distaste written on Silas's face, could almost hear the arguments that would come from the younger man word for word. Haegan had already thought them all himself. None of them mattered anymore. All that mattered was the Starborn.

They had to call it, to summon it, to face it.

And then kill it, of course.

"I am the last person to disparage the powers of the Cult of Stars, and we *will* need every advantage we can get to face the Starborn," Haegan said. "We'll present this to our people as an option to those who are willing."

Silas looked as though he were being asked to swallow a bucket of nails, but he nodded. "Of course, sir."

Haegan knew Silas would obey him without question once given an order, but whenever possible, he wanted his lieutenant to understand why he gave his orders. Mindless obedience was for the victims of Targan and the

Prisoner's mind control spell. From his fellow knights of the Exile Order, Haegan wanted belief. "It does not matter where a weapon comes from, Silas. Only how it is used." Hagen indicated Phoenix with a tilt of his chin. "Case in point."

Phoenix swallowed visibly as all eyes in the meeting fell on him. It was oddly surreal, seeing the glintchaser like this. As if he had been on their side all along.

"The armor and harnesses are ready. Both will enable full control of the Hearts, and modular integration with the new containment vessels, but the armor will make controlling multiple Hearts easy, and it's still enchanted armor all on its own. Full suite protective force, environmental proofing, and a strength increase of ten to one," Phoenix said. "The materials in the extractors still need time to catalyze, but they'll be ready soon. I've submitted my notes on the subject to Targan's team, but it's probably still mostly over their heads."

Targan pointedly ignored the last part. He had ordered Phoenix to document his process, but with production as the priority, Phoenix had still not had time to *explain* the documentation of his spellforging, and the Academy scholars' attempts to decode it on their own had been less than fruitful. Even bent to their will, Phoenix was the one holding the reins of spellforging. No doubt Targan found that infuriating.

"We have the vessels. Now all we need are the Hearts to put in them," Targan said.

"The team is already transferring the Hearts of Flames and Shadows into the new vessels," Phoenix reported. "As for the others . . ."

"The Heart of Light is still here at the Church," Salvione spoke up. "Its normal resting place is too secure to breach, even with my station, but I have heard that it will be taken out for a ritual meant to take place soon."

"What ritual?"

"Unclear," the clergywoman said. "It's not one of ours, and a vicar from another saint's church is performing it. But whatever it is, the Heart will be exposed. It will be our best chance to take it."

"Then we'll make plans to do so," Haegan said. "I still have the Heart of Force inside of myself. Snow possesses the Heart of Ice. And we now know that Lady Elizabeth wields the Heart of the Sky."

Phoenix's jaw tightened at the mention of his wife, but he made no comment. He was the reason they all knew that secret now. Haegan wondered how it had felt to divulge it. He found himself hoping it had hurt, and was briefly surprised. He had never harbored true animosity toward the Starbreakers, never relished the opportunity to hurt them. They were obstacles and opponents, but it wasn't supposed to be personal. But then again, they had killed him. Maybe he hadn't taken that as in stride as he'd thought.

"About the Winged Lady," Targan said with an annoyed sigh. "She was here at the Academy recently. Looking into *your* corpse, likely as a favor to Arakawa in exchange for help finding her husband."

"I warned you we'd draw attention taking him," Silas said.

"The Starbreakers have been chasing your order for months. Taking Phoenix wasn't going to meaningfully change that. But the whole point of you remaining in the shadows was to keep things obfuscated, and more to the point, keep attention off of *us*," Targan said.

The throbbing in Haegan's temples picked up with the bickering, and his stoic expression inched closer toward a grimace. Once again, his need for his allies' resources clashed with his intolerance for their egos.

"What can she learn?" Haegan asked, forcing them back to business.

"Nothing directly," Targan said. "I made sure the examiner wouldn't be able to talk. But if she gets close, she will know that she's found *something*. She could bring the Crown down on us."

When Targan said "us," he meant him, but Haegan took the threat seriously regardless. The Winged Lady was powerful, well-connected, and on a warpath. Dealing with her would have to be a top priority, or they would be risking everything. It might even be important enough for him to deal with the problem himself.

"Let me take care of her," a cold voice said, and Haegan's blood froze with it.

Everyone present, physically or otherwise, gawked as Snow strode into the room, leaving a trail of frost footprints in her wake. Her eyes were near solid wide, and ice clung to her cheeks and the edges of her clothes. She had given herself over to the cold, become an avatar of it. In this state, she was at her most detached. And her most deadly.

"How?" Haegan demanded. "I told you—"

"You told me to stay put until I was needed. I decided you probably needed me by now," Snow said, every word stated like it was obvious fact. "And I was right. If the Winged Lady is causing you problems, then I'm your best bet."

Silas scoffed. "That woman struck Ixnikol from the sky. You think you can deal with her?"

"You send me after her," Snow said, "and you won't have to worry about her looking for you anymore."

Haegan stared Snow down. Targan may have had ironclad faith in his spell, and both captured glinchasers had followed the commands that they'd been given, but the knight commander did not like the initiative the assassin had displayed in leaving her cell. He wanted to order her to return to her cell, and declare that he would deal with the Winged Lady himself.

But then he glanced around the table, and caught sight of the mark on Targan's forehead, and suddenly, he felt . . . lacking. Incomplete in power and focus. He was not at full strength, wouldn't be until Phoenix's work was complete. In the meantime, why not use the tools at his disposal?

Indeed, why not use every tool at his disposal?

The itch in his forehead grew stronger.

22

UNRIVALED

"What in the hells was that?"

After what had happened to Ryung, Elizabeth had gone straight to Ink. She was currently pacing around the High Inquisitive's office, unable to stop her hands from fidgeting, or her head from swiveling around, constantly looking for danger. Her heart had become a hummingbird's, practically drilling into her chest. She could still see the vacant look of Ryung's face. Still hear the faint pop of something inside his skull. Only it wasn't Ryung's face in her mind—it was Arman's.

She needed to act. To move. To get out of this office, which was too small and cramped and full of things that wouldn't help get her husband back.

"It's called a geas spell. Nasty curse of a thing that triggers when the victim does something the caster doesn't want them to," Ink said. "Will you stand still? You're giving me anxiety."

"Don't even," Elizabeth warned, jamming a finger in Ink's face. "Your boss did something with Haegan's body. He kidnapped my husband, and he's murdering people to keep it quiet. Give me one reason why I shouldn't put an arrow through every joint in his body and cook what's left of him with lightning."

"Besides that sounding impressively messy? We still don't know where he has your boy toy stowed away. If we move on him now, we could lose both of them," Ink said. In a rare show of humanity, Ink's expression softened. "I understand what you're dealing with—"

"Do you? Really?" Elizabeth snapped, and Ink's face went from comforting to admonishing so smoothly Elizabeth didn't see the transition.

"You know that I do."

Ink said it in a flat voice, but her eyes forced Elizabeth to recall a time not so long ago, when they had been inside each other's heads. Elizabeth, of course, knew better than anyone else alive what Ink had been through. What she cared about, what she feared. Ink had been forced to make tactical choices with the lives of people she loved in the balance too many times to count. It was easy for Elizabeth to forget all that when she needed something, *anything,* to be angry at. She was scared, and taking it out on a friend, and that wasn't fair.

Elizabeth sighed. "Sorry."

"Contrary to my typical presentation, I do have a heart," Ink said. "Give me some time. I'll figure out where Targan is keeping Phoenix. You'll get him back, and then we can bring the old man down. I promise."

Already, the nervous energy was building back up in her again just thinking about Arman in the hands of the Headmaster, but Elizabeth made sure to keep that energy pointed at the person deserving it. Targan was going to burn for this.

"You contact me the second you know," Elizabeth said, already halfway out Ink's window. Her ethereal wings sprouted from her back, and she took off into the evening skies over Sasel. She needed to clear her head, and get back in touch with Snow. She hadn't spoken to the assassin since that morning, but up until now, she'd been too busy with her own investigation to think about that. As she flew between the high rise towers of the city, rivers of flying skiffs beneath her and stars overhead, she activated her messenger coil.

"Snow, tell me you've got some good news."

Silence from the other side.

Frustration bubbled up in her, recalling the stories Arman had shared about Snow, and her tendency to leave her coil off at the worst possible times, always with the excuse of "focusing on the job."

"Chloe, so help me, if you don't put your coil back on and answer me, I will find you, and I will—"

She never got to finish her threat. For a split second, at the corner of her awareness, she felt a cold snap in the air, then something moving fast below her. And then, Snow was right in front of her, daggers flashing.

Elizabeth reacted on pure instinct, banking hard to one side as she unleashed a gust of wind to blast Snow away from her. Snow flew backward in a controlled tumble, vanishing out of the air and reappearing on the closest rooftop in a low crouch. Her weapons were still out.

"Snow, what the fuck?!" Elizabeth shouted. The wind carried her voice across the night air, letting Snow hear her even at their current distance.

"I got a new job," Snow said, her voice like shattering glass. "There are some very dangerous people who want you dead, Wings."

Elizabeth could have drawn her weapon, or flown away, or blown Snow off of the roof, but instead, she hovered, absolutely dumbstruck, half certain she was delirious. "Seriously? You pick now to go dirk on me? This isn't funny, Chloe!"

"It's not a joke." Snow twirled a throwing knife in her hand to hold it by the blade. "You're going to want to fight back."

Before the Heart of the Sky, before her training as a warden, Elizabeth had a knack for reading people's intentions, for knowing when they were lying and when they were sincere. With the Heart and that training, she'd only gotten better. Everything about Snow said she was being *deadly* serious. Snow's words promised violence, and Elizabeth believed her.

Which made absolutely no sense. She and Snow were friends. Only this morning, they'd been working together. She grasped for some kind of explanation: This wasn't Snow, but someone in disguise trying to throw her off. It was Snow, and she'd completely lost her mind. Snow had always been a traitor, and she'd been waiting quietly for months to strike for some hidden agenda.

She forced the guesses and confusion to the back of her mind as Snow threw a trio of blades and vanished. It didn't matter *why* this was happening.

It was happening. Whether it was Snow or an imposter, someone was picking a fight with the Winged Lady of Sasel. And if that's what they wanted, that was what they were going to get.

Wings sent out another gust to deflect the knives as she drew her swords. Snow reappeared on one rooftop, then another. On the third, a pillar of ice sprouted beneath her feet, catapulting her into the air as Wings dove to meet her. Their blades clashed only once before Snow vanished, and Wings felt the hairs on the back of her neck stand to attention. She spun around just in time to block the next strike as Snow blinked back into existence behind her, still in midair.

Then Snow kicked off of Wings's chest, backflipping away before letting herself plummet out of the sky. Wings was caught off guard, trying to work out what Snow's plan was in falling to her death, before she realized her swords were getting heavier.

Ice was rapidly spreading down the blades, racing for her hands. In another breath, she'd either have to drop the weapons or risk being frozen herself. Instead of doing either, Wings slammed the hilts of her weapons together, and in a flash of light, they transformed into a hunting bow, and the ice was dispersed. Still falling, Snow threw a dagger at the closest building. On contact, the weapon exploded into a pillar of ice that jutted out to catch her, and with one hand, she used it to turn her fall into a swing that catapulted her onto the side of another tower. She froze both her feet and one hand to the side of the building, sticking herself to it like a frozen spider. She'd only just stabilized when the arrows started coming.

Wings performed a flyby of the tower Snow was clinging to, outside of both knife and blink range, and loosed arrow after arrow. Even with them course correcting midflight, Snow dodged each shot, though two left deep gashes in the leather of her armor. As Wings banked around for another pass, Snow started sprinting across the side of the tower, leaving a trail of ice behind her until she kicked off the tower and into the air once again.

She blinked out of sight, and reappeared not on a rooftop or wall, but on the bow of a flying skiff as it sailed through the night sky above the city streets.

The passengers all shrieked in surprise while the pilot herself chose to swear and swerve out of the flow of other flying vehicles that wound through the airspace of Sasel like airborne streams.

Wings cursed. As long as Snow was in the mix of the air traffic, Wings couldn't risk shooting arrows or throwing out gusts of wind for fear of causing a midair collision. Snow meanwhile, had no such concerns, and threw another volley of knives at Wings, each one already coated in frost. They missed Wings, striking buildings or air travelers instead, and wherever the blades struck, ice spread at explosive speed.

Wings flew after Snow, bow transformed back into blades, but each time she got close, Snow blinked to the next flying skiff, or flying carpet, or saddled griffin. Each time startling whoever was already aboard it before throwing more blades at Wings.

Then she disappeared completely.

With the Heart of the Sky, Wings could sense disturbances in the air, and in battle, Snow always stuck out as a sharp cold spot in the air. But when Wings searched for that cold spot now, she immediately ran into a problem. Because Snow had been flinging around knives that spread her ice all over, the area was *full* of cold spots. Parsing out moving spots didn't help. Some clung to buildings, but others were carried along flying skiffs, and either could have been Snow. She tried listening for her, but the skies had been thrown into chaos, and picking out one soft moving assassin was impossible in the cacophony of confused passengers and panicking pilots.

Because their fight had been slowly trending downward as Snow repeatedly fell, Wings's first instinct was to search the flight lanes further below her. And in that split second where she was looking down, Snow dropped from the keel of an incoming skiff, silent as an owl diving for its prey.

Wings felt the incoming body on the wind soon enough to look up, but not soon enough to stop Snow from landing on her back and driving a dagger into her shoulder. Biting cold raced across Wings's skin as Snow spread ice across her body from the point of contact, and they listed to the side in the air as Wings struggled to adjust under the uneven weight.

Wings tried to use a gust to throw Snow off, but the assassin clung to her, welded on by the fast-spreading ice on Wings's body. Wings had seen Snow fight. She knew how quickly she could freeze a person once she had a blade in them. Knew she had seconds to do something.

So, with a furious beat of her ethereal wings, Wings climbed sharply in altitude, so that in a single breath they were high above the city. They hung in the air for a beat, Snow still clinging to her just as Wings had expected. Then, she tucked her wings in, and they dove.

The two of them plummeted together like hawks linked together in free fall, entering a spin as they fell faster and faster, sped along by Wings whipping the winds in a cyclone around them that held them even tighter together. Snow couldn't blink if she couldn't move, and Wings didn't want her going anywhere. Not yet. They spun and fell, spiraling so fast the world became a blur and Wings's stomach dropped into her feet.

And then, she unfurled, breaking hard and turning their drop into a dart to the side that saw them careening into the windows of a high-rise restaurant. Snow didn't have time to detach herself, and was practically glued to Wings by g-force even if she'd wanted to, so instead, she coated herself in an armor of ice, and braced for impact. Wings made sure that Snow hit the window first.

They went through in a crash that finally broke them apart and sent them both rolling across the floor in a shower of glass and ice, Snow colliding with a table, Wings with a bar counter. There were no customers inside, but there was a lone janitor, who immediately fled the area, leaving the two of them alone and sprawled on the floor in the darkened dining area, illuminated only by the stars and the lightstone of the city outside the windows.

Both of them groaned as they got to their feet. Wings was bleeding, mostly from her shoulder, but also from a few stray places where the glass had sliced her. Snow was in a similar state, nicked by arrows and battered from the impact of the landing. She favored her left leg as she stood, but in only a few seconds, the Heart of Ice numbed out the pain. More lingering, Wings knew, would be the disorientation from the dive. Wings's inner ears had adapted to flying maneuvers like that. Snow's hadn't.

That would buy her a second to recover, since her Servitor Heart wasn't nearly as good at blocking out pain as Snow's. And by now, Wings was certain that this was Snow. Nobody but the Cold-Blooded Killer could fight like her. Which just brought back all the questions of *why*.

"I ditched their ears in the landing, and we've got a few seconds before they get sight of us again," Snow said as she stood. "So listen close."

Wings had just enough time to ask "What?" before Snow blinked, disappearing from across the restaurant and reappearing right in front of her. Their weapons clashed in a brief dance of steel, until they briefly locked, Snow's Companion Piece holding off one of Elizabeth's blades.

"I know where they're keeping Phoenix."

Snow vanished, and Wings whirled in search of her. Knowing the tables and chairs crowded around them would provide too many places to hide, she let loose with a gale of wind that rippled out from her, taking every item of furniture, scrap of cloth, and piece of silverware scattering. Sure enough, Snow had been under one of the tables, crouched low. With her cover gone, she lunged forward. Wings leapt into the air, assisted by a flap of her wings, and delivered a flying kick that knocked Snow into a wall. Wings was on her in an instant, one arm to pin her, the other to hold a sword to the assassin's throat. At the same time, she felt the pinprick pressure of something sharp pressing against her abdomen. She didn't have to glance down to know Snow's knife was perfectly poised to stab her in the gut. Both of them went stock still. They had each other dead to rights.

"Targan's got some kind of mind control. It's strong. Don't take any chances," Snow said. "When I'm gone, check your pockets."

Wings blinked, trying to process what Snow was saying while also paying attention to the blade about to disembowel her. "Targan did this to you?"

"I've lost the element of surprise," Snow said, and it sounded like she was talking to herself, not Wings. "If I want to kill you, I need to retreat, and try again later."

Snow's arm moved in a blur, twisting out of Wings's pin and pushing her sword away. Wings spun with the momentum of the move, and came back around with swords held ready to continue the fight. But Snow was gone. Wings held herself at the ready for a few seconds, expecting a repeat of the last time Snow had disappeared. But no sneak attack came.

Slowly, keeping her senses open for even a whisper of movement, Wings sheathed her swords, and checked her pockets. One of them held a neatly folded piece of paper that hadn't been there before. When she unfolded it to read, she forgot how to breathe.

This is the most I could bend the control. Haegan's alive and remaking the Cult of Stars. Targan's working with him. So's my father. Arman is alive. They have him building something for them in our old headquarters in the Spoons.

Bring something to shield your mind.

Beyond that, Snow had included the address of the old Starbreakers' headquarters, along with best estimates of how many people Haegan's new Cult of Stars had inside, and the names of every face Snow had recognized. But Wings barely had eyes for those details. Her gaze fixated on her husband's name.

Relief coursed through her body. He was alive. She knew where he was. And anyone who got in between them, everyone Snow had named in her letter, was going to wish they had never been born.

23
THE FUTURE

Saint Avelina's Cathedral was the single largest building owned by any church in Corsar, with forty-nine separate high-rise spires connected to the main body by flying buttresses so large they included stairways inside of them. Every window was stained glass, the largest being a thirty-foot-tall rendition of Saint Avelina herself overlooking the nave, golden hair billowing across the glass. At night, the church was lit inside and out by lightstone fixtures ranging from carefully concealed strips to massive chandeliers. Even in places where there were no lightstones, one only had to touch the walls, and the stone itself would glow to illuminate the space.

That last feature was a factor of a very particular artifact, and Church's reason for selecting this place to cleanse Ruby's soul: the Heart of Light.

After the Servitor had been destroyed at Loraine, the Hearts that powered it had been divided up by the parties present, with the Heart of Light being given to the Church of Avelina, so they could make use of its natural amplification of divine magic. Whether it was healing prayers or calling forth divine radiance to blast and burn, divine magic just worked better with the Heart of Light around, and once it had been sequestered in the Church, the walls had gained their additional powers of illumination.

Church was one of the most powerful priests in Corsar, and Saint Beneger's domain of guidance and easing burdens was well-aligned with healing prayers. There were very few healers as potent as him, and with him on hand to resurrect Ruby the moment Daybreaker cleansed her, the odds were very good that she'd come back. But no matter how he tried to imagine it like an apothecary giving a medicine that temporarily stopped someone's heart, this was still *real* death, and it was cosmic law they were trying to circumvent. Church was not satisfied with "very good" odds for Ruby. So he wanted the Heart, and he wanted it *on hand*, as close as possible, to maximize its effects and Ruby's chances of surviving.

The Followers of Avelina did not normally take the Heart out of its holding place in the Church, but they had eventually agreed to find some time for Church and Ruby.

That time would be tomorrow morning, and so they were all staying the night in the cathedral to be ready to go as soon as the Church was. Everyone except for Brass, who hadn't been back to the capital city since the mess with Oblivion, and had been too excited to stay put. He'd left soon after they arrived, promising to be back and sober in time for the ritual, and disappeared to raise hell across Sasel.

"I still can't believe you talked them into it," Angel said.

"Bishop Sophia is a good friend," Church said.

"Uh-huh," Angel grunted, and took a sip of wine that had been so generously provided by their hosts. "Is she the one who sends you letters sprayed with perfume?"

"Yes. Why?"

Angel said nothing, just sipped from her cup and made meaningful eye contact with her asexual, aromantic friend until he took the hint. To his credit, it didn't take him as long as it used to.

"No, it's not like that," Church said. "We're friends. She's *joked* about wanting to marry me if no one else does by the time we're thirty and . . . she . . . wasn't joking, was she?"

Angel sipped her wine.

"I'm sure she knows about me," Church said. "She has to. I mean . . . I guess I never said. Oh, Beneger help me. Should I have said something?"

"You need to get in more bar fights, fuck up your face a bit," Angel advised. "Otherwise, this problem isn't going away for like, fifteen years, easy. Even then, you might age well."

"Sometimes," Church said, "I wonder if I have any idea what I'm doing."

"Oh, relax. You've got one romance-shaped blind spot. You're on top of most things," Angel reassured him. She stared down into her cup, looking down as if the alcohol had any answers the way she had so, so many times before. She wasn't getting drunk—the Church had not provided enough wine for that—but she had reached the stage in her drinking where she got pensive. "Figured yourself out pretty well after Relgen."

"You know, for the longest time, I thought that too. That I'd figured everything out after, found my place, and squared things away. But now, I don't know," Church said. "I love everything I've done in Aenerwin, and I don't regret a second of it. But ever since the whole Oblivion incident, I feel like I should be doing more. Like I *want* to do more."

"You thinking about getting back into the game?"

"No, not like that. I'm ready to be done fighting, I just . . ." Church searched for the right words to express what had been simmering inside him for months now. "I've been given a lot of power, and I don't think it was given to help the people of just one town. Helping rebuild Loraine after the Dread Knight attack has felt right. Helping Ruby feels right. And there's so many people out there who've had their lives upended by things they barely understand, like Ruby, like everyone in Loraine, and I just . . . I want to help."

"That sounds like you."

"What about you?" Church asked. "Have you figured out where you're going?"

Angel considered her cup. It needed refilling.

She had thought about where she was going. Had been thinking about it ever since defending Loraine from the Dread Knight. She should hate everything about that day. She'd faced down a horde of horrors, alone at first. She'd *died* that day and was only still breathing now thanks to Church.

And yet she had felt so perfectly at home on that battlefield. So completely herself as she *chose* to stare down the Dread Knight and its army and declare with her whole body, “Not these people. Not today. Not until you get through me.”

It felt *so good* to fight the good fight. Not stumble into it on occasion as a glintchaser, or rotely follow its traditions as a knight in an order, or hide from it in a bar, but really fight it with everything she had. That was who she was in her bones. It was where she belonged, and she knew it.

She refilled her cup. “Nope.”

Church waited for her to elaborate. She did not. Eventually, he yielded to her silence with a shrug. “Well, I hope someday you do.”

Angel scoffed, but nodded, and held out her drink. “To the future.”

Church, who didn’t have a cup, settled for fist-bumping the rim of Angel’s, and letting her drink for the both of them. “To the future.”

The dormitories in Saint Avelina’s Cathedral were twice the size of the ones in the Church of the Guiding Saint, with lightstone lamps instead of candles and a window that gave a breathtaking view of the capital city lights stretched out below Ruby.

More than that, while the Church of the Guiding Saint looked like a holy place, Avelina’s Cathedral felt like one. The very walls hummed with a sense of vitality and renewal. It was etched into every stone and arch. It practically cascaded off the sun-shield symbol of Saint Avelina that hung over the door.

It made her feel on edge.

Ruby had never really gone to church growing up in Olwin, but those places hadn’t made her uneasy like this one did. Never given her such a pervasive feeling of not belonging. But that might not have been the church’s fault.

Ruby stared down at her arms, which remained free of any kind of scars even after what she’d done in the clearing. She could still remember the feeling of the thorns pushing their way out. The thought made her skin itch.

Part of her was angry. This had all started because she'd been attacked and left to die, and yet because she'd accepted help from something that offered—something she couldn't even remember doing—she was cursed. Bound by some hellish magic that gave her power even as it ate at her soul, all because of some cosmic law bullshit not even Church seemed to be able to explain. It wasn't fair, and she wanted to hit whoever was responsible for those stupid laws over the head with a barstool.

But another part of her was afraid. Not of dying. But of this thing inside her, and of what it was doing to her. Every day, it grew harder and harder to tell its thoughts from her own. What if they were too late? What if she was already doomed?

Her unease, her anger, her fear. They ran circles in her mind, constantly chasing after each other and keeping her awake. She found herself walking for the door—to get some air, to get away, she didn't know. But when she opened it, she found herself intercepted by a familiar, wide-eyed face.

"Bart?"

"Ruby."

The fledgling paladin stood frozen in her door, one hand raised like he'd been about to knock, his eyes full of panic. But it was different from the look of fear she had seen so many times when he'd come to visit her in the night. This time, he almost looked . . . embarrassed.

"How long have you been standing there?" she asked.

"Uh. Not long," he lied.

She gave a half chuckle, and his face turned red as he hurried through an explanation..

"I wasn't trying to spy on you or anything. I was just . . . I was worried about you. With what happened in—"

"I'm sorry."

"I was going to say that must have been scary for you," Bart said, catching her off guard. "And the vicar's plan is . . . intense. And you've looked kind of anxious ever since we got here. You haven't really said anything since . . . you know. I wanted to make sure you were okay."

Ruby remembered the look on his face when she'd had him caught in a tangle of thorns. The fear on his face that had been *for* her. Not of her. She couldn't quite believe it, but there it was still. She nearly killed him a few hours ago, and he was at her door again, as concerned as he was every time before. She was a firebomb waiting to go off, sleeping under the same roof as him, and he was worried about *her*.

It was sweet, and more than a little comforting at a time when she felt less like a person and more like a curse. And as long as he still saw her as herself, she thought maybe that she could too.

"Anyway, I'm sorry for bothering you," he added, stepping back from the door. "I'll see you—"

"Bart."

"Yeah?"

She'd spent months quietly keeping Bart at arm's length, especially whenever he got worried about what was happening to her. Better to keep things to herself, she'd reasoned. Or maybe she hadn't reasoned it, and it was just a voice in her head twisting her own thoughts against her.

Either way, there was no point in trying to hide how bad things were now that everyone had seen it. And right now, she was desperate to not be alone with her own thoughts.

"Would you . . . stay with me for a little while?"

For an agonizing second, Bart stood stock-still, leaving Ruby with a knot in her stomach that wound itself tighter with every passing moment. She almost retracted the request and slammed the door in his face. Then, slowly, he nodded, and a weight lifted off her chest.

"Of course."

The thoughts of leaving that had carried her to the door vanished as she stepped back aside, letting him into the room and closing the door behind them. After a moment of Bart standing awkwardly in the center of the room, she took his hand, and the two of them sat down on the bed.

"You're not okay, are you?" he asked.

"No."

She figured that much had been obvious already, and yet, something about admitting it out loud made it feel different. More real. But maybe also less of a burden. She didn't have to hide anything anymore. No more fronts. No more lies. Just her, exactly as she was.

"You don't have to talk about it," Bart said.

She nodded her thanks. She squeezed his hand a little tighter, using him like an anchor and a reminder that she wasn't alone.

And true to his word, Bart didn't press her for a single answer. It made it easier to find the will to give them herself.

"I feel like I'm losing myself," she said. "Like I can't tell where I stop and it starts. Like maybe there's already no difference."

"There's a difference."

"How can you tell?"

"Because—" Bart paused, trying to choose his words carefully even as she could tell he had something he desperately wanted to blurt out. "Because I have lived next to you for months. And we've fought together and drank together, and I know what kind of a person you are. You're fearless, and fierce, and funny. When you smile, it's like you know you're about to win something. And maybe I don't actually know you all that well, and I know I don't even know your real name, but—"

"Cara."

Bart stopped. "What?"

"My real name. It's Cara."

She hadn't told anyone that in years. People asked, all the time. Especially in her old line of work. But she'd always dodged the question or just lied. She liked the layer of separation that came with using a fake name. It was why glintchaser nicknames had always made so much sense to her even as other people she knew dismissed or mocked them.

In a career where things could get very dangerous very quickly, it was just good for your sanity to keep some boundaries up, and keep a part of yourself safe from the rest of the world. But Bart wasn't the rest of the world. He wasn't even a fellow troublemaker like Brass.

Bart was different.

She twirled her hair around her fingers, a nervous habit since childhood. "I know yours, so . . . it's only fair."

She tugged him closer to her, resting her head on his shoulder as she looked out the window. A part of her was screaming in protest. She was showing too much, talking too much. That she couldn't trust someone who served an organization built to wipe out any trace of the very thing that was inside her. But she ignored it, choosing instead to focus on the warmth of his skin and the city lights and the stars.

She'd never dreamed she'd ever visit the kingdom's capital, and certainly never thought she'd get the chance to see it from a place like Avelina's Cathedral, high up in one of its tallest spires. It was beautiful. But when she glanced at Bart to see his reaction to it, she found him staring at her, like she was the city. He smiled at her, soft and hesitant, and she smiled back.

She kissed him then, under the lights. And for the first time in months, Cara was able to completely put her curse out of her mind.

24
BAIT

"This is a problem."

Snow was back in the mansion's meeting room with both Haegan and Silas, being debriefed on her attempt on Wings's life. The plan had been for her to take the lead with Silas providing both support and observation, but that had swiftly gone out the window as the fight rapidly outpaced Silas's ability to keep up, and Snow losing her messenger coil amid all the wind had meant Silas couldn't even hear the end of the fight, from which Snow had retreated without completing her assignment.

Her reasoning given was, straightforwardly, that she was an assassin, not a fighter. She killed underhandedly, with stealth and surprise as her greatest weapons. She'd gotten the drop on Wings, but they'd been in the Winged Lady's element, not Snow's, and once the fight drew out long enough to become a straight brawl, she was outmatched. It was run and try again, or die knowing she would most likely fail, and Haegan had not ordered her to throw her life away on this mission.

Silas wished he had.

"If you'd stayed close, I could have helped," Silas said.

Snow didn't even look in his direction as she said, "It's not my fault you couldn't keep up."

Not entirely, at any rate.

Snow didn't deliberately try to lose Silas—that would have been in direct defiance of her orders. She'd merely focused on fighting Wings over keeping close to him, and things had turned out how they did as a natural consequence. Working within Targan's mind control was a game of half-truths, bending rules, and finding gaps in her orders open to interpretation. But Snow was a practiced liar, especially to herself.

Ever the commander, Haegan took control of the conversation before the two of them could devolve into an argument. He wasn't a fool, and ever since Snow had independently decided to leave her cell to offer her services, he had been wary of exactly how firm Targan's control was over her. But he also knew she could still be useful. And until such time as she wasn't, Haegan did not intend to abandon a weapon as potent as the Cold-Blooded Killer.

"Regardless of how it happened, the fact remains that the Winged Lady is still active and working against us," Haegan said. "We need to act before our mission can be disrupted. Silas, send word to the other cells to begin moving out. To Sebastian's people as well. After that, I want you, Snow, and the twins getting ready to recover the Heart of Light from the cathedral first thing in the morning."

"Sir?"

Silas didn't elaborate any further than that, because he didn't need to. Haegan knew which part of his orders he wanted clarification on.

"We just received word," Haegan said. "The Starbreakers are the ones performing the ritual with the Heart. You'll need the assassin to help deal with her company." As if to settle the matter, Haegan turned his focus to Snow. "You will follow Silas's instructions as if they came from Targan or myself."

Snow grimaced, but nodded. "I will."

"What about the Lady?" Silas asked.

"Focus on the Heart," Haegan said. "Leave the Winged Lady to me."

Snow's information lined up with everything Elizabeth and Ink already knew, gave them Phoenix's location, and gave them the certainty to move against

Targan. Once Ink found a spell to shield their minds, the only thing that had stopped Elizabeth from flying directly to the Starbreakers' mansion had been her injuries, and Ink pointing out that the mansion was Academy property now, and if Haegan's order was using one such property, then every piece of property owned by Targan or the Academy was potentially suspect. With Sebastian Guerron and the Baron of Loraine involved, that only added to the number of suspect locations. A raid on one could alert the rest, or any of the others could serve as a fallback point for wherever they did raid. To properly stand a chance of catching Haegan, Targan, and all of their collaborators, they needed to hit every location at once, and not all of the locations were in the city.

It would be a massive undertaking. But when the Winged Lady of Sasel wanted something done, it got done. Elizabeth had skipped normal channels of communication, and gone straight to Lupolt, right hand of the King of Corsar himself. Once apprised of the situation, and reminded in very strong terms how much the Crown owed Elizabeth and Phoenix both, Lupolt had called in every knight at the crown's disposal and begun mobilizing royal army garrisons to work with local law enforcement. Ink herself sent a message to recruit her old company, the Cord of Aenwyn, to hit one of the locations on the southern coast. And Elizabeth had called Brass to get the Starbreakers in on the situation.

By the next morning, the living room of Ink's apartment had been transformed into a war council as she, Lupolt, and Elizabeth worked to coordinate a hastily assembled task force of knights, freelancers, soldiers, and town guards, all while trying to avoid making any moves that would alert their targets to what was coming.

Elizabeth had just finished talking with one of the independent knights when there was a knock at the door. Waiting outside, sporting a broad grin, wind-tousled hair, and a woman's scarf, was Brass. He looked like he'd left a party early and flown here on something fast with no protection from the wind.

"I hear we finally figured out which castle they're keeping our princess in?" Brass said by way of announcing himself.

"Brass," Elizabeth greeted. "Where's everyone else?"

"Ah, about that," Brass said. "I didn't tell them you called."

"What?"

"They were literally setting up Ruby's exorcism when you did, and that has to happen today," Brass said. "The kid's in bad shape. And I may have had something to do with that by taking her on too many adventures, so I didn't want them putting it off any more than we already had. Church and Angel need to be there. But I don't, so I'm here! They can save Ruby, we can save Phoenix, and everything'll be fine!"

"It can't wait?" she asked.

"She would have killed somebody if we hadn't stopped her."

That wasn't actually an answer to her question, which threatened to stoke her temper.

The part of Elizabeth that had been feverishly searching for her missing husband wanted to scream, throttle Brass, and fly straight to the remaining Starbreakers to demand their help in person. But there was something approaching real concern and regret in Brass's voice. Something so rare, it managed to delay her wrath. Didn't Ruby deserve to be saved just as much as Arman?

Ultimately, there just wasn't time to have this argument. Moving as many pieces as they were was noisy, and the longer they took to actually attack, the more they ran the risk of the enemy realizing what was happening and ruining everything.

Brass saw the acceptance on her face, and smiled. "So, who am I stabbing?"

Wings gave a frustrated sigh, and led Brass inside to show the organized chaos of their planning session. Two maps, one of the city, one of the kingdom, were splayed out on Ink's dining room table, each target location marked with pieces borrowed from Ink's third-favorite chess set.

Wings pointed at each chess piece in turn.

"Lupolt has the independent knights covering the other properties in Sasel, and Seven Gates and the Cord are splitting up to take the ones in the rest of Corsar. Ink is leading the team to arrest Targan. You and I are going after Phoenix."

That morning, as the sun began to rise over the city of Sasel, Church, Angel, Bart, Ruby, and Thalia all gathered in the largest ritual room of Saint Avelina's Cathedral. Even with Bart's visit, Ruby hadn't been able to get to sleep the night prior, and the early hour wasn't improving her mood any.

Brass had never come home, and responded to Church's attempts to contact him this morning via prayer with "Sorry, busy saving the day. Explain later, see you tonight!"

"I know I probably should have expected it, but I'm still disappointed in him," Church said. "I'm sorry, Ruby."

"It's fine," she lied.

It wasn't that she didn't like the others. Everyone present probably constituted the closest friends that she had left. But Ruby and Brass had always had a unique understanding. Every time she'd felt overwhelmed with what was happening to her, he had been the one to calm her down or make her feel better. Now, she was exhausted, deep inside a church that had her demonic influence more agitated than ever, staring down a ritual that was going to involve Angel killing her with an axe. Her nerves were on fire, and her whole body hummed on the verge of either fighting or fleeing.

She gave them all her bravest face regardless. Brass or no Brass, she was committed.

Bishop Sophia came in after them, gingerly carrying a narrow, two-foot bronze rod in both her hands. Tendrils of golden light came off the rod's surface in loops, and the glow that radiated from it made everything feel more vibrant and alive. With each step, the stone beneath the Bishop's feet lit up. Even contained as it was, the Heart of Light's power filled the space.

Church cleared his throat. "If we're all ready?"

25
SWITCH

Wings flew toward the Starbreakers' former mansion, staying high and keeping the sun at her back to avoid being spotted. Brass dangled from her arms, idly kicking his feet and watching the city pass beneath them, unbothered by the fact that the only thing keeping him from falling to his death was the strength in Wings's arms.

The world had shrunk to a single corridor of wind in Wings's mind, a straight path between her and Arman, without particular thought to what got in her way. The buzz of the protective spell Ink had thrown around her mind made her even more anxious. The closer she got, the faster she flew. Above them, the clouds grew dark and agitated, mirroring her mood. She could feel the gathering power in the air like a static hum that resonated in her bones. It begged her for release, for a target, and she had one.

"Ready?" Wings asked, her voice easily heard amid the cutting wind.

"Always."

She gauged the distance with an archer's eye, feeling the wind along their angle of approach and adjusting it with flicks of her will. Her grip on Brass tightened in anticipation. When they were directly above the mansion, they pulled sharply up, bringing them to a harsh stop. For a breath, their speed disappeared, and they hung in the air. Then, on Wings's exhale, she dropped Brass, and dove.

Wings and Brass shot down like missiles as Wings cut away the air resistance from underneath them. The mansion raced up to meet them at breakneck speed as they fell headfirst. At the last possible second, the wind gusted up to break their fall. They didn't stop falling, but they slowed enough to avoid injury as Wings flipped in midair to crash feetfirst through the mansion's windows. At the same time her feet connected, lightning struck.

The bolt flashed from the clouds overhead in a deafening boom that rattled windows for several blocks. Every ward and reinforcing magic on the glass shattered, and Wings and Brass tumbled inside in a glittering shower of razor-sharp shards, every single one of which was blown away from them as they landed with weapons at the ready.

There was no one in the hallway they landed in, but all down it, doors flung themselves open to see what the noise was. People, some armed, some not, emerged, and stared in shock and confusion at the knight and glintchaser.

"One chance," Wings said, nocking an arrow. "Where. Is. Phoenix?"

Ink was flanked on either side by half a dozen royal army soldiers as she ascended the Headmaster's tower. She considered them more for show than anything else, a way to demonstrate to Targan that she had the Crown behind her, and that if he wanted to resist, he would be defying His Royal Majesty Roland II, not High Inquisitive Kira Arakawa. It would be a test of how committed he was to this whole business, and if knowing the game was up would be enough to make him back down.

Privately, she suspected it wouldn't. As Headmaster of the Academy, Targan was quite possibly the second or third most politically powerful person in all of Corsar, depending on how much you valued the import of the Church of Avelina and its archbishop. His personal power was even greater. If anyone could expect to openly defy the King and get away with it, it would be Targan.

She wished she could have brought more mages for backup, but the list of them that could both be trusted and actually help against Targan had been exhausted arranging for the rest of the raids happening across the kingdom. She would have to be enough.

They stepped through the teleportation gate that carried them up to the top floors of the Headmaster's tower, and Ink silently commended the professionalism of the soldiers. None of them so much as balked at the crackling hole in space the gate created. They kept their heads high, and stepped through as calmly as if they were marching down the street.

Ink stood at the doors to Targan's office, considering her approach and what kind of foot to start the confrontation on. After only a moment's thought, she blew the doors off their hinges with a flick of her wrist. The pieces of the doors froze in midair before reassembling themselves into wholly repaired doors in the corner of the room, awaiting reinstallation. Targan sat at his desk, one hand lazily raised, the permanent frown lines of his face deeper than ever. His eyes flitted from Ink to the soldiers at her side, to the closing teleportation gate behind them.

Ink couldn't help but read the expression on his face. It wasn't surprise. It wasn't worry. It was affronted anger.

"Arakawa," Targan said. "Explain yourself."

If it had been just the two of them in the room, she might have explained herself with a lightning bolt. In a confrontation between them, she was the admittedly weaker party. Every second was a chance for him to ready himself, and the more prepared he was for this fight, the less of a chance she stood. But with the soldiers here, there was at least a chance of doing this cleanly and by the book. So, against her instincts, she took it.

"Headmaster," Ink said, adding a venomous sweetness to the title, "you're under arrest for . . . oh, take your pick. Come along, and I'll make sure the cell in Oblivion has lots of pillows for your bad back."

The frown lines on the old man somehow got even deeper. "Is that so?"

Again his eyes traced over the soldiers Ink had brought with her, the mundane spears in their hands, and then behind them at where the teleportation gate had been before it closed. She saw the look in his eyes a moment too late.

It said, *Is this all?*

The Headmaster stood up, and the world split in half.

Snow slid a pair of knives into the sheath on her thigh and double-checked the seal on the vials of mindfire antidote she had on her person. Of course the Prisoner had told Haegan's order how to make mindfire, and of course they were using it. True cultists like the Prisoner were immune, but since none of the team going to retrieve the Heart of Light had been marked, they were taking precautions.

She wondered how much longer there would be people in this order who needed to.

René and Rosa were with her in a lower-level room that had been converted into an armory, brushing their skin with desecrated water as a protection against the prayers they expected to have flung their way soon. It wouldn't last them long against someone like Church, but Snow didn't feel the need to warn them. They continually eyed her with disdain and suspicion, and they didn't offer her any of the water.

Whether or not she'd been dominated to their side now, Snow had come very close to killing both of them only a few months ago. She suspected they were still holding a grudge.

A cloud of crackling silver smoke formed in the center of the room, and Haegan and Silas both stepped out. Silas was still securing the straps of the case they would be using to carry the Heart onto his person, his motions frantic. Haegan wasn't looking at any of them, his eyes already fixated on a space behind them. The commander's usually well-maintained hair was disheveled, he wasn't wearing any of his armor, and the amulet he usually stored it in was missing from his chest.

"Sirs?" René asked, eyes wide.

"Stand ready," Haegan ordered, extending his hand outward and furrowing his brow in concentration.

Silas filled in the rest of the details as they waited for Haegan to open a portal. "Our location's been compromised. We're getting calls for help from our cells and allies all over the kingdom. It's a coordinated attack."

René balked. "Who? How?"

Rosa remained stern, and skipped straight to business. "What do we do?"

"We execute our mission," Silas said. "Retrieve the Heart, evade our attackers, and advance to Relgen. We have not come this far to be stopped."

The armory door burst open, a soldier of the order falling backward into it with a trio of arrows protruding from her chest. A moment later, just as Haegan summoned a cloud of crackling smoke large enough to walk through, Wings and Brass entered.

Wings drew her bowstring back, three arrows nocked at once, each one's tip glowing faintly green with a spark of druidic magic. René drew her daggers, Rosa her rapier, and Silas his quicksilver blades. Ice crawled across the edge of Companion Piece as Snow prepared to throw her own weapon. But then a pulse of pure force radiated out from Haegan, knocking everyone in the room away from him—his allies toward the smoke he'd summoned, Brass and Wings away from it.

"Go!" Hagen ordered.

Snow didn't hesitate. If she was off stealing from the Church for Haegan, she wasn't helping him fight Wings and Brass. She blinked as close to the portal as she could get and dashed the last few feet. Silas and the twins were slower to precede their commander into the portal, and in that opening, Brass saw an opportunity.

He surged forward, but not for Haegan. He made a beeline for the crackling smoke portal, hot on the heels of Haegan's underlings. Haegan reached out with the Heart of Force to hold Brass in place, only for arrows to shoot toward him. He halted them with a pulse of force, but each one exploded in a storm of razor-sharp needles of energy, disorienting him and slicing him with shallow cuts from head to toe. Any grip he had on Brass died before it formed, and the glintchaser gave Haegan a jaunty salute before jumping backward through the portal just before it closed.

Haegan suppressed a growl of frustration as he snatched another arrow in a telekinetic fist, and the next several that followed. This time he made sure to hold them far enough away to avoid the explosions of conjured needles.

"Mastery of the druidic arts and a Servitor Heart," Haegan noted. "What is it like, wielding the power that killed your friend?"

Wings froze, her next arrow already pulled back. "How . . .?"

"I have had unfettered access to both Phoenix and Snow. Everything they know, I know," Haegan said. "And I know we do not have to be enemies."

"You kidnapped my husband, and you had my friend try to kill me. If you want to make nice now, you can do it from behind bars."

"The Starbreakers would never work with me, and without the domination, I would not work with them. They're reckless, self-interested, and take no responsibility for their actions. Their mistakes killed my home, and they walked away. People like that cannot be trusted. At best, they can be used," Haegan said. "But you and I are knights of the Crown. We know what it means to fight for more than ourselves. To clean up others' mistakes. To use the powers of our enemies for the greater good."

At this, he pushed his hair back, revealing the fresh scar of a twelve-pointed star carved into his forehead, its lines still an angry red against his light skin. His eyes shone in a swirl of silver and purple, a mixture of the Cult of Stars and the Heart of Force shining through.

"I am about to become the most powerful man in Asher," Haegan said. "I can save this kingdom, this world. I can fix everything that is broken. The world is wild. I will tame it. The people are divided. I will unify them. The Stars seek to erase us. I will take this world from them, starting with what they took from us. Don't try to stop me. Not when we want the same thing."

Wings shook her head. "If you actually believe all that, then you really don't know the first thing about me. Or the world. Or the Starbreakers. Also, you aren't a knight." She stared at the fresh mark on his forehead. "Not anymore."

Haegan frowned. "When I first heard of you, I thought you would be the shining star of the next generation of knights," Haegan said. "The safe hands

I would be leaving the kingdom in when I retired. But watching you and your generation has only convinced me that if I want this kingdom protected, I have to do it myself."

His eyes shifted to pure silver, and a new cloud of crackling smoke opened up behind him. "Not all of the prongs of your attack on me are succeeding. But some are. I can't allow that. And I can't allow you to get in my way."

"Not your call," Wings said.

"From now on, everything is my call," Haegan said. He looked over her shoulder, and in an almost dismissive voice, said, "Kill her."

Wings felt the movement behind her before she processed the sound of the footsteps. As Haegan vanished in a cloud of silver smoke, she whirled and took aim—at Arman. He was dressed in his glintchaser armor, which still bore obvious scars of damage from his capture. His goggles hid his eyes, but the set of his features was one of unimaginable pain. The air carried the scent of him back to her, and he smelled exactly like he always did after spending too much time down in his workshop, like an overpowering concoction of smoke, metal, and sweat. She froze, pointing an arrow at the chest of the man she loved.

And in that instant of hesitation, he threw a fire sphere at her.

26

COMPLICATIONS

Church had a complicated relationship with resurrection. At the surface level, it was a miracle, plain and simple. A loved one brought back from the dead. Without it, Phoenix, Brass, and Angel would all be dead. But the world changed once reversing death became an option. It changed the way people saw Arno, and the way Arno saw himself. Suddenly, every death was his fault. Even—especially—the ones he couldn't reverse.

Because, worst of all, resurrection promised so much more than it could deliver. Desperate people imagined resurrection as a divine reset, turning back a person to before tragedy had struck them. The truth was closer to healing flesh that didn't want to heal and dragging a lost soul back to where it wasn't supposed to go. The longer a person was dead, the harder it was for them to come back. And the more damaged the body, the worse the odds, regardless of how much time had passed.

They were taking out as many of the risk factors as they possibly could for Ruby, and even still, Church was as worried as he always was before a resurrection. Maybe even more so, because what they were attempting felt wrong. Like they were somehow cheating the system.

And more to the point, he just didn't like killing people. He'd done it many times, always for good reasons, and yet it never sat right with him. He looked at Ruby and saw a healthy, innocent girl, and no amount of rationalizing and analogies to apothecaries stopping people's hearts made him feel better about this.

But Ruby was getting worse, and they were out of ideas.

So, with a sense of dread he couldn't shake, Church got to work. He placed a single, raw diamond the size of his fingernail into a jar of holy water, and with the first prayer in the ritual, dissolved it into the liquid with a flash of light. Then he drank it.

The mixture flowed through his body at an unnatural speed, looping through his veins and sinking into his flesh. In only a few seconds, his body felt solid and purified. Bishop Sophia handed Church the Heart of Light, and in the other, he clasped his priest's talisman.

Next to him, Angel's eyes flared into golden orbs, and a burning halo shimmered to life over her head. She held the axe Daybreaker in front of her, one hand on the hilt, one hand bracing just behind and below the head. As her body ignited in a corona of divine power, so did the weapon, until the edge of the axe-head became a crescent of white light. She aimed the edge just off center of Ruby's chest, right at the girl's heart.

Ruby stood in front of them, shifting nervously, Bart holding one of her hands, Thalia, the other. They were there to keep her steady, physically and emotionally, but in the moment, it was hard not to feel like they were actually there to keep her from running away.

"Close your eyes, kid," Angel suggested. Her voice echoed as if two of her were speaking at once, but it was the most subdued she'd ever sounded with that voice.

"Wait!" Ruby begged.

Church and Angel both faltered, exchanging a look.

"What's wrong?" Church asked.

"Nothing." Ruby shook her head, eyes frantic. "Something. I don't know. I don't—"

Bart gasped, and Thalia swore. Both of them pulled away from Ruby with bleeding hands as vines of razor-sharp thorns wound their way around Ruby's arms. Bishop Sophia spoke a prayer before anyone else could react, and golden wind whipped around Ruby in an instant, wrapping around her and holding her in place like a blanket of solid air. Ruby thrashed like a trapped animal, and the vines on her arms thrashed with her.

"What's—let go!"

"Girl, you need to calm down. You're going to hurt someone," Sophia said in her Bishop of Saint Avelina voice, equal parts soothing and authoritative.

Ruby's eyes locked on Angel. "You saved me. The Order of Saint Ricard was going to kill me and you saved me. Why are you killing me?"

"You know this is different," Angel said. She was trying to look Ruby in the eyes, but her instincts kept drawing her gaze to the thorns on her arms. They attempted to lash out, only to be held back by the bishop's prayer. If it weren't for that, they would already be dealing with a repeat of the incident in the woods. "Ruby, focus. Whatever that curse is telling you, it's lying."

"You're lying!" Ruby snapped. "You're all lying!"

"Church?" Angel's voice was urgent, asking for permission.

On a clinical level, Church understood what was happening. The demonic influence in Ruby could tell it was in danger of losing its prize, and was trying to defend itself, playing on her natural fears and insecurities. They needed to stop it, or it would only get worse, until Ruby became little more than its puppet or portal. She might already be on the verge of that very outcome. Brass wasn't here to talk her down this time. They needed to act, and they needed to act now.

But seeing the terror in Ruby's eyes, even manufactured and manipulated as it was, Church hesitated. And in that hesitation, Ruby lashed out.

"Let go!" she shouted, and her skin paled as her voice rang out with the command.

The weight of the Hell Tongue slammed into them all, though only Bishop Sophia had any kind of grip on her. Fortified as her mind was, the bishop did not release her grip. But under the sheer force of the demonic power, she wavered, and that was enough. Ruby broke free, banishing the grasping wind with a flex of her body.

"Help me!" Ruby screamed, and she wasn't talking to anyone in the room.

In a snap decision, Angel unleashed the blast from her axe. It came out as a focused beam, piercing Ruby straight through the heart. It left a neat wound, a hand tall and no thicker than the cutting edge of Daybreaker. Thanks to the cauterizing heat of the energy, it didn't even bleed. Ruby's body crumpled limply to the ground, her arms still bleeding from where the vines had sliced open her skin. Thalia covered her mouth in shock, and Bart staggered back a step.

Ruby was dead.

"Angel!" Church chided.

"Just get her back!" she snapped. A lecture was the last thing they needed right now.

Church gave her a look that said he clearly had more to say but he spoke the prayer for resurrection. In his hands, the Heart of Light flared as loops of divine light wrapped around Ruby's body. They sank into her skin, and shined through the hole Daybreaker had left in her chest as if a miniature sun had ignited inside her. Church's whole body shined in sympathy with Ruby's, and even with the reinforcement of the diamond water he'd taken, he felt the searing strain in every inch of his body as the stream of power Beneger fed him from Renalt transformed into a raging river. But it worked, and so did the Heart. With more ease than he'd ever experienced, Church healed flesh no longer meant to heal, and sought out Ruby's newly liberated soul.

His own presence connected with it, and for a flash of an instant, her consciousness was his.

She felt . . . free. As if she'd been weighed down by stones for months, and was only now escaping out from under them. She felt lighter than air, purer than a spring lake. And yet, there was what could only be described as spiritual scar tissue, a permanent mark of the chains that had bound her soul tightly enough to leave an engraving of its presence. It would always be there, but at the very least, it was purely her soul now.

Church felt a surge of relief that they'd accomplished that much. That relief turned to pure elation as he finished the prayer, the light faded, and Ruby gasped for breath.

It had worked.

Church staggered back, and Bishop Sophia caught him. He felt lightheaded and wobbly, all traces of the diamond water burned out of his body. He felt the unique exhaustion of divine exertion all the way down to his bones, but he smiled anyway. They'd done it.

"Ruby?" Bart was already at her side, helping her sit up. "Are you alright?"

Ruby's eyes shone in pure terror. "I'm sorry! I'm so sorry! I tried to fight it, but I couldn't think straight. It—"

"Take it easy," Angel said. Her halo had vanished, and she looked even more relieved than Church and Bart. "It's over now."

Ruby shook her head furiously. "No. Before you . . . I felt it. We were too late."

Bart's brow furrowed, and he turned to Church, but the priest and Angel were both staring at the blood Ruby's arms had dribbled onto the floor. It was only a tiny spatter. But it was starting to grow.

"Sophia," Church said. "You need to evacuate the cathedral. Worshippers, patients, noncombatants. All of them. Go!"

The bishop took off without a word of disagreement, already clutching her own saint's pendant. Church dug into his pocket for his Atreus amulet and summoned his armor onto his body. Angel gripped her axe tight in both hands, her halo re-igniting in an instant. They kept their eyes trained on the blood.

"What's going on?" Bart asked.

"The bond between Ruby and the demonic influence became strong enough to form a bridge. And she called for help," Church said. "Bart, take Ruby and Thalia back to the Star, and wait for us there!"

Before Bart could voice a complaint, the tiny spot of Ruby's blood swelled to the size of a small pond, and a geyser of red shot into the air as something leapt through. It landed with a thud that shook the floor, the stench of blood and rotting plants coiling off it.

It was shaped vaguely like a woman in a long dress, but the dress was a tangle of black moss, thorns, vines, and plant stems. The proportions were off, with shoulders twice as wide as the waist, and it didn't seem to have legs. Six golden cat's eyes spread out along its too-wide shoulders, and the jaws of a giant Venus flytrap served as both collar and neckline for its dress-like appearance. The teeth of those jaws created rows of spikes that framed a stiff, birch white face that looked exactly like Ruby's, but with massive red flower petals for hair.

The blood that had birthed it evaporated to coppery-smelling steam, though drips of it still fell from the demon's wet hide. By their nature, demons were corruptive, corrosive things, eating away at the world and turning it into a twisted reflection of themselves. And judging by the way dark roots were already beginning to spread out from where it stood, this one was strong.

When the demon spoke, its face did not move, though an opening near where its stomach was supposed to be did.

"Finally," it purred.

"Oh shit!"

The new voice drew every set of eyes upward toward its source where, on the balcony that overlooked the ritual room from high above, Brass stood, standing opposite a wary Silas, René, Rosa—and Snow.

"Hey guys!" Brass called down. "Bad time?"

"Brass?!" Church called out at the same time that Angel shouted, "Move!"

The demon surged forward like a swooping bat, ducking low as its dress of vines and moss flared out and then tucked back in for its charge. Angel swung with Daybreaker, and the demon met the attack with a flare of its billowing form as if sweeping out with a cape. A crash split the air where they met each other, echoing through the ritual room.

Angel was knocked back.

She swung her axe down, burying it into the ground and using it as an anchor to stop herself, but the demon was already sweeping toward her again in a zigzagging pattern. When it got close enough, its body billowed out and spun like a twirling dancer's skirt, and Angel's skin was sliced open as the curtain of thorns was dragged across her. Angel snarled in pain and let loose with a stream of divine light, but the demon folded up like a closing flower bud, and when Angel's blast subsided, there was only a scorch mark across the surface of the enormous petals it had wrapped its body in.

Up above on the balcony, the newest arrivals to the cathedral watched. René looked to Silas with uncertainty. They'd expected to have to contend with some of the Starbreakers, perhaps members of the Church of Avelina, not a demon, and certainly not one that could match the Starbreakers' infamous Sentinel.

"Sir?" she asked, looking for direction.

"We're here for the Heart," Silas said, though he said it with a scowl on his face. "Leave the demon to them!"

Rosa followed him off the balcony without a word. It was a drop of at least thirty feet, but before she hit the floor, the bracelet on her wrist flashed. Its twin on René's wrist echoed the display, and René teleported to her sister in midair. They kicked off each other, the force of Rosa's fall dispersed between them, and they landed at the same time in a low crouch, weapons at the ready, eyes locked on Church. Silas landed a second later, swinging down a length of quicksilver that transformed into a double-edged swordstaff once he reached the ground.

Church, still shaky from the resurrection, held out his hand, and summoned Zealot into it with a prayer.

Brass raced to follow Silas and the twins, only to have to stop as Snow blinked into his path with a dagger held out. He skidded to a stop only inches from running himself through on her outstretched blade, pivoted, and forced her back with his own sword. They reoriented themselves around each other, both in a fighting stance.

"I don't suppose you're in there somewhere, fighting to break free?" Brass said.

"I'm here," Snow said. "But I'm with them."

"That's a pity," Brass said, accepting that avenue as closed off. As Wings had described it, and as he now observed, Brass contended Snow was herself, just herself bent toward whatever her new controllers wanted. But Wings had also mentioned that Snow had been able to withdraw from the fight after giving herself an excuse to. He cocked his head and took a shot at giving her one now. "You do remember who taught you how to fight, right?"

Snow genuinely scowled at him, and Brass knew he'd chosen the wrong angle as she said, "You didn't teach me shit."

Behind him, Church could hear every clash between Angel and Ruby's demon. Their fight was blocking the way out for Sophia, and the only other path was to go straight through Silas and the twins. So with a prayer, he reached out to seize all of their minds to lock them in place. It was a strain to target three people so soon after the resurrection, and his body flushed with heat, but he powered through, locking his spiritual focus on them.

Nothing happened.

For an instant, he thought it was the strain, but as the prayer washed ineffectually over them, he felt a queasiness in his gut, as if he'd tasted something rancid. Experience took the guesswork out of the sensation. They'd used desecrated water. Beneger help him, he hated the stuff. In his mind, Zealot's disgust was almost deafening as the angel blade roared righteous condemnations.

As always, the sword's anger was infectious, and Church's heart pounded as he braced himself to meet them sword to sword while he worked up enough strength to burn through their unholy protections. But someone else got to them first.

Bart's body blazed with a corona of golden light as he rammed shoulder-first into René. He took slices across the face and arm for his obvious approach, but it almost didn't matter as the force of his charge took René off her feet and sent her flying backward. Rosa vanished in a flash, reappearing behind her sister to catch her before she collided with a stone wall. Silas tried to take a swing at Bart, but a spectral copy of Zealot manifested in the air in front of the boy, intercepting the strike and giving Bart time to get clear.

The young paladin came to a stop, unarmed, unarmored, the light gone from his body, but with his fists held at the ready. Bart ignored how much he was shaking, ignored the stinging pain and warm wetness on his face, and met the eyes of the twins. His intent was written on every inch of his body. If you want the vicar, you go through me.

The twins accepted his challenge without a word, dashing straight at him. Bart was just wondering how he could defend against two opponents at once with no weapon when a thorn-covered tendril cracked like a whip to strike, forcing René off course. Bart called divine strength back into his body and swung just as Rosa tried to stab him in the chest. His wild swing hit the edge of her weapon, and it was knocked from her hand with enough force to see it land clear across the room. She leapt back from him, just as another thorn whip slashed through where she'd just been standing.

The tendrils pulled back, and Bart's eyes went wide with terror as he saw them retract back into Ruby's arms. She met his eyes, gave him a "Save it for later" look, and turned her attention back to the twins.

"Back off," Ruby warned them. A new vine grew, slowly wrapping around her arm in preparation to be used. "Before someone gets hurt."

René reached Rosa's fallen sword, and held it out as her sister teleported to her side.

"We should say the same to you," Rosa said. "We want the heart. But we *will* go through you to get it."

Ruby clenched her fists and looked to Bart. His expression mirrored her thoughts. They were inexperienced as glintchasers. In their handful of outings, Brass had done the bulk of the work. In all likelihood, they were outclassed. But if they held the twins off, it gave Church and Angel that much less to deal with, and that could be all they needed to win.

"Try," Ruby said, with more confidence than she felt.

27
CASUALTIES

Ink only barely wove a shield spell in front of her in time as a scythe of purple energy tore out from Targan. It parted his desk down the middle, and proceeded to slice the room floor to ceiling as it raced straight at Ink. When it struck her shield, the power parted like a river against a stone, splashing out to either side of her. Every soldier she'd brought with her was sliced in half at the waist. A line of sunlight appeared across the entire ceiling, and chunks of plaster and stone rained down, falling into the new groove carved into the floor.

Targan didn't let up. Not moving from where he'd originally stood, he extended his palm, and in a blink, there were six Targans arranged in a circle around Ink, a crackling ball of violet light hovering in front of each of their hands. Ink rewove her shield from a flat disc in front of her into a dome of shimmering blue threads just as the Targans all fired on her at once. Six beams crashed into her shield dome, and the threads sustaining it immediately warped under the pressure. Ink knew she couldn't hold the shield, so she didn't try to.

Instead, she lashed out, expanding her dome of threads into a whirlwind of whips made of light. They sliced through five of the six Targans, and then kept going to cut crisscrossing gashes into everything around them. The last remaining Targan, who had still not moved from behind his now shredded desk, glanced up as the ceiling rumbled and collapsed into a shower of stone.

Both mages reacted with the same plan. Strands of light shot out from each of Ink's fingers, seeking out the largest chunks of masonry they could. With a yank, she whipped them all toward Targan. Meanwhile, the Headmaster raised his hand, and a cloud of debris gathered over his head in a swirling storm before he sent it all toward Ink in a tidal wave of stonework. The two attacks shattered against each other, leaving them standing in the remains of the Headmaster's office. Dust hung in the air from powderized stone, made hazier by the sunlight that now poured down on them. Overhead, the sound of an ongoing rockslide roared.

Ink looked up, and saw for the first time the scale of the gap between her and the Headmaster. He had sent a wall of debris from the falling ceiling to match her attack. But at the same time, he had held back, only sending a small portion of the debris he'd controlled at her. The bulk of the debris from the destroyed roof was swirling over their heads in a maelstrom of spinning stone, wood, and plaster. Ink's stomach dropped. It wasn't the scale of the spell that awed her. It was the ease. The control. Targan was holding an entire ceiling's worth of ammunition in the air, and he wasn't even exerting himself.

Without breaking his concentration on the maelstrom above them, Targan summoned six orbs of crackling violet energy, each one the size of a fist, that hovered over his head like a crown of inverted stars. Ink threw out a thread, but not at Targan. Instead, she lashed herself to one of the largest chunks of stone hurtling through the air, letting it yank her skyward. She needed distance, and a new plan.

With the aura of a man going for a stroll, Targan levitated into the air to follow her.

Wings conjured a wall of wind to divert the flames from the fire sphere's blast, though the resulting wall of flames blocked out her senses for a breath. Her mind, usually racing to keep pace with whatever fight she found herself in, felt scattered as it reeled from shock. If Arman had been anyone else, she would have already rushed in with swords flashing. But it was Arman. She couldn't just stab her husband. But if he was having the same crisis of conscience, he wasn't showing it. When the flames dispersed, three sparking metal discs were hurtling through the air toward her. She batted two aside with her bow, and ducked beneath the third.

Arman was sprinting, but not at her. Instead, he was running around the room, slapping box-shaped devices onto the walls as he went. Wings had no idea what they were, and she had a flash of regret for not taking a keener interest in Arman's spellforging. But whatever they did, she didn't intend to let them do it.

A quick sweep of the room let her spot three devices, and a fourth in Arman's hands. In a blur of motion, she drew and loosed four arrows. Each one found their target in the time it took Arman to take three steps. The pierced devices broke apart into sparks and metallic confetti, including the one still in his hand.

She was already drawing a fifth arrow when Arman pressed a glyph on his bracer. At her feet, the gravity discs she'd originally dodged pulsed in activation. They drew toward each other, and her toward them, in a sudden and violent burst of gravitational force. As they drew closer together, their effects amplified, until every sword, spear, and weapon rack in the room was hurtling toward her all at once.

Wings reacted on pure instinct. She let out a storm of wind that was closer to a shock wave in intensity, and the room rang out with a boom of thunder. The gravity discs broke apart, and the weapons and clutter that had been hurtling toward her now flew out from her in a storm of metal. Instant fear gripped her chest as she thought of Arman, too late to protect him from her own counter. But he already had a force shield up in front of him, deflecting half a dozen spear points and an errant shelf that had all careened toward him.

Relief flooded her, warring with her adrenaline. He was all right, but that had been too close. Arman was smart, and had his share of tricks, but she had a Servitor Heart on top of her own skill and powers as a warden. If this fight continued, she was going to hurt him. Protective instincts finally aligned with her combat ones, she exploded toward him in a burst of speed, and before he could move or even blink, she had him pinned to the wall, her bow pressed against his neck and wrists.

At this point, the fight was over. Wings was an archer and a swordswoman, and Arman worked with equations and delicate machinery. Beyond skill or power, she was physically stronger than him.

She felt a flash of hatred for Haegan as she was forced to hold the man she loved down like a struggling animal. It felt intrinsically wrong, him straining against her, kicking, fighting, losing.

"Arman, stop!" she begged. "It's me! It's Elizabeth! Whatever they did to you, you have to fight it!"

Wings couldn't see her husband's eyes through his goggles, but she could see the rest of his face. He didn't look like someone driven mad, or a vacant zombie, like people under mind control usually looked, but someone in the throes of grief.

Snow hadn't behaved like a typical victim of coercive magic either, but she'd clearly been working against whatever constraints were on her, and Arman wasn't. If Wings couldn't get him to snap out of it, she needed to restrain him and move on. But looking at him in obvious distress, imagining something twisting his mind and leaving him like this, she felt a desperate need to protect him, to save him.

She told herself there had to be something she could do. That there was some way to get him back, now, and stop this. And in that moment of desperately racking her brain for options, he croaked out, "I'm sorry."

He clenched his fist, and the seams in his armor turned yellow for a flash as electricity crackled across his entire body. Pressed against him, Wings seized as every nerve in her body felt briefly ignited, and she saw stars. She staggered back in a spasm, but Arman grabbed her by the shoulder, keeping the connection between them and continuing to lock her body up. With his free hand, he pulled out an engraving tool, wielding it like a dagger.

And she watched the face she'd gone to bed every night with for years prepare to kill her.

The room had descended into chaos, but Church couldn't afford to take his eyes off his opponent. Silas was a whirlwind with his quicksilver weapon. One moment, it would be a double-edged swordstaff. Next it would be a metal whip with a sword at the end. Then he'd get in close, and it would be two shortswords linked together by a cord between them. Even with Zealot helping to direct his movements, and its spectral copy harassing Silas at other angles, it was everything Church could do to keep up.

He wasn't used to fighting someone sword to sword like this, but Silas's desecrated water was holding out against Church's attempts to disperse it. Church's face was red, and he could feel the exhaustion of channeling divine power. If he could gather himself for a few breaths, he could build up something stronger to burn through the water, but he kept having to use smaller prayers to heal injuries, enhance his body, or return a blow.

All those little expenditures kept him in the fight, but kept him too spent to breach Silas's defense. It was a stalemate, but Church knew it couldn't last. The Heart of Light in his possession was making it significantly easier to heal himself, but even that added efficiency had its limits.

Then, Church heard Bart scream.

The young acolyte had René's dagger in his back. He threw a blind elbow, no divine reinforcement, forcing René back, and a moment later Ruby's thorn whips forced her even farther. Bart used a prayer to close up the wound immediately, but it was readily apparent that he and Ruby both were outclassed and running on even less time than Church.

The vicar stopped thinking about his own safety. He dropped every prayer he'd been using. When he took a cut from Silas on the leg or felt the tip of his sword pierce the chain mail in his armpit, he didn't heal the wounds. He pushed through the pain on nothing but his own grit, which made his form worse, and earned him further injuries. He took them all, until he'd bought as much time as he thought he could, and shouted a prayer at the top of his lungs.

There was a sizzling sound on Silas's skin as the protection of the desecrated water briefly resisted the prayer before being burned away. The prayer carried through, sinking into Silas's mind and turning his thoughts to lead. Silas's eyes widened in slow motion, and after a significant delay, he took a step back. René and Rosa had frozen entirely.

Church's exhaustion held him off from finishing Silas as the world spun, and he struggled to stay upright. For a second, he thought he had it. The bishop finally made it through, running to rally the rest of the cathedral against a potential demon incursion. Belatedly, Church regretted not giving her back the Heart of Light to get it clear of the fight as well. But there hadn't been time, at least not until—

The prayer broke, and his legs gave out from under him. His body and soul gave up as they both reached their limit. The resurrection, the fight, burning away the desecration, it had all been too much. Utterly spent, unable to stand, Church stared up at Silas in dread as the former knight shook himself free of the last of Church's influence, and moved in for the kill.

Ink wove shield spells into the sky, using them like platforms to stand on or kick off as she leapt and swung through the air, trying desperately to avoid Targan's onslaught. With a clench of his fist, a cloud of stone debris condensed all around her, trying to crush her from all sides. She responded with a web of threads, ensnaring each stone before using a pulse of lightning through the strings to powderize the lot of them.

Clouds of silver smoke billowed into being around him and Ink both, and he fired the violet stars hovering around him through the clouds closest to him. They emerged from the smoke surrounding Ink, shooting at her from half a dozen different angles.

She dispelled some, dodged others, but took a bad burn to the calf, and the platform she was standing on shattered like glass. She created a new one, bounced off it, and landed hard on the next.

His next blast pierced her straight through the chest, and the illusory decoy dissolved into motes of light. The real Ink came out of invisibility over his head, lashing out with another thread charged with lightning. Targan caught the spell on a ring of green energy he summoned around himself, dissolved it into essence, and then reformed it into a cloud of needles that shot toward Ink. Targan's hostile takeover spell was infamous for taking apart the offensive magic of his opponents and turning it against them. Ink had heard of it, but had hoped to slip past it by running the lightning through the threads instead of just firing it straight at him.

Instead, all she'd done was make it so she was being hit by electrified needles instead of a redirected lightning blast. They came too fast to properly shield herself against, so she had to make do with her own arms. It was like being struck by a hundred bees made out of fire, and she was left with dozens of tingling pinpricks all across her body.

She tumbled through the air, falling too erratically and fast to use a platform to save herself. Instead, she created a web of threads to catch her, anchoring it to the storm of stone Targan kept spinning around them. He could probably break the threads with enough force, or just drop the stones, but she had to try something.

He let her catch herself, even stopping the rotation of the debris cloud. He began directing the largest stones not being used as anchors by her web to fly at her. At first one at a time, then two, then three, until she was using a flurry of shields, whips, and lightning to keep the attacks at bay. It was an imperfect defense, and she took dozens of blows. With each one, the edges of the threads keeping her aloft fizzled, until finally a blow to her head disrupted the spell completely, and she fell back down to the tower below.

Targan stayed hovering, looking down on her as she struggled to pull herself to her feet. Behind him, every piece of remaining debris condensed into a single ball of rock. Then, it began to compress, smaller, and smaller, until it began to glow with heat and pressure. By then, it was the size of Targan. It shrank even further, turning from orange to yellow to white as it grew smaller and smaller, until, with a final, jerking shudder, it shrank to the size of a pinhead and exploded. The explosion froze when it had only expanded out to the size of a ball, a miniature sun held frozen by nothing but Targan's will.

He looked straight down at Ink, and frowned. "I'm disappointed in you, Arakawa. I thought you'd put up more of a fight than this."

Ink could feel a warm trickle of blood running down her forehead. She could feel all one thousand stinging pinpricks, and her leg throbbed as she tried to put weight on it. The top of the Headmaster's Tower was reduced to little more than a floating platform covered in deep slashes and listing to one side. There were smears of blood where the soldiers had fallen, but their bodies had been swept away or disintegrated by the fight. In contrast, the Headmaster didn't have so much as a scuff on his robes.

"I'm feeling magnanimous today," he went on. "If you were anyone else, I'd give you a choice between dying and submitting to a domination spell like your freelancer friends. But I think we both know which option you would choose."

Ink answered by tracing an arcane pattern through the air with her hands, lighting up a circle of glyphs around her feet. Slowly, the air around her began to shimmer in a fractal pattern. In that moment, too, she felt the gap between Targan and herself. He barely moved when casting. For most of her spells, she still needed the added focus of physical movement. It was slower, less efficient, and if Targan had taken her any more seriously, he could have obliterated her before she finished.

But he recognized the beginnings of a teleportation spell, saw a wounded woman trying to run, and flicked out a green beam to simply disrupt the spell and cut off her escape. She met the beam with a single thread of light, which shredded so violently under Targan's disruption that she lost a fingernail from the feedback. Targan raised an eyebrow, surprised she'd been able to throw out anything else mid-casting. She *was* rather proud of that. Casting multiple spells at once wasn't as easy as Targan made it look.

She finished her first spell and vanished in a shatter of light. Another shatter followed immediately after, above and behind Targan, and he turned in the air with a shield spell already in place in front of him to face—nothing.

He caught sight of a fading fractal pattern in the air, a faint whiff of ozone, all signs of a teleportation spell, but there was nothing but clear skies behind him. His shield dropped.

So did Ink's third spell.

Ink reappeared, her hastily woven invisibility falling apart. But it had done its job. By the time Targan could see her, she was close enough to punch him in the face. Targan was a more powerful mage, a more experienced spellcaster. But he had the body of an eighty-year-old man who had lived a sedentary life, and Ink was an ex-glintchaser with all the physical fitness and fighting instincts that required. When her fist connected, the fight was over.

Every shred of his concentration vanished. He might have regained it, except one of the things that concentration had been holding was the frozen starburst hovering over his head. Instead of a controlled, focused blast of energy, the ball simply detonated in the air. Ink wasn't even looking when it happened, too busy wrapping herself in threads to shield herself, and her vision still went white from the blast for a blink.

Her own attempt to shield herself was shredded apart by the blast, but she'd expected that much. She wasn't fazed to see Targan still alive either, though she had hoped otherwise. She sent a storm of threads as they fell, looping them around Targan's body and the jagged edges of the fast-approaching Headmaster's Tower, forming a tangled web. Just before they hit the ground, the threads all went taut.

Ink had her fall abruptly halted, and even with the threads stretching to disperse the force of the fall, she felt like the spell was about to tear her arms out of their sockets. She landed hard on the remains of the tower's top in a crouch, arms crossed in front of her chest, the lynchpin of a web of shining threads. Targan hung suspended in midair, the strands of the web wrapped around his limbs and throat. At a flex of her fingers, they tightened, digging into his skin until they drew blood.

His eyes had gone wide, with pain or panic. Probably both. His robes were burned half off him, exposing skin seared black, and blood streamed from his eyes, ears, and nose. Ink had known the blast would happen, been prepared for it. Targan was alive only thanks to the speed of his casting and the strength of his shield, but just barely.

"Kira," he croaked.

Ink gave him a venomous smile. "Targan."

Desperation showed on his face as his eyes flashed silver. Whatever he was trying, it took him longer than it took her to flex her middle finger, cinching the thread around his throat and slicing his head from his shoulders.

Brass and Snow traded blows in a blur of steel and shadows. She blinked all around him, froze the ground beneath his feet, fell back to throw knives and then closed the distance while he dodged. And no matter what she tried, Brass met it with a casual grace.

He hopped over patches of ice, once even leaping onto the balcony railing to avoid it and continuing to fight her even as he balanced atop it. He parried or ducked around every stab and slash, reading her intent with each blink. When they'd briefly fought a few months ago under very different circumstances, she'd managed to catch him off guard by blinking in place to trick him into expecting an attack from behind. This time, he met that trick with a palm strike to her chin.

A patch of ice formed over her lip to stop the bleeding where she'd bit it, and he flashed her an apologetic smile. And once again, Snow felt the true strength of the mental domination she'd been placed under. It didn't try to brute force her thoughts into submission. It didn't glaze her over or hollow her out. It twisted. It pulled. It tugged on who she was and adjusted her grasp on the world to lead her into justifying for herself what it wanted her to do.

The magic wanted her to obey Silas's commands, so it had twisted her perception of him in her mind until even now, even knowing in the back of her mind she was being controlled, she could only really think of him like a client she had decided to listen to. Fighting her friends? She'd already done that more than once, no mind control necessary. It was easy to tug her thoughts into being okay with doing it again. And now, she was under orders from Silas to kill anyone who got in their way. Brass was in her way. And it was painfully easy to want to kill Brass.

He was a conceited, self-aggrandizing, grandstanding, inconsiderate, easily distracted hedonist. As long as they'd known each other, he'd been getting them into trouble, blowing their money on whatever immediate pleasure he could find, and showing absolutely zero remorse for anything he did. Maybe, if he royally fucked up, you could get him to apologize for the trouble, but it was invariably followed by some variation on either "But at least everything turned out okay!" or "At least we'll get a decent story out of this!" And then, there was just his face. Brass had a cocky grin that was sculpted by the gods themselves to demand to be punched. He was wearing it now, telling her with a flash of his teeth that he was better than her in a fight, and he knew it, and in spite of the stakes of everything happening, he was having fun.

The spell seized those annoyances, fueled them with years of pent-up frustrations, and warped them in her mind into even bigger offenses than they actually were. Her anger cracked through the Heart of Ice's usual grip on her emotions, and the more that slid, the firmer the grip the mental domination had on her, until she genuinely believed with her whole being that Brass needed to die, right here, right now.

"You always do this," she said.

"Care to be more specific?"

She came at him again, though it was almost perfunctory. The attacks were slower, with fewer blinks between them, and Brass barely paid attention to the movements needed to counter them. His own attacks were equally halfhearted. It wasn't as if he wanted to kill her, and anyway, the conversation had his attention more than the fight now.

"You always make a mess of people's lives."

He parried another of her lazy strikes. "I prefer to think of myself as more of an enricher, but I admit it can get a bit—"

"Tell that to Ruby!" Snow shouted, her stoic mask shattering. She paused in her halfhearted assault to point out over the balcony to the fight happening below them, and then at Brass. "You dragged her into this world, and you didn't think for a second what the consequences would be. She was attacked because of you. She had to make a deal with a monster to survive because of you. She was lost, you held out glintchasing like it was the perfect escape, and now she's in so far over her head it'll be a miracle if she survives the day. Sound familiar?"

Brass froze. They weren't talking about Ruby anymore. "I thought we were past this."

"You stole me from life! You took me into a world you knew I wasn't prepared for, and then you abandoned me!"

"You were kidnapped! And I had a plan to save you!"

"You spent a week in orgies with Vera!"

"It was a complex plan!"

"So what? Once wasn't enough? You had to go and find another girl who didn't know better? Ruin her life too?"

Brass threw out his arms in indignation and pointed at himself. "Hold on, I didn't ruin anything. You were the one who wanted—"

His breath caught in his chest as Snow blinked in close, and stabbed him through the heart, exactly where he'd been pointing. His eyes blinked in surprise, staring first at the blade, then up at her. All traces of anger, of righteous indignation and moral outrage, had vanished from her face, replaced by a cold slate. He might have been better with a blade, but Snow was unmatched as an actress.

"You talk too much," she said flatly, and pushed him over the edge of the balcony.

Angel left a crater in the wall as she crashed into it, keeping her grip on Daybreaker only thanks to instincts that went deeper than her years of experience. The demon was in front of her in a blink, pinning her back against the wall before she could even finish peeling herself off of it.

"Poor little Sentinel," the demon rumbled in a twisted approximation of Ruby's voice, though it came from the mouth in its chest rather than the imitation face atop its shoulders. "You care so much about these little humans, don't you? Are you going to save them from me?"

It spun, throwing Angel into the ceiling. The demon leapt up after her, and when they met in midair, it twisted out of the way of Angel's wild swing to smack her back down into the floor. Angel fired another blast of light from her eyes, and again the demon curled in on itself, taking the blast with ease before landing on top of her with a thud that shook the ground.

It unfurled back into the loose approximation of a human woman, and bent over to meet Angel's eyes with the ones in its shoulders.

"Do you think that you can?" it crooned.

Angel tried to punch one of its eyes, but its body pulled back with unnatural swiftness and flexibility without getting off of her. Then its body flared out into thorn-tipped wings, and drove both of them straight into Angel's shoulders. She screamed.

"I am Carcenia, Rose of Death. She Who Birthed the Iron Scourge. I've killed hundreds of angels, Sentinel. But maybe you're better than your brothers and sisters. Stronger."

One of the wings withdrew and stabbed again, this time in her stomach.

"If you knew what was coming for this world, you would beg me to take it now, for what I will do will be a kindness by comparison. But you are nothing but a foolish puppet. So go on then." The demon's sickly sweet voice washed over Angel like a wave of rotting flowers. "Save them. Save anyone."

From beneath them both, roots of the demon's corrosive presence began to spread out, cracking stones. Feeling the roots wriggling beneath her made Angel's skin crawl, even distracted as she was by the agony in her gut. This was what happened when demons entered the world.

This thing, that had tormented Ruby for months, was going to spread like a disease, killing everything around it, inviting more of its kind to the world as its influence spread. They were in possibly the safest place for a demon incursion to happen, surrounded by servants and warriors of Saint Avelina. But by the same token, if the demon prevailed here, there was a very real possibility that there would be nothing left in Corsar to stop it.

She remembered how she'd felt facing the Dread Knight in Loraine. How right it had felt, even in death, to face evil and stop it before it could hurt someone else. She remembered, of all things, her conversation with Church last night, about what she wanted to do, to be. And through her pain, she made the silent vow that this demon would not touch anyone else.

The demon withdrew one of its wingtips, poising to stab her again. But when it drove down, Angel's hand snapped out to catch it.

She glared up at the demon with eyes like twin suns. She growled, "WATCH ME!"

Normally, when she spoke with her powers ignited, it sounded like there were two of her speaking at once. This time, it was one voice, and it echoed through the whole church. Her entire body flared with the intensity of an inferno, incinerating the surrounding roots, scorching the floor tiles beneath her, and bringing the ones she was touching to a bright orange glow. The demon retreated with a hiss, but Angel's grip on its wingtips was a burning vice.

Unable to flee or curl in on itself, the demon was left wide open as Angel let out a feral scream, and unleashed twin beams of light straight into its body. She put every ounce of her will, of her disgust for this monster, and her personal vow to protect into the blast. She felt close then, to something deeper in her power. Directed like this, backed by unwavering purpose, it felt more right, more natural, than ever before. The demon was blasted back, chunks of its charred flesh still in Angel's hands.

Angel rose to her feet, Daybreaker dragging across the floor in one hand. Guided as if by the memory of a dream, she held out her other, and a twin to the axe made of solid light flashed into her waiting palm. The wounds on her shoulders and stomach sealed themselves in seconds.

With another scream, Angel crashed into the demon in a burst of light.

The entire ritual room shook as the demon's body slammed into the wall, but just as it had it peeled itself out of the new crater in the wall, she struck again, this time knocking the demon back to the ground. She landed on top of it, a divine comet descending with axes raised.

Carcenia tried to block, so Angel's first attacks only tore into the wings of moss and vine it tried to shield itself with. More vines lashed out from its prone form, wrapping around Angel to try to fling her away. They held up under the sheer heat of Angel's skin, but were sliced to ribbons by her axes. Angel struck again and again, each blow hitting like a thunderclap and cracking more of the street beneath them until, finally, the demon's defense broke, and its body splayed out, a limp, pulpy mess. Three of its eyes were swollen shut as it glared up at the shining Sentinel.

"When you get back to the hells, tell them who sent you," Angel said. "Tell them that this world isn't yours to fuck with. And that as long as I'm here, it never will be."

With one last blow, she turned the demon to dust.

Her shoulders heaved from exertion as her halo faded, and smoke curled off her body. Though there was far less of it than normal, and in those last moments, it hadn't hurt like it usually had.

It was about then that Angel realized the entire room had gone silent. Everyone she could see—Starbreakers, allies, and enemies alike—had all been startled into a momentary peace, stunned by the display of raw power.

Silas and the twins stood ready and on guard, hesitant to move. Church was down. Ruby and Bart looked to be in bad shape, and grateful for the breather Angel's distraction had bought them. She doubted they'd be much help. But at the moment, if Angel had to take a three-on-one fight against Silas and his sidekicks, she liked her odds.

And then, Brass's dead body hit the ground.

Bart and Ruby froze. Church drew up short. Even Angel flinched. And as they all looked up to see where he'd fallen from, Snow struck.

She blinked into view right in the middle of the ritual room, and threw out her hands in opposite directions. Ice surged across the floor before spreading up and out into solid walls that engulfed four bodies at once. Bart and Ruby were both knocked over and pinned to the floor, with Ruby hitting her head hard on the way down and going out like a light. Church, who'd still been standing, was coated in it up to his chest, and the arm holding Zealot had been immobilized. Angel was encased from head to toe.

Silas and the twins had retreated on instinct when the ice had spread out, and now that all of their opponents had been immobilized, Snow could see the moment of consideration as they debated whether to finish all of them off while they were helpless.

"That won't hold any of them long, and we can't beat Angel," Snow snapped. "Grab the Heart and let's go."

Church started a prayer for strength, but stopped halfway through when Snow waved her hand, and the ice crawled farther up his body to cover his mouth.

"If I were you, I'd save your strength," Snow warned. With her eyes, she tried to indicate Brass's prone form.

Silas had ordered her to kill anyone who got in their way, and she'd already obeyed that command once. But as long as they were all pinned in ice, the others weren't in the way. It was the best she could do. Brass was dead, but in Saint Avelina's Cathedral with two of the most powerful priests in Corsar right there, he actually still had good odds of survival. As long as Silas ordered them all to take the Heart and leave, right now. Helpfully, while they all stood glaring at her, the ice encasing Angel gave a loud crack.

"René, the Heart. Rosa, our exit," Silas ordered, and the twins rushed to obey.

Inwardly, Snow breathed half of a sigh of relief. Only half, because Silas still hadn't ordered her to do anything. He'd just kept glaring at her.

"What?" she demanded.

"Don't move," he ordered.

Her body went still. Silas reached into the bag he'd brought with them and withdrew a cylindrical device Snow recognized. A lifetime ago, she and Phoenix had broken up over arguments centering on the device's function. On whether or not he should be trying to work out how to use it on her.

Instantly, her cold expression vanished. Snow wondered if Wings had passed word of her and Phoenix being mind controlled to the others, and if

Church could do anything about it. She only needed a blink of freedom, a breath without being bent by Targan's spell, and she could open Silas's throat. But she'd frozen Church's mouth shut, and thawing wasn't nearly as easy as freezing for her. Silently, she begged for Angel to struggle free faster, to force Silas to retreat now. To delay what the suppressed panic in her mind was sure was about to happen.

She couldn't bring herself to struggle against Silas's order directly, and she couldn't find any loophole or interpretation to slip out of its constraints. In a desperate bid, she tried to convince herself that being encased in ice was harmless enough to not count as attacking Silas, he'd only ordered her not to move, and that she'd have locked up any ally who was trying to do something she didn't want. But by the time she managed to send ice out from her foot to reach for him, he'd already activated the Servitor Heart extractor.

As Wings stared at the pointed tip of Arman's engraving tool, barely this side of conscious with electricity playing havoc with her nerves, she clawed desperately for options, and came up with only one. She couldn't move. But she had just enough affinity with lightning thanks to the Heart of the Sky that she could think.

With all the focus she could muster, she reached out to the air around them, and pushed it away. Not in anything as strong as a gust. She only moved it, until there was no air in the space around them whatsoever. Arman froze as he tried to take a breath and choked. He staggered back, breaking the connection and granting her a reprieve. He tried to get clear of the space of vacuum she'd made, but though she still couldn't move her body, she kept the airless pocket over him, following him as he staggered around the room, suffocating. And with no air to carry the sound, he did it in complete silence.

He dropped to the floor after only seconds of panicking for breath. He looked up at her, veins bulging, face tense, mouth agape. She could see the desperate, mortal terror in his eyes, and it tore her apart. She resisted the urge to shut her eyes. She had to watch, know exactly when he lost consciousness, if she wanted to avoid killing him. Finally, his body went limp. She knew him well enough to know he wasn't actually unconscious, just faking it to trick her into dropping the suffocation field early. A confused mix of admiration and desperate frustration took hold in her. Arman always fought to the very end—which was extremely unhelpful right now.

She held the field a few more seconds, until she could move her arms and legs again. Then, finally, she released her grip on the air.

Instantly, she was met by the loudest, shrillest sound she had ever heard. Attuned as she was to the air in that moment from controlling it so finely, her hearing was at its most sensitive, and the sound tore through her skull sharply enough to make her vision fuzz. She screamed in pain for a second until she could focus and pinpoint the source of the sound—one last device, dropped by Arman, its activation hidden by the vacuum bubble. Wings didn't trust herself to shoot it in her state, so she transformed her bow into swords, staggered over, and stabbed it.

It shut off instantly, but the ringing in her ears persisted, and she felt uncomfortably dizzy. Arman, she noted with intense relief, was unconscious but breathing. That at least had worked. Now, she just had to tie him up before he came to, wait for her accelerated healing from the Heart to fix her ears, and then she could get back to dealing with the rest of Haegan's forces here.

She felt rather than heard Haegan reappear behind her. The thud of his armored boots carried back to her, and she spun. Her swords were a bow again, and she fired from the floor. It whizzed half a foot to the side of his head. She was still too dizzy. Not that it would have mattered if she'd been on target.

Haegan stood covered head to toe in bulky, bronze-colored armor. Embedded in the chest were three glass orbs. Two of them glowed red and purple respectively, and the third orb held a swirling void of pure black shadows. The color and silhouette of the armor stirred something in Wings's memory that provoked a flash of urgency and danger unlike any other. She needed to move, to fight, and she needed to do it *now.*

Haegan held out a cylindrical device in front of him, and twisted it.

Wings felt something tear at her soul. She didn't hear herself scream, but she felt it. Pain exploded through her whole body, dropping her to her knees. Around her, wind whipped into a tornado, throwing about every loose object in the room. A steady stream of green light flowed out of her in a river, drifting into Haegan's device. It was like having her chest ripped open and her organs pulled out through the gaps between her ribs, though her actual flesh stayed perfectly pristine.

The only thing that changed were her eyes, which went from a swirling emerald green to a muted, sky blue. Eventually, the pain stopped. Her body felt like a dishrag that had been rung out, and she felt numb except for the sharp pain in her still-ringing ears. Once again, she couldn't move. She could barely think. She drew in a shaky breath, and felt *nothing*. No sense of the air around her, the contours of the room, the movements of others. It was just a breath. Her heartbeat, which had for years felt like a hummingbird's, now came so slowly for a moment she thought it had stopped altogether.

She gaped like a fish on dry land as Haegan looked from her to the device in his hands. He said something she couldn't hear, and jammed one end of the device into his armor's breastplate. The device pulsed with green power once, twice, and went dim. When he pulled his hand away, a new glowing green glass orb had joined the others already present. In that moment, as she realized what the orbs were, she understood why the armor had stirred her old memories.

It looked just like the Servitor.

28
RECOVERY

Bart was at Ruby's bedside when she woke up, back in a room in Saint Avelina's Cathedral. Her first thought, through a hazy, slowly recovering awareness, was that he looked a lot better than when she'd last seen him, bloody and struggling to stand after a bad fight with René and Rosa. It took her brain another second to register that she was also in much better shape than she had been, and a few more after that to realize that shouldn't have been a surprise. They'd been hurt in the middle of Saint Avelina's Cathedral, practically surrounded by people who could heal injuries with a word. Of course they were fine.

Except the last thing she remembered, Brass had fallen three stories, and Snow had buried the rest of them in ice. They'd been at the mercy of their enemies—at the Mercy of the Cold-Blooded Killer herself. In that respect, it was a miracle they were both still breathing.

Bart didn't have the expression of someone who'd been granted a miracle. He looked weary, like he'd spent a day getting nothing but bad news. His face and shoulders sagged with an exhausted weight, and when her eyes focused on him, the smile he gave her was tired and desperate.

"Hey," he said. "How are you feeling?"

"Could be worse," she said.

She cast a glance at her arms, to where the vines had burst from her skin.

As usual, there was no sign of where the skin had broken. Someone had even washed the blood off her arms and given her a new shirt with intact sleeves. But somehow, she could still feel them. Not in her flesh, but somewhere deeper inside herself. The demon's influence was gone, she was certain. But the changes that had already happened to her remained. Would maybe always remain. She wasn't sure how she felt about that. And for the moment, she had more pressing concerns.

She almost didn't want to ask, but forced the words out anyway. "What happened?"

"I couldn't see it, but after Snow pinned us down, they . . . did something to her. I think they were planning to kill all of us after, but Angel broke out, and they ran. They got the Heart," Bart said. His head hung low. "We lost."

The words conjured the image of a broken body clad in a crumpled purple coat. "Is Brass—?"

"He's fine," Bart hurried to answer. "The bishop was able to resurrect him in time. Actually, he's probably doing the best out of everyone right now."

"What's that supposed to mean?"

The weary shadow that hung over Bart's face deepened.

Ink's injuries were healed, and she'd changed into a fresh set of robes, but she still looked haggard. The illusion spell she usually wore over her hair had faded, and she hadn't spared the attention to reapply it. It hung unkempt, in its natural dark black color, and most of it was burnt split ends. Her eyes had bags under them, and she routinely found herself rubbing her face or temples, trying to fight off the mental and physical fatigue the priests' prayers hadn't fixed.

Among twelve other tasks meant to keep the Academy and kingdom from falling apart, she had Gamma brewing the strongest tea possible. She was going to need the caffeine. Today, and probably for the next several years, assuming they all survived that long.

The raid on Haegan and his order had been about as much of a disaster as possible. Out of all of their targets, only Ink's and the Cord of Aenwyn's had been successfully dealt with. The rest had fled or fought off the ambush, either by being a match for the forces sent in, or by the intervention of Haegan himself, who had arrived at nearly every battle that they'd actually had a chance of winning. The members of Seven Gates were all still recovering from their run-ins with him, though blessedly, they hadn't lost anyone. Two independent knights had fallen, along with the team of Academy mages Ink had assembled, and several dozen soldiers of the royal army.

They'd inflicted losses on the enemy, certainly. Weapons had been seized, and there were plenty of Haegan's followers now either dead or in custody. But the bulk had gotten away, including Haegan himself, who was now sporting a suit of armor handcrafted by Phoenix, and—what was it? *Six* Servitor Hearts? Force, Fire, Shadow, Sky, Ice, and Light, all held by one man.

The original Servitor hadn't even had that many, and it could have razed the kingdom. Now Haegan had six, and some plan for them involving the Starborn. What exactly that plan was, or where he and his order had disappeared to, she didn't know. Meanwhile, in the wake of the failed raid on his territory, the Baron of Loraine had risen in open revolt against the crown, and was already marching his garrisons on the surrounding region. Presumably, he would be making a play for power while the crown's forces were scattered and wounded, but maybe he was just a distraction. Maybe he was still working according to Haegan's plans, maybe he'd gone rogue. Neither Ink nor Lupolt could say for sure, because all of their agents were scattered and wounded.

"It's a complete fucking mess," she said to Lupolt, staring at the map of Corsar in front of her. She was in the war room of the Pearl Palace, trying to sort out their next move and going through reports from the raid as they came in. Lupolt still had his arm in a sling, having refused to see a healer while there were still other casualties to tend to.

"Is there *anything else* they told you about Haegan's plans?" Lupolt asked.

"Church, Brass, and Angel barely knew what was going on to begin with," Ink said. "Everyone with useful information is . . . still down, apparently."

A shred of sympathy sifted through the fatigue in her voice. She'd seen the condition of the others. Remembering that, she sighed. "They'll talk to us when they're ready. But the priest says they need time. And I'm inclined to agree."

Elizabeth ran into Church in the halls of Saint Avelina's Cathedral. Haegan had left both her and Arman alive, a fact that still astounded her. She could still see his face as he looked down on them both. She'd been sure then that they were dead. And then, he'd left. Like they weren't worth killing.

A part of herself she was trying to ignore agreed with him.

Things got fuzzy after she called for help with her messenger coil, but she remembered royal army soldiers arriving and carrying them both out, and the flying skiff ride to the cathedral. Most of the casualties from the failed raid were being brought here, and more were still coming in.

She tried to ignore the guilt that seized her chest when she thought of that. Haegan needed to be stopped. But she'd been the one to push for immediate action. With the Heart of the Sky flowing through her, she'd been filled with the desire to move, to do something. She'd been absolutely certain in her decisions.

Now, that absolute certainty was gone, and doubt was flooding the void it had left behind in her chest.

Church's face brightened when he saw her. "Elizabeth, you're up! How are you feeling?"

Elizabeth's face did the talking for her, and Church's friendly expression sobered.

"Is there anything you need?"

Elizabeth looked to the door in between them. "Arman said Snow isn't talking to anyone. Is this her room?"

Church glanced at the door. "Yes. I was actually just about to check on her."

"Let me."

She meant it to sound reassuring, but it came out more like a plea. Church nodded anyway, saying something about checking on the others and walking away. She breathed a sigh of relief. There was an unmistakable look of pity in the priest's eyes, but at least he hadn't fussed over her like Arman. Her husband's worrying was understandable, and under different circumstances, she would have let him fret as much as he needed to calm down. But not right now. Right now, she needed to feel useful, not fragile. And if there was any place she could be useful, it was here.

Taking in a deep breath that still felt too shallow, Elizabeth went inside.

A dark-haired woman with light skin and brown eyes sat on the room's windowsill, staring out at the city. She was dressed in simple, dark tights, and a matching long-sleeved undershirt. Her dyed, dark blue leathers and boots were sitting on a nightstand, neatly arranged, untouched. She twirled a familiar enchanted knife between her fingers without looking at it, and the Arcania lettering of Companion Piece's name glinted in the afternoon sun.

"Snow?"

It had been a full day since the raid. Their physical injuries were healed, and Church had even managed to painstakingly undo the damage done to Snow's and Arman's minds by the domination spell. But in that time, Snow hadn't said more than a handful of words to anyone. She had stayed in the room the Church of Avelina had given her, sulking in silence, barely moving.

The woman on the windowsill didn't reply. Elizabeth tried again. When she still got no answer, she tried a different name.

"Chloe?"

Chloe's body tensed, curling slightly in on itself. She drew in a sharp, ragged breath, and it came out shaky. Tears rolled down her cheeks without freezing for the duration of another half-strangled sob, and then Chloe wiped her eyes and straightened.

"What?"

Elizabeth blinked. The cold edge to Chloe's voice was *gone*. Instead of a vengeful ghost, she sounded . . . human. Alive. The change was so drastic it took Elizabeth a second to register the raw pain behind it, and remember why she was here.

“How are you feeling?” Elizabeth asked.

“Fine.” The answer was as brusque as it was expected. It was the same one Chloe had given everyone who’d asked. Everyone knew it was a lie, but Elizabeth knew exactly how much of a lie it was.

“Then you’re doing better than me,” she said.

“The extractor?” Chloe asked.

“No. Hurt like the hells, but it did what it was supposed to. Took the Heart without killing me.” Elizabeth paused to gather herself.

This was for Chloe’s benefit, but it was also for hers. She needed to get this off her chest, with someone who understood, who wouldn’t immediately devolve into guilt-racked sobs over it.

“I feel numb,” she said, and this time, she didn’t try to hide weakness in her voice. The soul-crushing emptiness. “When I had the Heart, I could feel everything. I could hear everything. I could *smell* everything. And now it’s all gone and it’s . . . suffocating. It’s like I went blind and deaf at the same time, and the world disappeared. I’m cut off. I keep getting startled by things behind me, everything feels too quiet, and if I look out that window at the sky, I think I’ll start crying, because I can’t *feel* it anymore.”

Her voice broke, even without looking at the sky. Avelina spare her, she’d been holding that in too long. She knew she *never* would have held in feelings like that with the Heart still inside her, and that realization drove the knife of its absence deeper.

“The worst part is what’s in my head,” Elizabeth went on once she’d mastered herself. “Before, it was always go, move, act, do. Now I’m thinking about everything, and I’m overthinking everything. Almost everything I have now, I got after the Heart. I got *because* of the Heart. My name. My job. My *marriage*. And so now I keep thinking, what happens now that the Heart’s gone? How much more am I going to lose without it?” She shook her head. “It’s stupid, and I hate it, and I hate even more that I would never think like this if I still had it.”

Elizabeth wasn't quite sure what to expect. Sullen silence, probably. Possibly dismissal. Mockery if Chloe was feeling particularly bitter. Just when she thought maybe sullen silence would win out, Chloe gave a scoff, and shook her head. Elizabeth cocked an eyebrow in challenge. But instead of saying anything cutting, the assassin squirmed uncomfortably for a moment, even casting a glance out the window as if plotting escape. Then the walls came down.

"It's nothing," she said. "Just . . . you're talking about how great the Heart was, and how it changed your life and you miss it so much, and I . . ." She trailed off, looking back out the window. "I think mine ruined my life."

She closed her eyes. Elizabeth waited for her to continue, afraid the slightest push might make Chloe close herself off again.

"It made everything so easy," she said eventually. "Not just the powers. I had an off switch for my feelings. No guilt, no fear, no pain, whenever I wanted. I didn't even have to force it out. I just had to let it happen. It was scary, at first. But then I'm using it in fights to stay focused. And then I'm using it during side jobs, so it doesn't bother me when a kid sees me kill their dad. And then I'm using it with Arman and the others. And the more I use it, the more I fight with them, because they're still people with feelings, and I'm not. And I don't want to think about how *that* feels, so I let the cold take that away too. And it takes, and it numbs, until I wasn't feeling anything. And I *liked* it that way. It made me feel *safe.* And it cost me everything."

Her brown eyes opened, and they were shining.

"Now all of a sudden, it's gone. I've got no safety. No protection. Just a decade of my own crap to deal with." She rolled her eyes in annoyance and shifted to staring at the ceiling. "And it doesn't help that now it's like all the feelings I have or ever had are just pouring out with no filter, and I keep fucking crying for no reason, and I'm *hot.* All. The time."

"You sound like me when I was pregnant."

"Fuck you."

Elizabeth laughed, and so did Chloe. Then they both cried, and then laughed about that. And in that shared cycle of laughing and crying, of commiseration and swapping stories, they both started to feel a little more like themselves.

"You're not going to lose your job," Chloe said. "Or Arman. Or any of it."

Elizabeth cocked her head in a silent, "How do you know?"

"The Heart didn't make you a different person," Chloe said. "Everything you did with it was already in you. It just brought it out. Besides, Arman was in love with you before the Heart."

"Really?"

"I think *he* might have been the last person to know. Even Church clocked it." A faint smile flickered on her lips, gone as quick as it came. Hesitantly, Chloe met Elizabeth's eyes. "How is he?"

Elizabeth tried to think of the best way to summarize the state her husband was in.

Arman was working.

Over the years, whenever things were going wrong in his life, Arman had learned to lean on work as a way to cope. It kept his mind focused, and it let him feel a measure of control over something. And that was something he desperately needed right now.

Even now, part of him was still trapped in the fight with Elizabeth.

He could recall with perfect, stomach-churning clarity, the plan he'd formulated to kill her.

She'll hesitate against me. Exploit that. She'll see any direct attack coming, so be indirect. Mislead her senses. She's fast. Strong. Smart. But she dies like anyone else.

Those were his thoughts. His memories of her in that moment. A problem to solve with murder as the solution. Even knowing his mind had been warped at the time, he couldn't help the disgust and shame that drowned him every time he thought about it.

And he couldn't *stop* thinking about it. It had haunted him from the moment he'd woken up in the cathedral.

Finding out she was still alive, that he'd failed in spite of his best efforts, had been only a partial comfort. The priests had healed her as best they could, but something had been ripped out of her that they couldn't replace. And he'd been the one to make it possible. He'd built the extractor. He'd distracted her enough to let Haegan use it—he'd nearly *killed* her. If she'd been any less resilient, any slower to react and adapt, Haegan would have pulled the Heart of the Sky out of a corpse.

Looking back on the time he'd spent with Elizabeth after he'd found her room in the cathedral, he wasn't sure he'd actually said anything other than "I love you" and "I'm sorry." Over and over again. He couldn't think of anything else to say.

He wasn't in Saint Avelina's Cathedral anymore. Instead, he'd returned to the workshop that had been his home and prison since his capture. Nobody had moved the tools and materials that Haegan's forces had left behind. There'd been too much else to worry about.

His heart was pounding, and his legs were shaking. But his hands were steady as he carefully assembled the pieces of the device he'd laid out in front of him. He'd had the idea for it percolating in the back of his mind months ago, and had started work on it in his spare time while under Haegan's thrall. It hadn't been finished in time for his fight with Elizabeth. But he could finish it now.

A single knock preceded the door opening, and Arman sat up, expecting to see Elizabeth. Instead, Angel stood in the doorway.

"Your wife said I'd find you here," Angel said, and panic gripped Arman's chest.

"Is something—"

"She's fine. Shut up."

The brusque interruption was like a slap to the face, and he went quiet. Angel looked around at the state of the room. It was a mess.

"Got word from Ink and Lupolt. Break's over. We've got shit to do."

"I'm not taking a break."

"Really? Kinda looks like it."

Arman set down his work a tad more aggressively than he meant to, and took a deep breath. He knew he wasn't actually angry at Angel. He was exhausted, and ashamed, and ready to snap, and she just happened to be the closest target. And she wasn't entirely wrong.

There were things he could have been doing besides spellforging. Problems he could have helped solve. But they would have involved talking to other people. Involved thinking about what had happened to him and the people who'd done it to him, and feeling hopelessly overwhelmed, and he didn't want any of that. So he'd come here instead. To work.

To hide.

"I almost killed my wife."

"Yeah, I heard," Angel said, unmoved. "You almost killed me once, and took you like seven years to get over it. On a tighter schedule this time. You good or not?"

Arman took a deep breath. "Not."

Angel shrugged as if she'd expected his answer. "For what it's worth, I get it. Something gets in your head, brings out a side of you you're not sure you like or trust, makes you feel like you don't know yourself? I've been there. A lot. Church and the others want to give you space to feel better. Maybe talk it out. Give you a hug. But my way's faster."

"What's your way?"

"Get angry. You feel guilty about what you did? Don't punish yourself. Punish the people who made you do it. All that pain you've got swirling in your chest? Give it to the people who deserve it. Anything else left over, stick it in a box, kick it under the bed, and deal with it when the world's not on fire."

"And that works?"

"It gets shit done," Angel said. "They don't need us to be emotionally stable. They need us to kick the bad guy's ass. Can you do that, or are you just going to sit down here and mope about it?"

Arman's gaze drifted back down to the device at the table. "When this is all over, we should both seriously consider therapy."

The device he'd been building was a weapon. It bore the same rotating cylindrical chamber as his old wand had, but rather than the straight-line design of a wand, he'd taken it in a new direction. It borrowed even more heavily from Old World designs than his previous builds had, shaped similar to a hand crossbow without limbs. He called it a gun.

Arman's doubts and guilt stepped aside, letting anger take their place. With the deft hands of a spellforger used to assembling in the heat of battle, Phoenix finished slotting in the final pieces, and took aim at a scrap piece of Servitor armor plated that had been left hanging on an abandoned rack. The cylinder spun, chambering the force cell, and Phoenix squeezed the trigger. The blast put a clean hole through the plate and left a scorch mark on the wall behind it.

It would be harder to punch a hole in the real thing, Phoenix knew. Guilt and anxiety still swirled at the back of his mind. But he had to admit, it had felt good to imagine that piece of plating as Haegan.

29
THE CULT

Haegan stood on the outermost walls of Relgen, overseeing the arrival of his new order. More and more of them arrived not on horses or in carts, but through cloud banks of crackling silver mists. Those were the ones who had joined him in tapping into the Cult of Stars' powers for the battles ahead of them.

Something in him had changed when he had taken that final step Targan had laid out for him, and carved the mark of the Stars into his forehead. Every slash of the twelve-pointed star felt as though he were cutting away at the restraints of something inside him, digging into himself to set it free.

At first, not much had changed. The itch in his forehead was relieved, but otherwise he'd felt the same. But then the enemy's attack had come, and forced him into action. Haegan had tapped into the power of the Stars more than he ever had before to teleport from one battle to the next, countering the enemy and providing avenues of escape for his people.

Before, that would have been taxing for him. But with the mark, it felt as though the more he used the power, the more he understood it, and the more he could accomplish with it. He had slipped further and further into it like a surprisingly endless pool, and he'd resurfaced on the other side a new man. The aches and pains of his body were gone. The fabric of space felt like a tactile thing to him now. A new connection had formed between him and something deeper. And it was powerful. Seeing those clouds of silver smoke, feeling them formed by others besides himself and knowing that others had found all those same benefits stirred something in Haegan, and the faint trace of a smile slipped through his stoic expression.

Standing next to him, Silas noticed. The young man wore one of the lesser projects they had "commissioned" from Phoenix—a harness capable of housing a single Servitor Heart. It was only an insurance policy, and currently sat empty. "I don't think I've seen you this happy in eight years."

Haegan hummed to himself. In his crusade to save humanity, he had gathered allies to him. But he had always felt alone. Silas followed him without question, believed in him, but did not understand him. Did not understand the truths Haegan did about the frailty of humanity, and the crushing, ordained inevitability the Stars represented. And he was Haegan's most loyal follower. René and Rosa, the next closest to him, had been motivated more by a love of Silas than any shared vision with Haegan. Guerron, Targan, the baron and the vicar, none of them understood anything beyond their own grabs for temporary power.

As the only one who had seen the full breadth of what was at stake, who walked the streets of Relgen and peeked beyond the veil of this world, Haegan had been separated from his fellows. He was the sole pillar that could direct so many disparate desires and agendas. For too long, he had been suffering under the weight of that.

Now there were truly others like him. There were others who *were* him, and he was them. He knew his fellow marked as he knew himself, and they knew him. Their lives and stories were one now, blended together in a single collective memory that stretched backward in an unbroken chain through everyone who had ever borne the mark of the Stars.

He recalled every time he had tried and failed to call the Starborn to Asher, recalled how many of those failures he'd met because of the Starbreakers. He recalled that final scheme, the knowledge of the Ending, seeding the knowledge of it in the Starbreakers and then coming to collect it once they'd retrieved it. He recalled the fear on all of their faces the moment they realized that after all their years of fighting and killing him, they'd failed, and the satisfaction it had brought him.

Haegan understood that those were not originally his memories. That it had been others who had borne the mark of the Stars that had seen and done those things. The Cult of the Stars. But now, all of their knowledge and power were his. He and the others were not *members* of an order. They each *were* the order.

And together, their order understood the Stars. They knew the only path forward for humanity was to face those stars, to reckon with them and meet their destiny. They all knew with perfectly equal certainty that this was something that could not be ignored or denied, only faced, and they were all as one in their commitment to facing it.

It made Haegan feel certain and whole in a way nothing else ever had.

Not all of the Exile Order had taken the mark, not all of them saw like Haegan did. But he and those like him could serve as the binding force of the motley army. An Order of Stars, guiding his exiles into the future. He liked the sound of that.

He realized he hadn't responded to Silas for some time now. "I'm not happy. Not yet. But I am . . . satisfied. To have come this far. To be as close as we are now to changing the world. And it feels right to be back here."

Besides Haegan's personal recruits, their ranks included Sebastian Guerron's personal freelancer company, the White Hawk. Unlike most bands that bore the name, the White Hawk was a true company of men and women with hundreds of members. Most of them were inexperienced thrill seekers and treasure hunters, but their veterans included people who had been glintchasers since before the Starbreakers' time. They had been enough to repel the enemy attack on them without Haegan's intervention. And thanks to their owner's fortune, and months of work on Haegan's part, all of them were well-equipped with Old World weaponry. Swords that could slice a target at a dozen paces, bows that could pierce through stone, armor that could wade through fire.

They also had a handful of Academy mages Targan had recruited before getting himself killed. Though there were less than a dozen of them, they had actually been some of the most rapid adopters of the cult's Starborn power, and shown the most proficiency with it. Haegan was looking forward to seeing what they could do in battle.

"You think we can then?" Silas asked. "That we'll be enough?"

They should have had the baron's militia with them as well, but the raid on their hideouts had spooked Hitzkoff, and the man had thrown himself into a preemptive clash with the throne. Once, that would have infuriated Haegan. The baron breaking away from the plan could have ruined everything. But in the face of the task before him now, Haegan found it hard to care. Whether the crown suppressed Hitzkoff or the baron somehow seized the throne, Haegan would be the one to truly decide the fate of humanity. Here, they would either conquer the Starborn, or be wiped out. Nothing else mattered.

Haegan felt the liberation of that wash through him like a cleansing tide, and he was able to look at the situation with new eyes. In the face of the Starborn, the baron's forces wouldn't make much of a difference either way. Numbers were not what they needed for this fight—it was raw power, and that was what the Servitor Hearts were for.

What Haegan was for.

"I think if we are not, nothing humanity can raise will be, and we're already dead," Haegan said.

Silas frowned, and Haegan felt a twinge of disappointment. There was that lack of understanding again. Silas would say nothing, would follow orders without question, but only Haegan and the marked understood that in the face of inevitable end, the only choice was to confront it, no matter the results. Perhaps Silas would come to understand. Perhaps he would die never knowing, but following Haegan to the bitter end regardless.

That would be enough. Because Haegan wasn't alone anymore, and there were still days before they were prepared to take the final plunge into the jaws of oblivion. There was time for Silas to see.

There was time for everyone to see.

30

ASSEMBLED

When Phoenix called them all together, he didn't assemble them in the cathedral, or the palace, or even the Rusted Star. Instead, he told his old companions to grab their things and meet him in their old mansion. Elizabeth waited with him in the dining room—one of the few rooms that had kept its function even after Haegan and his operation had moved in.

It still rubbed him raw to think that Haegan's operation had been right under their noses, hiding behind wards and securities he'd created himself, but he shoved that irritation to the back of his mind. A shadow still hung over Elizabeth's face, and he briefly remembered the other things he'd shoved to the back of his mind.

Later.

Brass arrived first, eyeliner reapplied, hair freshly cut, and bloodied outfit swapped out for a clean one. Church and Angel were right behind him. Both of them already had their angelic weapons on their hips. Bart and Ruby came in after, which surprised Phoenix, since he hadn't thought to invite them. But if Church and the others thought they were fit to be here, who was he to argue? Ink and Lupolt teleported into the room in a flash of light, bringing in a faint whiff of ozone. Phoenix hadn't thought to invite them to this meeting either, but Elizabeth had, and the wizard gave her an appreciative nod when they arrived. Snow arrived last, nowhere to be seen one second, standing in the corner with arms folded the next. Everyone gathered looked at him, which was fair, given that he'd called the meeting in the first place, but it still made his stomach churn. He broke eye contact with all of them and felt a little better. He ran a hand through his hair and ended up rubbing the back of his neck. As he always did when combating stress, he focused on the task in front of him.

For a moment, Phoenix was twenty years old again. He couldn't count how many times they'd met in this dining room to make a plan or discuss a job, and now here they all were again.

Then he remembered what they were up against now, and a different memory came to him. Of a war council room in the palace, crammed to bursting with freelancers and servants of the crown all gearing up to face down the Servitor. He'd led this group before, against an enemy just like this. Although now, the odds were much worse.

"Here's everything we know," he said. "Haegan's lost his mind. He and his order are effectively a new Cult of Stars. Whatever their original plan might have been, now they're hell-bent on summoning the Starborn to pick a fight with them." And here, he dropped the first new information. "And he's going to do it in Relgen."

Ink raised an eyebrow, but it was Lupolt who pounced on the claim first. "How do you know?"

"Haegan's pet cultist told Snow in so many words," Phoenix said. "The Cult of Stars kills to attract the Starborn's attention, but they'd never killed enough people to make it work. Until Relgen. 'The dead city in the mountains.' They couldn't have done it without us digging up the Ending first. And now the Cult wants to rub our noses in it by summoning the Starborn in the same place we helped them get its attention."

His expression briefly tinged with anger before sobering.

"If the cult is right, and Relgen's fall drew the Starborn to us, then the Hearts will absolutely give Haegan enough raw power to pull it the rest of the way into our world. If he does . . . we're all dead."

"So, what's the bad news?" Ruby asked with a forced chuckle.

Phoenix frowned, and spread out several sheets of paper all covered in hastily sketched diagrams and familiar hand's scrawl. They were his own notes from the design of Haegan's new armor. "Haegan had me build him a suit of armor from the remains of the original Servitor and the suit he'd already been using. At a base level, he'll have enhanced strength and stamina, and protection from magic.

Any prayers or spells trying to affect his mind or body will slide right off, and he'll be able to take a lot of punishment. The armor also lets him wield the power of all the Servitor Hearts he's collected. Essentially, he *is* the Servitor, but smarter, and with two more Hearts than the original. On his own, he might be one of the strongest things any of us have ever faced. And he's got a small army backing him. Compositionally, we're looking at trained fighters armed with Old World weapons, most of the White Hawk, and at least a few Academy-trained mages, any of whom could *also* have the powers of the Cult of Stars."

"I was joking."

"I do actually have good news," Phoenix said. He glanced down at the papers on the table. "I made Haegan's armor. I can unmake it."

"So, what, we hold him down while you take a screwdriver to him?" Brass asked.

"I'll be making weapons to disrupt his ability to use the armor," Phoenix said. "It won't be perfect, but it'll give us a fighting chance."

"How long will that take?" Church asked.

"Another day, at least," Phoenix said. "Luckily, Haegan and Targan were already kind enough to bring me all the tools and materials I need. My old workshop's downstairs, loaded and ready to go. I start working as soon as we leave this room, but there's only so much I can rush spellforging. But, Haegan's moving all of his people to Relgen, and even with some of them teleporting now, there's a limit to how fast he can move that many people. Once they're all gathered, it's not an instant thing setting up a ritual strong enough to let a Starborn into the world. We *should* have time for this."

"Always love to hear that word in a plan," Angel muttered.

"Most of us here fought the Servitor," Phoenix said, glancing briefly at Bart and Ruby. "You all remember how it went. Our only choice is to assume we have the time to prepare. If we fight Haegan without countermeasures, we won't stand a chance."

Phoenix was proud of himself for not commenting on their odds *with* countermeasures. It had taken him a few years, but he had learned that there was a time and place for the facts. That time was not when you were staring down impossible odds. He surveyed the faces of everyone present, trying to gauge their reactions. He was never the best at reading people, and he couldn't get much beyond a generally grim impression. Bart came the closest to looking outright terrified, visibly pale with wide eyes. Ruby's jaw was tense, and she was twirling her hair around one finger. Elizabeth's fingers twitched furiously. Angel was scowling, Church frowned, and even Brass's grin had downgraded to a halfhearted smirk. He guessed that they all had a good idea of their odds even without him spelling it out.

He was surprised when Snow was the one to break the silence, and then even more surprised by what she said.

"Most of the White Hawk are amateurs," she put in. "The rest aren't slouches, but they're still *corporate* glintchasers. No substitute for the real thing. Silas is the best fighter out of Haegan's people, and he isn't a match for any of us. Ink just took the title of strongest mage in Corsar, and I don't see any of the social rejects Targan found taking it from her. Some of them have cult powers too?" She shrugged. "We're the Starbreakers. Killing the Cult of Stars is what we do."

"We're not *all* Starbreakers, but otherwise, well said," Ink said. She eyed the diagrams and sketches Phoenix had laid out like a huntress examining her prey. "There are additional advantages I can contribute to the cause. A not insubstantial fraction of the royal artifact collection came from things the Academy confiscated from this very house after your fall from grace." Her face took on an amused smirk. "How would you all like your things back?"

At that, the Starbreakers collectively straightened. As the most accomplished glintchasers in Corsar, the Starbreakers had amassed a sizable collection of Old World artifacts over their seven-year-long career. They personally carried their most useful items with them on the job, but the bulk of everything they'd acquired had been stored in the house, and seized by the crown when the kingdom had found them partially to blame for the death of Relgen. It would be a fortune's worth of artifacts—and an arsenal's worth of weapons and armor.

"That . . . would help," Phoenix said.

"I'll put in an official requisition order to the crown at once," Ink said. She turned her head. "Lupolt?"

"I'll have everything delivered within the hour."

Ink beamed. "I love having him around. It makes everything so much faster."

"All right then," Phoenix said. "Everyone, gear up as soon as that gets here, and do anything else you need to get ready for a fight. This is our only shot, so we have to make it our absolute best. I'll have a progress update in about twelve hours, but for now, expect to leave in twenty-four. If you need me before then, you know where to find me."

31

FAREWELLS

Phoenix wasn't sure what time it was when he finished the countermeasures for Haegan's armor. His home workshop in Akers had a clock and automatically dimmed the lightstones after midnight, but he'd never installed anything like that in this space. The mansion's lab was the workshop of a younger man with nothing but free time, endless creative energy, and a girlfriend who kept even later hours than he did.

He'd missed being that younger man many times. Normally, spending hours tinkering away at a project like this made him feel closer to that version of himself, like he was recapturing a lost spark. Tonight, he felt like he was hiding. Burying himself in problems to solve so he could avoid the dark thoughts that still lingered in his mind.

Some of it was fresh. He'd almost killed his wife. He'd cost her her wings. He'd given Haegan all the tools he needed to kill them all. But some of the thoughts were old, long buried and resurrected by the mess they were in now. He'd gotten Elizabeth hurt by asking her to fight the Servitor with them. He'd failed to stop the Ending eight years ago.

He'd dug it up in the first place.

He was trying to listen to Angel's advice, to pack up the guilt and self-loathing into a box and kick it into a corner to deal with later, but he was having trouble keeping the box shut. And so working had become a shield to cower behind. That box contained a different man. The man who'd turned up sobbing on Elizabeth's doorstep, alone, exiled, and crushed beneath the weight of a dead city. He couldn't go back to that man. Not now. Not ever.

"Arman?"

Elizabeth's voice was like a lightning bolt to the chest. He flinched, and his heart jumped. It must have been late, if she was coming down to check on him. He didn't want to look at her. The focus his work had given him was already precarious, and her eyes could shatter it.

"The disruptors are finished and charging," he said, only daring to glance at her out of the corner of his eye. She was standing in the workshop doorway, carrying something.

"You're finished then?"

Technically yes. The devices he'd built could charge without any input from him, but he could monitor their progress, or double-check his math, maybe piece together more backups. His new weapon was already finished, but maybe he should do a quick disassembly to clean and fine-tune it. He could find something to do. Something to keep him focused, keep him moving.

"I'm not tired," he lied. She would want him to get some rest, and he really should *try* to sleep. But he still wasn't ready to stop working. "And I want to run some numbers before I turn in."

"*Arman.*"

Her voice was gentle, but firm, and left no room for argument. It told him in no uncertain terms that he wasn't getting away from her. He never could, of course. With a sigh, he set down his pencil, turned around—and froze in place.

A tiny baby girl, only a year old, was fidgeting in Elizabeth's arms, her green eyes bleary and half-closed. Robyn was tired, but already falling asleep. Elizabeth had to hold her stuffed owl in one hand. Elizabeth's eyes, back to their original blue, sparkled as they met his.

She smiled softly, and barely above a whisper, she said, "Come hold your daughter."

Any sense of work, of fighting, of being a glintchaser evaporated, and Arman floated forward slowly as if in a dream. His eyes never left Robyn. His arms reached out for her without his conscious input, and he cradled her against him. Elizabeth stayed close, resting her forehead softly against his.

The world shrank to nothing but his wife and daughter. The feel of them against him, soft as clouds. The smell of them, like a summer breeze. Only then, with everything else gone, did it truly hit him that he had been taken from his family, that he hadn't seen either of them in weeks. Now the reunion broke a dam inside him, and relief washed through him like a flood. His whole body shuddered as he cried.

Elizabeth rubbed small circles in the back of his neck and whispered softly to him. "Shh. We're here. You're here."

It steadied him. Filled him, like wind in sails. It was as if he'd been walking around with pieces missing from him, and now he was *whole* again. He hadn't even realized how much being pulled away from them had hurt him, how much Haegan had hurt him. But Elizabeth had, and known exactly how to fix it.

His family did what Angel had only tried at. They reoriented him and his priorities. They showed him what was important, and what wasn't, clearing his thoughts and crystallizing his resolve. His mistakes and failings weren't important. Elizabeth was important. Robyn was important. Haegan was not going to take them from him, or him from them, whether he had six Servitor Hearts or a thousand. And by every saint and star there was, he was not summoning a Starborn on Arman's watch.

Elizabeth saw the change in him, and smiled.

"Your family brought her," Elizabeth explained. "Your sister had them all on a skiff the minute I told them we'd found you."

"Layla's not going to like me going after the people I was just rescued from," Arman said. His sister had never approved his choice to become a freelancer, even before it had all gone horribly wrong. To her, it was nothing but asking for trouble.

"No, she won't," Elizabeth agreed.

A moment of silence passed between them before Arman dared to ask the question silently hanging over them. "Is she right?"

Elizabeth's fingers twitched, itching for the comfort of a bowstring. She gestured to their daughter with her head. "Could you look her in the eye, knowing you hadn't fought?"

"No."

Elizabeth nodded. "Neither could I."

Arman gingerly stroked his daughter's hair, and whispered to her in Gypic.

"My little star. We're going to fix the world for you."

"What's this do?" Thalia held up a glass orb the size of her fist, the latest object of curiosity she'd pulled out of the boxes of the Starbreakers' old equipment. The entire treasure trove was stacked up in a guest room in the Rusted Star. The collection taken from the manor largely represented a haul of backups, Phoenix's half-finished prototypes, and nostalgic keepsakes. There'd been a few gems, but the bulk of it now sat here in the Star, offering little more than fuel for Thalia's idle curiosity.

"Tap it on that gray circle," Angel instructed.

Thalia did so, and the orb gave off the steady white glow of lightstone as it levitated out of Thalia's hand, hovering at shoulder height. When Thalia stepped backward, it floated after her. When she stopped, so did the orb.

"That's fun," Thalia said. She poked the orb, and it bobbed in the air.

"It's junk," Angel said. "I think we took that off a wizard trying to make plants sentient?"

"Did he do it?"

"He never got the army of walking trees he wanted, but he had a pet shrub that could dance in its pot."

Thalia laughed, and that cracked Angel's stoically bored expression into a small smile. A moment of comfortable silence passed between them, as Thalia managed to deactivate the lightglobe and return it to its box, then came to sit on the bed with Angel.

"Copper for your thoughts?" Thalia asked.

"About what?"

Thalia shrugged. "Anything."

"Hmm." Angel considered for a moment. "Sorry. Banal thoughts are two glint a pop, and there's a premium on the profound ones."

"That sounds like overcharging."

"Is not. I've just been price gouged by shits like Brass who run their mouth for free."

Thalia laughed again, but the smile she wore after was smaller than before. "I'm scared."

Angel's lazy smile vanished, and she sat up straighter. A part of Thalia felt guilty for saying it, for ruining the easy mood of the evening, but she couldn't keep it down. Angel may have had practice staring down insurmountable danger, but Thalia didn't, and she wasn't sure practice would have helped her anyway. All of this—the impossible odds, the dizzying stakes, the dangerous magic—was normal to Angel in a way Thalia didn't think it would ever be for her.

"I'm not scared that Haegan's going to summon a star monster and end the world, or whatever he's doing," Thalia said. "I'd have to understand that to be scared of it. I'm scared for you. And I know how that sounds, but I've seen you dead once already. You aren't invincible, and these people are dangerous."

"I'll be fine," Angel stressed.

"Maybe. But maybe not. Neither of us know, and I'm not trying to talk you out of going or doing what you have to. I just need you to know that I'm scared."

"Look. Once Haegan and the Cult are buried, I promise to move the Star to the middle of bumfuck nowhere, or wherever you want, and we'll never have to deal with this bullshit again."

Thalia couldn't help the slight flutter in her chest at the way Angel phrased that, with the "we" and all the possibility that word contained. But the years had taught her there was a time to be gentle with Angel, and a time to be direct.

"Monica."

She breathed in the sound of her real name coming from Thalia. Whenever the other Starbreakers were around or involved, it was subconscious instinct to revert to her glintchaser name. To be the blunt instrument, the unbreakable wall, the occasional vessel of divine fury. She sometimes forgot that to Thalia, "Angel" was just a nickname her old companions called her. Being called by her real name made her feel so much . . . smaller. But not in a bad way, as if she were being diminished or belittled. It felt like a burden being lifted, like she was being given permission to stop being a towering figure of power and destruction and just be herself.

Thalia wore a proud but worried smile. "You are the most selfless, heroic person I have ever met. When you see people in danger, you can't not do something. That's not going to change. *You're* not going to change."

Monica's voice grew quiet. "I could."

"I don't want you to," Thalia said. "I want you to keep being this version of yourself. The version that cares. That likes who she is and what she does."

"So, what does that mean?" Monica asked.

"It means," Thalia said, taking a deep breath. "That I am going to be scared for you, probably for the rest of your life. Because somebody has to be, and maybe if you know that someone is, you'll actually remember to be careful out there. And then you'll come home."

Monica was quiet for a very long time as she stared into Thalia's eyes and saw how the adoration in them outweighed the fear. Her heart pounded in her chest, but for once, there wasn't a trace of divine power to it. It was such a small, mundane thing.

But she was a Sentinel. Some people couldn't even swing a blade hard enough to break her skin. She'd been bashed through brick walls, and come out the other side more annoyed than hurt. Someone who knew that, and worried anyway, touched her. It made her feel human, in a way nothing else did.

"I lost," she said, barely above a whisper.

Thalia blinked, but Monica kept talking before she could ask questions, because if she let herself stop now, she might never work up the courage to start again.

"The last time we fought in Relgen, I lost," she said. "The Cult had this enforcer leading the charge to steal the Ending. I went after him, Phoenix asked me if I needed backup. The others were already in their own fight. I thought they needed all the help they could get, and that I was fine on my own, so I told him no. And I lost. The Cult got past me, they got the Ending . . . and then we all lost."

Monica's hands flexed, remembering that day.

"Before that, with the Servitor? It kicked my ass. Me and the heavy hitters from half a dozen different companies all came at it. It killed everyone around me, and I couldn't do much more than get smacked around and watch before we finally brought it down. I've killed a lot of the Cult of Stars, but they're a pain in the ass, and if Phoenix says they're actually close to summoning a Starborn, then they're close.

"Any sane person would be fucking terrified going into this, but I'm just . . . ready," she continued. "The Cult's a disease. They get in people's heads and make them so afraid of the world and everything in it that they think the only solution is throwing ourselves at space monsters. They've killed, and they've hurt, and I want to stop them. I want them to never hurt anyone again, and I want it so bad that when I think about it, I start to shake. Stopping shit like them feels so right, but I don't feel heroic for it. I feel like I'm crazy."

Thalia placed a hand on her shoulder. "You're not crazy. Or if you are, it's a good kind."

Monica's chest loosened immensely, getting all of that out. But she had one last admission. Now, while she was still feeling open, and while they were both still safe and alive. "I really want to kiss you."

Thalia tucked some of her hair behind her ear. "What's stopping you?"

Now Monica felt heat rising, though it was still completely disconnected from her powers.

"I really don't know if I'm ever going to stop doing this. Fighting." Monica was restraining herself, but Thalia deserved a fair and honest warning of what she was getting into. "It's probably always going to be like this."

Thalia nodded, moving closer to her. "I know."

"I can't promise I'll come back. Not this time. Not any time."

She was close enough now that Monica could feel the warmth of her body even without touching her. "I know."

"You really deserve someone more normal than me."

"Monica." This time when Thalia said her name, her voice dropped a register, and it lacked any of the gentleness from before. "Kiss me."

So she did.

Arno knocked on the door of one of the mansion's bedrooms. If memory served, this one actually would have been Brass's room once, before the Academy had hollowed it out and then Haegan and his allies converted it into a sort of study. He entered only a moment later, and found Bart inside—along with Ruby.

She was half-sitting, half-leaning on a desk in one corner of the room, Bart standing in front of her, and when the vicar walked in, Bart took two steps away from her, and she stood up straighter. A pair of still smoldering, half-finished nails of the sort Brass liked to smoke sat in an ashtray on the edge of the desk, giving off a faint smell like burnt honey.

"Vicar," Bart greeted, unaccountably embarrassed. "What is it?"

Arno was surprised. Ruby had always seemed a little uncomfortable around Arno, but seeing Bart jumpy around him was new. It only took him a moment to piece things together—he had been their age once. Nerves always ran high before a battle, especially one this big with this much advance warning about how dangerous it was going to be. It was helpful to have someone to talk with, to keep yourself from drowning in your own thoughts, and Bart and Ruby were closer in age and experience to each other than they were to everyone else. It made sense they'd seek each other out, and conversations on the eve of a real battle could often be very personal things. The drug use fit the scenario as well, though for Bart's sake, Arno pretended not to notice that part.

"I didn't mean to intrude," Arno apologized. "I just wanted to talk for a minute, Bart."

"Sure," the youth said. He glanced back at Ruby. "I, uh . . . I'll be right back?"

"He will," Arno promised her.

"Sure." Ruby nodded, fingers drumming on the desk. "I'll be here."

Arno hadn't exactly intended it to play out this way, but he found himself taking Bart into the hall. The acolyte turned paladin threw one last anxious glance back at the door, as if expecting it to disappear behind him, before asking, "So . . .?"

"Bart, I want to apologize to you," Arno said. Bart looked confused. "I don't have the most favorable opinion on glintchasing. I know it can do real good, but as I've gotten older, I've started to focus on all the ways it goes wrong. How easily it turns messy and selfish. And because of all that, I didn't want this life for you. I think I wanted to give you the life that I wished I'd had instead. Something simple and small, helping people without all the danger and killing. And I never took into account that what might've been right for me isn't necessarily what's right for you. Everyone has a calling, Bart. Glint-chasing, fighting the good fight? It's not mine, not anymore. But it might be yours. That world needs people like you in it. And if you're going to do it, you might as well be equipped for it."

Arno slung the long, narrow case he'd been carrying off his shoulder, and flicked open its latches. Inside was a mace made of silver-white steel, grooves of yellow and purple energy running up its length before joining the flared head. The air around the weapon hummed like a struck tuning fork. As soon as Bart saw it, his eyes became transfixed.

"This was Angel's weapon, before we found Daybreaker," Arno said. "Phoenix called it a 'dispersal mace.' Angel just called it Crusher. It's light, can handle divine energy, and it hits like thunder."

He held the weapon case out to Bart, who gingerly reached out to take it. He stared at the weapon in quiet awe, and Arno could practically see the fantasies forming in the young man's mind.

"I want to give you Zealot too, one day," Arno said, hand resting on the angelic blade sheathed on his own belt. "But I do still need it this one last time. And it can be . . . a handful. I thought it best to start you with a weapon that doesn't have a mind of its own."

"Vicar, I . . . I don't know what to say," Bart said. "Thank you."

"Thank me by surviving this fight," Arno told him. "And by doing some good in the world."

Bart snapped Crusher's case closed with resolve. "I will. I promise."

Arno believed him. And he decided that if his life as a glintchaser had inspired this young man to grow into the hero Arno thought he could be, then maybe the legacy he'd left from all those years wasn't so bad after all.

"Good night, Bart," Arno said. "Renalt's strength to you."

"And his saint's guidance to you," Bart returned.

Bart hurried back to Brass's old room, where Ruby was still waiting for him, leaving Arno alone in the hall. The vicar's smile faltered slightly, thinking of the girl.

They had saved her, but it had been a near thing, and even now that her soul was free, her life would never be the same. She hadn't asked for any of this, but one chance encounter with disaster had nearly ruined her. He felt awful for all they'd put her through.

But he told himself that, in the end, they hadn't failed her. And they wouldn't fail anyone else tomorrow either.

It wasn't until he was halfway back to his own room that Arno remembered his previous conversation with Brass about Bart and Ruby, and an alternate explanation of what he'd walked in on earlier came to mind.

Oh.

The vicar briefly considered what, if anything, he should do with the realization. In the end, he simply kept walking, and tried not to think about it.

Snow had specifically paid for the Broken Cask to be empty tonight, so she felt a flash of irritation when somebody walked through the front door, until she realized who it was. Irritation was replaced by bemused resignation, and a small smile played across her lips.

"Hey stranger," Brass greeted.

Maybe it was the nostalgia of being back in the Broken Cask, maybe it was her still adjusting without the Heart of Ice, and maybe it was the bottle of wine she was halfway through, but Snow was actually happy to see Brass here.

It was probably the wine.

She met his eyes, gestured with her head to the bottle, and he grinned before taking a seat at the bar next to her. He produced his own wine glass, presumably from a bottomless pocket, and Snow poured him a drink.

"What are we drinking?" he asked.

"Guess."

Brass made a show of swirling the wine in his glass, breathing its scent, and taking an experimental sip. He smacked his lips. "Hernan Red, '98?"

"Riodante, '87."

"Ah, well, sommeliers are all bullshit artists anyway."

"You know, as a Siccaran, I think I'm legally obligated to kill you for saying that."

"Good thing you never let laws tell you what to do."

He smiled at her, and she rolled her eyes.

"Settling all right?" Brass asked.

"I finally stopped crying," Snow said. "I guess I feel more normal now. But also I've got no idea what that even means. And I'm still too fucking hot."

"Ain't that the truth." Brass winked, and she kicked him in the shin.

"Shut up," she said without malice. Brass laughed, even as he subtly shook out his leg.

"For what it's worth, you seem better," he said. "Happier, even."

"Hmm."

Snow didn't think happier was the right word for it. She felt much more aware of herself, and everyone around her, and she *cared* about everything more. But it was hard to be happy about getting her ass kicked and handing the enemy a weapon they were going to use to kill them all. Not to mention staring down another fight with that enemy only half as strong as she'd been before, and the knowledge that if they lost this time, it wasn't just one city that would fall. No, she wasn't happy. But it was easier to enjoy a friend and a glass of wine than before, and even the anticipation of a fight was carrying a thrill that it hadn't in ages. So there was that.

"Also, I always thought you looked better in black," Brass added after another sip of wine.

Snow was one of the few people who'd gotten a genuine upgrade out of their haul from the Academy. Shadedancer's Veil was a set of black leather armor, trimmed with midnight blue accents. It rendered her movements absolutely silent, let her walk on walls and ceilings, and gave her even greater mobility with her blinks. Not to mention it fit like a dream and had enough extra dimensional pocket space to contain an entire armory. It was leagues better than the armor she'd been wearing for years. But Phoenix had made the armor for her, and she intentionally hadn't worn it since they'd ended things.

That pettiness felt like it belonged to a different person. Neither she nor Phoenix were who they'd been back then, and now good armor was just good armor.

Brass had come out with a decent haul himself. A set of air walker boots that had the secondary benefit of just being a stylish pair of thigh-highs, a purple coat enchanted to be on par with armor for protection, and a belt full of bottomless pockets, which he'd stuffed with swords from his old collection.

"If you're going to keep flirting, I'm going to need another bottle," Snow said, walking behind the counter for just that. She'd only had Simon set aside the one—no sense in going into the fight of their lives hungover—but she knew where he kept the rest, and for her, nothing was ever locked.

"Make it two," Brass suggested, producing an already rolled nail. "I brought sober-ups."

"You know, I'm starting to remember why we were friends."

She took two bottles out of Simon's wine cabinet, left a stack of glint in their place, and poured new glasses for her and Brass. If she were honest with herself, she could admit that she wished the entire company was here. In the old days, the Starbreakers had always stuck close together in those moments just before big fights, as a way to savor all being together before everything hit the fan. One last drink, or meal, or shared campfire, just in case. Now that the Heart of Ice wasn't numbing everything, she wanted that feeling of closeness to others, craved it. And there was a real possibility that this could be their last chance. But in the absencc of a company, she settled for a partner.

They talked about everything, and nothing. Her family. His. Old times together, and things they'd gotten up to in their years apart. Whether or not losing the Heart had reignited any old flames for Phoenix—it hadn't—and how fucked it was they were going back to Relgen—very. They ran out of wine, climbed to a roof, and smoked something relaxing while staring at the moon and debating which saint was the hottest—Ellanour.

As far as last nights alive went, they could have done a lot worse.

32
THE CAVALRY

On a mountain ridge on the far north edge of Corsar, the Rusted Star rose out of the ground. When the Starbreakers walked out, they were greeted by a tiny, half-rotted wooden shack with the sign of Saint Beneger etched into the door. And despite themselves, and the near decade separating them all from this place, the five of them froze.

The shack was Saint Beneger's first temple. It was an anchor for the saint's power in the world. This was where, almost eight years ago, Church had teleported them in order to escape the death of Relgen. And it was where they'd torn each other apart. That was supposed to be behind them, but standing on that same ground left them all trapped in the ghost of that memory. For a breath, they were all thinking the same thing.

Please, let this time be different.

If they were alone, they might have just stood there, staring in silence. But Elizabeth came out behind them, followed by Bart, Ruby, and Thalia, and the presence of people without their shared scars was enough to bring the glintchasers back to focus.

The ruin that had once been the city of Relgen was visible from this distance. The day the city had fallen, you could have almost mistaken it for a whole, living place. The Ending only killed living things, leaving everything physical intact. Except for the crash site of the Rogue Imperia, everything in the city had been left untouched. Now, years later, there was no mistaking what it was. The banners that had once adorned the city walls had shredded away to tatters. Entire blocks of the city were blackened from fires that had been allowed to burn undisturbed, and structures had crumbled under eight years of neglect. To this day, nothing had grown in the circle of death that surrounded it, leaving the bordering terraces little more than barren plateaus.

At the same time, the city was more alive than it had been in years. Haegan's order were ants at this distance, but where they gathered, there was a suggestion of life and movement, and every so often, there was the brief flash of crackling silver smoke somewhere in the streets. As they watched, a building near the city's center crumbled down to its foundations.

"What are they doing?" Church asked.

Phoenix magnified his vision with his goggles to watch as men and women worked, some scouting, some demolishing buildings with magic, some tracing the pattern of massive arcane sigils into the streets. Finally, he spotted Haegan himself.

He stood at the top of a set of stairs that overlooked the city center, like an emperor surveying his domain. The gold and bronze Servitor armor made him into a towering figure, and the lights of six Servitor Hearts gleamed in the breastplate.

Silas stood stoic at Haegan's left side, hands folded behind his back. To Haegan's right stood a thin man in drab robes, hood pulled back to expose a forehead adorned with the ragged, twelve-pointed hallmark of the Cult of Stars that matched the one Haegan wore on his own forehead. Both of them wore the Servitor Heart harnesses Phoenix had made, which would let Haegan loan them a Heart's power if he chose.

"Clearing the field," Phoenix said. "They've got some big symbols to draw, and there are buildings in the way. Not to mention a group as big as theirs wants room to move and fight as a unit. They've got some skirmishing units scattered in the streets and rooftops, but it looks like they want the bulk of their forces standing and fighting."

"Could they actually do it?" Bart asked. "Kill the Starborn?"

"No," Phoenix said immediately. "What they've got could hold off an incursion of lesser Starborn, but if they make a hole big enough for a *real* one to come through—" He shook his head. "Haegan might be able to *hurt* it. But the Starborn could fight gods, and win."

"At least the old Cult was honest about feeding us all to the space squids," Brass said. "This whole 'blaze of glory' thing just seems like suicide with extra steps."

Before Angel could retort, there was a flash of light and Ink teleported onto the ridge with Gamma at her side, and eight more people behind them. The Cord of Aenwyn stood ready for battle, led by a tall, muscular man with dark skin, and short-cropped black hair. He wore a belt buckle shaped like the Arcane symbol for the number five, and sleeveless, white-and-bronze armor that exposed the tattoo of the Cord of Aenwyn's crossed spears and chains on his right shoulder.

"Quint," Phoenix greeted the Cord's leader with the firmest handshake he could muster. Quint's own grip still crushed his, and Phoenix suspected the man was holding back. "Thanks for taking the job."

"Thank the High Inquisitive," Quint said. "It's her payroll we're on."

"I couldn't very well let the Starbreakers take on the Servitor reborn without the Cord of Aenwyn to save them," Ink said. "Where would the symmetry be in that?"

Phoenix scoffed, but the battle of egos between the Starbreakers and the Cord had died a long time ago. Mostly. "It will be nice having you for backup. I know we had a lot more than just our two companies last time, but we're going to have to make up the difference with experience."

"Just two?" Quint asked Ink, who in turn asked Elizabeth, "You didn't tell him?"

Elizabeth shrugged even as her husband shot her a questioning look. "He had a lot on his plate."

"Didn't tell me what?" Phoenix asked.

She gave him an affectionate smile.

"While you were working, and the rest of you were off preparing to be big damn heroes, I decided to send out a few messages that the Starbreakers needed help."

At that moment, a bellowing roar echoed through the mountains. Every glintchaser on the mountain besides Bart and Ruby drew weapons, and only because they were too stunned to remember to brace for a fight. A massive, coppery blur shot overhead, banking into a hard turn before coming around, beating a pair of massive, leathery wings to slow its descent. Its reptilian head arced up in an arrogant display as it landed.

There was no mistaking the creature for anything but what it was—a juvenile dragon. And riding on its back were two people: A young, dark-skinned boy in leather armor, who dismounted first, and an elven woman with hair the color of an autumn forest, who let the young man assist her to the ground. As soon as the elf was clear of its back, the dragon surged forward to nuzzle into the waiting arms of Elizabeth.

"Hey Stixxy!" she laughed. "Did you miss me? Yes you did! Who's a good dragon?"

Phoenix recognized all of them immediately—Sinnodella, one of the last elves alive on Asher and Elizabeth's mentor. Stixaxlatl, her pet dragon. And—

"Dietrich?" Phoenix gawked.

The warden of Cutters Place gave a broad grin, and rested his hand on the axe-shortsword hybrid weapon Phoenix had made him only a few months ago. He was only nineteen, but he carried himself with swagger and pride that befit the protector of a burgeoning city on the edge of the Iron Forest. "I was in the neighborhood. And how could I say no to another chance to fight alongside my heroes?"

"Always a pleasure, Dietrich," Brass said fondly. "Who are you again?"

Before he could answer, a breeze swept through, carrying a fortune teller's card wreathed in pink light and depicting the image of a bird. It fluttered around for a moment, then suddenly fanned out into hundreds of cards that formed a swarming mass just before exploding in a puff of pink smoke. Where they had been now stood three women: there was Canvas, standing off to the side in her Academy robes, and with her were the two other surviving members of the Broken Spear. Standing front and center as she would at any opportunity, dressed as the sailing captain she'd been for the last decade, was Tarot, still holding a blazing pink playing card between her fingers. To the other side stood Faith, priestess of the Watcher, with her straight dark hair braided down her back and her priest's vestments worn in conjunction with chipped armor made of a monster's bones.

Elizabeth beamed to see the three other surviving members of her old company, and they grinned straight back. If not for the dragon still nuzzling her, she'd have already crushed them all in a group hug. Canvas and Faith decided to rush her for one instead.

"Sorry we're late," Tarot said as she tossed back her fiery red hair. "But you know we like to make an entrance."

As if taking that as a cue, golden rays of light shot down from the sky all around them, briefly bathing the ridge in a divine aura. When the light faded, the Order of Saint Ricard stood before all those gathered, each member standing where a beam of light had struck. Dozens of knights of the crown, wearing everything from chain mail to priest vestments to a thief's leathers. Hilda, the order's commander, exchanged a single nod with Angel before turning her attention to Phoenix.

"It is the charge of this Order to repel any invasion of the kingdom," Hilda declared, her golden hair still shining in the afterglow of her entrance. "Invasions of Starborn count."

Tarot stared at the single fortune teller's card in her hand and looked unaccountably upstaged.

Phoenix took in the influx of allies. This was so much more than he'd been expecting to work with. The weight that had been mounting on his shoulders from the moment he'd seen Saint Beneger's shack lifted. He was starting to believe they actually had a real chance, and he could see on the faces of the other Starbreakers that they thought so too. And then, he heard a horn blow, and he forgot all about breathing. The horn, deep and resonant, came from a lone figure clad in furs and chain mail, crouched at the crest of the mountain above their ridge. In the distance, more horns echoed the first. And then a lightning bolt shot down from the sky, striking less than a dozen feet from where Phoenix stood.

Where it had struck, a woman knelt, clutching a blue and yellow spear taller than her that crackled and popped with power. Sparks leapt from the head, and tendrils of lightning arced up the shaft and across her body. She wore fur-lined chain mail, adorned with blue and yellow decorations. Her hair was the color of burnt caramel, mostly hanging loose down to her shoulders, except for a portion that had been braided to wrap around her head and join together at the back.

She stood up after a moment, carrying herself like a queen, because that was what she was.

Immediately, every Starbreaker except for their leader broke out into a smile, though everyone but Church's had a malicious tint to it.

Phoenix's head whipped toward Elizabeth in shock. "You called Astrid?"

Elizabeth shrugged as if she didn't see the problem. "What? There's two monarchs on this continent who would let you borrow their army, and Roland's is busy."

Astrid Silverspear, queen of the Frelheim, gave Phoenix a warm smile, and he struggled to remind himself he was a grown man in a very serious situation, and did not have time to be flustered over seeing his first ex-girlfriend.

"Hello, *fyra,*" she said with a heavy northern accent. "Your wife tells me we have a world to save."

On the mountaintop where there had only been a single man before, slowly, more and more heads began to emerge. Frelheimer warriors, some clad in thick furs and armor, some with white hair and wearing almost nothing. All of them armed, all of them looking eager for a fight.

Phoenix cleared his throat. He had to admit, now he was feeling *much* better about their odds.

"You didn't think to mention any of this last night?" Phoenix asked Elizabeth.

In response, she gave him a triumphant grin. "You can say thank you."

"I love you."

"Close enough."

Phoenix turned his attention back to the city of Relgen, looking at it and the fight ahead of them with new eyes. They were still most likely outnumbered, especially when he factored in the strength Haegan himself represented, but now, they did have real numbers to work with. They had options, but also new challenges brought on by a larger group. For a few seconds, he stared silently, the rest of the world disappearing as he worked the puzzle over in his mind.

Then, with the eyes of his company, his wife, and all of their gathered friends and allies on him, he turned. "All right. Here's the plan."

33
SUMMONED

Even with hundreds of armed men and women gathered in its center, the city of Relgen was eerily quiet. The immediate area was clear of structures, leaving the Exile Order surrounded on all sides by silent facades and empty windows like the mountains surrounding a valley. Columns of putrid smoke rose up from the perimeter, where the partially mummified bodies that still littered the streets had been gathered and burned. The stench was carried around on a bitter, late autumn wind, which kicked up gray clouds as it whistled by. The streets and even some of the people had been dusted by a layer of ash and powderized stone, the remnants of buildings Haegan had obliterated to clear the field.

Teams of mages were positioned around the perimeter of the newly cleared city center, working to sketch out the massive arcane sigils necessary for the summoning they were attempting, while the bulk of their forces remained in a loose gathering in the center, ready to assemble into fighting ranks when the moment came.

Except for the mages, who would be working in concert to keep the Starborn contained within the summoning circle, the bulk of their forces would not be engaging the ultimate monster directly. They would only be doing battle with the lesser aberrations while Haegan faced the true threat himself. Still, the prospect of fighting even *near* a Starborn was weighing heavy on many of them, Silas included. They glanced nervously at the sky, fidgeted with their armor and weapons. Some bounced in place or went on short jogs. To their credit, no one ran off. But Silas knew they were afraid. The only ones who weren't were those followers who had adopted the power of the Cult of Stars, and Silas wasn't sure he found their placid eagerness reassuring either.

The unnatural stain that lingered in the city wasn't helping. There was a reason that even after the initial fall, Relgen had never been reclaimed. The land itself carried a haunted, unwelcoming edge to it.

Nothing grew in Relgen, nothing rotted naturally within it. Animals and even insects were completely absent. The whole place radiated a kind of sterile aura that suggested nothing living should ever be here. It got to Silas more than anything else. In the privacy of his own mind, he could admit that he didn't want to be here.

And yet, here he was.

Silas had known what he was signing up for from the moment Haegan emerged from the city of Relgen all those years ago, face streaked with tears, fists shaking, and swearing that he would change things, whatever the cost. They were fighting for a world where humanity wasn't constantly one artifact mishap or monstrous rampage away from a new collapse. He had known they would face both established powers in Corsar and existential threats from the Old World and beyond. But he had imagined fighting those battles alongside the Haegan he'd known then. The son of a soldier, the friend of his father, and the last knight of the Purple Rose. A man of such fire he could have snuffed out the hells themselves, such firm resolve that if a mountain fell on him, it would break into gravel. The Haegan who Silas had devoted himself to for all these years had been an unstoppable spear, driving forward toward his goals.

But things had changed. Haegan wasn't pushing forward. He was being pulled, inexorably, toward a terrible conclusion. Toward this conclusion.

Silas understood the shape Haegan's vision had taken. If the apocalypse was out there, hovering, waiting, why not turn and face it with everything you had? It had an appeal, fighting the danger instead of living like it didn't exist. He could get behind that, and had. But of late, there was a fatalism to

Haegan's outlook that left Silas uneasy. Sometimes, it felt as though Haegan honestly didn't care whether they won or lost at all.

How much of that had always been a part of who Haegan was? How much of it had come from his years spent preparing to fight to reclaim control of Asher's destiny? From his death at the hands of the Starbreakers? From the new mark on his forehead? Silas could only guess. But, standing at Haegan's side, looking out over the army they had assembled and armed, it was a little late to be getting cold feet. Silas may not be a true knight, but he was close enough that he would not let his dedication crumble in the face of fear or uncertainty. The fight was chosen. There was nothing to be done about it but win.

Rosa appeared in front of him in a cloud of crackling silver smoke, and Silas managed not to stare at the still fresh symbol of the Cult of Stars adorning her forehead. In a flash of light from Rosa's bracelet, René was at her side.

"All sigil teams have completed their work and are in position," Rosa reported.

"Squad leaders are all reporting ready for battle," René added. "But . . ."

Unlike Silas, she *did* glance at the mark on her sister's forehead. The one René had opted *not* to adopt. Silas had never had a hard time distinguishing the twins. Now, it seemed no one would.

"Go on," Silas said, getting her attention off the mark and on him.

"Two of our patrols haven't reported back in, both from southwestern blocks," René said.

"Bandits or ferals?" Silas asked.

There were a few people in Relgen. Some very desperate or very foolish criminals looking for places to hide or abandoned buildings to loot, and some insane vagrants who'd gone mad wandering the empty city and drinking in its hostile atmosphere. They'd had to deal with both sporadically while waiting for their forces to gather and setting up in the city center.

"Hard to say," René said. "We don't get much of either in that part of the city."

Silas tried to think of a scenario in which one of their patrols would be delayed and not signal an alert or call for help. His imagination proved lacking, but when he looked to Haegan for support, the commander and his Cult of Stars prisoner both were staring up at the sky as if transfixed.

"Now," the Prisoner said. "It should be now."

"Yes," Haegan agreed. "Silas, signal the order to form ranks."

Even with all his unease, Silas did not hesitate to obey. With the blow of a horn, and the launching of a crossbolt that burned green in the air, the Exile Order was called to action. Immediately, the men and women in the center of their formation began to arrange into squads and fighting lines. Around the perimeter, mages began work through the early steps of their joint summoning spell. The sigils around the city center lit up, causing the dusty streets to give off an off-white glow. All around, banks of crackling, silver smoke began to roll in like fog, hanging low to the ground while a matching cloud formed in the skies overhead.

Haegan himself wasn't needed yet, but already the Servitor Hearts in his chestplate shimmered as if waking up, and his eyes crackled the same colors as the smoke gathering. Silas cleared his throat.

"Sir? What about the missing patrols?" he asked. The commander had heard René's report, even if it had only been directed to Silas.

"Our people can take care of themselves," Haegan said. "And it will take more than bandits or vagrants to stop us now."

His eyes never left the cloud of silver smoke forming in the air as he spoke, and Silas knew from the certainty in his commander's voice that was the last word on the matter until the battle was over. He consoled himself that Haegan was, as always, right. There was no stopping this now.

As the silver smoke overhead swelled to encapsulate the city center that they'd cleared, Haegan stepped forward. In the distance, thunder pealed through the clouds. The wind picked up, and heat rose around Haegan even as frost formed on his armor. Every seam in his armor shined with brilliant golden light, and around him, shadows darkened. The crackling silver smoke in his eyes ran with streaks of purple, and veins of the same color energy rose in his skin. Instinctually, everyone around him, even the Prisoner, took several steps back.

"My brothers and sisters!" Haegan bellowed with a voice that echoed like thunder, filling the city. "For too long, we have clung to scraps. We have relied on scavengers and thieves to protect us from the very monsters they dig up, and our leaders have cowered behind walls while the world falls ever further into ruin. Starting today, the hiding ends. Starting today, we settle our claim to this world. Starting today, we face the Stars with eyes open!"

Haegan thrust his hands forward, and the Hearts in his chest became blazing suns of color as a beam of burning light tore from him, burrowing into the smoke cloud as lightning arced across the sky. All around the city center, the glow of the sigils went from off-white to brilliant violet as the summoning spell linked with Haegan's will and the power of all six Servitor Hearts. The cloud of silver smoke detonated, sending out a multicolored shock wave that passed overhead like a ripple. And where the cloud had been, now were cracks in the sky. They were jagged chasms and rivers of black that glowed purple at the edges, suspended unnaturally in the air above, and stretching out so that from the ground, they seemed to cover a quarter of the sky. And, very slowly, they were expanding. Below, the Exile Order let out a chorus of cheers and battle cries. At Haegan's side, Silas tightened his grip on his quicksilver swords, and the Prisoner grinned.

"Do you have any idea what a sky repairman costs these days?"

The voice of one man sounded muted coming off the back of Haegan's own booming proclamation, but Silas still recognized it, and immediately honed in on the source. One lone figure, marching straight up the middle of their forces formation. A gray cloak flew off the man's body, carried on the wind, revealing a bright purple outfit, thigh-high boots, and a shining war rapier held at the ready. His short brown curls had been coiffed and tossed to one side, matching his lopsided grin.

Brass shook his head and made a *tsk* sound, as if he were a disappointed parent. "Someone's going to have to pay for that."

He was less than two dozen feet from Silas and the others with Haegan. How he'd gotten that close without anyone seeing him or stopping him, Silas had no idea, but he wasn't going to let the Starbreaker take another step.

"Stop that man!" Silas shouted to the soldiers closest to Brass, even as he drew his own weapons and dashed out to meet him.

Brass only smirked as dozens of enemies converged on him. He feinted, sidestepped, and ducked, expertly weaving around the first few attempts to subdue him. His sword danced around him, never touching another person or even their weapon, and yet fending them all back. No one could parry his attacks, as he simply glided around every attempted defense and forced his opponents to dodge or be skewered.

Silas arrived only a moment before Rosa, who teleported in with another cloud of smoke, and René used her bracelet to teleport to her twin sister's side.

"Back!" Silas ordered the soldiers. He had dared to hope with numbers and arcane arms, the rank and file members of the order would be enough to take Brass. But if they weren't, he wanted them clear. He and the twins would need room to fight if they had any chance.

Silas struck first, using the quicksilver cord attached to his swords to swing them out like bladed whips—and they passed straight through Brass's chest as he made no move to defend himself.

Silas came to an abrupt halt as he stared at the image of Brass, which was already dissolving into the air. The illusory Brass winked, and Silas felt his stomach drop. A diversion. But where—

Snow stepped out of thin air behind Haegan, who only just brought up a hand in time to summon a gust of wind and deflect the fan of knives the assassin threw. Two of them exploded in midair as they careened off course, throwing shards of what looked like orange glass everywhere, while the third flew straight back into Snow's waiting hand even as the wind pushed her back. She blinked out of sight, gone as quick as she appeared.

At the same time, an arrow tipped with a glowing orange head sailed straight for Haegan's chest. It froze in midflight, suspended in Haegan's telekinetic grip.

A bolt of orange energy from the same direction slammed into Haegan, only an instant after he'd caught the arrow. His knees buckled, and the arrow clattered to the ground.

Haegan hit the ground with a sonorous clang, unable to support the weight of his own armor. The light of the Servitor Hearts, as well that of the street sigils and the edges of the cracks in the sky, all flickered with instability. The progress of the cracks' spread across the sky stuttered and slowed. A spike of alarm shot through Silas even as he scanned their surroundings for the next angle of attack.

Next to him, the Prisoner let out a dark chuckle. "Starbreakers."

The Heart of the Sky grew brighter on Haegan's chest even as the others continued to flicker. With obvious effort, he struggled to stand back up. He was doing something, Silas just had no idea *what.*

"Phoenix and the Winged Lady are on the rooftop to the south. I can't sense Snow, but the others are—" Haegan drew up short, surprised. "When did they get an *army*?"

Silas gaped in utter confusion, but before he could ask any questions, the fallen arrow Haegan had stopped earlier exploded in a burst of orange, and Haegan collapsed again. Silas was at his side in an instant.

"Sir?"

"Phoenix," Haegan growled, and it was all the explanation Silas needed. The spellforger had done something to Haegan's armor.

Haegan pulled the Heart of Flames and held it out to Silas. The situation was clear, they needed the Hearts' power now, and if Haegan couldn't use it, then Silas needed to supplement with his harness. Silas wasn't sure how he felt trusting a weapon made by Phoenix in that moment, but there wasn't much choice. For his part, Haegan looked ready to tear into the Starbreakers with his teeth, functioning armor or not. It wasn't exactly a comforting expression to see on his commander's face.

Fighting down his doubts, Silas seized the Heart of Flames. At the same time, war horns sounded, and a dragon roared.

34

BATTLE

The flattened city center exploded into a flurry of color and sound as Frelheimer warriors and knights of Saint Ricard clashed against the Exile Order. People teleported around the battlefield in clouds of smoke. Beams of divine light punched holes through armor. Balls of fire erupted in the middle of formations, and lightning crashed down from the sky.

Haegan's forces outnumbered the Starbreakers', but the Starbreakers' side was making up the difference with raw power. Stixaxlatl strafed the battlefield, spraying caustic acid from his jaws while Sinnodella, on his back, loosed arrows that exploded into showers of thorns as they flew. Drummer from the Cord of Aenwyn brought his warhammer down on the street, and the ground in front of him broke apart in a shock wave that toppled a dozen men. Naomi from the Order of Saint Ricard directed tiny orbs of divine light to dart through the enemy ranks, punching holes clean through anything they flew into.

Blocks away, Thalia and Gamma stood in the Rusted Star, watching a crude, illusory duplicate of the battle unfold, using a bird's-eye view to help the fighters on the ground spot and deal with problems before they could do any real damage.

Everything was going well. They'd caught the enemy by surprise—they'd been expecting an attack from the sky, not their flanks, and they were already most of the way to clearing a path for the heavy hitters to engage Haegan while he was still disabled. They took losses, but the enemy was losing more. Even though the cracks in the sky were still growing, Thalia felt like they were winning.

And then Haegan moved.

Phoenix had designed both Haegan's armor and Silas's harness, so he wasn't surprised when Haegan pulled the Heart of Flame out of his own breastplate and handed it to his lieutenant. That would bypass the disabling effect they'd saddled Haegan's armor with, and let Silas use the Heart, but it would still only be one active Heart instead of six. That was manageable.

But then Haegan disappeared in a flash of silver smoke, and Phoenix barely had time to process Gamma's warning over the coil that Haegan had moved before the knight commander appeared on the rooftop with him, and by then Haegan was already swinging a hammer.

"Shit!" Phoenix raised an arm, but even with his gauntlet's force shield, he was flung back. He half rolled, half staggered to his feet, inches from the edge of the roof, and only shooting out a line of spider silk kept him from teetering over the edge.

Next to him, Wings loosed an arrow into Haegan's back. The arrow didn't pierce the armor, but roots grew out from the shaft as it struck him, trying to wrap around his limbs and hold him in place. He tore them off with one hand and threw his hammer at her with the other.

"He's on us!" Phoenix shouted into the coil, before cycling his weapon and blasting Haegan with the highest power shot the gun could manage on short notice. At the same time, he fought down panic. He and Wings were *not* supposed to be the ones fighting Haegan head on.

His first shot managed to stagger Haegan, but the knight remained undeterred. Even as Phoenix kept up the barrage, Haegan summoned his hammer back to his hand, and swung. At first, Phoenix thought it would come up short. Then he noticed the Heart of the Sky on Haegan's chest blazing brighter than all the other Hearts. The hammer missed him, but the wall of wind that followed it lifted Phoenix off his feet and flung him from the roof like a rag doll.

To get a clear line of sight, he and Wings had taken up position on top of a seven-story building. He now wished they'd picked a shorter one. As he tumbled down, he had a moment where he could still see the roof, with Haegan and Wings both still on it. The moment stretched out in front of him in slow motion, as he imagined Wings facing down Haegan completely on her own. Desperately, he cycled his weapon's chamber, aimed—and fired another disruptor shot into Haegan's face. The knight caught the blast on his gauntlet, and the arcane carapace spasmed out from under his control. The Hearts flickered, and his stance buckled.

It was the most of an edge Phoenix could give her in the window of time he had. Catching himself with spider silk would have required giving up the shot on Haegan, and by the time he was able to use the silk line to climb back up, Wings might have already been dead. She'd still have to hold out on her own for a while, but at least now, she had a chance. That was all his Wings needed.

Sure enough, as Phoenix vanished beneath the edge of the roof, the last thing he saw was Wings transform her bow into swords and throw herself at Haegan.

Almost as soon as Haegan vanished, Silas saw a miniature sunburst from within the ranks of the Starbreakers' forces, and he recognized Angel instantly as she took off in the direction where Haegan had gone. Several others broke off from the battle to follow after her—enough for Silas to understand their true purpose.

They were here for Haegan, for the Hearts. The army of knights and warriors was just to keep Haegan's own order from reinforcing him. Any member of the Exile Order could fall in this battle. Most, Silas included, had been prepared to give their lives to this fight. But if Haegan fell, if they lost the power of the Servitor, then everything would be for nothing.

Thanks to the harness he wore and the handoff from Haegan, Silas felt the Heart of Flame's power blazing inside him. It urged him forward, stoked by his adrenaline. Rosa and René were with him. With the two of them at his side and the power of the Heart, they could break through to the other side of the battlefield and reinforce Haegan. The edges of his quicksilver swords glowed white hot, and he whipped one forward at the end of a long cord, intent to burn a path through to his commander. But before it could sear through an enemy's exposed back, a snow white sword blade darted out of the crowd to meet it, batting it off course.

Brass nimbly stepped out of the fray and into Silas's path, steam coming off his weapon as the blade visibly shrank. He shook his head. "Serves me right for using a sword made of ice." With a sigh, he tossed the weapon aside, and withdrew a new sword from a bottomless pocket at his hip, this one gleaming with a mirror's shine.

"Now, where do you think you're going?" he asked with a grin.

Months of frustration came to a boil as Silas set his sights on the real Brass, who became in that moment a symbol of every setback, every delay they had all suffered. And now, he was getting in between Silas and Haegan. But not for long.

Rosa acted before he could, a wicked sneer on her face. She sank down into the smoke that still gathered around their ankles like the ground had swallowed her, vanishing completely. She came back out a moment later, now behind Brass. The swordsman's grin never wavered, as he sidestepped a stab in the back without looking. Then, Snow blinked into sight, also behind him.

She met Rosa daggers against sword, forcing the younger woman back as Brass parried Silas's next few attacks. Brass's sword flashed red hot with each impact of steel, but the weapon held together. After a brief exchange, all parties fell back, Brass and Snow going back to back, Silas and the twins fanning out to encircle them.

"You could have stayed away," Silas said. "We let you live. You could have stood back, and let us finish this."

Brass's smile turned rueful. "We really couldn't. Starbreakers. Starborn summoning. It's a branding thing, I'm sure you understand."

"Your leader's drinking the Cult's piss by the gallon," Snow said. "If he summons a Starborn, he's not going to fight it, he's just going to be the first person it kills."

Brass held his blade forward in question as much in defense. "It's not too late to make the smart play here, Silas."

For a beat, Silas felt something in him slip. Snow's words had found a weak point in his resolve, striking at his unease over their involvement of the Cult of Stars. A seed of doubt, planted the very first time Haegan had explained to him where the silver smoke came from, watered every time Haegan had acted strange, was now beginning to flower. His worst fears whispered to him, and the image of the Cult of Stars' mark on Haegan's forehead hung heavy in his mind.

But then Silas remembered the last time he had abandoned Haegan to the Starbreakers. The day Haegan had died. He hadn't been with Haegan then, or when the Cult of Stars had attacked and forced their power onto him, or even walked the streets of Relgen alongside him. Silas could point to so many times he hadn't been by Haegan's side when he needed him most. And he couldn't help but think that if he had been there, Haegan wouldn't have died, wouldn't have needed to rely so heavily on powers like the Cult of Stars. Wouldn't seem so divorced from the man Silas had once followed without question. And he refused to fail Haegan again.

"I don't care about the Cult," Silas said. "I care about *him*. I *believe* in him."

Brass shrugged. "Well, so much for the smart play."

"You're all nothing but cowards," Rosa spat. "You only know how to protect yourselves and run away from the messes you make. We're different. We are knights, and we will change this world forever."

"You're delusional. And you're not knights," Snow said. "You're the Cult of Stars."

Rosa growled, but before any of them could move, a blackened, thorn-covered vine lashed out from the chaos of the battlefield. She had to turn to slice it out of the air, and then Bart tackled her shoulder first at a full sprint. Wearing chain mail, and fueling his body with divine power, he sent them both tumbling away. Ruby was on his heels, wielding tendrils of thorns like whips and immediately hounding René.

Silas swung with his own weapons to try to defend the twins, and in that opening, Snow and Brass moved as one to take him.

Back on a rooftop across the square, Wings came down on Haegan with both blades, aiming for the neck. She wasn't normally a decapitation person, but she was a mortal woman facing down a human Servitor. There was no room to hold back in this fight. And even still, she was too slow.

Haegan's gauntlet came up in time to block her, and then he drove the head of his hammer into her stomach. Without her own armor's enchantments, her ribs would have caved in. As it was, she had to roll with the hit, and was still winded and thrown back.

Blocking or parrying was out of the question, so instead she danced around him, slashing for any exposed joint in the armor as she dodged blows that cracked stone wherever they landed. She stayed alive, but she barely left a scratch. The entire time, she could feel the absence of the Heart of the Sky. She'd molded her entire fighting style around the speed it had given her, and without it, she felt like she was made of lead.

Her sword struck Haegan's gauntlet, the Heart of Ice flashed in his breastplate, and ice raced up her sword and crawled across her hand. The cold came as an instant, burning shock, and Wings let out a sharp gasp. The only reason she didn't drop the sword was that it had stuck frozen to her hand. Her next step came down unsteady on a patch of ice that had spread out from Haegan's boots, and she slipped. She knew, even as she fell, she was dead if she didn't do something drastic. She pulled an arrow from her quiver even as she hit the ground, and threw it. The explosive arrow detonated in Haegan's face, catching them both in a fireball.

Haegan staggered, and Wings rolled desperately away and onto her feet. Her armor was smoldering, and her skin screaming from new burns in a dozen places, but it beat being crushed to paste under Haegan's hammer. Transforming her swords back into a bow broke off the ice still clinging to one of them—taking some of her skin with it—and she loosed several arrows, each one expanding into a tangle of roots that wrapped around Haegan's body until finally, even he was struggling to move.

Wings stood in front of Haegan with an arrow drawn back, and for a moment, she wasn't standing on a roof in the ruins of Relgen, but on a street in Loraine, and instead of Haegan, she was staring down the Servitor itself. The roots holding him in place were already beginning to creak and snap under his strength. They wouldn't hold him, she was burned and bleeding, and the world around her had devolved into a war zone. Her body shook, and her hair was in her face. She loosed her last arrow at the eye slit of Haegan's helmet.

At the same time, the Heart of the Sky flashed green in his breastplate.

The air exploded out from around Haegan with the force of a thunderclap. Wings's arrow was knocked off course, bits of roots flew off him like shrapnel, and she was thrown off her feet. She loosed another arrow in desperation, but it was off by inches, and pinged off Haegan's helmet as he wrenched himself free of the remaining roots that bound him. As he did, all of the Servitor Hearts in his chest began to glow. The wind whipped into a frenzy, lifting Haegan into the air in an icy cyclone while overhead, the clouds rumbled, and all around, tiles of chunks of the roof were ripped into the air. Phoenix's disruptor shot had worn off. Out of time and staring down the Servitor armor's full power, Wings did the only thing she could think of.

She threw herself off the roof.

Wings shot out a vine arrow and used it to turn her fall into a swing as a torrent of lightning obliterated the rooftop, raining debris down on her. She crashed through the window of an adjacent building, rolled with the landing, and came up in a sprint. Outside, Haegan flew after her, and where he went, lightning followed. Glass and stone exploded around her as she ran, peppering her from all sides. She ignored it, making a beeline for another window at the far side of the room and diving out to finally reach the street level.

Haegan came around a moment later, still aloft in a cyclone of wind, ice, and stone. Looming high above, Wings expected more lightning, or maybe a blast from one of the other Hearts he had. Instead, he extended a hand toward the building she'd just escaped, which was already half crumbled from several lightning blasts. With a squeeze of his fist, he brought the entire thing down on top of her. There was nowhere to run. Nothing to hide behind. She brought up her arms to shield herself instinctually, no options left but to hope her armor would hold and someone would be able to dig her out when the fighting was over.

She thought of Phoenix, thrown from the roof in the fight. There hadn't been time to dwell on it earlier, but she hoped he'd survived. He had the tools to, but anything could happen in a fight. She thought of the other members of the Broken Spear, somewhere on the battlefield. They'd already lost one friend to the Servitor. Tarot would probably say they were cursed if they lost another. She thought of Robyn, still with Phoenix's family, and knew at least she would be taken care of.

And then there was only blinding light.

35

STARFALL

They arrived just barely in time. Relief and terror seized Church's heart in equal measure as Angel obliterated the debris raining down on Wings with a blast of divine light from her eyes, turning an avalanche of stone into a shower of gravel. Wings was alive. But that had been too close.

The priest readied Zealot, summoning a spectral copy of the sword in the air next to Haegan to attack. His attacks were joined almost immediately by the warbling barks of Phoenix's gun cracking off shot after shot as the spell-forger marched into view from behind a pile of rubble. He was covered in dust, but otherwise unharmed. That was two friends still alive.

Haegan retaliated almost instantly, calling down lightning, summoning surges of ice, and flinging objects with telekinesis. Angel stood her ground, enduring or punching through everything he threw at her, but the rest of them were forced to scatter and run as they fought, making themselves the most difficult targets they could. Phoenix and Wings peppered Haegan with arrows and force blasts while Church directed Zealot's copy to constantly harass him. None of the attacks individually did more than stagger him in the air for a breath, but together, they kept his attention scattered and his retaliation unfocused.

Church lobbed a grenade that carried the same disruptive power Phoenix and Wings had used in their weapons, but Haegan saw it coming. A gale-force wind knocked it off course before it ever got close, and it detonated in midair in a ball of orange light. The wave of ice Haegan sent in response left Church hunkered down behind a fallen piece of destroyed building, half-buried in a newly formed glacier. He had two more, but with how hard the wind was whipping, he didn't like his odds.

"I'm not going to be able to hit him with these!" Church shouted.

"My disruptor cell's empty!" Phoenix called back.

"Out of arrows too!" Wings shouted.

Most of the disruptors Phoenix had built were only designed to deliver a single pulse of energy. It would disable the armor's connection to the Hearts for a short time, but it would eventually wear off. He'd made spikes that could permanently disable it, if they were driven into the armor, but he'd only had time to make two, and given their limited supply, they'd been given to the two people most likely to be able to actually get close enough to use them. Snow had one, but she was somewhere else in this war zone. Angel had the other, but Haegan was out of her reach.

"We need to get him on the ground!" Phoenix shouted.

"Say no more!" Ink shouted.

She arrived in a shattering fractal pattern of light, dozens of threads already unspooling from her fingers. They flew out like lassos, wrapping and anchoring on a large chunk of debris on the ground, and then latching on to Haegan's arm. It wasn't enough to bring him down. But Ink had brought the rest of the Cord of Aenwyn with her.

Squid summoned an octopus tentacle that towered over all of them, and it wrapped around Haegan's other arm. He resisted, but the other members of the Cord hammered him with stone, flames, thunder, and poison gas until eventually, they'd finally overwhelmed him, and he was pulled to the ground.

Quint immediately pounced onto Haegan's back and drove a short spear into either side of his clavicle. The armor saved Haegan, but Quint used the still embedded spears as levers to drag Haegan the rest of the way to the ground. Phoenix and Wings joined in immediately, layering tree roots and spider silk into the snare to hold him down. Church's own prayers couldn't target Haegan directly through his armor's wards, so he focused on enhancing the strength of everyone else working to hold him. Together, they had him pinned a dozen different ways.

Angel sprinted forward, finally grabbing the disruptor spike off of her belt as she ran. Her eyes locked on to Haegan's struggling form, making eye contact through the slit of his helmet.

An inhuman roar echoed from inside Haegan's helmet. The sky flashed purple as he screamed, and a wave of force detonated out from him. The ground beneath him shattered to pieces, and a shock wave rippled out from him.

Everyone was flung off their feet as the streets were torn up, glass shattered, and the air was choked with debris. There was nothing but roaring destruction in their ears, and nothing but gray dust in their eyes.

Then came the lightning. Then sheets of ice. Then beams of light.

And finally, darkness and silence.

Angel was standing in a carpenter's workshop, which was odd, because a blink ago, she'd been blasted into next week by Haegan and buried under the building that had collapsed on top of her. An array of tools hung on one wall. A handmade shelf held boxes of nails, sheets of sandpaper, and jars of glue, paint, stain, and lacquer. Lumber pieces were arranged according to size in a corner. The light here had an off quality to it that made everything seem out of focus, and it all smelled of sweat, oil, and sawdust.

And in the center of the room, bent to examine the surface of a half-finished chair, was a dark-skinned, broadly-built man with a short, thick beard, and calluses on his calluses. Angel had never seen the man before, but she recognized Saint Beneger the Guide from how the steady impression of him matched what she always felt from Church's prayers. His presence explained a few things.

"Beneger," she said, more surprised than anything.

"There she is," Beneger said, grunting as he stood up straight. "Sorry to interrupt."

"Interrupt away," she said. She noticed that she didn't have any of the injuries she'd sustained in Haegan's onslaught. A thought occurred. "Am I dead?"

"Not yet," Beneger said casually. He held a measuring stick to the base of the chair, and began making small tick marks with a piece of charcoal. "Close though. And it seems to me you're in need of some guidance. That happens to be my specialty."

Angel gave a bitter laugh. What she needed was a new set of ribs. Guidance would have been nice sometime in the previous twenty years, while she flailed around desperately for a sense of self outside of being a Sentinel, and tried and failed to figure out what she was supposed to do with her life.

As if reading her thoughts, Beneger raised an eyebrow. "I sent you the best priest I've had in centuries to walk by your side for years. Not my fault you didn't listen."

Angel scoffed, though not as bitterly as the first laugh. "Fair, I guess. But why the face to face all of a sudden?"

Beneger's expression darkened for a moment. "Well. Arno is a tad preoccupied at the moment. And things are getting . . . urgent."

Angel frowned. "The Starborn?"

Instead of addressing the issue directly, Beneger flashed an enigmatic smile, and jerked his head in a beckoning motion. "Come here a moment, would you?"

Angel approached, because she didn't see what else to do in this situation, and Beneger reached for a handsaw. He indicated the chair base. "Hold that part there steady."

Angel wasn't sure why they were making a chair if things were *urgent*, but Beneger was a saint. They were, at the best of times, weird. So, while she held the base steady, he sawed away, slow and smooth, creating a space in the frame where he'd fit the next leg.

While they worked, he asked, "Do you know why there are saints?"

"Delegation," Angel said automatically. She'd been the apprentice of a paladin once, and she hadn't shirked *all* her religious studies back then. "The gods paint the big picture of what they want, the general plan, and the saints sort out all the small details. There's only so granular one god can make their focus, so they have a shit ton of saints to do it for them."

Beneger nodded thoughtfully. "That's all true. The finer details of things are our domain, and there are an awful lot of us specifically to keep the workload down. But it's more than that. It's not just that one god or even seven can't manage all the details. It's that they don't care."

Angel's eyes widened, and an instinct made her glance toward the sky. Beneger laughed.

"It's not blasphemy, Monica. It's the truth. The gods are too big. They *can't* care about small details. About individual human lives. Not like you or I can. We're the human element. The part that knows how to care."

He was looking straight at her now, taking a break from sawing. Angel felt uncomfortably bare under the saint's stare. Like he knew her too well.

"I'm not a saint," Angel said, noting the inclusiveness in his language. It sounded less certain than she meant it. She wasn't. She was a Sentinel, the soul of an angel in the body of a human. Specifically, an angel that had been unable to stand being in heaven, unable to interfere in mortal affairs except under the strict provisions of celestial law.

Beneger finished the corner he was working on, rotated the base, and started on the next. "Most angels don't understand Sentinels. They're fiercely loyal creatures, angels. They fight the good fight. Follow orders. But they're married to their sense of duty, and to them, Sentinels break from that duty. They abandon their post to fight like a mortal, and the other angels *can't* understand why."

He put the exact same emphasis on "can't" that he had when discussing the gods. That was all it took for the comparison to click, and Beneger smiled when he saw the recognition in her eyes.

"Sentinels," he said. "Have that human element. That extra something that means when they look at the world, and see all the evil and suffering afflicting people, they *care*. Not about the general cause of good versus evil. Not about some big picture. Sentinels care about people. About the little things. In a way only something mortal and human can. And when you care, you have to do something about it."

Angel felt something deep inside her shudder, as if a weight had fallen off her soul. All her life, Angel had seen the angelic side of her as something other. She'd thought of it similar to Ruby's possession—something that had left her infected with instincts and desires that weren't hers. Sometimes she ran from them, sometimes she embraced them, but she'd never truly felt like they were hers. Now, knowing that it had been not angelic instincts, but *human* ones, that had made her like this in the first place, everything seemed so much more . . . right.

As an angel, she was a soldier of the gods. As a person, she cared about other people. Not only were those sides not in conflict, they fed each other. She had experienced firsthand the truth of Beneger's words.

When you care, you have to do something about it.

It wasn't the mad zeal of an angel driving her into fights with demons and bloodsmoke rings. It was the empathy of a person with the power to do something about it.

Angel shook her head. "You're not even my saint."

It was Beneger's turn to scoff. "What, you think saints and mortals are exclusive partners?" He paused. "Well, some of them are weird that way. But I'm more practical, and I was the best saint in the neighborhood for the job. Ricard does send his regards."

His expression sobered.

"You wouldn't remember this. But when you died, and your friends had to resurrect you, Renalt offered you the option of whether to stay with them, or come back to the heavens. Can you guess what you told him?"

If Beneger didn't still have that all-knowing look on his face, Angel might have been tempted to say "To go screw himself?" but with that look, she couldn't help but answer honestly. Daybreaker was in her hands again.

"They still need me."

Church coughed, and tasted blood and grit. His lungs burned, and his eyes stung. Tears carved trails in the dust and soot that caked his face and armor, and he couldn't feel his legs.

The world had been bled of all color, rendering everything in shades of gray and leaving everything more than a few dozen feet from him shrouded in darkness. Occasionally, he saw a flash of lightning, or a beam of light, which appeared like stark white pillars in a sea of black, but even then, they were mostly silent, the crash of their power reduced to distant thuds and rumbles. A moment ago, the wind had been so loud it had been hard to think. Now he couldn't hear it at all, even as his hair was still buffeted by it.

It occurred to him, through a soup of pain in his head, that they were doing much better than the last time they'd fought the Servitor. By this time in the fight at Loraine, they'd already lost several people. They might have been losing people now, actually. It was hard to tell in the shroud of darkness the Heart of Shadows had made. His fingertips were tingling and he knew that was bad.

He clutched his saint's talisman and tried to speak a prayer to heal himself, but nothing happened. His voice sounded like it stopped dead only a few feet from him, swallowed up by the dark around him. An existential loneliness slowly dawned on him as he realized in this dark, not even Beneger could see or hear him. He was alone in the middle of a war zone, while all around him people were fighting and dying.

He tried the prayer again. And again. And again. He'd just given up on it and resigned to try and haul himself to his feet anyway when the darkness vanished. Sound and color crashed back into Church in a disorienting wall, and for a blink he couldn't make sense of any of it. Then Haegan planted an armored boot on his chest.

All around Church, a new city block of Relgen lay freshly devastated. Buildings were flattened, but unlike the neat clearing Haegan and his order had set up for their ritual, this was wild destruction. Rubble lay scattered all around in piles, mixed with sheets of ice and scorch-marked craters. Dust mixed with snowflakes and embers choked the air, flitting around in the still-whipping wind, and overhead, the cracks in the sky pulsed and rippled with violet power, eclipsing more of the storm-tossed sky with every second. Church couldn't see anyone else, but if they'd been caught in the wake of this devastation, he couldn't imagine they were doing any better than he was.

Haegan leaned his weight onto the foot he had on Church's chest until he loomed over him, dominating his vision. Church's armor immediately bent and buckled under the pressure, and his ribs began to scream in protest. Instinctively, he tried to shove Haegan's foot off of him, but he may as well have tried to move a mountain.

Haegan's eyes blazed with something that might have once been determination but had long since crossed the border into madness. Pebbles of debris floated around him as if gravity itself was breaking under the power he radiated. And there was a hatred in his eyes that chilled Church to recognize. He wasn't looking at Haegan. He was looking at a member of the Cult of Stars.

"You called yourselves the Starbreakers," Haegan intoned as if he were passing an order of execution. "You pretended to be protectors, but what did you ever really do to save us from the stars? What stand did you take? What sacrifices had to be made? None. Nothing. You spat in the face of the Starborn, and you left us to their wrath."

Haegan shoved his foot down harder, and when Church grunted in pain, he tasted blood in the back of his throat.

"I am better than you. Stronger than you. I will end our struggle for survival, and there will finally be peace," Haegan spat. With the gleeful smile of a fanatic, he added, "For fifteen years, you have been a thorn in my side. Today, I will finally be rid of you all."

With a sadistic calm that belonged exclusively to the Cult of Stars, Haegan began to cave Church's chest in.

And then the sky screamed.

Haegan's expression snapped into confusion and concern, and the pressure on Church's chest lightened as the former knight looked up. All across the battlefield, the pace of the battle slowed as others on both sides did the same. For a brief moment while Haegan was distracted, Church could breathe again. But at that moment, he forgot to pray.

Instead, the only word that came from his lips was, "No."

A wail that was and wasn't human echoed out over the city of Relgen as something slipped through the crack in the sky. It was the size of a horse, with leathery wings like a bat, but a body like a squid. Tentacles streamed behind it, a wide mouth ringed with rows of shark's teeth, and dozens of bulbous eyes clustered around its blunt head. It flapped awkwardly in the air, haphazardly as if unused to the weight of its body. Then came another, and another, and another. In seconds, the sky had started to swarm with them as they descended, all wailing in perfect unison.

Other *things* came through the cracks. Things made entirely of arms and hands that fell straight to the ground. Long, serpentine creatures with mouths down the lengths of their bodies that wriggled through the air like snakes in water. Spider-like monstrosities with a dozen legs made of blades pushed through one leg at a time before descending on strands of steel. The larger the creature that came through, the more difficulty it had, many of them getting stuck halfway until the part of the crack they were pushing through widened enough for them to escape. Some of them flew, some fell. Some of them looked the same as others, some were unique, but none of them looked like they should exist.

In their many run-ins with the Cult of Stars, the Starbreakers had dealt with more than just the cultists. Church knew exactly what he was looking at now. The lesser Starborn had started to come through the breach in the world Haegan and his order had created. And with it still growing, a true Starborn couldn't be far behind.

Church's messenger coil began to fill with chatter from Thalia and the other battlefield leaders as they desperately improvised a new plan and reported their situations.

Somewhere in the noise, Thalia asked for an update from those fighting Haegan. No one responded to her.

Phoenix, Wings, Angel, and the Cord of Aenwyn were all down. Anyone else who might have been strong enough to stand against Haegan was busy with cultists or lesser Starborn. As far as Church could tell, he was the only one still fighting the human Servitor, and "fighting" was being generous. If the heavens opened and Saint Beneger descended to bestow Church with a dozen miracles, he might be able to bring Haegan down, but even then, not easily, and not with enough left afterward to deal with this. They were running out of options and time. There was only one person who could stop this before it was too late.

"Haegan," Church coughed. "Look at the sky. Look around you. You're not saving the world from the Starborn. You're giving them exactly what they want. If they come here—"

"We will meet them! We will match them, or we will die trying!" Haegan snapped. He returned to pressing down on Church's chest with his boot, and the priest let out a choked scream as something crunched. "If humanity cannot hold this world, it does not deserve it! Let the Starborn take it from us if they can! Let oblivion come if it dares! I am ready!"

"Listen to yourself," Church insisted, even as every word felt like broken glass in his throat. "You were a good man once, Haegan. A knight. Are you talking like a knight now? Like someone who wants to protect people? Or are you talking like a cultist?"

Haegan frowned. More importantly, he didn't immediately cave Church's chest in. The priest clung to the hope that hesitation gave him like a lifeline and hauled on it for all he was worth.

"Don't let them win," Church pleaded. "Don't let them give us to those monsters."

Haegan was still for a long while. He looked from Church, to the sky, to the battle still raging behind them. Then, his face twitched, and Church's heart sank. All compassion, all concern, all humanity, had vanished from Haegan's eyes in a blink. There was only a manic emptiness. There was only the Cult of Stars.

"It's too late either way," he said. "You've lost, Starbreaker."

Church closed his eyes.

Beneger. We could really use a miracle right about now.

A streak of golden fire crashed into Haegan, tearing him away from Church and carrying him into the nearest building. There was a flash of light and a clang of metal so loud Church felt it in his teeth, and Haegan was launched into the sky. Before he'd even hit the apex of his flight, a golden streak shot up from the ground to meet him, stopping in the air above him as he rocketed upward. That was the first good look at Angel that Church got.

Her halo blazed white-gold, brighter than ever. The corona of golden light that usually roiled off her had expanded and unfurled into the shape of wings made of golden flames. Dazzling white-and-gold armor had formed over her chest and arms, and the rest of her clothes had shifted color to match. She held Daybreaker poised and ready to strike in one hand, and a twin of the weapon made of solid light in the other. Both weapons burned with the same divine flames as her new wings. When she struck Haegan, the explosion of light from the impact of the axes was like the birth of a new sun, and he fell to the earth like a comet.

Despite the pain still wracking his entire body, Church smiled.

That'll do.

Finally free of the shadow magic and able to breathe, Church said a prayer to heal the worst of his injuries. When his chest stopped burning, he crawled over to where Zealot was lying, and used it to shove himself to his feet. Immediately, the sword's voice filled his mind, demanding he throw himself into battle alongside the champion of the heavens to slay the enemy that had been tainted by the aberrations from beyond the farthest stars. Church sheathed the sword to shut it up, and staggered off in search of as many wounded as he could find.

Wings was lying in a pile of broken brick and shattered glass, her armor burned and warped, and too much blood running down her forehead. She'd been caught in the maelstrom of darkness and destruction that Haegan had unleashed, the same as everyone else. She hadn't even heard the lightning bolt that had detonated the ground to her right and sent her flying, it had just been darkness, biting cold winds, and then a flash of white, and the world went sideways.

Now the darkness was gone, and she had a halfway decent view of the battle in the sky raging between Angel and Haegan. The two crashed into each other again and again in the air, Angel a shining golden sun, Haegan a roiling maelstrom of destruction.

Wings had felt a brief pang of loss when Angel had burst from a distant pile of rubble and taken to the skies, but watching her now, the sheer power being exchanged between her and Haegan was nothing short of awe inspiring. Wings had seen Angel in a fight before, and this was nothing like that. This was bigger, brighter, and not to mention *airborne.*

Angel had never looked stronger, or more like her namesake. Or more in control. Angel had always blazed with power, like a raging, barely directed inferno. Now, the light coming off her was controlled and steady, only truly flaring when she struck.

Wings didn't understand it, but she was grateful for it. Whatever bottleneck Angel had broken through, it was saving all of their lives.

The backdrop of their battle was a dark sky, covered in pitch black cracks and increasingly filled by incomprehensible nightmares. Most of the creatures were simply descending on the city, turning more and more of the two amassed armies into allies trying desperately to defend themselves against a tide of horrors. But a few were already fanning out, flying off into the horizon or scurrying away from the chaos. With the detached, fragmented thinking that could only come from blood-loss-induced delirium, Wings noted that the world was going to have its hands full for a long time, exterminating everything that had slipped through the cracks today.

Assuming they all survived the day, anyway. If the baby Starborn were arriving, then the mother couldn't be far behind. Sure enough, her messenger coil crackled to life in her ear to confirm as much.

"We're running out of time," Phoenix grunted, and Wings had to close her eyes for a moment to savor the sheer relief that washed over her to hear his voice, even spoken through gritted teeth. *"Angel, you need to use the spike."*

"Lost it."

"What?"

"I. Lost. It." Every word was punctuated by another clash of Angel's axes against Haegan's armor, which were visible even at a distance thanks to the flashes of light each one produced. Haegan struck back, the crash of his hammer accompanied by a boom of thunder, and it was Angel's turn to fall to the ground, though she did it encased in ice. A moment later, the ice exploded.

Angel's next words came out with an annoyed grunt. *"Dropped it when he hit me in the blackout. Somewhere down there with you."*

Then she was back in the air and trading blows with Haegan. Phoenix's next few words came through more as static than intelligible sound. Wings knew her husband's voice well enough to discern the frustration in it, but she only truly caught the tail end.

"—can hear me, we need to find the disruptor and end this!"

"Can't see it here," Ink's voice came through, weak, but at least clear. *"Then again, I am* buried.*"*

"Angel, do you know where you landed?"

The sky exploded with the birth of a new sun as Haegan and Angel both unleashed beams of light at each other, and the clash in the middle briefly turned the world bright as midafternoon.

"She seems busy," came Church's exhausted observation.

"Thalia, did you see—?"

"I can't see anything *around Haegan right now. The Heart of Shadows is making it all a mess!"*

Wings blinked. She knew where Angel had landed. She'd seen where she'd burst out of the rubble. She knew. She could still help. She fingered her messenger coil, only to hiss in pain as the thing exploded in a shower of sparks. She yanked what was left of the device off her ear and threw it away, still smarting from the latest burn added to her collection. So much for telling them where it was. For the first time since coming to relative consciousness after Haegan's assault, Wings tried to sit up. She had to bite back a scream as her left leg shot through with the sharp pain of a break, and her head spun. She laid back down, trying to find a position that wouldn't make her leg seize in agony.

She reached for the pouch of materials she normally used to fuel the few druid spells she knew that didn't simply use her arrows as materials, hoping she still had enough lavender for a decent heal, and instead coming up with a pinch that could generously be stretched into minor pain relief. She used it anyway, focusing every ounce of the spell's power she could muster into her leg.

When she'd done all she could for herself, her next step was to find her bow, which she did after only a bit of searching, and use it as a crutch. She half stumbled, half crawled to where she'd seen Angel rise out of the rubble. It took agonizingly long. Above, Angel's battle with Haegan dragged on, the cracks in the skies widened, and monsters continued to pour into the world. The din of the battle in the city had begun to shift in pitch, as more and more of its sound became dominated by desperate screams. Every crash, every inhuman shriek, spurred her forward. This madness had to stop, and it needed to stop *now*.

She reached the spot. She lost track of time as she sifted through debris, as the world faded to nothing but that patch of ruined streets. And then she found it. A single metal spike, slightly smaller than a dagger, engraved along its sides with arcane sigils that gave off a faint orange glow.

"Found it!" she shouted, immediately holding it up. "I found it!"

She looked around, and the surge of triumph she felt died in her chest. No one was anywhere near her. She spotted the dusty red form of Phoenix crouched in the rubble, but he was hundreds of yards away, unloading a jet of flame on a lesser Starborn that had wandered from the main battlefield. Church was off in a completely different direction, bent over the body of someone she couldn't recognize. If Angel heard her up in the sky, she gave no sign of it as she continued her duel with Haegan.

Wings was alone, surrounded by a battle that felt like the end of the world, with the key to stopping it in her hands, and there was nothing she could do about it. Her grip on the disruptor spike tightened. If not for its presence in her hand, her fingers would have been twitching furiously, the way they always did when they longed for the comfort of a bowstring.

At that thought, Wings hit on one last, desperate idea. She reached back into her quiver for an arrow, and broke the head off. With a quick spell, she caused the broken shaft to regrow around a *new* head—the disruptor spike. The weight was all wrong for an arrow, but she didn't care. Her bow was heavy enough to make it work, and her arms were still working just fine.

She nocked the arrow and took aim at Haegan. She had to relax the string almost immediately to wipe blood out of her eye, and when she pulled back again, she became aware that maybe her arms weren't actually fine as she saw the tip of the spike tremble on her bow. Haegan was a tiny bronze figure at the center of a storm in her vision. The winds were whipped into an absolute mess, and she reminded herself to account for that.

The world narrowed down to the point of her arrow, and the bronze armor of her target. The armor born from the Servitor. She'd nearly died in the original Servitor's attack. Nearly. But instead of dying, she'd come out the other side stronger than ever, newly infused with a Servitor Heart. The Heart of the Sky was gone from her now. But the strength she'd earned on that hellish day, paid for in blood, was still inside her. She drew in a sharp breath, held it, and forced her shaking arms still with pure will.

Her arrow flew.

Her shot found Haegan just under his right arm and stuck. The human Servitor seized up in midair, and Angel did not waste an instant. She struck hard and fast, batting Haegan back and forth across the sky, constantly zipping through the air to meet him, each hit producing a flare of light and taking another piece from his armor until, with a blow that cleaved off half of his helmet, she sent him crashing down.

She landed on top of him feet first, driving him even further into the ground.

Ruby and Bart were keeping René and Rosa busy, and gods bless them for it, because Snow and Brass had their hands full with Silas. The blades whipping around Silas on the end of their quicksilver cords had become a white-hot whirlwind, and the ground was covered in still-glowing grooves his swipes had carved into the street. Fire trailed off the weapons and him as he moved, spraying out to extend his reach.

Snow missed the Heart of Ice more than ever. The air was scorching hot, and her armor sported a dozen burns just from where his blows had gotten *close*. She threw a pair of knives at Silas, and his red-hot swords sliced them both in half. Brass parried his counter attack, but got the end of his own sword cleaved off for his trouble.

Snow threw a smoke bomb at Silas's feet just to get a moment to catch her breath, but he blindly threw out fire through the smoke, and she had to keep dodging to avoid getting a hole seared through her spine.

"Thalia, send somebody to give us a hand here, now!" Snow barked into her messenger coil.

"Broken Spear, can you—"

Tarot cut Thalia off before she could finish. *"Killing something, hold please!"*

Someone else cut in saying they could see Silas and were on their way, but Snow didn't recognize the voice and didn't bother asking for clarification. She knew all of their actually powerful allies. If a stranger was coming to help them, it had to be one of the cannon-fodder nobodies. She and Brass were on their own.

"New plan," Snow said to Brass over the coil. "I've still got the disruptor spike. Keep his eyes on you, and I'll shove it into his harness."

"Aren't we supposed to use that on the big man? And will that even work on him?"

"If you've got a better idea, let's hear it."

"I'll get his eyes on me then."

"Good boy."

Snow was already replacing one of her knives with the spike. As the smoke cleared and Brass rushed forward to engage Silas, Snow blinked away to find cover and wait for an opening. Brass, as ever, put on a master's performance with his sword. He stepped and wove with effortless grace, made three moves for every two Silas made, and always made sure that he never parried an attack with the same part of his blade twice, minimizing the damage his weapon took from the sheer heat. Only Silas's raw firepower kept Brass back. Snow watched the pair dance, waiting for her moment.

And then a monster came down on top of them.

It was mess of a thing, some nightmarish cross between a spider and a flock of bats. It already had an arrow through its middle when it crashed to the ground near them, but its wounded shrieks made Snow's blood run cold.

It had been a long time since she'd seen the monsters this close without the Heart of Ice's numbing protection. The occasional nightmares she still had hadn't done them justice. She'd thought she could handle it when the sky first opened up, but the monsters had been comfortably far away. This one was right in front of her. She blinked in close before she could think and killed it with a quick stab to something fleshy. She'd hoped to stem the old fear that was already flooding her veins before it became a problem, but when she drew her focus back to the fight between Brass and Silas, it only got worse.

Brass had seen the creature's crash landing, same as her, and though he put up an unflappable front, Snow knew he'd found the monsters just as disturbing as any of them. So when he'd heard one so close, he'd taken his eyes off of Silas to look. It was only a second's waver in attention, but Silas hadn't lost focus at all.

Snow watched in slow motion as Brass tried to bring his sword up to parry Silas's incoming thrust, already knowing he was too late. The white-hot blade was diving straight for his heart, and it may as well have been her own for how sharp and real the spike of alarm in her chest felt. Unadulterated panic roared through her entire body, so immediate and intense her eyes watered and her heart stopped. Before she could even register her reaction, she'd already blinked out of cover.

Snow reappeared in the space between Brass and Silas, all but throwing herself on top of Silas's thrusting arm even as she shoved both men away from each other. It was like tackling a bonfire, and the ensuing pain was immediate and searing. An instant later, Snow was lying on the floor with smoke and the smell of burnt flesh curling off her. She screamed, dropping the disruptor spike and clutching her stomach where the worst of the burns were.

Silas recovered his stance as quickly as he could. Brass recovered quicker. He stomped on the tip of the disruptor spike, flipping it up and into his hand and thrusting it straight into the center of Silas's harness. The flames rolling off of Silas guttered out in an instant, and in the shocked second from him that followed, Brass swiped his sword across his neck.

Silas froze in place, and coughed once as a river of blood began to flow from a new slit in his throat. He grabbed desperately at it, and Brass dismissively kicked him in the chest to go finish dying somewhere he wouldn't be in the way.

Brass was already at Snow's side.

"Easy, easy," he said, taking her into his arms. After a bit of fishing around in his coat's bottomless pockets, he found a bottle of something that could help. "Nice save as usual, Snowflake."

She held back a scream as he applied a salve to her burns, and her grip on his coat turned her knuckles white. She remembered this exact pain from the last time he'd used this salve on her, years and a lifetime ago. It wouldn't heal wounds, but it would stop them from killing her for a while.

"Next time," she hissed. "Pay attention."

He chuckled, but the mirth of it didn't reach his eyes. "Promise."

For a few seconds, Snow only whimpered as he continued to treat her wounds and rattled off constant reassurances that she was going to be fine. Eventually, her body stopped shaking quite so violently, and her grip loosened from white-knuckled to merely vice-like.

"I know it's currently raining monsters, but I could really use a priest right about now," Brass said into his messenger coil. "Church? Saint Ricard lady? Anybody?"

Snow didn't hear the response over the coil, but from the way Brass's expression turned annoyed and he looked around as if surveying his options, she doubted it had been a helpful one. So, no healers available, her covered in burns, and nightmares raining from the sky. Snow knew better than to tempt fate by wondering if things could get any worse.

But it turned out that fate didn't need tempting.

As soon as Phoenix had limped over to join the others at the crater Angel had pounded Haegan into, he switched power cell chambers in his weapon and immediately set to work on the chestplate of Haegan's armor with the cutting torch setting.

"What are you doing?" Angel asked.

"The Hearts are the only thing strong enough to close those cracks in the sky quickly," Phoenix said without stopping. "The armor's too damaged, so I need to jerry-rig a new control system for them that won't make anybody's bones explode, and then we can use them to shut that rift before—"

The words stuck in Phoenix's throat as every molecule of air around him suddenly became a thousand times heavier. He was instantly floored, as his awareness was overwhelmed by an inescapable sense of pressure coming down on top of him.

At the same time, the inside of his head began to scream, as if his brain were trying to tunnel out of his skull in every direction at once. From the air to the earth, the world itself hummed like a struck gong, and everything briefly went silent. Even the shrieking of the lesser Starborn stopped for a moment. Everything was muted, and overwritten by something that was less voice and more impression.

I hear you.

Phoenix lay on the floor screaming and clutching his temples until Church's hands found his head. Warm relief passed through him a moment later, and the pain in his brain faded to a dull ache. He met the priest's eyes, and saw they were full of absolute terror. Nearby, Angel glared up at the sky with her jaw clenched.

Above, the cracks had bled together, until there was no more sky, only an endless black blanket drawn over their heads as far as the eye could see in any direction. All across the battlefield, fighting had stopped. The luckiest people were still looking around in confusion. Others stared at the sky, transfixed. The least fortunate were lying on the ground screaming and writhing as Phoenix had been only a second ago. Another impression sang through the world. conveying its meaning straight into the conscious understanding of everyone in the city, and miles beyond it.

Now be silent.

The first black tendril from the sky came down. It started like a pillar of solid night, but quickly began to twist and snake, making hard right angle turns, folding in on itself, or splitting to go in two directions at once. It spread out as it descended, like a rapidly expanding root system of absolute abyss. When its farthest reaching piece made contact with the earth, and eclipsed an area the size of a sporting field, everyone within fifty yards of it instantly exploded. Dozens, maybe hundreds of lives, erased in a shower of pink mist. It happened in a blink.

Those outside the immediate death radius fell over, joining those who had already succumbed to the screams. As the Starborn's presence in the world grew, the effect spread. One by one, scattered all through the crowd, but predominantly in the parts of it that had been the Exile Order, people's heads began to explode.

The lesser Starborn whipped into a frenzy, diving on anything still alive, and creating a whole new wave of screaming and panic.

Phoenix felt himself hollow out as he watched. He didn't make a sound. No one with him did. They all stood silent, and watched as the Starborn began to wipe out humanity with nothing more than the weight of its existence. Sound became nothing but a whine in his ears, until a cough came from behind him, and Phoenix remembered that Haegan was still trapped in the half-destroyed Servitor armor.

The former knight was bleeding from his eyes, his mouth, his ears, and most severely from the mark of the Cult of Stars on his forehead. He hadn't taken his vacant stare off of the sky.

"What have I done?" he whispered.

Then his skull exploded.

36
THE ENDING

Ruby limped into the Rusted Star, supporting an exhausted Bart. The novice paladin's face was flushed from divine overexertion, and he was only kept upright by his arm around Ruby's shoulders and hers around his waist. Dietrich came up behind them, streaks of dried blood running from his eyes and nose, and one of his arms in an improvised sling made out of a cloak that wasn't his. Gamma, who'd left the Star to come get them, brought up the rear of their procession, carrying René over his shoulder with the one arm he hadn't lost in battle. She was bound with black, thorn-covered vines, face was covered in a half-smeared splatter of blood, shouting her sister's name in between violent sobs. Ruby found herself surprisingly sympathetic for a woman who'd tried to kill them—it was hard not to, after they'd all watched Rosa's head explode.

But as bad as the five of them looked, the situation inside the Rusted Star looked worse.

Every table and chair in the place was gone, smashed and repurposed into splints and stretchers, and every square foot of extra space that had been made was packed with casualties from the battle. Frelheimer warriors and soldiers of the Exile Order lay side by side on the floor, thin blood-stained blankets beneath them, all screaming in pain, madness, or both. The air reeked with the stench of every bodily fluid mingled together.

The Order of Saint Ricard's knights and priests worked alongside Frelheimer healers and Exile surgeons, hurriedly darting around the cramped space to tend to people as fast as they could. Every one of them looked as though they were hanging on by a thread, and more than a few had half-dried streaks of blood running down their own faces.

Ruby and the others were barely through the door before Naomi, the priest from the Order of Saint Ricard, started shouting at them.

"Is there anyone else behind you?" she asked. "Did you see anyone else out there?"

"No one sane," Ruby said.

In the immediate aftermath of the Starborn's arrival, everyone with a working messenger coil had gotten the same command from Phoenix: Run. Grab whoever you can, get as far away from Relgen as possible, and whatever you do, don't look at the sky.

Naomi saw the harrowed truth of Ruby's words in her eyes and gave a grim nod. She pointed first at the still-screaming René and then at what could generously be called an open space on the floor. "Put her over there and find somewhere to stand out of the way. Thalia!"

The bartender was behind the bar, hands braced on the counter. Her head and right arm were bandaged, and from the look on her face she was struggling to stay upright. But she nodded when Naomi shouted her name, and called back, "Close it up!"

Naomi shut the tavern's doors, and shouted for everyone to hang on. Ruby couldn't tell how many people actually heard her over the cacophony of the wounded, because almost nobody actually followed the priest's instructions by the time the bar began to shake. Ruby had just enough time to lean her weight against the wall for support before the entire tavern dropped into the earth.

The tavern went dark for a few moments, during which time the screaming from the wounded redoubled. Then the sensation of falling stopped, and everything steadied.

"All right, everyone, let's move!" Naomi shouted.

The assembled menagerie of healers were already at work, scooping up the wounded with blankets, lengths of broken table, or just by hand, and carrying them out of the Rusted Star in a hurried queue. From how efficiently everyone moved, it was clear this wasn't the first or even second time they'd had to do this. Someone carried René off, but even after all the trouble they'd gone through to save her from Relgen, Ruby found it hard to care where they were taking her. There was too much going on, too much still to do, to worry about the fate of a single exile.

Bart got as far as the second "w" in "Where are we?" before he passed out, and Ruby nearly fell from the surprise of suddenly having to carry him in full armor. Dietrich caught her with an outstretched arm, and she nodded her thanks. Ruby looked around, unsure what to do with Bart now, especially with every healer in the tavern busy evacuating the building. Eventually, she found the only person in the room who wasn't busy: Thalia.

The bartender was three shades paler than usual, and wasn't so much standing behind the bar as leaning over it, half-collapsed on the counter and staring miserably into the middle distance. She looked like she wanted to vomit.

"Thalia? What's going on? Where's everyone going?"

Thalia blinked several times and visibly tried to steady herself before answering. "Dropping the wounded off where there's more resources to help them. We're in . . ." she paused to remember, ". . . Silverspear. Astrid's city. Most of the wounded in this trip were hers. We dropped some others off in Aenerwin, and back at the . . . at Ricard's place."

"What happened to you?" Ruby asked.

Thalia tried to summon a weary smile, and failed. "Tripped over my own feet when the Starborn hit. Broke some glass. I'm fine. Sit down somewhere. When the healers get back, we're tunnelporting again. Meeting up with the others."

"Where are they?" Ruby asked.

Thalia was a long time in answering. "Outside the city."

Ruby physically recoiled at the thought of going back anywhere near Relgen, and Thalia noticed.

"You can get off here, if you want," Thalia offered.

Ruby forced herself to shake her head. If the Starbreakers were still there, they had a good reason. And if there was anything to be done about the Starborn, she wanted to be a part of it.

When the healers finished their drop off and came shuffling back inside, Thalia called out for someone to double-check the doors, braced her hands on the bar once again, and willed the Rusted Star back down into the earth.

They came out on the same mountain ridge where they'd first arrived to scout out Relgen, right next to the old shack. Ruby followed the flow of people milling out of the Rusted Star, and mentally braced for what was waiting for her outside.

The sky was a curtain of unnatural, liquid black, and yet it was as easy to see as if it were broad daylight. The wind that had once whipped through the mountains had gone completely still and silent, leaving the stale air hanging around them. The city of Relgen was still there in the distance, but now it was tangled in a net of black tendrils that had slowly descended down upon it. They were spreading out from the city now, marking the surrounding land with veins of darkness. The tendrils closest to the city center, the first to have emerged, had begun to grow mottled gray skin over them. Crackling silver smoke billowed through every street, spilled out of the walls from every break and window like smoky waterfalls, and fanned out around the city in a hazy lake.

The scale of it defied her ability to grasp, and Ruby forced herself to never look at any one spot for too long or think too hard about what she was really looking at. It was like the feeling of standing at the base of the mountain and staring up at the top, so staggeringly high up she couldn't properly take it in, only a thousand times worse, because it was bigger than a mountain and malicious and was *alive* and what did that word even mean when—

Ruby squeezed her eyes shut, and counted backwards from ten. Focused on the numbers, small and simple and concrete.

Ten. Nine. Eight . . .

She resolved to stop looking directly at the Starborn.

Instead, she found the Starbreakers, who were all loosely gathered near the edge of the ridge overlooking the city. Church knelt with eyes closed and his back to Relgen, side by side with Hilda from the Order of Saint Ricard and Faith from the Broken Spear, as the three quietly prayed. Phoenix and Wings sat next to each other on the floor, heads resting against each other, holding hands. Snow, Brass, Canvas, and Tarot were sitting in a circle, staring at the ground and smoking, with Snow hugging her knees and slowly rocking herself. Angel stood next to Astrid Silverspear, Queen of the Frelheim, as they both watched the Starborn slowly unfurling over the world with disapproving glares.

Sinnodella was a ways from the others, stroking Stixaxlatl's snout and whispering softly to try to soothe the very agitated dragon. Ink and Quint were also somewhat removed from the group, with Ink leaning back into Quint as he held her against him. She idly reached behind her to stroke his cheek as she watched everyone else. He never took his eyes off her.

There were still a few Frelheimer warriors gathered, standing a respectful distance from their queen, and some knights from the Order of Saint Ricard who had no skill in healing. To Ruby's half surprise, she also saw members of the White Hawk, the company that had sided with Haegan, and some of his gray-adorned Exiles. Not many, but enough to notice, and they'd formed a secondary clique in the gathering on the other side of an invisible dividing line.

Phoenix stood up when he registered the Rusted Star's arrival, and most everyone else turned from what they were doing to look at the people coming out of the tavern expectantly.

"Last trip's done," Thalia reported. "We got out everyone we could."

"What do we do now?" Ruby asked, unable to stop herself from blurting out the question.

She expected orders, or a plan, maybe a quip from Brass about breaking for lunch. Instead, Phoenix's already downcast expression sank into something like a final, apologetic resignation.

"All your people are out, Astrid," he said to the Queen of the Frelheim. "Go home. Be with your family."

"I will stay with you until the end. You may yet have need of me," she said. "And if not, this is as good a place to die as any."

The spellforger sighed, and held up his wrist. His gauntlet projected an illusory image of a globe, of Asher, as a layer of black spread across it. Symbols most of them couldn't understand flashed next to the display, but he translated in a despondent voice.

"The Starborn encompasses the planet in six hours. Even if it doesn't immediately kill everything under its shadow . . ." Phoenix shook his head and dispersed the display. "We stayed to make sure we got out everyone we could. But we've got six hours left with our daughter. We can't throw those away. There's enough room in the Star for everyone here, and we can take you anywhere you want to go. If you need a recommendation, Xykesh and Kaberon will probably be the last places—"

"That's *it*?"

Every head spun to Ruby. She was surprised by how loud her voice had come out, but, though her heart pounded in her chest, she was undeterred by the sea of eyes suddenly on her.

"Kid—" Brass began, but Ruby cut him off.

"You're the Starbreakers! It's a Starborn! This is supposed to be your whole thing! You can't . . . you have to do something! There has to be something! A spell, a thing, the Hearts—Can't we just reverse whatever the cult did and send it away? Or fight it? Or—"

Everyone kept staring at her with sad expressions. *Poor girl*, their eyes said. *She looks so afraid. She sounds so desperate.*

Well, she was afraid, and she was desperate, and she responded to it the way she always did—by kicking and screaming. She found Brass in the sea of faces and fixed him with a glare. "All those stories of the glory days. All those times you five did the impossible. All those times you won when you should have died. Where are *those* Starbreakers?"

"They're standing *right here*," Phoenix said without an ounce of reassurance. The defeat in his face was gone, but only because it had been replaced by bitterness. The look in his eyes reminded Ruby of a wounded animal—in pain, and about to lash out. "We were good at what we did, but in case you forgot, or Brass just failed to mention it, we *lost*. The last time we came to Relgen, we lost, the city died, and we couldn't fix it."

"So you're just going to give up?"

"There's nothing else to do!" Phoenix shouted. "We tried to stop this. That was our shot, and we blew it, again. We lost, *again*. Maybe, if there was more time, we could try to find a portal to another world and run far enough away to survive, but there isn't enough time for that, and *this* world is *done*! The Starborn is here, we can't send it back, and there isn't enough firepower on this planet to take it out. It's over."

Every word Phoenix fired out came loaded with eight years of pain and failure, of having already been in this exact spot before. And they carried a certainty in them that struck Ruby in her core. The last pillar of hope she'd been holding on to, the image of the Starbreakers as implacable heroes who could solve any problem, crumbled.

Relgen loomed in the distance behind Phoenix, caught in the Starborn's slowly expanding grasp. Ruby remembered watching people explode just from being near it.

From looking at it. And the fight finally left her.

It was over.

They lost.

"Eight years," Church said, "and nothing's changed."

"Maybe we *should* try for a new world," Brass mused. "That'd sorta close the circle, wouldn't it?"

Snow gave a dark laugh, and even Phoenix scoffed. In the last fall of Relgen, Church had used a prayer to pull them out just before the Ending had wiped out every living thing in the city. Fleeing the planet before the Starborn could do the same to it would be oddly poetic.

But Phoenix shook his head.

"I actually did consider it," he said, though he didn't sound hopeful. "Ran through some options in my head, waiting for the Star to get back."

"And?" Angel asked.

He shook his head. "There's no time. Natural rifts are too random to know where to find one. If there's a mage powerful enough to punch through themselves, I don't know them, and a group effort takes too long and too much to set up. There's probably all sorts of artifacts that could pull it off, but those aren't just lying . . . around . . ."

Phoenix's face slackened for a moment, and then his brow furrowed. He started to pace. The ridge fell silent, as everyone who knew Phoenix held their breath, and watched from the outside as pieces fit into place in his mind.

Then, he cackled like a madman.

"Well, don't hog all the good news to yourself," Brass said.

Phoenix shook his head. "Oh, it's *not* good news. But it is a chance."

"That sounds like good news," Wings said.

Angel rolled her shoulders out. Snow took a long, hard drag from the nail she'd been smoking, and stood up. Church clutched his saint's talisman for comfort and set his jaw. Brass only grinned.

"There *is* enough firepower on the planet to take out the Starborn," Phoenix said. "Something that doesn't work on a level of physical destruction, that kills as a point of fact. And the Starborn is already sitting right on top of it."

Phoenix stood at the edge of the ridge now, staring not at the Starborn, but at the city of Relgen itself. At a specific spot along the city's walls, where, eight years ago, a skyship had crash-landed.

"Kill it with the thing that brought it here in the first place." Phoenix spoke as if to carve the words into reality itself. "The Ending."

37

THE HEROES

Church and the others listened with rapt attention as Phoenix laid out the plan for them over the course of the thirty-yard walk back to the Rusted Star, during which he was also frantically assembling, repairing, and adjusting his gear. Everyone else hurried to follow after him, with the other Starbreakers leading the pack. Though he looked manic, they all knew the "walk, talk, and tinker" stage was always where Phoenix did his best work.

"We'll have to go in shielded," he began as he dug out fresh power cells for his pistol. "The Starborn's existence strains the mind, and it'll only get worse the closer we get and the longer we're exposed. Church, work with the other priests, spread out the load. Try to get everyone, but if you have to, prioritize people who've already been exposed the most. They're the most vulnerable."

"Skip me," Angel volunteered immediately. "I don't need it."

"Are you sure?" Church asked.

"Yes." The resolve on her face left no room for debate.

Phoenix ignored them, still talking, but moving on to disassembling a device for its parts. "I'll use the information the scanners gathered to map out the Rogue Imperia's location in the city, and we use the Star to tunnelport right to it. We split up from there. Most of us take up a defensive position around the Star to hold off any lesser Starborn, while a small group of us goes into the ship to retrieve the Ending. Once we have it, we all fall back into the Star and get the hells out. I rearm the Ending, we tunnelport in one last time to get it in position, get clear of the blast radius, watch the explosion."

"We'd probably look cooler if we didn't watch it," Brass said. Snow gave him an incredulous look, and he shrugged. "Just saying."

"Not that I think anyone here isn't ready to do their part," Wings said, "but if the goal is to get in and out as quickly as possible, are you sure we should take a group this big?"

Phoenix looked over the assembled allies following them into the Rusted Star: The Cord of Aenwyn and the Broken Spear. Hilda and the Order of Saint Ricard. Astrid and her bravest warriors. Sinnodella and Stixaxlatl. Gamma. Dietrich. Ruby. He grimaced.

"Honestly?" he said. "I'm worried it's not big enough."

"It'll be fine," Brass offered up. "This is a great plan. Maybe even your best."

"Only if it works," Phoenix muttered.

"Look at it this way: if we all die, that was probably gonna happen anyway. So really, there's no pressure at all."

Church wasn't sure he agreed with that, and from the looks on everyone else's faces, neither did they. But the last of their allies had filtered in, and the doors were shut. The decision wrote itself onto Phoenix's expression, and Church read it clear as day.

While Church left to speak with the other priests, Angel shoved her way through to the bar, braced herself on the counter, and looked to Phoenix expectantly. He pulled up the illusory map of the city of Relgen from his gauntlet's projector, and highlighted the relevant spot in red. She stared for a moment to fix the spot in her mind, nodded, and mentally ordered the tavern to move.

That was as far as they got into the plan without problems.

When the Rusted Star lurched into the ground as it had hundreds of times before, something went wrong. There was an earsplitting screech like nails on a chalkboard, and a violent impact as if the tavern had struck something. Everything and everyone was thrown, all sense of up and down vanished, and bodies and debris tumbled as the tavern spun, rocked, and finally stopped with a crash that split the floorboards, cracked the support beams, and shattered what little glass remained from the Starborn's arrival.

Groans and shouts filled the tavern's interior, intercut with agitated roars from Stixaxlatl. When the world finally stopped spinning, Church crawled out from underneath a fallen knight of Saint Ricard's and struggled to stand. He nearly lost his balance from sheer disorientation when he realized the entire tavern was now lying on its side. The walls had become the floor and ceiling, and the ceiling and floor the walls. Light was streaming in from the windows that weren't facing the ground, so they'd resurfaced, they'd just done it very wrong. Church had to resist the urge to use a healing prayer on those sprawled around him, who were also struggling to stand up. They were rattled, but everyone was still conscious and moving, and he would need to save his strength, especially if his suspicions of what had just happened were right.

"Did we . . . hit something?" Brass asked from underneath a pile of other freelancers.

"No," Angel grunted. "Something hit us."

The tavern shuddered again, and this time when it lurched, it went upward. As if it were being lifted up off the ground. Church's blood went cold, suspicions confirmed.

"Shields, now!" he shouted.

There wasn't time to be organized about it. Church, Naomi, Faith, and every other person who could muster enough divine energy for a mental shield threw out protections according to their own target selection, and prayed they didn't overlap too much. Church shielded himself, Phoenix, Snow, and Brass, purging the hazy protections Brass and Snow's drug use had erected and replacing it with a solid wall of divine will. Angel, he left alone, trusting her assessment of her own mind.

If anyone could resist the mental pressure of a Starborn, it was her, and every scrap of power counted. It ended up being balanced out when he threw a protection over Wings, and felt his energy crash into Faith's as she did the same. He had other overlaps as he expanded out from his priority targets to anyone near him, and some other priest thought they were closer or more responsible for this or that person. It was sloppy, wasteful, and probably had still left some people unprotected, but they were out of time. The tavern's entire structure had started to creak.

"Everybody out!" Phoenix shouted.

Some people dove for windows. Angel kicked a hole in the wall. Church scrambled for the front doors, which were now in the center of the floor, and jumped. He fell three stories toward a cobblestone street beneath a void black sky, surrounded on all sides by shrieking monsters. Without turning his head, he saw a mound of gray slime the size of an elephant, twisted bodies with six leathery wings instead of limbs, and hulking monstrosities with spikes instead of eyes. But the worst thing he saw as the Rusted Star rose up away from him was what was holding it.

Tentacle wasn't the right word for it. It was a pillar of gray flesh, streaked through with stripes of endless, empty black, and it rose so high into the sky Church couldn't see where it ended. He did see the part of it that had spread out to clamp onto the top of the Rusted Star, picking it up like a child might a playset. As it lifted, the clamp grip it had on the tavern squashed and spread, until it had become a giant gray lasso wrapped around the entire building. Then, with a squeeze, it shattered the Rusted Star to pieces.

The tavern detonated in a burst of stone and primal magic so loud and bright that Church spent the rest of his fall blind and deaf. His armor's enchantments took the brunt of the impact, but his head was still ringing, and it took him a few seconds to work up the courage to stand. In that time, something warm and wet started to rain down.

The limb the Starborn had extended to crush the Rusted Star now ended in a ragged stump of black that rained thick ichor down on all of them. It had the consistency of jelly, the color of onyx, and it smelled like a rotting corpse covered in cheap perfume. For a moment, Church was too stunned to form a coherent thought.

Angel's not going to be happy, was the first one that actually got through. On its heels, *We actually hurt it.*

A swell of hope and pride surged up in Church as he marveled at the aberrant gore raining down on them. The Starborn could bleed.

The elation was short-lived.

A cursory look around told him they had made it to Relgen. Even to the general area Phoenix had mapped for Angel. But it also told him that they were completely surrounded by monsters, who were all shrieking in sympathetic pain and rage. Church couldn't count them all. He wasn't sure he wanted to. Pressure mounted against thc barrier of his mental shield, and the world reverberated with the Starborn's intent. There was no sound, but its message was unmistakable.

You will be silent.

No heads exploded, but several people fell to their knees screaming, and those that were still standing grimaced in visible discomfort. For his part, Church felt like someone had just hit him in the temples with a pair of hammers. The biggest of the monsters charged forward, bellowing with a maw that could swallow a person whole. Several people brought spells and weapons to bear on it, but one person reacted faster than all the rest.

Astrid Silverspear shot forward, carried on a bolt of lightning with her spear, and she slammed the spearpoint into the creature's domed head with a boom of thunder. It was a dozen times her size, and yet when she struck, *it* was the one thrown back and driven into the ground, tearing a furlough through the street as it went. When it finally came to a stop dozens of feet back, she yanked her spear free of its head and stabbed again. Lightning arced from her weapon, striking out at the dozen lesser Starborn that had begun to converge on her, turning them all to charred husks.

She ripped her spear free again, addressed everyone in a voice that matched the thunder of her weapon.

"We have our mission! Clear a path to the weapon! Hold the line!" She raised her spear high into the air, and screamed, "For the Frelheim!"

The Frelheimer warriors still standing raised their weapons and joined her war cry. As they gathered themselves up to charge into the fray, Hilda drew her own sword.

"For Ricard! For Renalt!" she bellowed.

One by one, the battle cries went up as the Starbreakers' allies threw themselves into one last fight against the end of the world.

"Showtime, ladies!"

"Cord! Advance!"

"For Corsar!"

As everyone surged forward, five individuals remained, subconsciously pulled toward each other instead of the enemy. Church met the eyes of each of his companions in turn. Snow, grimly determined. Angel, already seething with divine light. Brass, smiling as wide as ever. Phoenix, focused entirely on the looming shape of a massive crashed skyship, half-buried in the crater of its own landing.

The spellforger pulled his goggles down. "Let's go to work."

Alongside the others, the Starbreakers charged.

In the mad chaos that followed, Church only caught snippets of the fighting around him, focused as he was on maintaining his mental barriers on the others. But everywhere he looked, people were putting up the fight of their lives.

Angel took to the air in a burst of light, Daybreaker in one hand, an axe made of light in the other, and beams of divine fury streaming from her eyes. Where she looked, monsters died. Sinnodella and Stixaxlatl flew alongside her, with the dragon rending through targets with its claws and acid breath, and the druid effortlessly healing any wound it incurred fighting. When a giant flying centipede came their way, Angel didn't hesitate to fly straight through it, gouging a massive hole through its body and roasting it from the inside out.

On the ground, Phoenix threw out a gravity disc as Brass sprinted at a towering monstrosity that left craters with every step. The device pulsed just as Brass jumped, taking him all the way up to its head and putting him in a perfect position to slice cleanly through the back of its neck. He landed gracefully, taking a bow as the creature fell. Snow immediately blinked into position behind him to skewer the skull of something that had been about to eat him while his back was turned.

A tangle of Ink's glowing blue threads bound a different monster like a bird ready for the oven, and Quint leapt forward to land on its head and drive a spear through its exposed brain. Wings fought alongside the rest of the Broken Spear as easily as if she'd never left the company. Hilda and the Order of Saint Ricard fought like a wall of steel and blessmetal, carving through the enemy on the ground with weapons that shone with divine light. Astrid and her warriors, by contrast, fought like demons, hurling themselves at lesser Starborn and hacking away in imitation of their Queen, whose lightning spear launched her from monster to monster.

Ruby summoned such a tangle of black thorns they almost resembled a giant grasping fist, and she used them to help Gamma, who was trying to keep a gargantuan Starborn pinned down with his freezing blasts while Dietrich slashed away at its back.

And all of them were only keeping the thing immobilized and distracted to give Bart time to gather power into a hammer blow that set off a full-blown thunderclap when he struck, leaving a hole and shower of gore where its chest used to be.

Their force was small, and the longer they fought, the more creatures began to come up from behind them, but they were still making progress, tearing toward the Rogue Imperia, which seemed to grow closer and larger with every abomination felled.

Church himself was limited by necessity. Keeping as many people mentally shielded as he was meant he had little energy or focus to spare on other prayers, and he stuck mostly to using Zealot to fight his way forward. Even conserving his energy, he was starting to feel the early signs of divine overexertion. He felt hot, lightheaded, and his heart was beating fast even for a battle. The pressure he'd felt in his skull from the Starborn had lessened, but it hadn't gone away.

By some miracle, he made it to the wreck of the Rogue Imperia still standing unassisted, though he immediately collapsed into a crouch behind cover as soon as he did. The other Starbreakers were already there, save for Angel, who remained in the air.

She provided support for the others, who were slowly rearranging themselves into a defensive ring around the ship to fend off the horde of monsters that was coming in on all sides now. There were at least three people with real battlefield command experience on their side, but Astrid had taken charge of the whole operation by virtue of shouting first and loudest, and being the one with lightning coming off her with every attack.

"How are you holding up, Church?" Phoenix asked.

"Tired," he said. "But managing."

"If you can't keep up the shield, we're done," Snow said.

"I guess I'll have to keep it up then." He gave her an exhausted but earnest smile. "I don't have much else in me, but I have this."

"I'll stay and make sure nothing bothers him," Brass said. "You two go get our bomb."

Above, Angel gave a feral cry as she dove down into the fray on the ground, relieving some of the pressure on a beleaguered Order of Saint Ricard, but leaving Sinnodella and Stixaxlatl alone in the air. Wings and the Broken Spear tried to pivot to cover her, but that put more pressure on the Cord of Aenwyn to hold their own part of the line without their support. Nobody was overwhelmed yet, but from the sheer number of horrors coming in from all directions, it was clear that the momentum of the battle was shifting, and the longer they were forced to stay in one place, the greater their chances of being overrun.

"Maybe be quick about it?" Brass offered.

Phoenix nodded. With the fire cell of his weapon set to high intensity and minimal range, he cut a hole in the ship's hull, and kicked it in to create an entrance.

Then he and Snow both disappeared into the ship.

Brass moved to stand between Church and the rest of the battle, indicating with his eyes for Church to stay down and save his strength.

"Just between us, how long do you actually think you can keep the shields up?" Brass asked.

Church's grip on Zealot tightened. "As long as I have to."

The interior of the Rogue Imperia was dark, but that wasn't a problem for Phoenix or Snow as he set his goggles to night vision, and she simply relied on eyesight that had adapted to darkness after years of using shadow blinks.

"Do you know where we're going?" Snow asked.

"I still have the ship's layout stored from last time," Phoenix said, tapping the command glyphs on his bracer to pull up the illusory map. "And I remember where we left the Ending."

The illusory miniature replica of the Rogue Imperia hovered over Phoenix's wrist, two points marked in red. One just inside the hull, and one deeper in, near what would have been the cargo hold. Given where they were, and the angle the ship had crashed at, they were in for a climb. Once Phoenix mapped out their heading, they moved, Snow disappearing in a blink, and Phoenix shooting a line of spider silk to haul himself upward.

They went quickly but carefully, conscious of the fragile state of some of the wreckage, and the constant threat of the battle outside disturbing something or spilling in after them. Now was not the time to make a rookie mistake and be buried by ceiling collapse, and they both knew it. But even rushed, the two of them were old hands at exactly this sort of exploration. Almost instinctively, they knew where they could step without falling through the floor, what doorways could and couldn't be trusted, and when to expect unwelcome surprises.

When they ran into an automated security system in a part of the ship that still had power and were caged in by a cage of lightning, Phoenix disabled it. When a starfish-shaped monster jumped out of the walls, Snow stabbed it. When something big outside slammed into the ship and a part of the ceiling collapsed, Snow blinked next to Phoenix while he threw up a force shield over the both of them. All told, it was a completely average delve into a ruin, practically identical to the dozens they'd performed over the course of their careers. Phoenix almost felt bad about the both of them being down here, since he felt sure either of them could have gone through this alone without a hitch.

True to Phoenix's predictions, they found the Ending exactly where they'd left it eight years ago, in the hold of the Rogue Imperia. It was a surprisingly delicate device. It looked like a white ceramic lotus flower, roughly two feet across in size. The ship's crash had tossed it around, and with the whole chamber now tilted at a forty-five-degree angle, it was upside down and slid up against a wall. But there wasn't a scratch on it.

Phoenix didn't waste a second, turning it over and running an arcane scan of it with his bracer to see what state it was in. If they'd come all this way for a broken hunk of metal, he wasn't sure what he'd do. The scan took an agonizing six seconds, during which time he couldn't breathe. But finally, his bracer began to display all the relevant information it had collected in a spread of arcane glyphs. He let out the breath he'd been holding, but he was far from relieved.

"Well?" Snow asked.

"The underlying structure of its firing mechanisms are all still functional, but it's got no power," Phoenix said. He started taking out his supplies. Tools. Components. Then, from one pouch at the back of his belt, he withdrew six glass orbs, each of which glowed a different color except for the one that was an orb of pure black. The Servitor Hearts, pried out of Haegan's armor. "These should be enough to get it restarted."

"Okay," Snow said. "So what's the problem?"

"The problem," Phoenix said with a heavy sigh, "is that I still don't fully understand its triggering sequence. That was why I couldn't disarm it last time."

"We came all this way for a bomb you don't know how to set off?"

"No, I can set it off," Phoenix said. He *still* didn't sound relieved. "I just . . . once I arm it, it's armed and firing. No remote detonation. No way to build in a longer delay between pushing the button and the blast going off. And we lost Angel's bar."

Phoenix saw the sudden, grim understanding write itself on Snow's face. The Rusted Star had been their exit strategy. Without it, or a way to control when the device went off, they were stuck inside the Ending's blast radius.

"So what do we do?" she asked.

Phoenix grimaced and took up his tools. "We hope I'm a faster learner now than I was at twenty-four."

Snow nodded. "You work. I'll tell the others."

"Snow."

She froze just before she could blink away. Phoenix's eyes were hidden behind his goggles, but his expression was plain all the same. "If I can't figure this out—"

"Figure it out."

And then she was gone.

38
COMPANY

Early on, Brass had been a little disappointed in his role. While everyone else got to slice up extra-dimensional monstrosities—and Quint in particular started to pull ahead of him in kill count—Brass had to hang back, and keep Church protected. Now, Church was important to the plan of not having their heads popped like grapes by a stray glance from the giant space monster, and if Brass had to babysit anyone, he was glad it was Church and not Erik Erikson or whatever Frelheimer Warrior Number Six's actual name was. But he had been a bit bored hanging on the back line.

He was no longer bored.

Brass wielded a sword in each hand as he did his best to protect several different priests, including Church, Naomi, Faith, and some others he hadn't had time to come up with names for. One by one, they'd all started to suffer the same exhaustion as Church from keeping the rest of the fighters mentally shielded from the constant pressure of the Starborn, which even Brass was starting to feel as a dull ache behind his eyes. They were all just inside the entrance Phoenix had cut into the Rogue Imperia, sitting against the bulkhead, eyes closed, breathing heavy.

He took what he assumed was the head off of one monster, skewered another through the middle, and kicked a third as it leapt at him. His boots were enchanted to absorb the shock of a fall, but Brass had found the enchantment was also helpful for planting a kick on a charging horror without being toppled, and he was at the point where he was having to squeeze every advantage he could out of the situation. So was everyone else.

Snow blinked back into sight next to Wings, who Brass had been fighting alongside for the last few minutes, and handed her a handful of arrows that were covered in black ichor.

"All I could find," Snow said by way of apology.

"Thanks." Wings stuffed them into her quiver, not seeming to mind the black blood that coated them. Probably because she and the rest of them were all covered in the stuff by this point. She immediately loosed one, taking out a multi-limbed monstrosity that had been crawling across the Rogue Imperia's hull to come up behind them. "Hanging in there?"

"Not much choice," Snow said. She was down to her last dagger, Companion Piece, and the liquid rope launcher built into her armor's bracer. "Your husband needs to work faster."

"Why is he always 'my husband' whenever people get upset? He's *your* companion."

"He's running out of time is what he is," Snow said.

The defensive line they'd established hadn't collapsed, but it had been forced back as casualties had started to mount. Mostly injuries or exhaustion so far, but there were already a few dead. Everyone fought more or less with their backs to the Rogue Imperia now, with Hilda and Quint coordinating efforts to rotate fighters in and out of the front to give people time to rest. Even Angel had been told to take a break at one point. She probably wouldn't have listened, except she'd just fallen out of the sky and had smoke coming off her, so she'd actually stayed down and let herself be dragged back to recover. She'd gone back out since, but she hadn't transformed back into her full-wrath-of-the-heavens state.

Stixaxlatl was out of the air. Tarot was out of cards. Gamma had lost his other arm. The barricade of stone and glowing thread the Cord of Aenwyn had erected was broken in several places, and even Astrid had stopped hurling herself at the enemy like a human lightning bolt. Things weren't looking great.

So, naturally, they got worse.

One of the priests taking refuge inside the Rogue Imperia, a Frelheimer, finally reached their limit, and slumped over, unconscious and bleeding from the nose. Without the priest's protection, a swath of the fighters on the frontline immediately doubled over, clutching their heads in pain. Some of them were instantly mobbed and mauled, but some managed to stagger to safety or even to continue to defend themselves. Until they looked up. Once they did that, they screamed, fell to their knees, or began clawing at their own faces. Some went for all three at once. People near them who were still shielded turned, distracted or trying to get the vulnerable to safety, and inevitably exposed themselves in the process.

The line collapsed, and the monsters that had followed the Starborn into the world surged forward.

Astrid sounded a retreat, and even managed to make it a fighting one as everyone withdrew closer and closer to the Rogue Imperia's carved-out entrance. One by one, they retreated into the ship, until Astrid herself finally came in, and Drummer from the Cord of Aenwyn called up a wall of stone to seal the entrance.

That simply, the fighting paused, as if a switch had been thrown. Darkness enveloped them all, and all noise from the monsters outside became muffled and distant. After the mad cacophony of battle, the sudden quiet was almost deafening, even though there was still plenty of noise in the form of moaning and labored breathing.

Tiny globes of light began to appear, fluttering into the air and spreading out in the dark chamber like a swarm of fireflies until there were enough for everyone to dimly see. Sinnodella lowered her hand after finishing the conjuration and sat down next to Stixaxlatl to begin mending its injured wing once more. The dragon was not the only one wounded.

From outside, they could still hear banging on the hull echoing all around them as the ship's hull was swarmed. The Rogue Imperia was not a whole, intact ship, but a massive wreckage. There would be ways for the smaller creatures to find their way inside. And if they tried, the bigger ones could probably smash their way in. They had, at best, bought themselves a few minutes. And sealed off any hope of escape.

Astrid tapped her spear to the floor once, a queen calling a court to order, and everyone grew silent as the ring of the metal reverberated through the chamber. Even the sounds from the wounded and maddened lessened. She stared down Snow, Angel, and Brass each in turn, finding them in the room. "I will stay here. You need to tell Arman that it is time."

"I'll come," Wings said immediately, and no one protested.

"Me too." Church grunted as he hauled himself unsteadily to his feet. This time, Brass and Angel tried to raise an objection, but Church cut them off.

"We started this together," he said. "I want to end it together too."

All arguments dried up. With one last shared look, the Starbreakers and Wings walked out.

They found Phoenix exactly where Snow had left him, in the middle of a scene that was all too familiar to Brass. Phoenix was hunched over the Ending, a dozen different arcane displays and threads hovering in the air around him, desperately working at the problem of the device, frantic with the knowledge that he was running out of time. The sight of it stopped the Starbreakers in their tracks, and their reaction was all it took to clue Wings into what this must have reminded them of.

Suddenly, none of them, not even Brass, looked like they could speak. So Wings was the one to clear her throat.

"Arman."

He didn't look up from his work. "I don't have it yet."

She knelt down next to him, and rested a hand on his shoulder. His hands stopped working, but his whole body continued to shake. She said nothing, only squeezed his shoulder hard enough to anchor him in the moment instead of inside his own head, and remember the world around him.

Phoenix was a smart man. He would know what it meant that they were all here instead of outside fighting. He pulled something out of his pocket. A glass orb that glowed swirling emerald green. The Heart of the Sky, sealed and contained.

"The power source is actually really efficient. I didn't even need to use all the Hearts to get it going again," Phoenix said. His grip on the orb tightened. "I was going to find a way to give it back to you."

Wings rested her hand on her husband's, covering up the Heart of the Sky. She used her other to push his goggles off of his face, and look him in the eyes. There was a ring of grime around them in the shape of the goggles. "You're the only heart I need."

He looked at her, and then at his company. "I'm sorry."

"What are you sorry about?" Brass asked, voice subdued as he plopped himself down on the floor with them. "We're about to save the world, right?"

Angel snorted, and shook her head. "Guess we are."

She knelt down with them. Church followed her. And so did Snow. Phoenix sighed, and tapped his messenger coil.

"Ink, how many people could you teleport out of here, right now?"

"If I were willing to risk an aneurysm and didn't care where I ended up?" Ink came through, her usual smug superiority replaced with exhausted resignation. *"Myself."*

Phoenix had expected an answer along those lines. Teleporting got harder with both distance and the number of passengers, and Ink had just been through back-to-back battles against Haegan and the Starborn's horde. But it had been worth an ask.

"Better odds of survival than staying here," Phoenix pointed out.

There was a long pause from Ink.

"I could have worse company to die with."

Brass didn't know all of Ink's story. But he knew enough to imagine her with her fingers interlaced with Quint's when she said that, while they sat with the rest of the Cord of Aenwyn. Most glintchasers didn't live to see retirement. They died, usually violently, miles from home, and often for no good reason.

In comparison, everyone here had a pretty good run. Brass sifted through his own thoughts for the places he hadn't been to, drugs he hadn't tried, and sexual acts he'd yet to perform. There were a few heartbreakers on that list, and he'd been hoping to get everyone something nice for Frostfall this year, but on the whole, he supposed he couldn't complain.

And then Phoenix said, "No."

Brass cocked his head. "We're not saving the world?"

Phoenix ignored him, shoving away from the group and digging into his bottomless bag until he found what he was looking for. With a grunt, he hauled out his sky surfer, and immediately began unfolding its mast and sail.

"Arman?" Wings asked.

"Phoenix?" Snow prompted.

"There's *one* last option," Phoenix said. "It's an Avelina thread, and I could be dead wrong, but if I'm right—"

"About *what?*" Angel snapped. She always hated it when he started skipping steps in his explanations.

"The Starborn's coming through the rift, right? The more it comes through, the more influence it's been exerting. Why? Why couldn't it exert full influence through the open rift from its side of it? What if it can't? If the rift somehow interferes with arcane energy flows like a screen or a filter, and we set the Ending off on *its* side of the rift before it can come all the way through, the blast *might* not cross back over to this side."

There was a moment of silence as what Phoenix was saying, and the course of action he was currently implying, hit them. Then everyone was on their feet.

"Okay," Angel said. "Prime that shit, and I'll fly it up."

"You'd never get through the lessers on your own," Phoenix said. "We go up together. I can carry the Ending on the surfer and fight, and you can cover me."

"There's room for two on that thing," Brass said. "I can take a swing at anything that gets too friendly with you."

Church shook his head. "I have to be the one riding with Phoenix."

"You can barely stand," Snow pointed out.

"Maintaining a shield will be easier if I'm closer, and you *need* a shield if you're getting that close to it," Church said. "It has to be me."

Snow frowned, then looked to Angel. "If you can carry me up until we hit flyers, I can keep up on my own from there."

Angel raised an eyebrow, but only shrugged her agreement.

Brass sighed, and started digging in its coat. "No, it's fine, I think I've still got—ah!" He withdrew another sword from his coat's bottomless pockets, this one with a cross guard molded into the shape of a pair of wings. "All right, ready to fly."

"Hey—" Wings started to protest.

"I'm sorry." Phoenix cut her off. "No room. No time. If I don't come back—"

She cut him off straight back by kissing him hard on the mouth. "You're coming back," she declared.

He only nodded, pulled his goggles down, and stared at the ceiling. "Angel? We're going to need an exit."

"Yeah, yeah," Angel said as she began to glow once again. "Stand back."

Beams of light shot from her eyes, and she swept them in a quick circle before cutting them off. A moment later, three circles of metal fell to the floor, and there was a clear exit tunnel leading out of the Rogue Imperia, still glowing hot around the edges and wide enough for the sky surfer to fly through. Light exploded from her body once again, her wings and halo reappeared, and after grabbing Snow by her armor, she took off into the air.

Phoenix cast one last look over his shoulder at Wings. "I love you."

He made one last adjustment to the Ending, and then abruptly, its magic began to warm up, coming off in slowly spinning loops of white light. Then he and Church were on the sky surfer with the Ending, taking off after Angel and Snow.

Brass gave Wings a sympathetic smile. "Sorry. Sword only seats one."

She shook her head. "Go. I'll catch up."

Brass had no idea how she planned on doing that, but grinned anyway. He knew he wouldn't miss this for the world, and was glad that Wings wouldn't either. He pointed his blade straight up, and the winged sword chimed like a bell before he was whisked skyward.

39
EMBERS

Silas was dying, and the world was dying with him. Up until a moment ago, Silas had been furious with the Starbreakers, and everyone they'd brought with them. He and Haegan and the rest of the Exile Order were fighting for the future of humanity, and the Starbreakers had spat in their face. The Exile Order was here to *kill* the Starborn, and the Starbreakers had tried to stop them. Brass had opened his throat, and Silas had fallen to the ground full of righteous indignation.

But then the sky had truly parted, and Silas had seen what the Starborn was. The vastness of it. The impossibility. Then he'd understood. The Exile Order were not the heroes of this story. They were the fools who had just doomed the world with their hubris.

Understood was the wrong word. The more Silas thought about it, the more he had to concede that, deep down, he had always known that they were not on the right side of this conflict. Nothing they'd done had felt right, but for a while he'd been able to convince himself of the necessity of it. He'd wrapped himself in Haegan's conviction, his certainty. His madness. Haegan had been Silas's hero.

But how could he be anything but mad for wanting *this*? And in the absence of that necessity, of his belief in Haegan, Silas was left only with the knowledge that he should have known better.

He was drifting. He wondered how much of that was blood loss, and how much came from his own loosening grip on sanity. You could not stare into the Starborn and not lose your mind. And he couldn't look away. Distantly, a part of his mind was screaming that he knew battlefield healing. That he could staunch the bleeding in his neck and save himself. But he struggled to see the point of it. They were all already dead. They had been from the moment the Starborn had learned that this world existed. All Silas and his brothers and sisters in arms had done was speed up the process.

Something grabbed him, pulling him deeper into the crackling silver smoke that still covered the floor, and for a moment, everything went silver as it swallowed him whole. It was over only an instant later, and he tumbled out of the smoke and into the ruined remains of what had once been a cathedral.

More blood ran from his neck, and in his shock, survival instincts won out over nihilism, and he clutched the wound to try and keep the last of his life from flowing out of him. Panic seized him. He had seconds to live if he didn't think of something.

Someone kicked him, and he rolled onto his back, too weak to resist. Then, the Prisoner was on top of him. Silas saw the burning zeal of the man's eyes, so intense it bordered on ecstasy. His grin stretched unnaturally wide across his face, made even more unhinged-looking by the blood that ran from his eyes, his nose, and the twelve-pointed star on his forehead. Droplets of the blood hit Silas in the face as the cultist leaned in close to him.

"Very good," the Prisoner said. "I have done very good so far, little knight, and the rightful owners of this world have come to reassert their claim. But the work is not done."

Rage rekindled inside of Silas. This man was the Cult of Stars. He was responsible for leading Haegan astray, for turning them all into an instrument of humanity's end. This was all his fault. Silas clawed at him with one hand, going for his eyes.

The Prisoner leaned out of the way easily, and pinned Silas's arm down with one hand. Silas couldn't take the other off his neck.

"There are still some who will resist the truth of the universe. They must not be allowed to upset the natural order of things again," the Prisoner said. "And for that, I will need this."

The Prisoner pulled out the spike Brass had driven into Silas's Servitor harness and plucked out the Servitor Heart. Silas didn't have the strength to fight him, though he did try. With horror, he watched the cultist plant the Heart into his own harness and saw the angry red Servitor Heart pulse with power as it came under the control of a new will.

"This will do nicely. Goodbye, little knight."

Then the Prisoner faded back into the silver smoke, and the smoke itself retreated from the ruined cathedral, leaving Silas alone to die.

40
THE STARBREAKERS

The Starbreakers flew almost straight up. Angel took the lead, golden wings spread, Daybreaker in one hand, Snow in the other. Phoenix kept the sky surfer close behind them, steering with one hand while keeping his pistol at the ready. Church was anchored to the surfer by the board's enchantment, which left his hands free to hold onto the Ending, just in case. The weapon's magic was still slowly whirring to life, but the loops of light coming off it were building in intensity with every passing second. Brass brought up the rear of their formation, holding on to his sword like his life depended on it.

Above them, the Starborn was a wall of endless void and patchy gray skin expansive enough to fill the sky to the horizon. And in between were hundreds of malformed shapes, flapping, floating, and flailing through the air. No two of them were the same arrangement of body parts and materials, but all of them were unnatural and angry, and together they formed a twisted cloud of teeth, claws, and tentacles.

"That is a lot of monsters!" Brass shouted to be heard above the wind.

"We don't have to kill them, we just have to punch through!" Phoenix said. "Angel clears the path, we keep them off of her, we don't slow down!"

The gap between them and the monsters shrank even faster as some of the lesser Starborn began to dive down. They all sighted their first targets, each picking a different section out of the mob.

Except for Church, who had his eyes squeezed shut as they climbed higher and faster. He wasn't just fighting against divine overexertion. He also hated flying.

"We're all going to fucking die," Snow muttered.

"What?" Angel asked.

Snow reversed her grip on her dagger. "I said throw me!"

So Angel did. And then the monsters were everywhere.

Flung by Angel like a sack of potatoes, Snow sailed straight into something resembling a giant bat, immediately digging her dagger into the membrane of its wing and using the leverage and her momentum to swing onto its back. With one stab to the back of what looked like the head, the creature went limp, and began to fall. She jumped off it almost as quickly as she'd found purchase and disappeared in a shadow blink. She reappeared onto the next closest monster, poised to strike. She kept pace with the others, blinking from one enemy to the next, only sticking to it long enough to deliver a stab and find her next unwitting platform.

As soon as she was free of Snow, Angel resummoned an axe of light to pair with Daybreaker into her off hand and set to work. Her every swing carried a wave of golden light with it that scythed through otherworldly abominations like they were made of paper. One monster up ahead shuddered its bulbous body, releasing clusters of red-hot polyps from its hide that came down at her like a rain of arrows. Phoenix shot one with a force blast, and it exploded in a ball of fire, setting off a chain reaction that saw the entire attack erased long before it reached Angel. She responded by punching a hole through the creature with the beams from her eyes, which caused the rest of the creature to explode.

Brass fell past her, slicing a monster in half as he went by. With another flick of the blade, he changed his flight's direction, dodging a spray of some no-doubt incredibly deadly bile a monster tried to vomit up at him. His next shift in direction sent him dropping straight down onto the back of another monster, this one big enough that when he sank his blade into it, it didn't seem to notice. It was chasing after the others though, so Brass opted to simply keep his sword in it and go along for the ride until he saw something else coming for Angel's blind spot, and let his sword whisk him off to meet it. He did all of this while alternating between profuse cursing, whooping at the top of his lungs, and laughing uncontrollably.

Phoenix was sweeping his pistol back and forth, spewing fire in every direction he could to keep them from being overwhelmed. In the moments where they had any breathing room, he switched back to force blasts and peppered the horde in front of them, but the blasts had little effect unless he set the gun to its highest intensity, and that would empty the cell in seconds. Not a huge problem, but he was dangerously low on supplies, and between shooting and steering, he didn't have a hand free to reload a cell anyway. No sooner did he think that when he had to eject his entire spider-silk cell in one shot to quickly entangle and drop a monster that had closed in on them terrifyingly fast.

They were making progress, but the deeper they pushed, the more surrounded they became. Snow was having to blink more and more to avoid getting overwhelmed. Angel's attention was split in too many directions, and no amount of devastation she wrought created much space for long. In desperation, Phoenix talked Church through digging into his belt for a fire sphere and arming the weapon. Church didn't even need to throw it, just let it go, and the ensuing explosion that went off behind them took a cluster of monsters with it.

Brass was the first one to fumble.

The enemies had become so densely packed that he was having trouble using his sword to maneuver, and during an attempted sideways dash to evade an attack, he put himself right into the path of another creature that snatched him up in a set of oversized talons. He sliced himself free in seconds, but by then, he had fallen too far behind, and he was cut off from the rest of the group. Snow found herself caught in a similar position only a few seconds later, wrapped in the tail of a flying snake-thing that dragged her down and away as she fought to free herself. The pressure on Angel increased with only Phoenix covering her, and for a moment, he lost sight of her in the swarm that converged on her. What happened next made Phoenix feel like an idiot forever comparing anything Angel had done to a sun. Next to what she did in that moment, every display of power she'd shown before looked like a candle.

A pillar of light, equal in size to any one of the Starborn's tendrils, burst into being, drawing a golden seam across the entire sky that stretched all the way up to the rift above and down to the ground below. Phoenix's goggles tried to keep up with the light, filtering it out as much as they could, and he was still blinded for a few terrifying blinks. When the light faded, and he could see, Angel was dropping like a stone through a suddenly empty sky.

Her voice came weakly through the coil. *"Go—"*

And then her body fell past them toward the earth.

"I've got her!" Snow and Brass said over the coil at the same time.

Phoenix hadn't stopped flying, and as soon as he heard that, he didn't spare Angel another glance. She'd created a massive clearing in the horde, and a straight shot all the way to the rift. It was already starting to fill in, but he could tell the lesser Starborn would close in too slowly. They were going to make it.

"Church, get ready to throw it!" he shouted, never taking his eyes off that last stretch of distance between them and the rift. Between them, and saving everyone. They were going to do it.

And then Church flung Phoenix off of the sky surfer.

The sky surfer could only anchor one person on to its board, and that person had been Church. Phoenix had been keeping his footing on the board through a mix of balance, grip on the controls, and controlling the angle of their climb. So when Church threw all his weight into a hard yank and hip toss, Phoenix was off the board before he'd even realized what was happening. And by the time he did, the Starborn's tendril had already smacked the sky surfer like a person might swat at a fly.

Phoenix hadn't even seen the blow coming, but Church had, just in time to fling Phoenix to safety.

But Church was still anchored to the sky surfer. Throwing Phoenix had also thrown it off course, so instead of being instantly obliterated by a direct hit from the Starborn itself, the flying board only barely clipped the edge of the outstretched limb. That was still enough to send it careening out of control. It spun and flipped, still traveling upward thanks to its momentum. And instead of throwing the Ending across the threshold and flying away, the sky surfer crossed the threshold entirely, taking Church and the Ending with it.

41

THRESHOLD

Church wasn't sure he'd ever been as exhausted as he was from trying to keep up the Starbreakers' mental shields against the Starborn. The weight of it had turned into someone piling granite bricks inside his skull. The feeling of divine overexertion, like heatstroke mixed with a crash at the end of a sugar high, had left him on the edge of delirious. But still he held on.

As someone without any real interest in romance, Church had once asked Phoenix to explain what exactly it meant to him. According to Phoenix, romantic feelings were a mix of strong desire for and adoration of another person. You wanted to be around them, because they made you happy, they were important to you, and everything about what made them who they were brought you joy. The world seemed more right when you were with them, and you wanted to do everything you could to make their lives better. Partly because you wanted to reciprocate how much better they made your life, and partly because you wanted good things for them.

After that conversation, Church thought he understood why romantic relationships didn't seem to click for him. The feelings Phoenix had described hadn't sounded all that special; Church felt that way about everyone.

It was why he loved helping people so much. Why he'd dedicated his life to it. Why he'd stuck with the Starbreakers for so long, even when the work stopped calling to him. Because in spite of all their differences, being with the

Starbreakers made Church happy. They were important to him. The world felt more right when they were together, and he wanted to do everything he could to make their lives better. Because they had made his life so much better, and because they deserved it.

When Relgen had fallen, and they'd all fought and disbanded, Church had thought for a long time that bond had been tainted by blood and pain. That all he could do was move on, and do better with others moving forward. But these last few months of being back in each other's lives had reaffirmed everything Church had ever felt about his companions and then some. They could get distracted, and lose their way at times, but the world was better for having them in it.

And he'd remembered something else from the old days in the company. From their best days, when they fought not to enrich themselves, but to make the world a better, safer place. If the Starbreakers were taking care of everyone else, someone needed to take care of the Starbreakers. And that, Church had decided all those years ago, was his job.

He did what he could to keep them, if not on the straight and narrow, at least going its general direction. He healed their wounds and defended their souls as the needs arose. And if it looked like they were going to get themselves killed, he would find a way to save them.

He'd remembered it when they were sitting around the Ending. When he realized that, technically, they'd won the day the moment they'd gotten Phoenix to the weapon.

The world would be safe from the Starborn. The only lives that still hung in the balance, futures uncertain, had been that of the Starbreakers, and all the other souls that had been brave enough to follow them back into the path of a living apocalypse. He'd recognized then, how ready they all were to give their lives, and been profoundly struck by the desire to make sure they didn't have to.

It was what had compelled him to use the prayer to get them out of Relgen all those years ago. It was what had given him the will to keep the mental shield up even when his brain felt like it might cook from the effort. And it was what had forced him to open his eyes and watch Phoenix's back, even though he hated flying.

He'd seen the Starborn's tendril coming in to swat at them. He'd *felt* the animosity of the thing build in the air and push against the mental barrier he'd erected. The massive, mottled gray-and-black thing looked more like a towering organic superstructure than an appendage. And it moved so fast. He didn't have time to warn Phoenix, and anyway, he wasn't sure he could form words or draw enough breath to shout. But he could jerk his body, shift his weight hard enough to get his friend clear.

Then everything had been swallowed by black.

Church felt every mental shield he'd been holding up vanish in an instant, and a cold shiver ran through his body as he looked on an endless sea of true nothingness. His body felt unsettlingly light, as if something he always carried with him was suddenly gone, and he knew at once that his connection to Renalt and Saint Beneger had been severed. He was completely alone. Until he wasn't.

YOU DISTURB THE SILENCE.

Existential pain flared through Church—mind, body, and soul. He felt intrinsically wrong on every level. He did not belong. He should not exist. He tried to scream, but no sound came from his mouth. He thrashed, but there was nothing solid to touch. Not even a feeling of air on his skin. The only sensation of any kind was the pain of the Starborn's displeasure.

YOUR EXISTENCE IS A FLAW. I WILL CORRECT IT.

Church felt himself being pulled apart. Unwritten. Unmade. He understood himself as an imperfection in a sheet of smooth glass, an unwanted ripple on the surface of a still pond. He was a disruption in the perfect order of the universe, and it was not just him. Humanity. Mortal life. The gods that shepherded it. Anything that was not the Starborn was wrong, always buzzing at the edges of the Starborn's awareness and agitating it, keeping it from sleeping or thinking.

Once, the Starborn had not known the source of its displeasure. The chaotic static of life had become like so much background noise to it, that it could not even sort where it came from or where to begin. But then, a stutter. A tiny shift in the noise that carried a note of perfection. Of silence. It had heard the fall of Relgen in the sudden silence of so many lives snuffed out at once. And it had come to inspect it. To understand what had dampened the noise, and how more silence might be made. Until it understood.

It had not seen a way to reach out to touch the world, but it had waited and studied, searching for a way in. And, almost instantly from its perspective, a way had emerged, and practically drawn it in. Now, at last, there would be silence. It had only to reach out a little further now. But something had come through the other way. A single, muted note of existence. Insignificant, but tinged by the power of the Starborn's oldest surviving enemies.

Church. Church was the note. The enemies were the gods.

The priest fought to remember himself, his existence, his purpose. He breathed, and he wasn't sure if it was an actual breath or only remembering what it felt like to breathe, but in that moment there was no difference. It was a halt in the process of being silenced.

And with his awareness briefly free of pain, he felt something else. A static, pricking sensation from an energy brushing over him. It was so subtle, that if he'd had any other sensation to experience, he might not have noticed it, but here in the Starborn's home, he could feel it. The Ending's power was still building, still coming closer and closer to a cascade of power that could kill even the Starborn.

Unfortunately, the Starborn noticed too.

YOU STRIKE AT ME. I DO NOT ALLOW IT.

And then, it wasn't just Church being unmade, but the Ending too. He felt the titanic, all-consuming presence wrap around him and the device both. He could see it fuzzing at the edges. He saw himself fading away, and his heart clenched. They were so close. It was about to go off, he was sure. He just needed to buy a little more time.

Instinctively, he tried to pray. To call up resilience to resist the Starborn's erasure of him, or some kind of shield to protect the Ending. Nothing happened. He felt not even a ghost of Beneger's presence.

YOUR SAINT CANNOT HEAR YOU. YOUR GODS WILL NOT COME.

All this time, Church had not been hearing the Starborn's words so much as experiencing them. They wrote themselves into his consciousness, into his understanding of reality. The Starborn did not speak. The Starborn was.

And it knew it. It didn't just look down on Church, but on all of humanity, on the gods and their saints. In its words, in its will, Church could feel its contempt for everything that was not itself. For all of its size, its conceptual weight, its reality-warping presence, at its core, Church saw only an arrogant, selfish creature that would slaughter billions on a whim to have its way. And Church refused to let it go unchallenged.

"Won't come?" Church asked, and there was sound to his voice. The Starborn recoiled at it like a person might at the sting of an insect.

A warmth spread through Church's body, starting in his chest and spreading out across every inch of his body. Where it went, strength flowed through, a sudden, endless reserve of power. His whole body shone with white-gold light, and Church felt at his back a presence that could match the Starborn. And he knew this was not Beneger.

"I am a servant of Renalt, god of strength and justice," Church intoned. "Where I go, he is with me!"

And with no prayer, and no intercession of a saint on his behalf, Church called the power of a god. A pulse of golden light radiated out from him, pushing back against the Starborn. The Ending took on solid form, his own pain vanished, and he could feel his own existence solidifying. The Starborn pushed back almost immediately, and Church knew he couldn't hold the creature back for long at all. But he also knew he didn't have to.

The Ending had continued to charge, and was even now too bright to look at. Just as it had been right before—

Something yanked Church backward, and a strange sensation crawled across his skin as he felt himself pulled across a threshold, and suddenly, there was air again, and sound, and oh Renalt, he was so, so tired. The boundless strength and power evaporated from him, coming off him as a shower of glittering lights trailing away from him as he was pulled back into the physical world, and the waiting arms of Phoenix.

"Got him!" Phoenix shouted.

Church blinked, already feeling himself sliding into unconsciousness. Dimly, he registered that Phoenix was bleeding from the nose and eyes, and that they were now on the back of a dragon. Wings was there, shouting for it to dive down, and it listened to her. Church registered this, and looked back to the rift in the sky. He could just make out the brilliant point of white light that was the Ending, surrounded by the black of the Starborn.

The last thing he saw before passing out was that white light detonating.

42
THE VICTORS

When Church went through the rift, Phoenix's first thought was that it should have been him. Privately, he'd thought it might come down to something like this. A scenario where one of them would have to make the sacrifice for everyone else. To give their life so everyone else could live. Brass certainly wasn't going to do it. Neither would Snow. Church or Angel would be willing, but Phoenix had quietly decided that if it came to it, if it had to be anyone, it would be him. He knew how the Ending worked. He'd been the one who'd failed to disarm it last time. This was his second chance. He couldn't let anyone else pay the price for it.

Except Church went and tried to anyway, hurling Phoenix clear of a Starborn's attack and then disappearing through a tear in reality. Phoenix's heart had stopped as he fell back to Asher.

Then a brass-colored blur had practically slammed into him in midair, and a familiar grip clasped him by the arm and swung him onto the back of a dragon as naturally as if they were helping him onto a horse.

"Gotcha!" Wings shouted.

The instant elation that hit Phoenix was almost dizzying. He wasn't afraid of falling to his death—he had ways to save himself. But he was terrified that Church was about to die in his place, and there was nothing he could do about it.

"We need to go back for Church!" he shouted.

Wings didn't question him, just turned Stixaxlatl with her hips. Phoenix, finally with his hands free, frantically reloaded the spider-silk cell in his weapon.

When they were close enough to the rift, and he could just make out a humanoid figure on the other side of it, he fired out a line and yanked.

He hauled Church back across dimensions like a fisherman pulling a catch out of the water, and Wings angled their flight to close the gap with him until Phoenix snatched him out of the air and into his arms.

"Got him! Drop!"

Wings immediately put Stixaxlatl into a dive. Behind them, on the other side of the rift between worlds, the Ending set off. It turned out that Phoenix's hypothesis about the rift had been half-right. The barrier did interfere with the Ending's power, but instead of stopping it from coming over to their side, it had only blunted the blast for them. Some of the power came through, and where it passed, lesser Starborn seized up and went limp. But it didn't travel nearly as far as it should have, and with Stixaxlatl's speed, they outflew it.

The dragon struggled to pull out of the dive, and its efforts made Phoenix's stomach climb into his skull, but he barely noticed.

All around him, dead monsters were falling out of the sky, and not just the one's killed by the Ending. Several of the creatures went into fitful shrieks before exploding into gore, even though they'd been outside the blast radius. The black void substance of the Starborn's form shriveled up and vanished, leaving huge sloughs of gray flesh behind that, now unsupported, fell to the earth in horrifying crashes.

Some of those bits had been above them, and they rained down black blood in buckets on all of them.

Phoenix still couldn't bring himself to care.

They'd killed a Starborn.

They'd done it.

They'd won.

It was raining gore, and Snow was laughing. She couldn't remember the last time she'd felt as *alive* as she did then, standing in the middle of a ruined city, surrounded by monster corpses, getting drenched in ichor. It wasn't just as if a weight had fallen off her shoulders. It was like a weight had been taken off the entire world. Like something had been pressing down on everyone and everything, and only now were they taking their first real, full breath. And it felt so good.

She wanted to dance. To cheer. To kiss somebody. Brass was next to her, grinning just as wide, and it was either him or the still unconscious Angel lying in the mud next to them. She grabbed Brass by the shirt and went for it, and he went along without a second's hesitation, spinning them. He tasted like iron, sweat, and bad decisions, and she didn't care at all.

They'd fought a space god and lived. And *won.* Nothing else mattered.

"Oh gods," Angel muttered. "I couldn't have just died? I had to wake up to this?"

Snow and Brass broke apart laughing, and Angel grumbled something about them dying in a hole that made them laugh harder. The black rain slowly petered out to a drizzle.

Above, the rift in the sky had already started to close, breaking up from a solid sheet of black back into cracks in the sky, through which they could just make out traces of sky tinged by sunset.

A shadow of a dragon fell over them as Stixaxlatl came in for a landing with three people on its back. Phoenix and Church didn't dismount so much as tumble off the dragon's back, with Church as dead weight and Phoenix failing to support him. Snow laughed all over again, and her chest felt full to bursting. This was what she'd really been missing out on with the Heart of Ice. Pure, unadulterated joy. A relish for being alive in a world that kept trying to kill them, and kept failing.

Wings helped Phoenix to his feet, and Church groaned.

"Did . . . did we win?"

They all looked at each other, all disbelief and idiot grins, and Phoenix nodded. "Yeah. We won."

"And thank the gods for it, because I have to *piss*!" Brass announced, immediately sauntering off toward the closest rock big enough to do his business behind. "Back in sixty!"

Snow shook her head, even as she took mental stock of herself and realized she herself desperately needed food, a bath, and a drink or twelve followed by a month of uninterrupted sleep.

"We should probably wash this stuff off," Phoenix said, noting the black ichor that had soaked all of them. "Preferably with holy water."

"Someone else can make it," Church moaned, eyes closed. "I'm not using another prayer for a week." One of his eyes opened and found Phoenix. "You saved me."

Phoenix smiled. "I had to pay you back for last time."

Church chuckled in acknowledgement as Phoenix put one hand to his messenger coil. "Whoever can still hear me, it's Phoenix. It's over. The Starborn—"

His words were swallowed up as a burst of flames washed over them.

For the second time that day, Snow's body screamed in protest at the burns covering her. She couldn't be sure, but she thought she might have hit her head in the blast. The blast. What had happened? Where were they?

She opened her eyes, struggled to push herself up to her feet and only got as far as lifting her head. None of the others had fared any better than Snow. Phoenix was lying on top of Wings, the back of his coat and armor half melted. Stixaxlatl was hysteric with pain, halfway to fleeing. Church had lost pieces of his chain mail and was writhing in pain. Angel was lying face down in the dirt, not moving. Flames still licked the ground around them.

A lone figure strode toward them, the Heart of Flames a red glow burning at the center of his chest. For a moment, Snow thought the figure was Silas, here out of a misplaced desire for revenge. But it wasn't Silas. It was the cultist prisoner Snow had encountered in the mansion's lower levels.

His thin, frail body was shaking, and his eyes were bloodshot. Trails of dried blood ran down his face in dark red streaks. Fire licked up his arms, and pooled in his palms.

"You. Ruined. Everything!" the Prisoner said. "You . . . abominations! You perversions of the natural order! We are pests! Cosmic intruders in the properties of true power! It is our place to die! And you dared to take an immortal life to preserve your own putrid existence!"

He threw out his hands, sending another wave of flames. Phoenix weakly put up an arm on instinct, and his force shield sputtered to life long enough to blunt the attack before flickering out. Instead of being completely incinerated, Phoenix fell back screaming, his arm smoking. Stixaxlatl only fled farther away from the flames. Without Wings or Sinnodella to guide him, the young dragon was too ruled by its base instincts, and those instincts were being overwhelmed by pain and fear.

"Years of effort! Of maneuvering in the darkness!" the Prisoner screamed. "Rebuilding my numbers after your purges! Everywhere I went! Every step I took! You were there, haunting me! Killing me!"

Church coughed and tried to stand. The Prisoner directed his next blast at him.

"I have suffered your interference for too long! Today, I rid myself of you all! Today, the Starbreakers burn!"

"Hard pass!"

A knife sank into the Prisoner's wrist, and he howled like an animal as Brass dropped down from the air straight on top of him. When the Prisoner threw fire at him, Brass flicked his winged sword, and neatly dodged the blast with a shift in the direction of his fall.

He landed next to Phoenix in a low crouch before kicking the spellforger in one direction and rolling in the other, letting another blast of fire pass between them. He came up holding his sword in one hand, and Phoenix's gun in the other.

He pulled the trigger, and a line of spider silk shot out, hitting the Prisoner in the face.

Brass had been hoping for a force blast, but played the hand he'd been dealt, hooking his leg around the silk line and stomping down hard to yank the Prisoner toward him. He went for a killing thrust, but the Prisoner reacted with blind rage and fire to match, and one of the crescents of flames that lashed out from him sliced clean through Brass's blade. The flames burned the spider silk off of the Prisoner's face, just in time for him to see Brass, now with his coat removed and wrapped around his fist, throw a punch.

Their exchange was brief. Brass punched with his protected fist, and the Prisoner sprayed fire in every direction. Brass dodged each one, but even avoiding being incinerated, his coat still caught fire in the exchange in seconds, and he had to retreat and hurriedly shake it off his hand.

Brass shot another shot of spider silk from Phoenix's gun, but not at the Prisoner. Instead, the line found Companion Piece, which was resting just a few feet from Snow. Without fully understanding why, she tried to dive for the weapon before Brass could pull it away. But she was too hurt, and too slow. With the silk, Brass yanked the dagger into his waiting hand, and Snow's fingers found only dirt and ash.

Brass came at the Prisoner again, weaving his slashes and stabs around the inferno that spewed from the cultist. Several of his attacks landed, but the Prisoner was still one of the Cult of Stars. He felt no pain from the injuries Brass gave him, and the Heart of Flames sealed most as soon as they were made. And meanwhile, Brass took burn after burn. With every new singe or sear, the other Starbreakers cringed. But what had them most terrified was how quiet Brass had gotten. There were no dismissive jokes at the Prisoner's expense, no line about the others being free to tag in anytime. Only grunts, and hisses of pain.

Still shaking with pain from his burns, Phoenix started rummaging through his pockets for something, anything useful. Wings called to Stixaxlatl, trying to get the dragon to calm down, turn back, and help. Church grit his teeth, trying to master himself long enough to think straight. Agonizingly slow, Angel stirred in the dirt. Snow's whole body shuddered as she tried to shadow blink, but she went nowhere as pain wracked her from head to toe and wisps of shadow curled uselessly off her. They were all too injured to do much of anything, but they struggled anyway, because none of them could just lie there and watch Brass fight a losing battle alone.

Snow tried to blink again, heart hammering in her chest. It failed, but this time, the Prisoner took notice of her. He turned, and she saw her death in the flames that licked up his arms.

Brass threw Companion Piece, and a cloud of silver smoke appeared in the air to swallow the knife in mid-flight. Brass dodged it when it came flying out of another cloud that materialized in front of him, but he didn't dodge the single, thin steak of flames that the Prisoner shot out at the same time, spearing him through the chest.

"NO!" Snow screamed.

Brass let out a gasp, and his eyes went wide. His stagger turned into him tripping over his own feet, and in his ensuing fall he didn't drop Phoenix's gun so much as fling it away. He landed hard with a smoking hole in his chest, breaths coming out shaky and uneven. As the Prisoner came to loom over him, Snow caught Brass's eye, expecting to see shock or mortal terror in his gaze.

He winked at her.

"You are finished," the Prisoner snarled.

Lying on the ground with a smoking hole in his chest, Brass gave a weak smile. "Well, that's embarrassing. I swear, I usually last longer than this."

Snow saw the plan at the same moment everyone else did. Phoenix's gun lay only a few feet from him now. Church found himself a similar distance away from Zealot, laying fallen on the ground. Angel was groaning, halfway to conscious, taking in the scene around her. The layout of the fight had created a line, running through Snow, the Prisoner, and Companion Piece, laying just a short distance away after Brass had dodged it. He couldn't call it back into his hand, but she could. The madman's full attention was on Brass, face twisted by contemptuous fury. The rest of them had an opening.

The Prisoner leveled a flaming finger like an executioner's blade. "You were always the most infuriating."

"I do my best."

Snow thrust out her hand, calling Companion Piece back to her. But if she stayed lying on the ground, the blade's flight would be too low to the ground to kill the Prisoner, so she tried to stand. Pain made her lurch, and the Prisoner whirled on her again. He fired the shot meant for Brass, but her body gave out underneath her and she dropped, avoiding the hit. Companion Piece whizzed harmlessly between his ankles.

He'd have burned her alive in the next breath, but at that same moment, Brass clicked his boot heel against the ground, extending the hidden blade in the toe, and kicked up to drive it squarely into the man's taint. The Prisoner howled in pain, and instead of a single finger, he waved his whole arm, throwing down a curtain of fire on top of Brass in retaliation.

Snow threw Companion Piece the instant it reached her hand. At the same time, a blast of force caught the Prisoner in the chest, knocking him backward and impaling him from behind on the spectral copy of Zealot that materialized behind him. Twin beams of light punched through his chest at the same time that Snow's dagger sank into the twelve-pointed star on his forehead. All the flames on the Prisoner went out in an instant. He hung limp for a moment, held up by the sword of golden light that had run him through. When the sword's image faded to nothing, he collapsed, dead.

The Starbreakers surrounded him, all still prone. Phoenix had his gun in hand, Wings next to him and holding his arm to keep it steady. Church's fingers were wrapped around Zealot's blade. Divine light faded from Angel's eyes as her power retreated.

They had all been too slow.

The Prisoner was dead. But of Brass, nothing remained but ashes already being carried away on the breeze.

They stared in mute shock. For a few seconds, nobody moved. Nobody breathed. When Snow finally could, she screamed at the top of her lungs.

"BRASS!"

43
THE TAVERN

The Old Spot wasn't much, as far as taverns went. It had a chicken coop out back, wooden tables and stools for a few dozen people at once, bunks for about half that in a common room upstairs, and a decently clever name painted onto the wooden sign mounted over the front door. It sat smack dab in the middle of fucking and nowhere in a stretch of nothing that would have been abandoned and swallowed by the wilderness an age and a half ago, except that it also sat just off Future's Road, so it was actually a fairly well-traveled stretch of nothing. Turns out, people still have to pass through nowhere in order to get somewhere.

Chloe wished she could count herself among the patrons of the Old Spot trying to get somewhere. For the last few weeks, she and Brass hadn't been going anywhere but away—away from her old home, away from her father's men, and away from the gang that had tried to kidnap her and hold her for ransom. A gang, incidentally, that Brass had all but abandoned her to for months. He'd rescued her eventually, but only after Chloe had been forced to learn the skills of a thief just to survive her imprisonment.

It was a point of tension between them. One that still brokered the occasional fight—like the one they were having now.

"I get that you're still mad," Brass said. "But it all worked out in the end! We got you out, Vane and all the other bastards are dead, and you turned out to be even more of a badass than I thought you would."

"And you turned out to be even more of a jackass than I thought you would."

"Come on, Snowflake—"

"I told you to stop calling me that," Chloe snapped. "My name is Snow."

Chloe expected some kind of retort or snide jab from Brass about her new freelancing moniker, so she was surprised when his face suddenly grew soberly sincere.

"You're right," he said. "I'm sorry."

Chloe blinked, then scowled. Somehow, Brass being genuine and apologetic was more infuriating than his usual glib remarks. "What are you doing?"

"You know, I'm not always up to something. Sometimes I'm just trying to be nice," Brass said. Chloe's face marked just how much she believed him, and he sighed in exasperation. "Look, do you really want to keep fighting about this"—he lowered his voice to conspiratorial murmur—"or do you want to check out the mark that just walked in?"

Chloe's body tensed with sudden, reflexive excitement at Brass's tone and that wonderfully alluring word, "mark." They promised a scheme, a tidy profit, and the thrill of pulling off a job. She reminded herself that she was still mad at Brass, and that she was a professional now, not the spoiled rich girl full of wanderlust she'd been when they met. She forced herself to relax.

She didn't turn around—giving away interest in a target like that was an amateur move, and she didn't make those anymore. Instead, she glanced down as Brass discreetly pulled a hand mirror out of his jacket pocket and rested it on the table at the perfect angle to give her a view of the man who'd just walked into the Old Spot.

"Man" was probably a strong word. His caramel skin was smooth, clear of both wrinkles and any sort of facial hair. He wore a dark red traveler's cloak, too thick for the season and too big on him, and it didn't do much to hide his skinny frame. His dark hair the kind of short you could only get from a barber, which meant he couldn't have been on the road long.

A wide-eyed mix of excitement and uncertainty was plastered across his face, and that expression infected everything else he did. The overly curious way his gaze swept the room and the nervous smile he wore like a shield made him look awkward, but it was the massive, overstuffed backpack and old crossbow two sizes too big for him that really made him stand out as completely and totally out of his depth. The boy might have been around Chloe's age, but one look at him, and she knew she'd seen more in the last year than he'd seen in his entire life.

After a trepidatious look around, he made his way over to the bar. Along the way, the crossbow hanging from his backpack bumped into at least three different people. He stopped to apologize every time.

"Him?" Chloe asked.

"Are you kidding me? He's perfect. Look at him," Brass said. "New clothes, fresh face, overstuffed bag, and absolutely no self-awareness. He doesn't have the first idea what kind of world he's walking around in. He's like a baby carrying a giant wallet."

"You're way too fixated on the backpack," Chloe said immediately. "It could be full of bullshit."

"Bag of bullshit's worth more than nothing. Besides, we're traveling a little light ourselves these days. Maybe we could use some bullshit."

Chloe considered telling Brass this was a waste of time, but when she thought about it, she was forced to admit they weren't doing anything else right now. A small opportunity was better than no opportunity, and if nothing else, stealing was fun.

"Okay, so what's the plan?"

"I've got a few ideas: We could leave, disguise ourselves, come back posing as knights hunting for a stolen artifact. We ask to see his bag, accuse him of stealing something, and then . . . what are you doing?"

Chloe paused partway through partially unlacing the top of her shirt. "Not everything needs to be complicated. I'll distract him, you take his stuff."

Brass gave an apprehensive look, like he agreed with her but didn't want to. "Isn't that a little . . . obvious?"

She took another glance at the awkward boy's reflection in Brass's mirror. "I don't think anything is obvious to this guy."

Brass looked like he wanted to say something, but then his eyes widened a fraction, and he hurriedly slapped down the mirror and slid it back into his jacket as discreetly as he could. "Shit. He looked at us. Act casual."

"I've been acting casual."

"Excuse me."

Chloe turned around as their target smothered any plan in the cradle by walking up to them before they could work out their first move. Internally, she was panicking. She'd already been plotting out her approach, first moves, but now that the conversation wasn't on her terms, she found herself scrambling to adjust her plan.

Externally, she remained perfectly composed.

The boy froze when she met his eyes, and any worries Chloe had about being able to pull one over on him vanished in an instant. She had him, hook, line, and sinker.

"I—" He cleared his throat and tried again. "I was told that you two might be able to help me."

"Well, we are very helpful people," Brass said. "What can we do for you, Mr. . . . ?"

The boy brightened instantly, standing up a little straighter as a hint of pride tinged his expression. "You can call me Phoenix."

Chloe knew there were people with that name, but he said it with the obvious air of someone offering up a pseudonym. And not just any pseudonym, but one he was putting on for show, as if it made him more impressive. Almost like—

It all clicked into place for Snow at once. The wide-eyed enthusiasm. The overpacked bag. The out of place crossbow. The flashy fake name.

Avelina spare her, he wanted to be a glintchaser.

Chloe did her best to hide a sudden cringe of embarrassment. Is this how she'd looked to Brass when she'd first started? Had she really seemed this naive? This out of her depth? No, she couldn't have.

A shared look with Brass confirmed he'd made the same assessment of their new friend, and reached a similar conclusion: this was going to be too easy.

"Really?" Brass said. "Well, nice to meet you, Phoenix. I'm Brass, and this is my lovely assistant, Snow."

"Pleasure to meet you," Snow added as she found her footing. She tried to keep the breathy undertone subtle. She didn't want to come on too strong, or that might give the game away. She did make sure to eye him up and down and tilt her head in a show of interest though. "Why don't you sit down and tell us what we can do for you."

"Phoenix" didn't need any further convincing, pulling up a chair and immediately launching into what might as well have been his life story. He was a scholar from the Infinite Library on a research trip, looking for a ruin he thought was somewhere in Central Corsar.

At first, Chloe didn't really pay attention to the details. But Phoenix just kept providing so many of them, going on about the history of the Arcane Empire, and something called a spellforger and someone named Vulcan, and honestly Chloe still wasn't absorbing the details, but she did find herself oddly and surprisingly absorbed into the telling of them.

However naive he might be about the real world and the business he was trying to break into, Phoenix knew what he was talking about. The puppy-dog-like excitement he'd shown for his surroundings morphed into a deeper, more nuanced enthusiasm that came with real expertise on something, and it drew her and Brass both in to listen.

Phoenix claimed there was some important Old World artifact—she really had failed to absorb the details—in a specific ruin he'd mapped out the location of and cross-referenced local stories to confirm the existence of. The locals called it Aenerwin's Run, a little fortress sitting on a lakeside island accessible only by bridge. And he was looking to hire some extra hands to help him delve into that ruin.

He offered to pay them glint up front and at the job's end, as well as a more than generous share of any other saleable loot they found in the ruin, as long as he got to keep the specific artifact he was after if they found it. As far as negotiations went, Phoenix had played things pretty awfully. He tipped his hand too much as to what he was after, and what was really valuable on this delve. Depending on what the prize was, he'd either set awful terms for himself, or awful terms for them, and the latter was a short recipe to get robbed as soon as the job was done.

And that was if they didn't just rob him now, which was still an option in Chloe's mind. Admittedly interesting as his historical treatise had been, Phoenix was still a potential mark before he was a potential employer.

"I'm sorry to interrupt, but did you say you were going to Aenerwin's Run?"

Chloe felt a twinge of irritation as a new fresh-faced young man approached their table, this one even younger and more naive-looking than Phoenix. He had a short but thick head of auburn hair that looked a little shaggy, like he'd been cutting it himself, faintly tanned skin, and he wore an old brown priest's cloak over a sailor's clothes, and a sword belt that looked like he'd had to loop it around himself twice to tie it to a reasonable length. His attire said traveling priest, but if the boy was old enough to be ordained, Chloe was a spinster. Chloe wanted to tell him politely but firmly to mind his own business, but before she could, Phoenix answered first.

"You've heard of it?"

The younger boy nodded. "A friend and I are headed that way. Apparently some, uh, criminals were using it to hide some of their stolen goods, but something else has moved into the ruins and scared them off."

Phoenix frowned. "What kind of something else?"

"I don't know. Something dangerous, I suppose? The stories we heard said it was shooting magic at people who tried to cross the bridge into the ruin."

"Well, that's . . . a development," Phoenix said. Then, because apparently he had no sense, he started divulging everything he'd told Snow and Brass to this new stranger. "I think that ruin is the final resting place of the Imperial spellforger Invidiar Vulcan. If I can find any of his old materials, it could revolutionize how we interact with Old World artifacts."

"Oh, uh, wow. That, seems nice?" the younger boy said. "I don't know what that means, but if you're going to the ruin too, would you mind if we came with you?"

Phoenix hesitated, looking back to Chloe and Brass. "It's all right with me, but—"

"Let them tag along," Brass said, once again before Chloe could tell the newcomer to leave. "The more the merrier."

Chloe gave Brass a look that said, "Seriously?" and he answered with a wink that translated loosely to "Trust me."

She knew Brass well enough by now to know that nobody should ever listen to that wink, but she also couldn't contradict him in front of Phoenix without raising unwanted suspicion. Phoenix looked to them with undisguised excitement.

"So you'll take the job?"

"We're glintchasers," Brass said. "We take most any job, if the price is right. And yours sounds plenty right to me."

"That's great!" Phoenix said. "How soon can we leave?"

"No time like the present," Brass said. "You go find our new friend's other friend, we'll settle up our tab, and we can hit the road. No time to waste, daylight's burning!"

The new boy led Phoenix over to an older, taller girl with dark skin, curly hair, arms that looked like they could bench both boys put together. Chloe didn't catch much of what was said between them, but she did catch the girl's name.

Angel.

Chloe didn't pay them any further mind. For the moment, they weren't the problem. "How did we go from robbing one idiot to agreeing to delve a ruin with three of them?"

Brass shrugged, seemingly unbothered. "Best case scenario, this guy's lead's actually worth something, and we get an easy score of sweet loot. And if the lead's shit, we're still getting paid, and we can always rob all three of them blind afterward."

"I don't know."

"Come on," Brass pressed. "What's the worst that could happen?"

44

FALLOUT

"BRASS!"

Snow's heart seized in her chest as Brass's ashes blew away in the wind, and before she was consciously aware of what she was doing, she'd crawled to what little remained of him. Her fingers clenched in the blackish-gray dust, as if she could somehow squeeze him back into being whole again.

"No," she whimpered. "No, no, no."

She looked around to the rest of her company; none of them were moving. Only staring in mute shock.

"Church!" She called the priest's name like a drowning woman begging for a lifeline.

Church's eyes fell when Snow called for him. He knew what she wanted. And they all knew he couldn't do it.

"Chloe . . ." He used her real name, trying to console her.

"No!" She knew what he would say. You couldn't resurrect someone without a body. She didn't care.

"No. Do something. You have to do something. We have to . . . to . . ."

Phoenix and Wings knelt down next to her. His left arm was badly burned, and so was her right, but they draped the others around her shoulders, pulling her into a silent embrace. Whatever last threads of blind desperation had been holding her together snapped. Her body gave out, and she sagged into them as she began to sob. She gripped the front of Phoenix's coat for dear life as her whole body shook with every ragged breath and keening cry. Holding her tight, Phoenix and Wings cried too.

Not far away, there came a din of noise. Shouts and cheers. Horns blowing. People banging on their shields and armor. The sounds of victory. Everyone still alive in the city, and maybe everyone within several hundred miles, was celebrating. The Starborn, was gone. As far as everyone else was concerned, the day was won.

Church joined Snow, Phoenix, and Wings on the ground in a clatter of metal on metal, resting a gauntlet on Snow's shoulder and pressing his forehead into hers as tears flowed freely down his face. Some of the pain from their injuries subsided as he whispered a prayer. It soothed their burns, but did nothing to affect the stabbing agony in their chests, or the roiling nausea in their stomachs.

Angel was the last to come. Her brow was furrowed and her eyes were aimed at the ground. Of all of them, she was the least physically hurt. The soot and ichor hadn't even clung all that much to her white-and-gold armor, which only made the splashes of it that did stand out all the more. Her curly hair had gone stringy, matted with blood and sweat. For a while, she just stood over them, staring at the ground and not saying anything.

Eventually, something in the Sentinel snapped, and she kicked a nearby stone pillar in half. She punched what was left of it, shattering all but a stump of it to rumble. Then she beat the last stump of the stone with her fists until it was gravel. Only then, chest heaving, did she drop down next to the others, leaning her back against them. She still didn't look at any of them.

The world was saved. The sky was back to the color it was supposed to be. After so long living in the shadow of failure, the Starbreakers had triumphed.

And Brass was gone.

45
THE FUNERAL

It was a cold day in the city of Sasel. An overcast autumn sky hung over the city, turning the sea a shade of mourning gray and rendering the normally glittering harbor into a mass of cramped boats and folded sails. Even the airborne traffic lanes of flying vehicles that normally snaked through the skies between the spires of glass and stone moved at a languid pace, seemingly depopulated by a city's collective decision to stay home.

And yet, there was still beauty to be found in the city. Even on the cloudiest day, Sasel remained the Jewel of the Coast. The soaring heights of its buildings and its long, rippling banners retained the same aspirational majesty that characterized the city at its best, and the wind-tossed waves that battered the coast seemed to do so with an energy that defied the gloom, remaining loud and moving on a day that might otherwise have felt quiet and still.

Arno stood on the rooftop garden of Saint Avelina's Cathedral, taking it all in. His eyes were glossy from holding back tears. Sasel was sometimes called the City of Yesterday and Tomorrow for how readily it incorporated Old World technology into the everyday lives of the citizenry. It was a place that both harkened back to a past, and promised to use the best of that past to lead into the future. It was a city of possibility and ambition. A city of dreams.

Brass had loved it here.

With all the contradictory and blatantly false histories he'd provided them with over the years, the Starbreakers didn't actually know where Brass was from. In point of fact, they didn't even know his real name. Brass had always been insistent that he didn't want to be anyone other than the person he was now. In truth, it was genuinely difficult to imagine that Brass had ever been anything other than Brass.

But it meant that they couldn't hold a funeral or place a headstone where he'd been born, as was Corsan tradition. So instead, they'd come here, to the city where Snow had first discovered him, and where they'd all spent most of their years together.

It was the best place they could think of to say goodbye.

All four of them were dressed in black. Stripped of their armor and weapons, shrouded in grief, with no mission or objective in front of them, they ceased being the Starbreakers. Church, Snow, Phoenix, and Angel had been left behind somewhere in the ruins of Relgen. On that rooftop, there was only Arno, Chloe, Arman, and Monica.

Arman wore a long coat over a set of dark clothes and a vest. His dark hair and beard had been combed into submission, and frown lines marred his face. Monica wore a shawl over a floor-length dress and sandals. Her hair had been woven into braids and done up in a bun that sat high on her head, held in place by a golden hairpiece. Chloe had dressed sharply in a short jacket and pants, dark hair pulled back into a Siccaran braid, pale skin blending into the overcast sky behind her. Arno himself was adorned in his funerary priest vestments, a black-and-white version of his normal white and blue.

Arman and Monica were both taking in the view like Arno was, but Chloe had her back turned to the city, her eyes on the ground. There was no one on the rooftop but the four of them.

"Are we doing this or not?" Monica asked, breaking the heavy silence that had begun to hang over them.

That did the trick of dragging them back to the present, and Arno cleared his throat. "Arman?"

Arman withdrew a small urn from the bottomless interior pocket on his coat, and handed it to Arno. The priest cradled it in both his hands as the rest of his friends gathered in a loose circle around him. Arno looked around.

"Does anyone want to say something?"

Monica went first.

"So long, asshole," she said, waving to the urn. "Amazed it took you this long to get yourself killed." She paused for a moment, before adding in a much softer voice. "Sorry for not killing that bastard quicker. And thanks. For something, probably . . . for a lot of somethings."

She looked around, silently demanding that someone else go.

Arman took a deep breath, stuffed his hands in his pockets, and stood up straight. "I think if I sat down and did the math, I would be annoyed with Brass more often than I wasn't. He was cocky. Impulsive. Rude. Hedonistic. At times, even callous. He almost never took anything seriously, and he had absolutely no restraint about when and where he stuck his dick in things. He got us into trouble more times than I can count.

"And for all of that, he might have been my best friend," Arman admitted. "He got us out of trouble almost as often as he got us into it. He always believed in me, even when I didn't. He taught me things about the world, and about myself. And he never lived a single day of his life with regrets. I was always kind of jealous of him for that.

"I don't think I've ever met someone more meant to be a glintchaser than Brass. He loved this life. He loved the novelty, the adventure. He loved the risks, and the rewards. And he loved this company. More than any of us." Arman took a break to clear his throat and wipe the corners of his eyes. Something was in them. "So, math or not. I'm going to miss him."

As the speech gave way to silence, all eyes turned to Chloe. She'd yet to take her eyes off the urn since Arman had taken it out. Now, noticing everyone was looking at her, she shook her head. She picked a point somewhere behind Arman's head to stare at, and whispered, "No."

Monica gave her a dirty look, as if to say, *Come on, even I said something.* But Chloe ignored her, and eventually, the group's expectations relented.

With everyone else having said their peace, Arno cleared his throat for the third and final time, and spoke Brass's last rites in the language of the gods.

"You who have fallen in a search for adventure
Know that you are remembered
Strength to your soul in the journey that follows
To break and turn any that would bind your will.
May your pockets be full as you face the Reaper
May your heart guide you to where you're meant to be
Step out from this world, and into the next
To find your next adventure, everlasting."

Gingerly, Arno removed the lid on the urn. The wind immediately picked up, and without Arno having to tilt the urn at all, the ashes that were all that remained of Brass lifted up out of the urn to join the passing breeze, while the urn itself let out a long, low note. The ashes took on a faint golden glitter as they scattered into the wind, as Arno's words passed off one final divine blessing to the Starbreaker's swordsman.

"I've never heard you use that prayer before," Arman noted.

Arno shrugged. "Well, he didn't die peacefully. But I don't think Brass would have liked the warrior's last rites either, so . . . I made something up."

Arman raised an eyebrow, looking ever so slightly alarmed. "Does it still count if you do that?"

Arman had eyes and ears. He would have seen the telltale divine light in Brass's ashes, and no natural wind reached into an urn to carry away the ashes inside while playing a perfectly pitched musical note. But he'd also had enough lectures on the nature of divine prayers from Arno, and the priest knew that from the outside, something wasn't adding up.

"It does when I do it," Arno said.

That should have just raised further questions, but Arno spoke with a quiet finality that signaled the topic was done, and Arman didn't protest or question. He gave only a shrug to say that he didn't understand what Arno meant, but trusted him regardless.

"What did you say?" Monica asked.

"Normally last rites are all about peace and reassurance, but Brass always treated peace and quiet like it was the plague. I tried to come up with something that was more about celebrating life and finding something new in the after."

Arman nodded his appreciation. "He would have liked that."

"Bullshit," Monica said. "He'd have hated all of this."

Arman reconsidered. "Yeah, he probably would."

Chloe made a bitter exhalation that might have been a laugh and shook her head, but otherwise still said nothing.

Arno wore a sad smile, agreeing that Monica was right. Brass probably would have called them all too dour for a day ostensibly about him—and thrown in a simile involving some kind of sex act. But funeral rites were for the living as much as the dead. And it was hard not to be dour when saying goodbye.

That being said, it would have been a betrayal to Brass's memory to spend all day in this kind of mood, so now that last rites had been spoken, Arno used a thread of divine power to reach out into the world, until he could connect his soul to another, somewhere else in the city, and send a message.

We're ready.

All around them, the air began to break up into geometric fractals, while at their feet, arcane glyph patterns began to form in a circle. The four of them gathered close to make sure they were all inside the spell, and then let themselves be teleported away.

46
THE SAINTS

In a stomach-twisting blink, the Starbreakers went from the roof of Saint Avelina's cathedral to the entryway of the Broken Cask, halfway across the city.

Even if you ignored the usual standard for glintchasers—which was dying alone and unburied a hundred miles from home—Brass's funeral had a packed after-party. Knights, priests, glintchasers, privateers, Academy mages, an ancient druid, a foreign queen, and even a few sex workers were all in attendance. Some of the people were there to remember Brass. Others had merely come to pay their respects to the rest of the Starbreakers.

The Broken Cask was not the tavern where they had all first met, but it was the first tavern the Starbreakers had ever stayed in when they'd come to Sasel as a company, and over the course of their careers it had become their home away from home. Some of their best barfights, one-night stands, and drunken sing-alongs had happened in this bar. There had been no other choice of where to have this party.

The Cask was one of the few taverns in Sasel that didn't use lightstone, instead making do with lanterns and the light of its twin fireplaces. It gave the place a warm glow, accentuated by the deep, rustic hues of its wood-paneled construction. Under normal circumstances, it was a place of music and laughter.

Now, the tavern was silent.

All eyes in the room were on the Starbreakers. Some concerned, some admiring, some longing for comfort. Arman had shrunk under so many gazes at once. In his element, in the field, he could give orders with complete confidence. Outside of it, was another story. Chloe's eyes were on the floor, occasionally darting to the closest exit. Only Monica stood tall and met the stares of everyone else in the room, but she didn't say anything. Arno was about to break the silence, but someone else beat him to it.

The sound of struck steel rang out as Astrid brought her spear's butt down. The spearhead danced with sparks of stored lightning, and all the air in the room crackled as she shouted. "The battle is won, and we are alive! We are here, not only to mourn the passing of friends, but to celebrate their achievements, and the gift they gave us with their sacrifice," she said.

She held her spear tight in one hand, and in the other, she raised a tankard. "To the fallen. To victory! To the Starbreakers!"

Everyone in attendance echoed her with each toast, and on the third, broke into brief applause. The tension in the room died with it. Like a slumbering giant shaking off sleep, the Broken Cask slowly came back to life as people resumed sharing stories, singing songs, and taking full advantage of the free booze. With one last shared glance between them, the Starbreakers scattered into the party.

Elizabeth found Arman almost immediately and pulled him into a fierce embrace. He returned it, burying his face in her hair. She kissed his forehead, and whispered something to him that made him hug her even tighter. They wouldn't stay at the party long. They had a daughter to get home to.

Monica meandered through the party with a drink in hand, offering noncommittal remarks or intimidating silence to people who talked to her for a while. But before long, she found herself leaning against a wall at the edge of the party, Thalia by her side. They chatted idly about Brass, Monica pointed out and identified the strangers to Thalia, and, after a few minutes of hesitation and side-eyeing, Monica put her arm around Thalia. The bartender smiled, wrapping her own arm around Monica's waist.

Chloe had vanished without a word.

Arno walked a circuit of the bar, accepting condolences and offering them in return, thanking everyone who'd been at the battle for Relgen, and catching up with old faces. He accepted a drink someone offered him out of politeness, but after a single exploratory sip that burned fiercely, he gave up on it. Reflexively, he made a mental note to offer it to Brass when he saw him, and instantly felt a renewed pang of loss.

That was the thing about it. When you lost someone, you didn't simply lose them once. You lost them over and over again, every time you thought about them, saw or did something that should have included them, and then had to remember that they were gone.

This was not his first funeral, or even his first time losing someone he cared deeply about. This wasn't even his first time mourning the loss of Brass, if he counted the Starbreakers' original disbanding.

But it didn't make this time any easier.

"This one's for you, Brass," the priest whispered, and downed the rest of his cup.

Two hours, six more drinks, and a tavern-wide rendition of all twelve verses of *The March of Everwinter* later, Arno found himself getting some air outside the Cask, while Arman and Elizabeth went home and Monica continued to do her best to drink the Queen of the Frelheim under the table.

The overcast day had given way to a foggy night, which turned the light of buildings and flying traffic overhead into a blurry, multicolored haze. The traffic in the skies and streets had thinned out, leaving the streets in eerie silence for blocks at a time before being suddenly broken by a flying skiff or carriage speeding by. Arno could see his breath.

He didn't feel cold. And for as much as the drinks burned going down, Arno wasn't so much as lightheaded.

He felt Beneger arrive before he saw him. There was a spike of anticipation, as if he'd just heard someone knock on his front door, a sense of reassuring familiarity, and the world felt steadier. More solid, as if it had all been reinforced.

And then he was there, standing next to Arno.

The Guiding Saint was dressed like any other citizen of the city out for a walk at night after work, with a long, thick coat wrapped tight around him, and bits of sawdust still in his beard. In the saint's presence, the light became softer, and everything beyond their immediate surroundings slipped out of focus. The workshop scents of oil and sweat overpowered the usual damp, coastal air of the city.

Before, whenever Arno had spoken to Beneger, he had felt just a little out of place. The saint had carried an aura of otherness, of separation. Something from another place and time, made of something different than the stuff that made up Arno.

That feeling was gone now.

"Beautiful night out," Beneger observed, casual as ever.

"I guess so," Arno said. He looked up into the hazy, blank sky. "It feels a little wrong after everything we've been through, but I actually still prefer nights with stars."

"Nothing wrong about it. Stars aren't inherently evil. Over in Gypten, they call saints stars. People look up in the sky, and get to see them hanging in the sky, shining down, guiding their way through the desert." Beneger smiled fondly. "Nice image, that."

"Are they, really?" Arno asked. "The stars, I mean. Are they . . . saints?"

"Oh, some of them, sure. Saints shape culture, culture shapes saints. Most of what you're looking at up there are other worlds, other places. But Gypic saints—stars—they always make sure to put a light up in the sky for their followers to point to. It can get a little involved, actually. You should see the arguments they get into over constellations."

Arno wanted to share in the amused smile on Beneger's face. Instead, with no small amount of fear, he asked, "Am I going to?"

Beneger's smile shrank to something more gentle, but did not disappear. "That's up to you."

"What happened?" Arno asked. "What . . . am I now?"

"You tell me."

Arno took a deep breath, going back to a moment he had been trying very hard to forget. "When I went up against the Starborn, I called on Renalt's power, on my own. No prayer, no help from you. I just . . . used it."

The void of the Starborn had been closing in around him, cutting him off from his saint, trying to erase his existence. There had been no intermediary to bridge the gap between Renalt's power and him. He had been alone. And faced with the end, not just of himself, but of everything, he had refused to accept it.

He hadn't asked for power. He had declared it was his.

Beneger nodded.

Arno shook his head. "But that's what saints do."

"It is."

Beneger's simple acknowledgement answered Arno's next question before he could ask it. He'd suspected it these last few days, as he recovered from the battle and processed what he'd done. But now there was no denying.

Arno Farnese was a saint.

"How?"

"The same way it happened for everyone else. Gods can't notice a single person. What they can notice are people who become something greater than themselves. People who become the embodiment of an idea. People who mean something."

"Then . . ." Arno hesitated, unsure if he wanted the answer to this question. "What do I mean?"

"Arno," Beneger said, sounding disappointed for the first time in the conversation. "Why would you ever need someone else to tell you that?"

Arno sighed. "I just . . . I don't know how I'm supposed to do what you or Avelina do. Embody something as big as guidance or hope."

"Well don't go thinking of it like that," Beneger said. "For starters, the job doesn't have to be as broad as you think. I've known plenty of saints who became the patron of one family or place, never expanded past that, and there's no shame in it. But even Avelina and I aren't as broad as you think. Guidance is a big idea. Too big, even for a saint. I'm not the saint of guidance. I'm the saint of guiding people to their callings." Beneger met Arno's eyes for emphasis. "I help people become who they were always meant to be."

Arno's chest tightened in a complicated knot of pride and anxiety, mixed with another pang of grief. Brass had believed Arno was meant for great things too.

"So. What now, oh student of mine?" Beneger asked, and the usual irony he placed on the word "student" was replaced with a genuine, gentle admiration.

As he had so many times over the years, Arno felt something click when Beneger asked him that question. It always made him reframe his thinking, taking him away from abstract ideas and pointing him toward action.

In the autumn night air, Arno considered what he wanted to do next. Funnily enough, his first thoughts were of Bart and Ruby. The two had come a long way from where they'd started, but there was still a lot Arno could teach Bart about the world he was stepping into, and Ruby still needed her soul cleansed of demonic influence. After all the turmoil the last year had brought them, Arno wanted to make sure they both landed on their feet, with a real future ahead of them. He thought about Loraine, which was still recovering from the Dread Knight's attack, and which was sure to suffer even further now that its baron had risen up against the crown. Without Haegan, that uprising was doomed to fail, but it would be a messy process. And when the dust finally settled, the people of that town would need help more than ever.

He thought of Relgen, a city wiped out and abandoned after everything the Cult of Stars had done to it, and the instability its fall had brought on the whole kingdom. Hundreds of thousands displaced. Rampant lawlessness. Crown forces strained to their limit to keep people protected.

And he thought of his old company. Chloe, who wasn't sleeping and barely ate. Monica, who was out of a job and a home. Arman, adrift for years and revived by danger that had passed.

So many people, their lives all thrown into disarray by one disaster or another. They needed peace. Stability. They needed to rebuild.

"I think I know what I'm the saint of," Arno said. "And I definitely know where I want to start."

47
THAW

For however much it looked like an ordinary house, Arman's home in the village of Akers was the next thing to a fortress. Its timbers were physically reinforced with the protective magic Arman usually wove into armor. Every door and window was enchanted with a seal that meant they would only open to people Arman allowed. Wards rendered the house impenetrable to scrying magic, and the walls and ceilings were a network of traps and defensive armaments.

If Chloe were anyone else, she wouldn't have made it inside.

But she'd honed her skills in countless Old World ruins, where arcane security measures were more common than intact upholstery. And more than her professional skills, she knew Arman. So she fooled the seals, anticipated every trap, and passed through the halls without detection. She walked in pitch darkness, eyes adapted to shadows, steps quieter than a whisper. Until, finally, she found herself alone in the dark of Arman's workshop.

It was smaller than the one he'd built for himself in the mansion, back in the old days. But instead of reducing the scale of his work, he'd just increased the clutter. Upstairs, she'd been careful to watch her step to avoid tripping any wards or stepping on a child's toy.

In the workshop, it was difficult to find anywhere to step at all. It smelled like machine oil and ozone, and even with the lights off, the room was dimly lit by the faint glow of a dozen different magical devices in various states of assembly.

Chloe's eyes fell onto the glow of one object in particular, and her breath caught in her throat. Sitting between a damaged plate armor chest piece and a loose stack of scrawled notes was a glass orb, slightly smaller than her fist, that gave off an iridescent, pale blue light.

The Heart of Ice.

Hesitantly, she plucked the Heart off the worktable it had been left on. The glass was cold to the touch, but the shiver that ran down her spine had nothing to do with that.

For over a decade, Chloe had been infused with the Heart's power. It had taken her from a talented thief and glintchaser and turned her into the Cold-Blooded Killer. She'd been practically unstoppable. And it had numbed everything. Fear. Pain. Doubt.

Joy.

Pleasure.

Love.

Then she'd gotten all those feelings back, just in time to watch Brass die right in front of her—defending her.

She'd told herself that it was a question of practicality. That she'd based her whole fighting style off the Heart's powers, and not having it was tripping her up. That she lived a dangerous life, and she needed every weapon she could get. But the truth was so much more pathetic.

Brass was gone, and the grief of it tore at her every day. It was agony, and she wanted it to stop.

The Heart could make it stop.

The lights in the workshop came on, and Chloe drew a dagger on instinct. Behind, standing placid as if he'd been there the whole time, was Arno. He wasn't wearing his clothes from the funeral, or even his normal priest's vestments, but the simple wools and linens he'd worn as a freelancer whenever he wasn't in armor. Somehow, looking at him, the world seemed out of focus, like Arno was the only real thing in the room, and everything else was an illusion.

"How did you get here?" she asked.

"I can appear to people I have a strong enough connection to."

"Since when?"

"Since the Starborn."

Chloe nodded, having quietly suspected something had changed in Arno since the battle in Relgen, and now having a good guess at what. She wondered if any of the others knew. "What do you want?"

"To help," Arno said.

Chloe's reflexive response, that she was fine, that she didn't need help, was already on her tongue when she heard the door to the workshop open. She flinched, and Arno wore a guilty expression that answered her previous thought.

The others did know—because he'd gone to them first.

Two people descended the stairs.

Monica's face was stone as she took in the scene with arms folded. Arman wore open worry on his face. They stared at her for a moment before catching sight of the Heart of Ice in her hands. Arman stiffened, and did a bad job of hiding it.

"Chloe," he said, and he spoke her name with a familiarity only he could have. He didn't ask her if she was okay, because she wasn't. He didn't ask what was wrong, because she'd deny anything was. Instead he asked, "What are you doing?"

She could answer bluntly and literally, avoid the real question. But Arno had chosen his weapons well. Arman had been a weakness in Chloe's walls even when she'd had the Heart of Ice. Without it to reinforce her defenses, he shattered them with a look.

"I just want it to stop," she choked out. Like a dam bursting, everything she'd been holding back since before the funeral came tumbling out all at once. "I can't sleep. I can't eat. He looked me right in the face before he died, and he fucking winked at me, like he had it all figured out. Like it was going to be okay. And then he was gone. I was too slow, and I missed, and he's dead because of me."

She slammed the Heart of Ice on the worktable. It didn't break. She slammed it on the table again. Not even a crack. Monica closed the distance, putting one hand on her shoulder, and resting the other on top of her hand holding the Heart. Firm as stone, and yet still gentle. Chloe tried to glare but was caught off guard by the naked empathy in Monica's eyes.

She'd been too slow too. They all had.

More of the fight bled out of Chloe, and she sagged against the table.

"That fucking idiot," Chloe said. "Why did he have to be so stupid?"

"Because he was Brass."

"It hurts."

"I know."

"He was my friend."

"I know."

Monica's voice echoed the pain in Chloe's own chest, and in that connection, she found the permission to cry. And Monica and the others all cried with her. It was like dropping a set of weights that had been dumped onto her shoulders, and the intensity of release that came with it left her physically shaking.

It all hurt so much. But at the same time, it felt good, so impossibly good, to not be alone in that hurt. To not be alone in life. The Heart of Ice fell out of Chloe's hand, and she let herself hug her friends. The orb hit the ground, rolled somewhere under a bench. And that was the last thought she paid the damn thing.

"It's so fucking much. All the time," Chloe cried into someone's shoulder. They were all holding each other too close to tell whose it was.

"Welcome back to being human," Monica said.

Chloe gave a short, bittersweet laugh. And there in Arman's workshop, wrapped in each other's arms, the Starbreakers finally let go of the crisis. Of all the lingering wounds between them. Of the last eight years. And they let tomorrow come.

48
THE HERO

Traditionally, a knighting ceremony was done before a grand audience in the Pearl Palace's great hall, with hundreds in attendance, from the council, to the nobility, to the knights who would be serving alongside the newly appointed, to their friends and family

Given the people being inducted, Roland and Lupolt had opted for an alternative ceremony. The council and nobility were absent, the knightly presence had been scaled back to a single representative per order, and each inductee had been permitted only a single guest.

Gathered before the throne of Corsar were two dozen men and women, their numbers comprised of former members of the Exile Order, freelancers from the White Hawk, and even a few Frelheimer warriors.

Several of these people only a few months ago had been traitors to the crown. But when the Starborn had come, each and every one of them had fought, not only to escape, but as part of the Starbreakers' push to retrieve and use the Ending. In a very real sense, everyone present had helped save the world.

Lupolt had still protested rather strongly against the decision. But he'd been overruled by both Roland, and a newly christened saint. And in the end, even he agreed that after everything that had happened in the last year, the ranks of Corsar's knights were in desperate need of revitalization.

The Starbreakers had also been offered knighthoods, for the second time. But out of the four, only one stood in the lineup now.

Monica wore the armor she had summoned during her battle with Haegan, shining white and gold inlaid with intricate, angelic designs. Daybreaker hung on her back, and her hair had been braided and wrapped into a partial bun, with the excess falling down the back of her neck.

Elizabeth stood before them, wearing a new set of leather and steel armor that featured a glowing green orb at the center of its breastplate. The Winged Lady was back, and today, it was her honor and duty to swear in Corsar's next generation of defenders.

She went down the line and asked each one, "Do you swear to Renalt to serve the crown faithfully, to defend the kingdom and its people, with honor, diligence, and pride, in as great a capacity as you can, for as long as you live?"

Each man or woman nodded, responded that they swore, and stepped forward to kneel before Roland, who ceremonially lowered his sword to each of their shoulders.

Some of them would be joining the knightly orders: the Seven Gates of Sasel, the Order of Saint Ricard, or even the newly recommissioned Knights of the Purple Rose. The rest would become independent knights, itinerant protectors who went wherever the crown needed them. Which, given the state of things, was everywhere.

Then Elizabeth reached Monica at the end of the line and asked, "Do you, Monica Falone, swear to Renalt to serve the crown faithfully, to defend the kingdom and its people, with honor, diligence, and pride, in as great a capacity as you can, for as long as you live?"

Monica cocked her head as if thinking it over, looked to Roland, and shrugged. "Nah."

Elizabeth's eyes widened as she bit back a laugh. The rest of the room let out a mix of gasps and muted swears. Lupolt looked ready to flip a table. Roland, to his credit, only quirked an eyebrow.

The king's right hand stepped forward, seething. "Did you really attend this ceremony just to—"

“I came here to tell you I’m not swearing any oath, or following anyone’s orders. I’m done with other people telling me how to live. I’m going where I want, when I want.” Monica had initially made eye contact with Lupolt to match him glare for glare, but she’d quickly turned her attention to the king. He had yet to say anything. Everyone was staring at her now, but she kept her eyes on his. “But I am here to help. However I can, as long as I can. So when you need me, call. I’ll be there.”

“So long as Corsar can consider you a friend, that is good enough for me,” Roland said. “You have nothing but my gratitude and my trust.”

“Good. Just do me a favor, and don’t call for . . . two weeks?” Then she gave a half bow combined with a jaunty salute, and walked off, slowing only for a quick, “Say hi to the kid for me,” to Elizabeth, who nodded. By now, the Winged Lady was beaming.

“If I may ask,” Roland said just before she left. “Where are you off to in such a hurry?”

Monica grinned as she came to stand next to Thalia, her chosen guest for the ceremony. “I’ve got a date.”

She scooped a laughing Thalia into her arms as if she weighed nothing at all. Then a pair of wings made of golden light unfurled from her back, and she took off, shattering a window on her way out.

49

THE TEACHER

Arman stood in the middle of campus at the Tarsim Academy of Arcane Arts, just in front of its newest addition. Like every building at the Academy, the new hall's architecture had been modeled off the structure of arcane sigils. The arches and triangles of its facade evoked stability, transference, and recombination. Arman regretted coming already, and that was before the hall's front doors opened, and the Academy's new Headmistress sauntered out. Ink had never been humble before, and she hadn't seen her promotion as any reason to start. The triple-layered silk robes, each sporting subtle luminescent designs and gold leaf trim, made her look like an empress, and her unnaturally blue eyes shone brighter than ever.

"Phoenix! There you are," she greeted, as if she'd been waiting for him and not the other way around.

"I'm retired," he said reflexively.

"Of course. Arman. Well, don't just stand there. Come in. We've got a lot to get through, and I've got another meeting right after this."

Arman considered walking away, just to spite her. But he'd agreed to this for a reason. And Ink would never get to that reason if he didn't play along first. Sighing deeply, he followed the Headmistress inside.

"Construction still isn't technically complete yet, and I suspect it's going to undergo serious renovations even after its official opening. But it's ready for early previews," Ink said of the hall as they stepped in a wide but empty grand entryway with a vaulted ceiling, full of thin glass columns, pedestals awaiting display objects, and an indoor fountain still dry and missing its crowning decoration.

Every path out of the entry went through wide double doors, made to accommodate either dense crowds or massive objects, and long, unbroken bands of lightstone encircled the edges of the ceiling, flooding the room with white light. It was a barren space now, but it stood ready and eager to be filled.

She led him through the halls—spacious, well lit, but with a workman quality distinct from the pristine foyer. These were halls made to take a beating, and to be easy to clean while also accepting they would never truly be clean. There were a few standard lecture halls, a larger auditorium structured for academic demonstrations, and an empty area with drop sheet-covered furniture that would eventually be faculty offices and conference space. There were dozens of workrooms, all mostly empty, but unmistakable for their size and space allocations to shelves, workbenches, and storage.

In short, it was a new hall at the Academy. One more geared towards practical experimentation than most, but nothing that immediately made it seem worth the extended tour. Arman was starting to run out of patience when Ink brought them to a room that stopped his heart.

It was like someone had taken apart his workshop from the Starbreakers' manor and reassembled it in this room. It wasn't one to one. All the equipment present was too polished and unused. Some of it was the wrong size, the arrangement of the space was different, and there was one crystalizer in the back that would explode if anyone tried to use it. But it was still undeniably a spellforger's workshop modeled off his own.

His blood ran briefly cold. "What is this?"

"You like it?" Ink asked nonchalantly as she looked around. Her smile had grown sharper. "I had it put together from the information you gave Targan and your assistants during your stint with Haegan's troupe. I'm sure you have notes, but I think it turned out quite well for what we had to go on and how little we still understand."

Arman tried several responses in his head. Most of them fizzled into incoherence partway through. The room suddenly felt too small, and he wanted to leave.

"This . . . this isn't what we talked about."

"And so it isn't," Ink said. She turned on her heel, walking through the workshop to a door on the other side. "Right this way."

It took him an incredulous second to follow. The next room was the largest they'd been to aside from the foyer, covered in floor-to-ceiling shelves with large round drafting tables taking up the center. Some of the shelves were mundane wood, but others were Old World construction, slotted full of weavebooks, semi-solid-state compendiums, and even a repository. One of the tables was full of the devices needed to access the ancient media, some of it looking freshly refurbished, other pieces looking like they'd been pulled from a ruin yesterday.

"Here it is," Ink said. "Everything we have on spellforging. Bits and pieces recovered from ruins or on loan from other collections. Theories and treatises written by enterprising scholars. And of course, copies of your work, and all of the attempts to decipher them."

Ink had invited Arman here to discuss the subject of the materials he'd provided Targan. Arman had asked about them being returned to him, or destroyed. Ink had deflected, and now he understood why.

The new hall had everything the Academy would need to start its foray into spellforging. After fifteen years of keeping the craft secret, the seal was going to break.

"So, you called me here just to gloat?"

"Would you believe I called you here to beg?"

"No."

"Fair enough. I wouldn't beg. But I will ask," Ink said. "Hear me out, before you say no and storm off."

He wanted to say no out of spite, but he was still too off-balance for any kind of quick response. No words wanted to come out, and Ink took the opening.

"There's no unlighting the beacon. Nobody's cracked spellforging yet, even with everything Targan took from you. But we will. It'll take a year, five, maybe ten if the team turns out incompetent, but no matter what, it's happening, whether you want it to or not," Ink said. Her voice was surprisingly gentle. There wasn't much gloating in it—there might not have been any, but Arman's ability to read people was rooted in pattern recognition, and it was impossible for him not to imagine Ink as smug. "But if I have a choice between cracking it without you, or exploring it with you, I know which one I want." And here came the strangest part for both of them. Sincere flattery. "Without you, we'll remake mistakes you've already learned from. We'll be slower, directionless, and significantly more likely to blow up this nice building and everyone in it. This whole enterprise is safer and cleaner with an expert at the wheel, and for all practical purposes, you're the only expert there is."

It struck Arman then how different this was from when Targan had asked for his help disguised as Ink. The Headmaster had played into how Arman would have thought Ink would ask for help—like the action physically disgusted her.

The reality was . . . disarmingly genuine.

The ice that had been running through his blood began to thaw. He found it easier to think in complete sentences again, instead of abstract puzzle configurations. He stopped pacing. He hadn't even noticed he was doing it.

"You hate me," he said, trying to make the puzzle make sense.

Ink shrugged. "Of course I do. You can *almost* keep up with me."

Arman scoffed.

"Ask yourself, honestly," Ink pressed, "is there anyone else in the world you would trust to run this program better than you?"

Ever since Relgen, Arman had been struggling to trust himself with anything other than idle tinkering he did in his basement. In the back of his mind, he'd always known someday spellforging would make its way into the world, whether he kept his oath or not. But he'd always told himself that whatever happened when it did wouldn't be on him. He'd done his part to keep the craft contained, to keep humanity from having access to the mechanisms that had ruined the elves.

Targan had disagreed on the matter. The argument had only sounded bitter coming from the old man.

But Ink had shifted the phrasing of it just enough. Even if he didn't feel up to the task himself, who was he comfortable handing the reins of an arcane revolution to?

And had he really been keeping his hands clean? Was doing nothing when he had the chance really any different from condoning what someone did in his absence? Or was he only hiding from the daunting responsibility of it all?

"I want to personally vet everyone we bring into the program. Staff and students."

"As the Department Head, final say on all hiring and admission decisions is yours. Though I really would advise delegating that as soon as you have a team you can trust. I imagine you'll have better things to do than read admissions essays."

"I'm not going to be anyone's puppet. If this place is going to be mine, it's going to be *mine.*"

"The only people with any authority over you or your work will be myself, and Roland, and we both know better than to try to control you."

"What about your High Inquisitive? Will I have to answer to them too?"

"If a matter concerning her purview arises in your department, perhaps. But if you try to tell me that you don't trust Kaila Blackrock, I'm telling your wife."

Arman blinked, considered his options in the situation, and moved on without protest.

"I won't make anything I'm not comfortable putting out into the world. And I won't let anyone else in the program do it either."

"I look forward to seeing where you draw those lines." She smiled, and one last time, he considered whether this was a good idea. If he could stomach having Ink as his boss.

He thought of a small, green-eyed little girl, who he'd held and promised to fix the world for. He thought of his younger self, so confident in his vow to defend a secret to his dying days. And he knew immediately who he'd rather disappoint.

"All right. I'm in."

"Then may I be the first to say, welcome aboard, Professor Meshar."

The headmistress extended her hand, and Arman shook it.

50
THE PATRON

Considering he was part of a conspiracy against the crown, Sebastian Guerron was lucky to have dodged Oblivion. He was living in a small house on the coast, just north of Sasel, overlooking rocky cliffs. He had a bedroom, a bathroom, and even a modest study. He wore no chains or prison rags, instead dressed in plain but well-made cottons and wools. The small staff would cook his meals, clean his rooms, and even bring him news of the outside and new materials to entertain himself.

But every door and window was locked and sealed by magic. The walls and furniture were reinforced with defensive enchantments, and wards prevented any form of teleportation or supernatural communication. Comfortable as he might have been, Chloe's father was still imprisoned.

Chloe sat in a simple wooden chair directly across from him, wearing a midnight blue dress set with onyx stones, hands folded neatly in her lap. At the moment, she bore an uncanny resemblance to her mother.

"Your testimony worked," Chloe reported to him. "Mom's been cleared of all charges, and family assets were released and turned over to the two of us."

Chloe read the tension in her father, interpreted it with years of practice. He was glad his wife and daughter would be taken care of. But it burned him that he could do nothing to affect their situation. That they would go on without him.

She answered his first question before he could ask it, because she knew him, and knew he wouldn't like the answer.

"The White Hawk's been dissolved," Chloe said. "We terminated all contracts, and turned over any personal property in the company headquarters to the crown. Mom's going through the inventory of all company property for what to keep and what to liquidate, which will probably take her the rest of the month."

Her father's whole body shook, and a vein bulged in his temple. He wanted to shout, but even imprisoned, he clung to his self-image of a man in control. He spoke with the artificially measured tone of someone restraining their own temper.

"That company was our family's primary source of income."

"The company's all either dead or locked in Oblivion, thanks to you," Chloe said. "It was a done thing. We just made it official."

"I suppose you and your mother think you can simply live frugally then?" His tone made it clear how naive he thought that would be.

"No. I've got expensive tastes, and Mom's worse," Chloe said. "I'm sponsoring a new company. Maybe several, eventually. They did repeal the Act of Relgen, so the freelancer business is about to be booming. But I've found some promising talents with good branding, and I think they're a good place to start."

"If you were just going to go into the same business, why hamper yourself by starting over? The White Hawk is already established. It has a reputation."

"That reputation is tanked, and you know it," Snow said. "Besides. You don't care about us being able to leverage a reputation. You care that the White Hawk was yours, and I'm replacing it with something that's mine."

Chloe's father had been confined here for months, but this was her first visit. She was severely out of practice dealing with her raw, full emotions, and it had taken her this long to work out what it was she felt every time she thought about him.

It was layered. It hurt, but in a way that was twisted up with a bittersweet warmth. The two feelings were as inseparable as they were vivid.

Betrayal. Not the purely pragmatic reality of it—one party's trust being answered with another's bad faith—she could recognize that even with the Heart of Ice in her. This was something so much worse. Less concrete, but so much more real. The breach of something that should have been precious.

"You used to be my hero," she said. "I thought it was Mom's fault you stopped seeing what really mattered, that you only cared about reputation and money. But then you threw in with Haegan. Even after he almost had me killed. Even after he turned my brain inside out. And I figured out the truth."

"Chloe, I am sorry about what happened. But as soon as I became involved, I did everything I could to make sure you were protected. Everything I ever did, I did for you and your mother."

"No, you did it for yourself," Chloe said. "Mom is a bitch, but she cares so much about money and reputation because she wants to be comfortable. You care about it because you want to be important. You're not a hero, and you never were. Because you only care about saving the day so long as you get the credit for the saving."

"Mom can have whatever reason she likes for staying in the business, but I'm not doing this for money, or reputation," Chloe said. And then came another swell of emotions, far more easy to identify. Grief. And pride. "I'm doing this . . . because somewhere out there, there's a little girl who's realizing that her hero isn't real either. But she still wants to believe that the adventure is real.

That heroes are real, even if hers wasn't. And I believe in *her*."

She stood to leave, having said her piece. Her father did not take the hint, standing up as if he could follow her out. For him, the conversation was not over. Would not be, until he had won it. She reached out a finger, tapping the invisible barrier separating them. The control glyph lit up red, and when Sebastian's lips moved, she heard nothing. He, however, would still hear her.

"Mom's visiting on Sixday. I'll have something nice for you to wear sent over," she said. Her voice was tighter than she'd meant it to be as she choked back a sudden urge to cry. Not over her father. But over the image she'd conjured in her memory, of the next girl to share a start like hers.

There had been someone else with her, the day her adventure had started. She wasn't just getting into this business to sponsor the next her, but also the next *him*.

And there was one more thing she still had to do for him.

51
THE REBUILDER

Arno stood on the same ridge where he had once watched Relgen die, and now with pride watched it come back to life.

For the first time in eight years, the road to Relgen was well-traveled. Carpenters and masons brought wagonloads of construction materials in a steady stream, and following them came their families to keep them company, cooks and innkeepers to feed and house them, and merchants to sell them their necessities. And as more and more people arrived, the Church of Saint Arno was there to coordinate and direct them.

Tents of every size were being pitched everywhere, growing the camp that had sprung up around the walls, but already some of the buildings just inside the city gate had new occupants. Out in the surrounding landscape, druids and clerics worked side by side to restore life to the land and soil, with some particularly industrious farmers already toiling in the terraced fields that had seen the earliest efforts. And here and there, scattered among the workers, entrepreneurs, opportunists, and clergy, were freelancers.

They were a vast minority of the ruintown's population, but they served as private security, patrolled the outskirts for wandering monsters, and even delved into the city itself. A lot of strange and dangerous things had made the dead streets of Relgen their home over the years, and someone had to clear them out if they were ever going to rebuild.

And that was what Arno—what his church—would do. First here, and then wherever disaster struck. They would be there to clean up the mess of disaster and ruin, bring protection and relief, and get people back on their feet. It was an ambitious mission in some respects, but Arno hoped it would only be needed at this scale every so often. The rest of the time, they would focus on smaller, personal disasters. The Church of Saint Arno would make sure that the worst day of a person's life was not the end of it.

Next to the newly christened saint, Arman let out a low whistle. "You know, I think this might be the first ruintown in history created to resettle a place instead of strip it to the bone. Not bad, for a retired glintchaser."

"Everyone has to start somewhere."

"Start? Are you planning on overtaking Avelina someday?"

Arno shuddered. "Gods, no. Putting aside that my mission's much more niche than hers, I don't know how she does it, having that many followers. I've only got a handful, and the prayers still give me headaches if too many come at once."

"Is that normal?" Arman asked, briefly worried for his friend, before feeling stupid for worrying. Arno was effectively immortal now.

"Beneger says it's because I became a saint while I was still alive," Arno explained. "It's supposed to get easier. Hopefully quickly."

"Hopefully," Arman echoed. "Genuinely, it looks like you're off to a great start. I'm kind of jealous."

Arno raised an eyebrow. "Everything going all right at work?"

"Yeah," Arman said, unconvincingly. "Ink—Kira's been good on her word. I've had my pick of staff and students. I've got a pretty good first batch, people I think I can trust, plenty of room to work. I just . . ."

Arno waited while his friend searched for the right words. Arman shook his head, looked at the ground and back up at Relgen, kicked at the fresh snow.

"I don't regret taking the job," he said eventually. "I think, in their own twisted way, Haegan and Targan were right. I did abandon the world, and sitting on spellforging and letting other people decide what happens to it helps no one and doesn't even keep my hands clean. Like it or not, this is my responsibility. I'm ready for that.

"But I look at all the safeties I'm putting in place, all the groundwork I'm doing to make sure we don't just end up like the elves, and sometimes I wonder what's the point. Maybe I can keep things under control while I'm around, maybe I even manage to teach the generation after me to be smart. But what about two generations down? Three? Ten? How long before everything I worked for comes undone, someone builds a mad king a crate full of Endings, and we get a new Collapse? At least you'll be around to keep an eye on what you leave behind."

"You know, saints can fall out of influence. Clergy membership can decline, beliefs can fall out of favor, politics can shut down organizations," Arno said. "What I build has just as much a chance of failing as what you do."

Arman scoffed. "Well, that's comforting."

"What I mean is, everything ends, eventually. Maybe tomorrow, maybe ten years, maybe a thousand. But I don't think that's what matters," Arno said. "If there's one thing I learned from Brass, it's that every day is beautiful, whether or not you know you'll get another one. If what we do buys the world even one more day after we're gone, I think we'll still have done something that matters."

Arman thought it over as he watched the city of Relgen be put back together brick by brick. He considered the life he had, his family and friends. He thought of the mesmerizing joy of tinkering with spellforging projects and theory, and the chance he now had to share that with others.

He thought of the wonders he'd seen, the lives he'd touched, the monsters he'd slain. He asked himself what it was worth to have even just one more day.

Arno was right. Even one day would matter.

And they were going to give the world so much more than one day.

"You know, it just occurred to me," Arman said. "Does this conversation count as me praying?"

"Oh gods," Arno muttered. "Don't you start too."

They laughed, and stayed on the ridge for a while, talking about everything and nothing. But eventually, they said their goodbyes, promising to meet up again later, hopefully with the others next time.

Arno watched Arman leave on the sky surfer, as he had eight years ago on this very ridge. But this time, there was a smile on his face. It had taken them eight years to rebuild, but the worst day of the Starbreakers' lives hadn't been the end of them after all. They were alive, thriving, and all leaving a mark on the world they could be proud of.

All but one of them. But Brass had made his mark a long time ago; he'd just made it on all of them.

52
THE LEGACY

Bart walked through the cellblocks of Oblivion, trying to match the nonchalant energy of his guard escort. The obsidian halls felt too close, and his saint too far, but he didn't let his discomfort show. One of Brass's many lessons in their excursions: never let them see you sweat.

It helped that this was the light-security cellblock. The people here were guilty of crimes worth being imprisoned in Oblivion for, but they were only a limited physical or flight risk. Of course, light security in Oblivion still meant being practically entombed in layers of enchanted steel and stone, stranded on an island in the middle of some of the most treacherous waters on Asher.

He'd had to pull strings to get here, and he still hadn't quite processed that he was able to call in favors from the Headmistress of the Academy and the crown of Corsar. But that was the life he'd stepped into.

They reached the cell they'd come for, and the guard stepped back a respectful distance, while still being close enough to hear everything and intervene if something went wrong.

René sat inside the cell, dressed in the rag uniform of most inmates here, head slumped, back against the far wall. There was a single spatial shackle around her ankle that chained her to the wall, to prevent teleportation. It was an unnecessary precaution. René hadn't been the twin who gained the Cult's powers.

"It's René, right?"

The woman looked up, and, getting his first good look at her that wasn't in the middle of a fight, Bart realized she must have been around his and Cara's age.

"What do you want?"

Bart cut straight to the honest heart of the matter. A tendency he'd picked up from his time under Arno's tutelage. "I came to see if I could take you out of here."

René's face scrunched. "What for?"

"You wanted to be a knight once. You wanted to help people. As bad as some of the things you did were, at the end of the day, they all came from that. Plenty of Haegan's exiles didn't become full cultists. But you didn't just not take the plunge. You knew something was wrong."

René bristled at the mention of Haegan and the Cult of Stars. Bart noticed.

"I think you deserve a chance to help people without being duped into following a bunch of Starborn cultists."

"And what? You want me to follow you instead? A bunch of glintchasers?"

"Company of glintchasers," Bart corrected confidently.

René made a disgusted noise in the back of her throat, muttering something about crows. Bart knew convincing René wouldn't be easy. But he'd come prepared.

"Haegan had a lot of allies in his plan. Not all of them died at Relgen. Some of them didn't make it to the city at all. They're on the run, hiding or fighting, and there's a bounty on all of them. There's also the lesser Starborn that came through the tear in reality that didn't die when the big one did. They've been spreading out. Even multiplying in some places. The things that killed your sister, the people responsible for bringing them into the world? They're still out there. We're going after them. And I thought you'd like to come."

René did a bad job of hiding the flare of pain and rage that shot up through her, and Bart felt a pang of guilt at exploiting that pain. But he was trying to offer René a fresh start, and he didn't want her to throw it away without giving it real thought. This was how he made sure she actually considered the offer.

He knew it worked when, instead of telling him off or cursing at him, she said, "You don't know me."

That wasn't a no, and he gave her a reserved smile. Echoing something he'd heard from a friend, he said, "I'd hardly call us strangers. In fact, I think after you do something as intimate as fighting to the death with someone, you get to know them at least a little."

René stared at him with equal parts bafflement and contempt. "If we had been fighting to the death, you'd be dead."

"Maybe," he said, with a tone that said he disagreed but was humoring her. It was a front, and she saw through it. He changed the subject. "My saint believes that the worst day of a person's life shouldn't ruin them forever. He believes in fresh starts. Second chances. And so do I."

"Which saint?"

"You probably wouldn't have heard of him. He's new."

René remained incredulously contemptuous for a little while, glaring at him. But the longer she stared, the less she found in Bart to doubt. He meant it. All of it. There was an earnest integrity to him that reminded her . . . not *of* Silas. Maybe, who she'd thought Silas had been.

She took another look at her surroundings. She thought about the people who had lured her sister to her death. Then she met the paladin's eyes, and nodded.

Once all the particulars were settled with the warden, René and Bart stepped through the teleportation gate to leave Oblivion, and were greeted by three other faces René was vaguely familiar with. There was the pale girl with the demon thorns who'd always traveled with Bart, the cobbled together autostruct who had carried her off the battlefield at Relgen, and a dark-skinned young man sporting some kind of enchanted combination axe-shortsword she remembered seeing at some point in all the fighting.

"René," Bart introduced. "This is Cara, Dietrich, and Gamma."

"It's Ruby and Thorn on the job, though," Dietrich said.

"The Court spare me," René muttered. "I'm not going to have to use a . . . nickname, am I?"

"Sorry," Ruby apologized. "Part of the gig."

René looked to Bart for confirmation, who gave a semi-apologetic shrug. "My real name's Bart. But while we're working, you can call me Copper."

René sighed, already beginning to question her decision. If not for how good the sun felt on her skin after months in Oblivion, she might have been tempted to walk back through the gate.

"So. What's this *company's* name then?"

The other three human members shared a small smile between them, like they were fondly remembering something. Gamma remained outwardly stoic.

"It's still pending our sponsor's approval. But we were thinking of calling ourselves The Starbreakers."

53

THE FRIEND

The village had grown in the years since she'd been here last. There were two horses in town instead of only one. A group of children ran around nearby, playing a game of tag. The last time she'd set foot in this place, most of them hadn't even been born. Such a carefree sight struck her as odd until she reminded herself that this place was about as removed from the broader affairs of the kingdom as you could get without leaving the country altogether.

The road wasn't a road, but a mud path worn in the fresh snow, and she walked it wrapped in a cloak that blended well with the locals. Everyone was bundled against the winter chill, wearing clothes sewn in their own homes.

She had to ask for directions to the right house. The person she asked was friendly, but glanced somewhat incredulously at her boots. Why would someone with shoes that nice need to see the village cobbler?

The house was a squat thing, and to her eyes, not nearly large enough to serve as both business and family home. But everything was smaller here. Somehow, everyone in places like this just made do with less.

It was a simple, quiet, peaceful place. As had been the case the first time she'd been here, she understood instantly both why everyone here was happy, and why Brass had left.

She reached the house, knocked five times in the same rhythm he had, and waited.

An older woman answered the door. She was a plump, soft figure. Most of her hair was still its natural brown, but some gray had begun to sneak in. She kept it tied up, but the curls of it still cascaded down her back. Her face had a natural smile to it that briefly lit up when she recognized Chloe, but quickly vanished when she processed Chloe's expression.

The woman called for her husband instantly, who was only just behind her, putting a pair of winter shoes together on the dining table. He was a tall, wiry man, whose gnarled hands remained dexterous and sure in their work. Together, they made such an ordinary pair. There were couples like this in every village, in every province. They were no one. And everyone.

When the man saw Snow, his face followed the same trajectory as his wife's.

The former assassin suppressed the urge to run. Tears were already brimming in her eyes. But she had to stay. Had to do this. None of the other Starbreakers knew about this place, knew about any of this. Because if anyone did, it would tarnish the purity of what Brass was. She was the only one who could deliver this message.

She cleared her throat and said, "I'm here about your son."

AFTER

The city of Sasel stretched out before the Starbreakers as they sat perched on the roof of a manor house they didn't own. A sea of tiny lightstone blips mirrored the starry sky above, and the full moon bathed the night in a soft glow, made softer by the haze in their vision. A breeze from the coast swept over them, bringing in a hint of the ocean that swirled with the smell of alcohol on their breath.

Brass poured another drink for himself out of their stolen bottle of Silk Tongue Gin. He was three drinks ahead of everybody else, yet still had the balance to stand on the slope of the roof. Church watched him with equal parts dread and respect. Even hammered and swaying on his feet, the duelist's balance was impeccable.

He held the bottle out to Church, and the young cleric shook his head. "Uh, no, no thanks. I think, um, I think I've had enough."

"Lightweight." Brass rolled his eyes, but withdrew the bottle and plopped down. "I need a new drinking buddy. All my old one does is make moony eyes at her boy toy."

"Screw you." Snow gave Brass the finger, but didn't move from her position, nestled in Phoenix's arms with her back against his chest and his coat draped over her shoulders.

Brass held up his hands.

"No offense meant. You two keep enjoying your honeymoon. Drinks are just more fun with friends."

"I drink," Angel said.

"I need a drinking buddy who likes *me," Brass amended.*

Angel offered an apologetic shrug, before swiping the gin from him anyway and taking a drink straight from the bottle. It didn't burn going down so much as tickle, and left a bittersweet aftertaste. For whatever else she could say about Brass, he could pick out some good stuff.

The bottle traveled back and forth down the line of the glintchasers as they stared out over the royal capital, drinking in the view. Even Church eventually dared to take another sip.

When they'd arrived in Sasel a month ago, they were nobodies. A band of punk kids trying to get rich just like every other freelancer company that passed through. Now, they were heroes. Honored and esteemed by the king and queen themselves. It came with some money sure, but nothing they couldn't burn through. What mattered was the name recognition. The clout. From this day forward, when people in Corsar heard the name "The Starbreakers," they would know who that meant.

That was what they were celebrating. More than another job done, more than surviving another brush with death, they were celebrating new opportunities. Off the back of a win like this, they could become something. And that made anything feel possible.

"Do you think people in Aenerwin will hear about this?" Church asked. Out of all of them, he'd been the most reserved about their success, but even his voice carried an unmistakable tinge of pride.

"Everyone's *gonna hear about this," Angel said.*

"What do you guys wanna spend the money on?" Brass asked. "Because I've got ideas. I've got many, very good ideas."

"We're not burning it all on hookers and hash," Angel said.

". . . I have a few other ideas."

"We could afford to stay in some nicer places for a while," Phoenix said, running through the list of future expenditures he kept in his head. "Replace equipment we lost. Buy some horses, so we don't have to rent or walk everywhere—"

"You're so sensible, it's heartbreaking," Brass said, shoulders sagging in disappointment.

"We could buy a house," Church offered, almost too quiet to hear.

Four heads swiveled toward him in unison, and the priest in training shriveled under the attention.

"Well, you know. It could be nice, having like . . . a base to come back to. That's ours. We could get mail delivered there. We could put stuff there we don't want to carry. And Phoenix is always talking about wanting an actual workshop."

"That's . . . actually not a bad idea," Snow said.

"I haven't lived in a house since I was fourteen," Angel said.

She gave no further opinion on the subject, but her eyes flitted across the others before staring down at her shoes. That expression was the closest Angel usually came to expressing sentiment. She'd never say it outright, but she liked the idea too.

Snow nudged their leader and accountant to get his opinion. Phoenix mulled it over. "I mean . . . we could probably afford it right now, depending on where we were looking."

"Fuck it, let's buy this one," Angel said, slapping the roof they were sitting on. "It's got a good view."

"And we've already spilled booze on it," Snow added. "It's practically ours already."

Phoenix let out a half laugh. It was almost certainly the gin talking, but he saw no flaws in that logic. "Guess we'll talk to whoever owns this place in the morning and see if they're selling."

Church sighed, imagining the reactions of his friends and mentors back at his home temple if they could see him now. A glintchaser, a hero, and a soon-to-be property owner. A wistful smile traced across his lips thinking of them. "Do you guys ever think about what you'll do after this?"

"I've got some letters to send to a few big names in town," Phoenix said. "They'd never give us a second look before, but now we could have some real clients on our hands. And that's not even mentioning the sites I still want to check out for ourselves. South of the river, there's—"

"No, not that," Church said. He was surprised at himself for interrupting Phoenix. He also blamed it on the gin. "I mean . . . after, *after. Like . . . when you're done being a glintchaser."*

A contemplative hush fell over the group. For Phoenix, it was just him trying to organize his thoughts amid a slush of alcohol. But for the others, it was the first time any of them had actually given serious thought to the idea. All of them had become glintchasers more or less for the sake of it. Planning for life beyond it hadn't really come up, not when they'd been too busy thinking about how to get through the next week.

But now, they were over the hump of obscurity and inexperience that crushed most companies. If they kept up this kind of momentum, they were looking at particularly lucrative careers. The kind of money freelancers could make if they didn't get themselves killed could set a person up for just about anything.

"I'm going to open my own wing of the Library," Phoenix said. Unlike the others, he had given this subject some thought. "It's gonna be a special section, all about the history of freelancing. And I'm gonna commission a book about us to put in it."

"You wanna put us in a history book?" Angel asked.

"I'll tell them to make you sound good," Phoenix assured her.

"Ooh," Brass excitedly chimed in. "Don't get a priest to write it. They always skip the good stuff and give Renalt all the credit. Hire a bard." He snapped his fingers in revelation. "Hire an Iandran bard."

"What?"

"Come on, they eat the stuff we do up out there," Brass insisted. "Plus, they never skimp on sex and violence. We could have a play written about us! We could have a series of plays. Comedies, adventures, romances! Maybe a tragedy. Those always win awards."

"Brass, I wanted a book, not a play."

"Commission both! You might as well."

"Hey," Snow whispered, tugging on Phoenix's collar to get his attention. "Is there room in that library wing for an artifact collection?"

Phoenix cocked his head for a moment, until he realized what Snow was implying. "Absolutely."

Snow smiled, and tugged on Phoenix's collar again, this time pulling him into a kiss as she pictured their future. Someday, when they were finally too old or too rich to keep freelancing, she'd build a collection that would make her father's look like a drawer full of knickknacks. And when she and Phoenix got married, they wouldn't have a marriage anything like her parents'. They'd be happy, stay happy, forever.

Angel rolled her eyes at the two of them, and folded her arms, thinking of her own answer. Finally, after another minute and another turn with the gin, she had it.

"I'm gonna open a bar," she said. "All the great companies meet in a tavern. So that's what I'm gonna do. I'm gonna open a bar, and it's gonna be the place where glintchasers can meet, and form up, and then come back from a ruin and blow all their cash on me. And any time there's a problem, I can send them *to deal with it."*

"I'm going to build an orphanage," Church said, suddenly silencing everyone. "I've been out of official church structure so long, I don't know if I could fit back in. But I want to do something helpful." Drunk tears were rapidly forming in his eyes. "I just . . . it took me so long to find a place in this world for me. And I want . . . I want to give some kids what I didn't have, before I met all of you."

"Uh. Shit. That's . . . really nice," Angel said, suddenly uncomfortable. She looked to the others for help, but Snow and Phoenix were both avoiding eye contact and Brass was stifling laughter.

Before she could think of what to say, Church closed the distance with her, draping his arms over her.

"You guys are the best friends I ever had," he said. "And I love you all so much. I would do anything for all of you."

"Oh my gods, he's a sad *drunk," Brass said. "I always wondered what Drunk Church was like, but this is even funnier than I thought it'd be."*

"Fuck you," Angel scolded him.

"No, it's adorable," Brass said, sitting down on the other side of Church and throwing an arm around him. "And also definitely the nicest thing he'll ever say to me. I love you too, buddy."

After a few seconds, Brass realized that now everyone was staring at him. After a few more, he managed to piece together why.

"Oh. Yeah, no," he waved his hand dismissively. "I support all your dreams, but I'm not doing anything after this."

"What? You're retiring to somewhere tropical and sitting drunk on a beach for the rest of your life?" Snow asked incredulously.

"Heaven and hells no," Brass said. "I mean . . . I'm never *giving this up. This feeling. This gig. I've got no idea what next week's going to be. We could fight a giant snake, or steal something for a wizard. We could find some Old World sap's long lost secret stash and be the first people in a thousand years to get high off magic elf drugs."*

"Old World empires only completely collapsed seven centuries ago," Phoenix corrected.

"Not the point," Brass said. "I just mean . . . This is it, you know? This is all I ever wanted, right here."

He sighed. Perhaps the most content sound any of them had ever heard a person make. A drunk, blissful smile took over his face as he looked out over the city, and the endless possibilities of the future.

"I'm going to do this for the rest of my life."

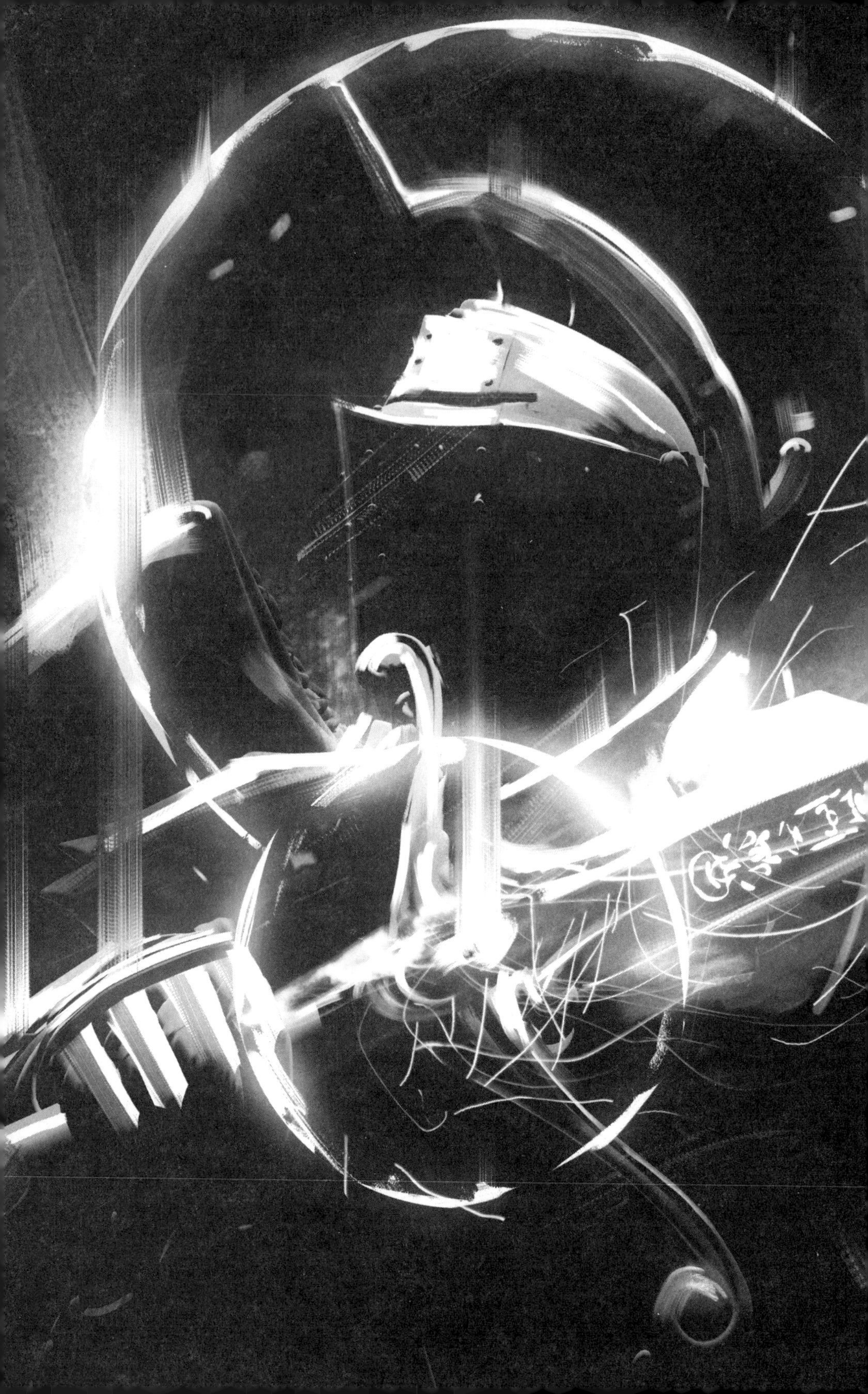

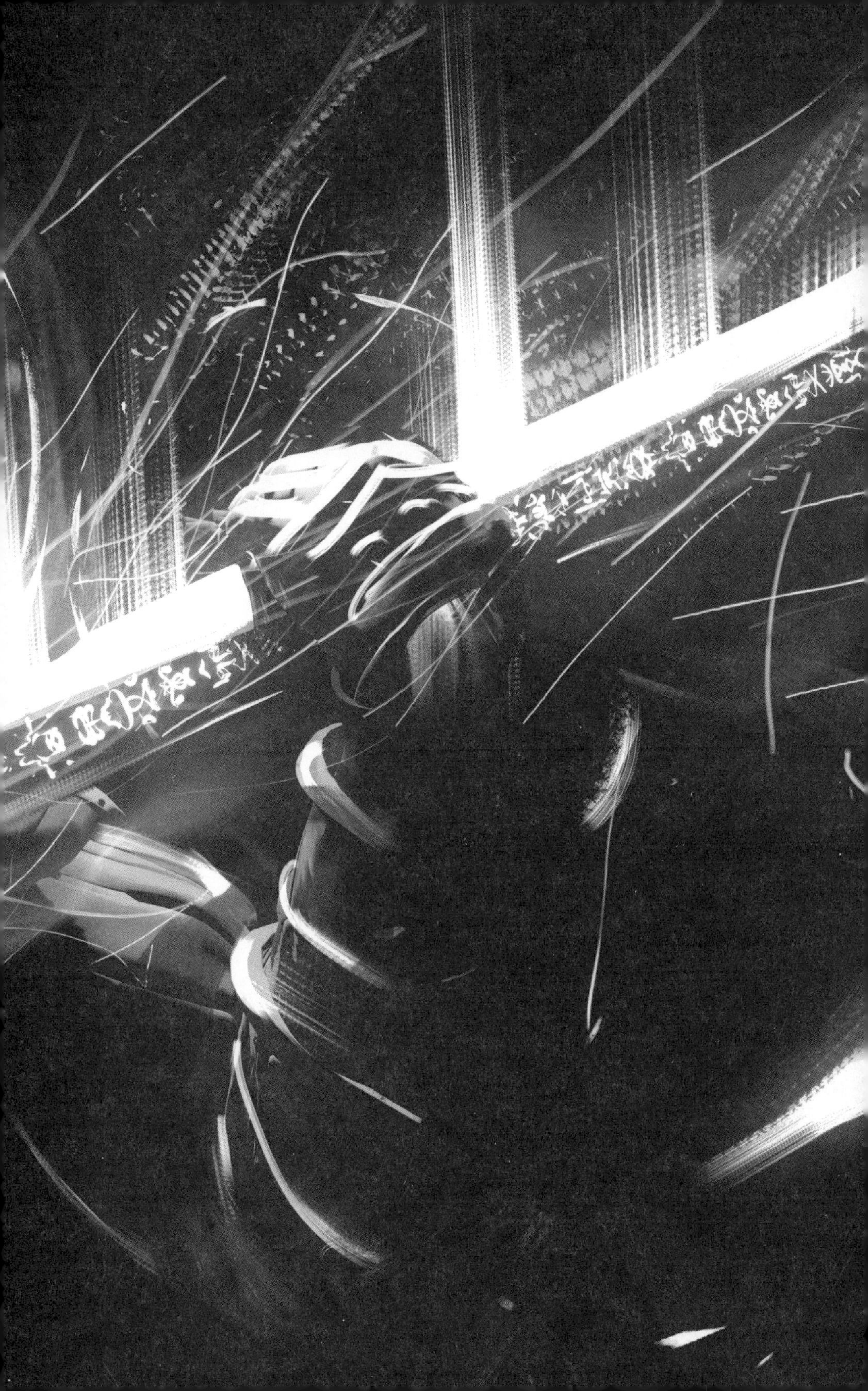

GLOSSARY

CHARACTERS

Arman "Phoenix" Meshar: Former Starbreaker and scholar of the Infinite Library. Sole keeper of the secrets of spellforging in Corsar. Husband of Elizabeth, father of Robyn, and ex-lover to Snow.

Arno "Church" Farnese: Former Starbreaker, priest of Saint Beneger the Guide, and the vicar of the Church of the Guiding Saint in Aenerwin.

Astrid Silverspear: Queen of the Frelheim and Phoenix's first love.

Bart: Paladin in training who was once an acolyte at the Church of the Guiding Saint.

Bishop Sophia: Leader of the Church of Saint Avelina. Arno's friend.

Brass: Former Starbreaker of unparalleled hedonism, irresponsibility, and skill with a blade.

Chloe "Snow" Guerron: Former heiress and Starbreaker, now a notorious assassin. Possesses the Heart of Ice. Ex-lover to Phoenix.

Dietrich: Warden of Cutters Place, a village on the edge of the Iron Forest. Rescued by the Starbreakers as a child, and helped Phoenix and Wings defeat Edelfric as an adult.

The Dread Knight: Fallen spirit housed in a cursed helmet that sought a war with humanity and raised an army of undead to attack the town of Loraine.

Edelfric: Former servant of King Roland I, transformed in death into a plant monster and the Scourge of the Iron Forest. Eventually slain by Dietrich with the help of Phoenix and Wings.

Elizabeth "Wings"/"Sable" Meshar: Former member of the Broken Spear. Now a skilled archer, practitioner of druidic magics, knight of the crown, wife of Arman, and mother of Robyn. Possesses the Heart of the Sky.

Faith: The former priest of the Broken Spear. Officiated Arman and Elizabeth's wedding.

Gamma: Autostruct belonging to the Academy, formerly attached to the Golden Shield, and now a direct servant of Ink.

Hilda: Commander of the Order of Saint Ricard, daughter of Sir Richard, and Angel's former training partner and lover.

Sir Haegan of Whiteborough: Silas Lamark's mentor. A former knight of the city of Relgen who witnessed its fall and swore to make Corsar strong enough to prevent anything like it from happening again. Stole the Heart of Force from the Academy and put out a contract on several individuals connected to the Servitor Hearts, including the Starbreakers. Killed by the Starbreakers.

Kaila "Canvas" Blackrock: Former member of the Broken Spear and now mage at the Academy. Unable to speak, communicating instead in illusions and sign language.

King Roland: Former king of Corsar, born in the city of Relgen. Abdicated the throne after the city's fall and passed soon after.

King Roland II: Current king of Corsar, son of Roland. Unable to walk unassisted after an attack by Kurien in his youth.

Kira "Ink" Arakawa: High Inquisitive of the Academy, formerly a member of the Cord of Aenwyn, and a powerful wizard. Brought the stolen secrets of Hidoran wizards to Corsar.

Kurien: Notorious masked murderer who earned her reputation as the Prince Killer by targeting the heirs of nobility. Stopped from murdering multiple world leaders by the Starbreakers.

Lupolt: Advisor, attendant, and bodyguard to King Roland II. His sister died in the fall of Relgen.

Monica "Angel" Falone: Former Starbreaker with the divine powers of a Sentinel, and the owner of the Rusted Star tavern.

Naomi: Priest of Saint Robyn, member of the Order of Saint Ricard, and Hilda's current lover.

Queen Katherine: Former queen of Corsar, and the mother of Roland II.

Quint: Former prince of the kingdom of Kaberon, now the leader of the Cord of Aenwyn. Ex-lover to Ink.

Renalt: Corsan god of truth, justice, and benevolent strength, and the patron deity of the kingdom.

René and Rosa: Twin sisters who work for Silas Lamark.

Sir Richard: Hilda's father and the person who trained Hilda and Angel to become paladins. Killed in battle defending the girls.

Robyn Meshar: Daughter of Arman/Phoenix and Elizabeth/Wings.

Ronan "Pitch" Highwater: Former member of the Cord of Aenwyn turned assassin, who burned down the Crimson Lilac brothel in pursuit of a contract on the Starbreakers. Possessed the Heart of Flames until it was taken by Silas. Died when he lost the Heart.

Ruby: Former escort at Crimson Lilac. Left to die in a fire by Pitch and had her prayers for salvation answered by a demon. Granted power in exchange for enduring the demon's corrupting influence.

Saint Avelina: Saint of Hope, and servant of Renalt. Patron of the largest church in Corsar.

Saint Beneger: Saint of Guidance, and a servant of Renalt. Followed by Arno.

Saint Ricard: Saint of Vigilance, and a servant of Renalt. Patron of the Order of Saint Ricard.

Saint Robyn: Saint of Rebellion, and a servant of Renalt. Followed by Naomi, a priest in the Order of Saint Ricard.

Sebastian Guerron: Chloe's father, one of the richest men in Corsar, and the owner and patron of the White Hawk.

Silas Lamark: Former knight who worked for Sir Haegan, and has since taken up his mentor's mission of remaking the nation of Corsar.

Simon: Server at the Broken Cask, de-aged by a witch's curse, and only just now reaching adolescence for the second time.
Sinnodella: Elf who lives in the forests of Corsar and trained a young Elizabeth in druidic magics.
Stixaxlatl: Adolescent dragon that lives with Sinnodella.
Tarot: Former member of the Broken Spear, specializing in card-based magic spells.
Thalia: Bartender of the Rusted Star.
Vera: Former owner of the Crimson Lilac, a brothel that was burned down by Pitch.

LOCATIONS AND ORGANIZATIONS

The Academy: The Tarsim Academy of Arcane Studies, better known simply as "the Academy," located in the capital city of Sasel. The foremost institute of magical knowledge and study in Corsar, and one of the greatest in the world.
Aenerwin: Town where Arno currently lives, site of the Church of the Guiding Saint, and the first town the Starbreakers ever saved from the Cult of Stars.
Akers: Small village on the outskirts of the city of Olwin, where Arman and Elizabeth Meshar live.
Asher: Name of the world.
The Broken Cask: Tavern in the city of Sasel, formerly frequented by the Starbreakers.
The Broken Spear: All-female freelancer company Elizabeth Meshar previously belonged to, during which time she used the name "Sable." Now disbanded.
Church of the Guiding Saint: Church in Aenerwin dedicated to Saint Beneger the Guide.
The Church of Saint Avelina: Largest church in Corsar, better known simply as "The Church."
Clocktower: Criminal organization that facilitated the hits on the former Starbreakers, and clashed with the company many times in the past.

Cord of Aenwyn: Internationally traveling freelancer company that developed a bitter rivalry with the Starbreakers. Currently led by Quint, with former members including Ink and Pitch.

Corsar: Kingdom now ruled by Roland II. Only recently unified by the previous reign of Roland I and Katherine of Sasel, and still reeling from the fall of the city of Relgen.

Costera: Continent that Corsar, Parthica, and the Frelheim all occupy.

Crimson Lilac: Vera's former luxury hotel and brothel in Olwin that was burned down by Pitch.

The Cult of Stars: Cult dedicated to the return of the Starborn. The Starbreakers earned their name by foiling their schemes and hunting their members years ago. Thought to have been wiped out by the fall of Relgen.

Disassembly Council: Council within the Academy tasked with keeping dangerous artifacts secured from the rest of the world, and destroying them when possible.

Faceless: Gray-skinned, shapeshifting, telepathic beings believed to come from another world.

The Frelheim: Frigid kingdom to the north of Corsar where humans and dwarves coexist.

Future's Road: Artery that links Corsar's capital city (Sasel) to the rest of the interior.

Hidora: Great empire of the Far West, and the former home of Kira Arakawa.

Gypten: One of the nations present at the summit in Nikos. A land of deserts, mountains, and elemental rifts, fueled by trade and ruled by the sultan. The native homeland of Arman's family.

Her Lady's City: Shorthand for Her Lady Excellent's City of Corrinverno, the capital city of the Iandran Empire.

Iandra: One of the nations present at the summit in Nikos. The self-proclaimed center of the world, famous for its passionate people and their love of the arts. Arno Farnese's birthplace.

Infinite Library: One of the greatest repositories of knowledge in Asher, situated off the coast of Corsar. The place where Arman Meshar worked and studied before becoming a freelancer.

Nikos: Capital of Parthica, and the host city of the first international summit of Asher.

Oblivion: Prison of incredibly advanced physical and arcane security features, where the most dangerous criminals and monsters are kept.

Olwin: Largest city in Corsar's interior now that Relgen has fallen. Home to countless refugees from the area surrounding the fallen city.

The Order of Saint Ricard: Knightly order responsible for defending Corsar from foreign invasion and monitoring the conduct of its rulers.

Parthica: Nation bordering Corsar with elected leaders and strong military and philosophical traditions.

Pearl Palace: Home palace of King Roland II.

The Purple Rose: Knightly order responsible for defending Relgen and the surrounding territory.

Relgen: Formerly the military capital of Corsar and Bastion of the North. Its entire population was wiped out by an Old World weapon during the Starbreakers' final mission together as a company.

Rusted Star: Tavern owned by Monica.

Saint Avelina's Cathedral: Headquarters of the Church of Saint Avelina, located in Sasel.

Sanctum of the Oracle: Great Old World machine housed in a floating fortress of ice and rock, built to provide perfect knowledge of the past, present, and future. Home of the Oracle.

Sasel: Capital of the kingdom of Corsar; City of Yesterday and Tomorrow, Jewel of the Coast.

Seven Gates: Order of knights who serve the crown.

The White Hawk: Corporate freelancer company owned and sponsored by Sebastian Guerron.

OTHER TERMS

Company: Most common name given to a group of freelancers who work and travel together.

Crow: Colloquial, semi-derogatory name for freelancers used most commonly in Iandra.

Extractor: Device created by Phoenix to siphon the energy of a Servitor Heart. Only a few unused models remain, held by the Academy in the event of their need.

Freelancer: Itinerant mercenary-explorer, who finds employment in everything from delving into Old World ruins, recovering artifacts, hunting monsters, and serving as hired muscle. Infamous in many places for bringing trouble wherever they go, but nevertheless invaluable for their skills and expertise.

Glint: Corsan currency.

Glintchaser: Colloquial, semi-derogatory name for freelancers used most commonly in Corsar.

Hell Tongue: Fiendish power to control others with verbal commands.

The Old World: Days when the elves ruled an empire of several worlds that included Asher, and humans were little more than servants.

Paladin: One who is trained to funnel divine power into their body and weapons.

Sentinel: Angel who incarnates in human form to battle evil on the mortal plane, forgetting its previous life as an angel in the process.

The Servitor: War machine of the Old World, which rampaged through Corsar until stopped by a joint effort of multiple freelancer companies and the forces of the crown.

Spellforging: Old World practice used to create arcane machines and weapons.

Starborn: Ancient cosmic beings from beyond the farthest human understandings of the universe, believed by some to have existed before the gods.

Servitor Heart: A power source of the Servitor, each one keyed to a specific type of power, such as Force, Flames, Ice, Sky, or Shadows.

ABOUT THE AUTHOR

Elijah Menchaca is a Puerto-Rican author born and raised in Bakersfield, California, and has been writing and telling stories since he was five. He's moved all around the country to chase some dreams and learn how to put his own pants on.

So far, he's discovered a love for *Dungeons & Dragons*, graduated from the University of Louisville with a BA in History and a minor in creative writing, begun a career in teaching, and has now concluded his debut fantasy series, Glintchasers, which began in 2021 with the release of *They Met in a Tavern*. As far as dream chasing goes, things are well in hand.

He's still working on the pants thing.

ACKNOWLEDGMENTS

Even though I'd always set out to write these books as an expression of feelings about the trajectory my life had been taking, I never expected the journey of this story and my own to end up as parallel as they have. This series, and this book, are about rebuilding. About finding purpose and meaning after you survive the worst day of your life.

This book was written during my own personal Relgen. And I took no small comfort and catharsis in this story about people getting the chance to right some wrongs, change for the better, and build new lives. I hope this journey has meant something to you too.

As usual, I could not have done this alone.

So, thank you to the CamCat team for giving me the chance to give this story its proper conclusion.

In particular, thank you to Sue Arroyo, publisher, CEO, and inspiration. The world would be diminished for her passing, were it not already made so much better by all the good she brought into it.

Thank you to my editor Bridget McFadden. You're a joy to work with, and I'm so happy I got to close out the story we started. Hopefully I wasn't too much of a diva over the interrobangs.

Thank you to Megan McCarter, who allowed herself to be spoiled for this book so I could have a sounding board. To Mason Chernosky and Victor

Kalinyak, for putting a roof over my head and giving me the help I needed to get back on my feet.

I want to thank God for this life, my family for their never ending support, Taylor Swift for providing the soundtrack, and Panic! At The Disco for giving me Brass.

A sincere thank you, and my deepest apologies, to the person without whom these books would not exist. I wish you nothing but the best.

And of course, thank you, dear reader. The work is not complete until it finds its way to you. And now that it has, we did it. We made it to the end. I hope you enjoyed the story.

I'll see you in the next one.

If you enjoyed
Elijah Menchaca's *They Played Their Role*,
consider leaving us a review
to help our authors.

And check out
Meredith R. Lyons' *A Dagger of Lightning*.

CHAPTER 1

If you don't know where you're going, fine, just make sure you know what you're looking for. —Solange Delaney

"Im. Imogen! You're okay. You're alright, you're okay."

I awoke gasping, my ears throbbing as if my heart had established satellite locations. My eyes immediately locked onto a familiar shape, the feather swaying back and forth, dangling from the chain on our ceiling fan. *I'm safe. I'm in bed. With Keane. I'm okay.*

The orange glow of a street lamp filtered in through the open curtains. I reached up and lightly clasped Keane's forearm, his warm palm still gripping my shoulder, although he had stopped shaking me. I turned my head toward him, trying to take slower breaths. He'd angled himself just far enough away so that I wouldn't accidentally strike him. I must have been flailing.

"I'm awake. Sorry. Was I loud?" I never remembered these dreams when I woke. Only a sensation of falling and some vague knowledge that my grandfather had been there, either falling with me, or trying to keep me from falling, or . . . something . . .

"You didn't shout or anything this time, just thrashed around." Keane flopped back onto the pillows, sliding an arm beneath me and hauling me to his side. I let him, even though I was very warm and wanted air. The sheets beneath me were damp with sweat. I shoved the comforter down to my waist.

"Sorry I woke you. I've been trying to rest my ankle and didn't run yesterday." I always slept better if I were exhausted. I didn't process emotions the way most people did, and if I were unable to channel them physically, they liked to ambush me when I was unconscious.

"That's alright," Keane sighed, trailing his fingertips up and down my arm. Keane had been a good friend since college. Neither of us had ever married, in spite of cycling through many long-term relationships.

At some point, after spending a mutual friend's wedding together as bridesmaid and groomsman for the umpteenth time, Keane had suggested that if we hadn't found anyone by forty, we should just wed each other. I'd drunkenly agreed.

Now I was forty-five, Keane was nearly fifty, and six months ago he'd finally gotten my yes. I accepted a ring after insisting upon dating first, living together first, then living together for at least a year . . . until I'd run out of excuses. There were none. Keane was great. We got along great. Sex wasn't bad. Cohabitating was cheaper and made maintaining a home easier. And it was nice being on his insurance plan.

Settling, Imogen. You're settling is what you're doing. She'd been gone sixteen years and I could still *hear* my grandmother's exhale, could practically see her tossing a gauzy scarf over a small-boned shoulder as she gave me a *look* from beneath her lashes.

But what was wrong with that at my age? I'd come to the conclusion that 'true love' was a fantasy—although my grandparents had sure seemed to have it. Perhaps it wasn't in the cards for everyone. I'd looked around long enough. Fortunately, I'd never wanted kids, so I'd never felt that pressure.

"So, what are your plans for today?" Keane yawned, still lightly stroking my arm.

My stomach tightened. He had some kind of agenda. "Some more job applications, maybe—"

"You know, you don't have to get a job right away—"

"I *want* a job. I need to contribute—"

"I know, Im, and you will, but you don't need one in the next twenty-four hours. Your dad's coming in next week, and," he rolled toward me, pulling me even closer, "the guest room is still a mess."

My eyes dropped away from his. I turned my face skyward again and focused on the feather. "I know." The guest room would have been nice if it weren't for the large pile of cardboard boxes. All mine.

I *had* tried to whittle them down. But I didn't know what I'd need. I didn't know where I'd fit in this new place. Keane had received a dream job offer in New Orleans. He'd convinced me that this would be a great life for both of us. Wasn't I tired of the cold in Chicago? Wasn't I able to find friends wherever I went? Weren't we going to get married now? I had no good arguments, so I went with him. It made sense. We were engaged. Why not? I rolled my shoulders against the tightness threatening, trying to make a little more space between us. I didn't want to go through the boxes downstairs. Going through them meant getting rid of them, and I hated to let go of those little parts of myself.

I'd never found my calling. I liked to hop around. I was good at a lot of things, never great at any one thing. I never had a "tribe," but I was good at getting along. I'd find a job here too. Find things to like about it. I was good at adapting. I could wedge myself in.

Grandma would have told me to keep searching. *You're different, Imogen, and that's okay. But you have a place. We all do. You'll know it when you find it. Just keep looking*. Well, she wasn't here. Besides, maybe this would be it.

"Okay," I said, taking a deep breath. "I'll go through the boxes today. Try to put some away."

"You could make a donation pile too," Keane said, pulling the covers back up around us. "What about all that martial arts stuff? You haven't fought in over a decade."

Something twisted at my center. "I liked fighting though," I said quietly. I had loved sparring. It was another effective outlet for emotions packed down too tightly. And I'd been good at it. Although I was technically too old to fight competitively anymore, I could still train. "Maybe we could find a place here, we could do it together—"

Keane chuckled. "I'm still sore from soccer two days ago." He yawned again and pulled me even closer, eliminating any space I'd created by wrapping his arms around me. He pressed a kiss to my forehead, one hand rubbing my back. "You know, I was thinking when your dad's here next week, we could set a date for the wedding. Like, an actual date. Maybe something in the fall."

I felt myself go rigid in his arms. "Not the fall," I said. Keane's hand stilled on my back, but he didn't let me go. This was the only thing I had ever pushed back on consistently.

"Imogen—"

"My grandma disappeared in the fall. I don't like the fall."

"Imogen." Impatience simmered under his voice. "Everyone on Earth has lost a grandparent—"

"Lost, yes, had one disappear, no."

His chest inflated against my arms where I was still smashed against him. He exhaled slowly. "She was one-hundred-and-two, Im. You know she died. She probably left because your grandpa had just passed on and—"

"Her car was still there. All her stuff was still there. And she left me that message." The muscles between my shoulder blades tightened painfully.

Keane sighed. "She was quoting Stephen King—"

I knew exactly where this conversation was going and how I would feel afterward, but I couldn't help it, I took the bait. "No, she said, 'There might be other worlds to see,' not 'There are other worlds than these,' there's a diff—"

"So she misquoted—" Keane cut himself off when I started pushing out of his embrace. "Okay, baby." His voice lifted on the second word like he was asking a question. He held me slightly away, pushed my short hair back from my face, then tilted my chin up so I was forced to look at him. "I know you don't like to talk about this, so I'm not going to push it but… it's always something. First, you wanted to wait until I was sure about the job, then you wanted to wait until after the move, and now I just feel like you're making excuses."

"Just not the fall," I said. "Any other season—"

"How about this summer then?"

It was already June. Summer was technically days away.

"You want to get married in summer in New Orleans?" Honestly, this far south it felt like summer had been sitting on us for months already.

He didn't answer, just stared into my eyes, his fingers still at my chin, his arm at my waist, still holding me to him. Keane knew how to wear me down. If it was this important to him… what difference did it really make when it happened?

"Fine. Summer," I said, although a surge of distress simmered beneath my skin. "We can talk about it when dad's here."

"Really?" Keane grinned, the corners of his eyes crinkling. My heart softened. He really was a handsome guy. And he was good to me.

"Really," I said, smiling back.

He kissed me softly. "I love you, Imogen."

"I love you, too." The words came easy. We'd been saying them to each other as friends for decades. I forced another smile, the distress coalescing into eels tossing against my stomach. "I'm gonna head out for my run. The sun's gonna come up soon."

"Okay." He gave me a squeeze and released me. Keane knew what I was doing. And he was letting me. "Text me when you're close and I'll go out and get coffee for us." He snuggled back into the downy comforter.

"'Kay." I rolled out of bed and padded to the dresser in the soft brown light of near dawn. I snatched up some running shorts, a sports bra, and socks and slipped into the bathroom to get dressed. My sore Achilles still ached in spite of my rest day, but I ignored it. I couldn't get out of the house fast enough.

I stopped long enough to do a few heel drops on the front step to warm up my ankle before setting out, but that was it. The sky had lightened to pink by the time I hit the pavement. I loved the warm June mornings. Although I was leery of hurricane season, I couldn't complain about being warm all the time. No more treadmill-exclusive winters. I took off toward the levee. Running along the top at dawn was my new favorite way to greet the day.

I tried to shake off the tension from this morning's conversation as I ran. No one understood how hard I had taken my grandma's disappearance. We'd had a different bond. Even my father had said that he felt like an interloper sometimes when it was just the three of us together. I had a nagging feeling that Keane had used that attachment when he suggested the fall to push me into a summer wedding. I shoved that thought away. If he had, it was done now.

My mother had died when I was eight, which was about when I'd stopped emoting in the 'normal way.' I had to let it out physically. Running, fighting, acting. I wasn't a cryer and I wasn't a talker. I think it was one of the things Keane liked about me. If something upset me, I waited until I felt safe to let it out, or I channeled it through my body.

Not for the first time, I wished my grandma was around so I could run this wedding thing by her. Ask her why I had these conflicting feelings about what was so obviously the right decision. I mean, I'd already followed the guy across the country.

Keep looking, Imogen, she would level her green eyes at me. *Keep exploring. No need to pin yourself down to this one. You've got time. I don't care what anyone says.*

Nevermind that she'd met my grandfather at eighteen and married him shortly after. Well, look where all that exploring had landed me. I had the most eclectic resume on the planet and was now a forty-five-year-old fiancée.

"Get outta my head, Grandma. Keane's great and I'm doing this." I turned up my music, ignored my aching ankle, and picked up the pace. Running was one thing I'd always done, always loved, and always been good at. And Keane was obviously the right choice. Wasn't he?

I'd only logged about three miles when I had to stop to stretch my protesting Achilles and glanced up at the rising sun. Good clouds today. I pulled my phone out of its pouch to take a picture and noticed a text message. Odd for this early. Maybe Keane needed something. I clicked on the app and my heart lifted a bit when I saw it was Al from our soccer team.

I liked Al, although I was surprised to receive a text from him at dawn. Keane and I had joined a rec league this spring to meet people and Al was another charming newcomer. We'd gotten close with the team and I'd enjoyed harmlessly flirting with Al, even though I was probably technically old enough to be his mother. He gave back as good as he got, which was fun for me, and he and Keane got along like a house on fire. Didn't hurt that he was easy on the eyes and fun to talk to. The first time the three of us had hung out alone, we'd stayed up until midnight. My 5 a.m. run the next morning had been rough, but I hadn't regretted it.

Al: Hey! I know it's early, but since you're an early bird, I took a chance you might be up. You feel like meeting for some coffee? My treat.

My finger hovered over the screen and I started walking toward the next trailhead, almost absently. Keane was supposed to get coffee for us later. But Al had never asked me to coffee before. Maybe he needed to talk. And if I were being honest with myself, I wanted someone to talk to who wasn't Keane. Seeing Al was always fun. It would give my morning a lift. And I was feeling a little reckless.

Me: I am up! On a levee run actually. Which coffee shop are you going to? I'm less than a mile from the next trailhead and I could run there.

Al: What trailhead are you near? I'll come meet you. We can go together!

Directions given, I tucked my phone away and continued my run, my pace a bit faster—in spite of my Achilles—in anticipation of seeing my friend. *Calm down,* I told the tendon. *We'll have a shorter run than planned and a nice rest at coffee.*

When I approached the trailhead, Al was already waiting. He waved.

I waved back, slowing to a walk as I reached him. Strolling toward me. Wearing . . . a tunic and pants? Odd. His long blond hair was pulled neatly back and he was sporting the laid-back grin of a confident twenty-something without a care in the world. It was impossible not to smile back.

I pulled my earbuds out of my ears and tucked them into the pouch with my phone, shutting off the music. "Hey! Fancy meeting you here. Do you live or . . . work around here?" I gestured to his attire. Come to think of it, Al had never mentioned where he worked or what he even did.

"Not exactly." He smiled and reached for my left hand as if to shake, which I automatically extended. He cupped it in both of his.

I laughed. "Sorry if my hand is sweaty."

"It's not." His amber eyes glittered. The wind blew his earthy, sandalwood scent in my direction. I was positive that I smelled of nothing but sweat, but if he noticed, he didn't seem to mind. "I'm glad you were out. Thanks for meeting up."

"Sure, how can I help?" I pushed sweaty strands of my choppy, chin-length hair out of my face with my free hand and planted my foot on a rock, taking advantage of the pause to stretch again. He clocked the movement.

"Ankle?"

"Always." I smiled, pulling slightly on my hand. He gave it a squeeze and let go. His eyes dropped to my engagement ring as his fingers brushed over it. "Ankle, shoulder, uterus . . . getting old is no fun."

He moved closer. "Maybe I can help with that."

"With . . . my ankle?" I stepped away from the rock, fiddling with the zipper on my pouch, a warning bell pinging. Was this weird? It felt weird. I glanced around for Al's car and realized there wasn't one. Had he walked here?

"Among other things." His gaze flicked to my fidgeting hands then bounced up to my face. Something flashed behind his eyes. "How'd you like to know more about your grandmother?"

I froze. My stomach turned in on itself. "What are you talking about?" I tried to remember if I'd ever talked to Al about her, riffled through my memories of post-game bar visits.

Al cleared his throat, eyes on my nervous fingers, speaking quickly as if he could sense that I was ready to bolt. "I knew her. And I know you want to know where she went and where she came from. I can tell you everything about her."

I stilled, my heart hammering. How was it possible that Keane and I had just been talking about her and Al would show up minutes later claiming to know what happened to her? Grandma would have called it a sign.

VISIT US ONLINE FOR MORE BOOKS TO LIVE IN:
CAMCATBOOKS.COM

SIGN UP FOR CAMCAT'S FICTION NEWSLETTER FOR
COVER REVEALS, EBOOK DEALS, AND MORE EXCLUSIVE CONTENT.

CamCatBooks

@CamCatBooks

@CamCat_Books

@CamCatBooks